MW00834097

Also by Alexandra Allred

Damaged Goods - When Joanna Lucas moves to a small town to escape a scandal and a scoundrel, she finds herself in trouble again when she befriends a stripper-turned-Mormon, a one-legged woman thanks to a loose tiger, and a dirty-minded troublemaker with a love of inane questions, and they take on an industrial town. Erin Brockovich has nothing on these ladies!
Prepare to laugh out loud and cheer them on as they set out to right a terrible wrong . . . no matter how outlandish things get.

White Trash - <u>White Trash</u> is a fast-paced, laugh-out-loud book that serves as a bitter social commentary on American hypocrisies and prejudices. As a small police department works the biggest whodunit in Granby history, a startling underworld of domestic abuse, gunrunning, drug use, illicit sex, and child molestation is revealed. It's a story that neatly summarizes the reality of every American small town peopled with neighbors you can't get away from, you can't stop talking about, and you may not want to leave.

Roadkill - When bodies of women are dumped along the rural roads outside Columbus, Ohio, Allie Lindell is determined to find the killer. This journalist turned stay-at-home mom, slowly losing her mind to Disney tunes, knows there is only one thing she can do—solve the murders with a little help from her reluctant sister, her sidekick neighbor, and her ballsy former co-worker.
Roadkill is the funny, sometimes aggravating, ultimately heartwarming story of a woman trying to give everything to her kids, keep the love of her partner, and not lose herself in the process.

Sweetbreath - When the president of Sweets Sullivan is found dead, everyone is all too ready to believe it was a suicide–everyone but Allie Lindell. Restless and feeling a bit like she's *just* an at-home mom, Allie misses the crazy deadlines, office banter, even rush hour traffic. The former obituary writer for *The Columbus Dispatch* with a mind for murder refuses to let diaper duty and nap time keep her away. As Allie gets closer to the truth, her relationship with her life partner begins to unravel and she is forced to make a choice. This time, however, her sweet tooth might get her killed.
Sweetbreath is the second mystery of the Allie Lindell series–a story of family secrets, murder, crooked insurance schemes, drugs, chocolate cravings and chocolate-chocolate chip cookies that are to die for. Who can resist?

She Cries

By
Alexandra Allred

TWCS PUBLISHING HOUSE

First published by The Writer's Coffee Shop, 2014

The Writer's Coffee Shop
(Australia)   PO Box 447 Cherrybrook NSW 2126
(USA)   PO Box 2116 Waxahachie TX 75168

Paperback ISBN- 978-1-61213-210-5
E-book ISBN- 978-1-61213-211-2

A CIP catalogue record for this book is available from the US Congress Library.

Cover image by: © istockphoto.com / KKIDD
Cover design by: Jennifer McGuire

www.thewriterscoffeeshop.com/aallred

For true loves everywhere

Prelude

Despite his popularity, or maybe because of it, Jeremy Connors was a man out of control. He needed a constant rush of adrenaline. He thrived on excitement, anger, pain—especially pain. He lived and played to the absolute extremes of his physical and emotional endurance, and, as a result, he was a star.

Fans adored him and reveled in his chest-pounding, fist-pumping grandstanding each time he shut down the opposing offense and sent opposing players off the field on stretchers. Like the fans, sports writers and broadcasters couldn't get enough of Connors, and everyone agreed there was no other player like him. Connors dominated plays, dominated players, and dominated games. He ruled the field.

Except tonight—the single most important night of his career, and he hadn't been able to do a damn thing. The normally unstoppable safety for the Boston Rebels, the normally indomitable force known as Jeremy Connors had been stopped cold. Rendered ineffectual. Reduced to an afterthought in the game—*the* game. The greatest show on earth. The Super Bowl.

Playing in the biggest, grandest sporting event in the world—and winning —was to have been Connors' time to seal his place as a football legend; his opportunity to garner even more endorsements, sponsors, and commercials; his right to demand an even bigger salary, a better contract. Most important, this was to have been his night to claim the one accolade which had so far eluded him—a Super Bowl championship ring. He should have been basking in all the glory and adulation that the ring and his celebrity status entitled him. It should have been his. This was to have been his night to shine.

Instead, he had been forced to suffer the humiliation, in front of millions, of helplessly watching the seconds slowly tick off the game clock. He hadn't bothered to go out onto the field to congratulate the other team or to grant any interviews. Instead, even before the clock ticked down to zero,

Connors had headed straight for the locker room to shower and change and get the hell out of there.

From this night there would be no turning back.

* * * *

As he sped back to the hotel, pushing his sports car to its limits, his pulse raced and his fury was palpable. He wasn't accustomed to feeling powerless or humiliated. After several moments of deep thought, he decided that the last time he had felt this way had to have been the game against Washington Carver when he'd been a junior in high school. The outcome of the game had determined which school moved on to state, but his team just hadn't been able to deliver. He had been double-teamed the entire night and unable to shut down a single play. Washington Carver's quarterback had been on a roll, firing rockets to his receivers with such precision and power that there had been no denying them. It had been their night, their game, and their shot at the state championship. And, just like this night, all he'd been able to do was watch as the minutes had ticked off the clock, and the other team had sailed to victory. He had been furious with his own team. How he had hated them. He had hated everyone—his coach, his booty calls, his teammates whining about injuries—real or imagined. But he hadn't hated the other team. No, for them, he'd only had admiration. Power always had to be respected, and he owed them the acknowledgement of a well-played game.

He'd grudgingly felt the same admiration for the victors tonight. Not that he'd shared that feeling with anyone. He had been too devastated. He was still Jeremy Connors, and he ruled off the field just as he usually did on. All he had to do to dull these unbearable feelings of powerlessness and impotence was to find the right quarry—the right woman to sacrifice to his ego and anger. And finding a woman, any woman, was never difficult for Connors.

In fact, she found him.

Even after such a humiliating loss, the throngs of adoring fans still filled the hotel lobby. Mostly women, of course, but she stood out. An Amazon at almost six feet tall in heels, she was confident and bold as she approached him and let him know—let everyone know—that she wanted him. She was exotic-looking with an olive complexion and thick, black hair that fell to the middle of her back. When she laughed, she flipped her hair and looked around to see who was watching. She touched his arm and then his chest lightly, letting any and all females know "this one is mine."

And he let her.

The rage was still there, but it shifted as he enjoyed the show as much as the rest of the crowd. He knew how different she would be when he was done with her, and satisfaction was a great partner to anger. He was going to have a good time, releasing all his energy, frustrations, and fury into and on to her.

* * * *

He threw her against the wall and smiled as she first groaned and then crumpled with a whimper to the floor. He watched as she rolled over onto her hands and knees. She never looked up but he imagined how her face looked.

Scared.

Hurt.

Pretty.

Defenseless.

From rage comes power, and he wasn't a kid anymore, licking his wounds from a high school game. This was the big time and he played for keeps. He played for the big bucks and the spotlight. He played for power and for women.

He remembered that night against Washington Carver again. It hadn't even been ten years ago when sweet little Ashley Williams tried to console him after the game. He'd pounded her. He'd ravaged her. He'd had her begging for mercy—his mercy. He'd dominated and controlled her and did what he'd wanted with her until, at last, he was done with her.

Pound, dominate, control—that was how the game was played. It was how he was designed.

Only later, when he had finally calmed himself, had he been able to take stock of the damage, and he'd gathered her in his arms and consoled her.

He'd always read the local papers about his performance on the field after each game and noted the injuries he had inflicted on others. An immense feeling of satisfaction came from knowing he had single-handedly benched players—*talented* players—for a game or, if it was a good night, a season. He was the dominator. The enforcer.

But females were different.

They were different in a way he could not explain. Of course, there was the obvious. They were softer, more fragile. Unlike an opposing player looking to test his mettle against the likes of Connors, females expected to be dominated.

This one started to crawl toward the door, and he put his foot in the small of her back and pushed down. It was like stepping on a paper bag—all air.

She had nothing left to give and fell flat, crying softly.

"Please, don't hurt me. Just let me go." Her voice was muffled in the hotel room carpet. "I won't tell anyone. I swear, I won't say a word."

He laughed.

He couldn't figure women. Who wouldn't tell the world she had been screwed by Jeremy Connors? Wasn't that the whole point of coming up here? She had wanted so badly to be with him and now she was playing the victim. Well, he wasn't buying it.

He never bought it.

He had made the circle from New York to Hollywood. There wasn't a woman in the free world who knocked on his door without knowing she was in for a wild ride. Sometimes he might get too carried away, but he was always forgiven. Either he had handled it himself, or his agent had cleaned up the mess, but they had always come back. They always wanted more of the kid.

He'd said again and again to agents and teammates alike, *that's the way of women*. They wanted to be dominated. They wanted to be forced. They wanted to be controlled. It dated back to the beginning of mankind. And it was why they always singled out professional athletes. Women craved power—specifically, women craved men with power.

Men were straightforward. On the field, men came at him every day with the clear desire to knock his head off his shoulders, take out a knee, and bring him down at any cost. But women? They never came straight at you. They tried to blindside. Ambush. They wanted you to come inside them, maybe get knocked up for the sole purpose of getting hooked up. They wanted the power of saying they had had Jeremy Connors.

And not just Connors. He'd seen it a million times with his teammates. Some sweet thing would come on to a guy whom everyone knew was married with kids. She'd throw her panties in his face and promise him a night of wild, unbridled sex—no strings attached. Some really meant *no strings*. They just wanted to have a celebrity tussle with them for the thrill of telling others. But there were so many more who had agendas.

She rolled over, looking at him with large brown eyes. She was gorgeous. Glossy black hair was matted to one side of her face, which was flushed and sweaty. Her mouth was drawn close, making her red lips look twice as thick and juicy, and he stared at their luscious and inviting fullness, smiling.

Her shirt—such as it was—was falling off her shoulders, exposing large, firm breasts.

Connors stiffened.

By glory, this is why the woman was made.

Her long, smooth, bare legs were clenched tight at the knees, but he already knew what was there. He had visited her sweet spot and would again. He had punished her for the game lost, for the way he had been shut down, for the way he had been forced, before millions, to watch the clock tick off.

She crossed one arm over her breasts, trying to conceal them, while she used the other to push her weight up.

He waited patiently.

She tried to slide against the wall, eyes on him, as she felt her way to the door.

"Where are you going, baby?" he asked in a deep, smooth voice.

Her mouth trembled. Those sweet, puffy lips trembled at him, beckoning him.

"Hmm?" He raised his eyebrows and enjoyed it all—the smell of sex, the sheen of sweat covering her body, the rigid tension in her muscles, the huge eyes, the mussed hair. He let her slide a little farther away and gain more confidence as she closed the distance to the hotel room door.

When she had approached him in the hotel lobby and made her intentions known, he had pulled her in close and whispered in her ear. She had smelled so good, but her response had been even better.

She had moaned, closing her eyes for a moment, and smiled a lazy, seductive smile, letting everyone in the lobby know what was happening.

She was aching to be with him. Holding her that tightly, he had felt it pouring off her.

Hell, people had felt it all the way across the lobby.

"You change your mind, baby? You don't wanna play anymore?" he murmured.

She whimpered. She cried something about wanting to go home. It was hard to understand. Her voice was high-pitched. Tiny. She sounded like a little girl. But he knew it was all part of the game women like her liked to play. His smile broadened as he moved in, and she froze. She drew in a quick, sharp breath, and the sound rushed through his brain. She was paralyzed with anticipation, trying to figure out what he was going to do to her next. He was in complete control of this game.

"Oh, no, baby girl. We got so much more to do." He leaned in, grabbing a handful of that gorgeous, thick hair.

Chapter One

Samuel Spann dragged his fingers across his face as he listened to the sports channel happily weighing in.

"In another late-night skirmish that no doubt has his legal team scrambling, Jeremy Connors was arrested last night for disorderly conduct at a gentlemen's pub in Atlanta. Reportedly visiting a relative in the peach state, Connors couldn't help but check out the local talent at the Bay-at-the-Moon Lounge for Men," the commentator said and chuckled as his co-anchor grinned and shook his head.

Sam leaned back in his leather chair, grimacing at the wide screen in his office.

Beside the plasma television with remote in hand, stood another member of Jeremy Connors' damage control team, Mike Waters. He didn't look at the television but stood staring at his colleagues.

". . . in a string of violent behavior . . ." The commentator continued to offer details Sam did not want to hear.

"Turn that off," Sam said and sighed.

"This is unbelievable!" Mike paced the large room. "Sam, this is all we're doing. I can't stay on top of what he's going to do next. Hell, forget the case, I'm spending countless hours on just damage control. Last night, he's arrested in Atlanta. Two days ago it was a brawl in a bar and . . ." He snapped his fingers and pointed at Sam as if that would help him to remember. "Before that . . . a fight with some guy in Boston." Mike shook his head again. "Sam, we can't keep doing this."

Sam watched Mike's struggle.

A bulldog of a man standing six feet tall with sandy blond hair, Mike had been a football star in high school—his glory days—and smitten with the idea of working closely with one of the best professional football players alive on what had been heralded as the criminal court case of the decade.

Jeremy Connors stood accused of raping a woman named Jessica Stanten, a well-known socialite-turned-sports-agent. Her past was stellar—all-American, graduated cum laude from Stanford, two serious relationships, no other known sexual activity. Mike had wanted a slam dunk. He'd wanted to show the ranks of Jackson, Keller & Whiteman that he was partner material, but Connors was making it nearly impossible.

"Ed, tell me this is all just another great miscarriage of justice," Sam said and sat forward in his chair, focusing on Ed Slader.

Ed, like Sam and Mike, was a big man—tall, big-boned, fair-skinned, yet he was completely content to sit back and watch the show rather than get his hands dirty. He wasn't afraid of hard work; rather, he preferred to think of himself as the *cleanup crew*—sweep in at the last moment to tidy the mess no one else could manage.

"Isn't all of this a great miscarriage of justice?" Mike asked as he paced. "I mean, come on! These women know exactly what they're getting into when they climb into bed with him. They know exactly what they're getting into with every bed they climb into. They want sex with a superstar. Period. Now, this guy—"

"I think the victims would have something to say about that," Ed said quietly. Two sets of eyes snapped in his direction, and Ed shrugged. "Sorry. A ridiculous figure of speech."

"There are no victims here," Sam said, shoving papers aside as he came to his feet. "Let's get that clear right now."

"I just meant that the guy from that bar—"

Sam threw up a hand. "Ahh, don't want to hear it. I don't want nor do I need to know the details. I know exactly how it all went down. Some asshole wanted to compare balls with Jeremy. Guy's sitting there, tipping back one too many while he watches some little honey he's got no chance of ever laying, and in comes Jeremy Connors. So he starts something up. You know, a little show for the guys, a little show for the dancers. How many times does Jeremy have to put up with this?" As he talked, he moved around his desk, hands clasped together, working the scenario the same way he had countless times in front of a jury.

Ed and Mike made eye contact, and Ed settled into the leather sofa with a slight smile curling the edges of his lips as the master worked the room.

"Let's be sure of this, the only victim here is the athlete himself. How many times does he have to be challenged, slandered, shouted at, and berated all because he's a gifted athlete?" Sam stopped for a moment, digesting his own words.

In truth, he was sick and tired of the way athletes behaved. They achieved any sort of star status, and their egos took over with a self-inflated sense of entitlement that took a previously sane, talented player and turned him into an I'm-above-the-law moron. There was no getting around it—Jeremy Connors was a giant pain in the ass, and Sam couldn't wait to be done with the case. But this was what he did best.

"Mike, you're on this latest . . . situation. I want it handled and case closed by the end of the week. Pay out whoever you need to and shut this thing down. No press, no interviews. Nothing. It didn't happen. *Capiche?*"

Mike nodded and Sam turned to Ed.

"Ed, this has nothing to do with Jessica Stanten."

"Our lady-in-wait," Ed said on cue.

Chuckles reverberated across the room.

"Yes," Sam said with a nod. "Keep digging. Let's remember, gentlemen, we're the victims here." Sam glanced back toward the television. The story of Jeremy Connors' latest escapade was long over, but the memory of it lingered. He sighed. "We're the victims."

Lady-in-wait was a term Sam had created. Coined specifically for Jessica Stanten, but others fell nicely into the category. Jessica was no more a victim in all this than Jeremy. Sam had seen it time and again. Women seduced athletes and wound up playing the innocent to some alleged foul play all for the name of money. Big money. They weren't victims. They were merely lying in wait for the next sucker. In fact, it was funny to Sam how these women portrayed themselves. Only when they did not get what they wanted did they play the victim. Otherwise, they were stalkers. They knew travel schedules, where the team stayed, and favorite hangouts. These women, these *ladies-in-wait*, were far more aggressive than any paparazzi had ever aspired to be.

It was a position Sam took in law school and one that landed him with the prestigious Jackson, Keller & Whiteman, a dinosaur-run firm that had cemented itself with labor disputes in the early 1940s but had recently shifted its focus and efforts on entertainment industry cases, following the big bucks, high profiles, and publicity-generated cases. Initially, that had meant focusing on paternity suits and divorces of the well known and well paid. The cases were no brainers that benefitted everyone, even the athletes. But in the past decade, the cases had become much more challenging—and disturbing—as the behavior of professional athletes had worsened exponentially, but the public had continued to tolerate the behavior. Jackson, Keller & Whiteman had gone from divorce to defending professional athletes accused of murder, rape, tax evasion, and drug possession.

"Ed, talk to me about Carmen Hernandez," Sam said but any further discussion was interrupted by the light rap on his office door.

Sam's assistant, Lisa, a neat and pleasant woman, poked her head into the office. "I'm sorry, Sam. Mr. Whiteman is on the phone."

Sam shot a look of concern at Ed then Mike.

The big guy didn't call down unless there were congratulations or someone was losing a job. On this day, or any day since he had taken the Connors case, there wasn't anything to celebrate.

He cringed and moved gingerly toward the phone, aware of all the eyes on his back. Ignoring them, he asked Lisa. "He say what he wants?"

"He's been watching the news," she said flatly.

Sam lost a step.

"This thing is getting out of control," Mike said with a groan. He threw himself onto the sofa next to Ed and collapsed his head into his hands. "The Connors case is becoming unmanageable."

"That's your department, Mike. Manage him" Ed said and Mike glared.

Even as Sam picked up the phone, he heard Mike complaining about playing babysitter. It had become the second most popular topic between Mike and Ed—who was going to look after the prima donna athlete while they worked the case.

Sam grunted softly and ran his hand across his throat to get Mike to stop so that he could hear Mr. Whiteman outline how he wanted Sam to handle the Connors case, but the fact was Mr. Whiteman really had no idea of who and what Jeremy Connors was. He was an atypical client. Connors didn't care how the case was handled. He just wanted to have fun. He believed that if he threw money at the situation others could resolve it while he continued tearing up the lines on the field and destroying lives off it.

Mike and Ed angrily lowered their voices, bickering back and forth while Sam tried to placate Mr. Whiteman enough to get back to the more important discussion at hand.

"Thankfully, I don't answer to you." Ed furrowed his brows as his voice rose and he waved Mike off.

"This is a team effort, man." Mike said. "I'm busting my ass trying to pin this guy down." He fell back into the folds of the couch. "It's not like I'm asking him to . . . to *kill* someone or run naked through the streets. Although, I'm sure he'd do it, given the chance. Hell, I'm just asking him to stay out of trouble and he can't do it. He's such a giant ass, he can't do it. He just thinks—"

"He thinks we'll take care of whatever mess he creates," Sam said, finishing the sentence.

Ed and Mike turned in unison.

Gently, Sam lowered the phone onto its cradle and sighed.

No one spoke for a moment.

Today lawyers had to be spin doctors, sugarcoating the outrageous behavior of athletes, the excessive salaries, and demanding audiences to their advantage. It was something Sam had mastered, and it was why he had been assigned as lead council for the Connors case, but even the higher powers that be could see that Connors was on a one-man crusade to sabotage his own case. The latest barroom brawl was an annoyance to be sure, but manageable. The Carmen Hernandez situation had yet to be settled and, of course, Jessica Stanten was ongoing, but they had reached a boiling point. There could be no more distractions, no more scrapes with the law, and no more potential lawsuits—however unreasonable. Anything in print looked bad for the Connors team.

Sam punched the intercom button on his phone.

"Lisa, find me a resort. Some out of the way, never-heard-of-it resort where there are no reporters, no bars, and for Hell's sakes, no women."

"Sam, what are you doing?" Mike asked. His voice deepened and he glanced at Ed, the nudge for a little support clear in his look.

"Actually, I know of a place," Lisa said with a hint of laughter in her voice. "I'll be right in."

"Never-heard-of-it resort? Talk to me, bro. What are we doing?" Mike said and patted the desktop.

"You know what we're doing. It's called damage control. You said you wanted help with it, well here you go," Sam said. "I don't like it any more than you but we're going to have to work out of the office. If we can't keep our boy from, uh, finding trouble, we'll take him somewhere where trouble can't be found."

Mike's mouth dropped open as Lisa entered, smiling.

"My brother-in-law has this insane notion that he wants to do a cattle drive up in some place in Utah. You're gone for, like, ten days or something. No phones, no television. You drive a herd from some ranch in Horse Canyon to somewhere in Colorado with a couple of ranch hands," she said and shrugged. "But he can't do it. It's pretty expensive. It's some old refurbished turn-of-the-century farmhouse. You know, the real deal, but done up all fancy. Real pricey." She placed a pamphlet on Sam's desk.

Ed was on his feet, waving his hands. "Oh, ho, there, cowgirl." While there was laughter in his voice, his eyes were wide with worry. "I may be a Texas boy, but I'm no cowboy and have no desire to be. Let's talk Bahamas, Jamaica . . . the Cayman Islands even. Poolside service, maid service, umbrella drinks."

Sam scoffed and rubbed his forehead. "You're missing the point. We're trying to avoid crowds." He nodded toward Lisa. "Sounds good. Get me more details." Briefly, Sam eyed the pamphlet and then tossed it to Mike.

She nodded, slipping away under the glare of both Ed and Mike.

"A cattle drive?" Mike said and laughed. "You're *not* serious. A cattle drive?"

"Look, I'm not saying we have to participate. I'm sure we can sit around the ol' campfire while the others, I dunno, drive the herd. We'll pay top dollar for their facilities. I'm sure that's all they care about. Point is—"

"We fall off the map." Mike shook his head.

This was supposed to be the case that put them *on* the map.

"Exactly. So, switching gears . . ." Sam looked at Ed who seemed enthralled by something he was reading. "Tell me something about Carmen Hernandez."

Carmen Hernandez, a pretty twenty-four year old, had filed a paternity suit against Jeremy Connors in the last twenty-four hours. One more distraction for the jury, one more storyline for the newspapers, one more sound bite for the late night news, and one more joke for the talk show hosts. All that was known about her was that she worked as a cocktail waitress, pulling down a meager twelve thousand dollars a year while raising a two-year-old daughter, and now she was pregnant with Connors' baby, or so she claimed.

"We've got Dilmont working it," Mike said. "She's in Chicago, living with her parents. We really don't know who she is yet."

"Well, we need to. Quickly." Sam crossed his arms and scowled. "With all the talking she's been doing to the press, we need to find something damaging and take her out of the equation."

"Look, about this cattle drive thing." Ed brandished the pamphlet in his hand and shook his head as he pointed at the picture of the ranch featured on the cover.

"We're doing it. Pack your boots," Sam said.

Mike snorted and Sam eyed him.

"You, too, big boy. When was the last time you threw a leg over a horse?"

"Whoa, I don't mind saying it. I fear the equine."

Sam covered the grin that popped up at the image of the two hundred and seventy-five-pound Mike on a horse. He was pretty sure the equine feared Mike as well. The former college ball player had shifted most of his weight to his stomach. Although powerfully built and surprisingly agile on the racquetball court, Mike was all belly and no outdoorsman.

Reluctantly, the men left Sam's office, and as Sam watched them go, he couldn't stifle the chuckles any longer, amused at the prospect of big Mike and Ed riding horses.

He fingered the files on his desk, but there was nothing amusing about the case.

A picture caught his eye and he studied it a moment.

Jessica Stanten.

She was lovely. A lady-in-wait.

He sighed.

She had known before she'd bedded Connors what kind of a man he was. She had known he was a player when she'd seduced him in the hotel lobby. She had known of his reputation on and off the field and had known him to be volatile.

Hell, everyone knew!

Everyone knew about Connors' infamous bar fights, wild parties, and destruction of hotel rooms. Sam would argue to his death that Jessica Stanten, *the alleged rape victim*, was nothing more than a lady-in-wait.

There was no denying that a rape kit showed trauma to her body. She had been brutally mistreated by someone, but that didn't mean that Connors was the culprit. In fact, Connors' semen was not the only thing found inside her. There had also been traces of a condom, and Jeremy didn't use condoms, indicating there had to have been another man. Her character and sexual history would play a huge factor. Although she had initially appeared wholesome, Sam intended to change that. He would argue that Jessica Stanten had been around the block quite a few times and liked rough sex. He would argue that she knew exactly what she was getting into when she went upstairs with the notorious playboy. As for the bruises and tearing . . .

He shrugged. Did he really know that was the doing of his client? She'd been with at least one other man that night. Possibly two. They were still hunting for others, but even if it was just one, he would be able to prove his point. Connors was just one man in her little game to collect money.

Carmen Hernandez posed another problem. They didn't know much about her beyond her being a hard-working, divorced mom, a good Catholic girl, a regular girl next door.

Still, if she was such a good girl, why was she sleeping with the likes of Jeremy Connors?

Whatever the answers, he needed to get Connors away from everything and everyone. He needed to remove distractions, temptations, and any further disruptions from the case, and where better than the middle of nowhere?

Chapter Two

According to Connors' version of events, Jessica Stanten had been the aggressor in bed and out. Although she had a sweet, baby doll kind of face with big eyes and a full mouth accentuated by makeup, she had said things to Jeremy that he couldn't believe. She had told him how she wanted him, wanted it rough, wanted him to force her down, wanted to feel every inch of him. She had said she wanted the bed to rock, the headboard to slam against the wall, and she wanted him to teach her a lesson.

That was what she had said, over and over again. "Teach me, baby! Teach me a lesson."

She had wanted to be punished and dominated the way women like her do. She had wanted a man in bed who was in complete control, and Connors was in total control. They had both known that she had been helpless to stop what she had put in motion and she'd loved it. She had moaned for him and tilted her head back, arching for him, writhing for him in a way that made him want her even more and she had urged him on every bit of the way. And when it was done and he had slowed his rhythm, she had been begging for more again.

She had loved the way he smelled, the way he covered her entire body, the way his right arm wrapped around her, the way he had total dominance over her. She had squealed and wiggled in such a way that she had gotten him going again, and just like she'd asked—no *begged*—he had rocked the furniture. She had driven him to near madness until, finally, they had both collapsed. And then, according to Connors, she'd begun to laugh.

It had been a weird kind of laugh, he'd said. *Part exhaustion, but part something else. Like she was a little nutty or something. She said she'd be good to go again after she got some rest.*

He hadn't been able to. He had to get some sleep before catching the next flight home. It had been that awkward time that he'd never enjoyed.

No matter how good the sex, no matter how hot the woman, there always came that time when he needed to send the woman packing so he could get some shut-eye.

Like so many women before her, that had made her mad.

These women always got upset when he kicked them out after a romp. But he didn't care. They were strangers, and there was no way he was going to share his sleep time with someone he didn't know. Some of the groupies were scary weird, psycho stalker types.

She had ranted on about how he shouldn't treat her that way, he'd said.

He had told her how good she was and all the things women liked to hear but had kept her moving toward the door until he had been able to shut her out of the room and go to bed.

That, Connors had said, *was the last time he had seen Jessica Stanten.*

Sam read the notes again. There was no way this girl was naïve. Judging by witness accounts of how she was dressed and comments she'd made in the bar while waiting for the team to arrive at the hotel, as well as the very descriptive liaison between Stanten and Connors, she was no girl next door. But Sam worried about the female reaction to this case. He had listened to the way the women in his own office talked. Their responses had been guarded, careful not to insult Jeremy Connors or the legal defense. Still, he had sensed tension. If just one woman on the jury felt as strongly as some of the women in the office about the naivety or accountability issues, they were screwed.

No, Stanten was not naïve or innocent. She got what she came for, and after Connors had given her the boot, she had gone looking for more somewhere else and gotten beaten up.

Sam rocked back in his chair, staring at the desktop.

What was her motive? Anger?

If Connors had let her sleep the night with him, she wouldn't have been brutalized. It was also certainly an ego thing as well. There were dozens of witnesses in the bar who verified she had spoken openly about getting to know Connors. Some might even say she'd bragged. She hadn't anticipated being used and tossed to the side. Accusing him of rape made him pay twice—for humiliating her and for setting her outside to be abused by another.

He picked up a pencil and began to doodle when Mike poked his head into the office again. "Got a minute?"

Sam nodded.

Mike sauntered in, huffing loudly to announce his displeasure with something. He thumped a rolled up magazine against his hip, strode up to the desk, plopped the magazine before Sam, and snapped his hand back in a grand fashion.

Always the showman.

Sam pressed the pencil between his lips and picked up the magazine.

"Another damned women's magazine," Mike said, falling back into a chair. "Let me tell you this, women are damned hypocrites! They talk about respect and how to be treated by a man but have you seen their magazines? All they talk about is sex, how to have it, who to have it with, about jumping *his* bones, and all kinds of crap. Not to mention, almost every picture of a woman in these magazines is naked. They look at each other naked!"

Sam stared at Mike, letting him vent.

With an added huff, Mike waved his finger toward the magazine in Sam's hands. "It's Jessica's version. The true story. The untold story. Crock of shit. Read it. Read it." Mike slammed into the chair's back, crossing his arms and sighing loudly.

Sam glanced at the headlines.

VIOLENCE AMONG ATHLETES! YOU COULD BE NEXT!

Next to the bold caption was a picture of a large, well-muscled man strangling a helpless woman.

Sam rubbed his temple.

"She's saying she went to talk to Connors, try to persuade him to sign with her as a sports agent, even says she tried to appeal to his feminine side or some crap like that—"

"This isn't new." Sam let the magazine fall back on his desk.

He didn't need to read it. He'd heard it all before. Stanten claimed she was a sports agent and had wanted to talk Connors into signing with her but things turned ugly as soon as she got behind closed doors.

"Ah, but read on. They've got like fifteen examples of other athletes convicted of raping some innocent hotel-hopping groupie," Mike said, leaning forward and flipping the pages so hard and fast they popped as they whipped past Sam's nose.

"I don't need to read it, Mike. I hear it all day. So do you. But does this article talk about the second semen sample? Anything about our interview with the ex-boyfriend?"

Mike shot to his feet, his eyes full of hope. "We got a second semen sample?"

Sam knitted his brows, scowling. "Please! It's the next conclusion. We have evidence of a condom. We know Connors didn't wear a condom and we have the ex-boyfriend, Ted Nehoff, stating that he had . . . what was it?" Sam leaned forward, shuffling through his paperwork. He pulled out the paper he wanted and passed it to Mike. "He testified that Stanten used sex as a vehicle to get what she wanted but he refused to commit."

Mike nodded as he read the report.

They had discussed the particular use of the phrase "used sex as a vehicle to get what she wants." That would bode well in court.

"She's a whore," Mike said, thinking out loud.

Internally, Sam winced. It wasn't an argument he particularly liked, but he wasn't above using it for the sake of making an impression. He nodded in agreement with Mike. "Don't lose sight of that. She used sex to get what she wanted. For two and a half years, she used sex to try to get ol' Ted to commit to the relationship. Finally, he was tired of the games and said no more. She'd hit a wall. This only *after* she'd been kicked out of Connors' bed. I mean, look at her, Mike. She's gorgeous. I'll wager she's not used to being treated that way and she kind of flipped out."

What he didn't like was the fact that Ted Nehoff claimed to have had sex with Stanten before she went to see Jeremy Connors. It was a definite problem. There was no history of violence with Nehoff and nearly two-dozen witnesses who could track most of his comings and goings the evening of the alleged rape, including the time frame he had been with Jessica Stanten. What Sam needed was evidence of a third partner.

"But there's also the issue of the hotel room," Mike said as he went back to the magazine and flipped to a page. Even upside down, he knew right where the paragraph was and poked at it.

Sam let his eyes follow Mike's finger.

"Stanten claims that someone came in behind Connors and cleaned the room." Mike reminded Sam of Jessica's argument and Sam laughed.

"Of course she's saying that. She *has* to say that! Hell, Mike, what's she gonna say? That she was brutally raped and fought for her life but the room was immaculate? Nope. That dog don't hunt."

The Houston police had checked out the room and found no evidence of a crime scene, no blood, no ejaculation, no broken furniture—nothing to support the story that Jessica Stanten had presented to them. No staff members had reported anything out of the ordinary. No hotel guests had complained of loud noises. A professional cleaning crew and an investigative team had found nothing out of the ordinary, which only fueled the argument presented by Jackson, Keller & Whiteman that nothing had happened. Certainly, no crime had been committed.

"I still don't like it," Mike said, shaking his head. "Look at this. They got themselves a little poll here." He poked the magazine again. "Look how many women think he's guilty! Look how many think he's getting away with a crime simply because he's a celebrity. Damned bitches!"

"It's just a poll," Sam said, trying to placate Mike. He needed to keep Mike focused on the facts, keep him bloodthirsty and on the hunt.

For the most part, Sam had been pleased with the way the case was going, but there had been some sticking points. Jessica Stanten had claimed to be the victim of not only rape but of sabotage as well. Someone from the office of Jackson, Keller & Whiteman had leaked information about Stanten and her family. It had been all over *The Chronicle* the next morning and ballooned from there. While Jackson, Keller & Whiteman had vehemently denied any knowledge of this action, Mike had appeared far too pleased with the fallout. Sports fans around the nation had called Stanten's home. She had had to move, change cell numbers, quit one job, and been fired from another.

Sam had seen her parents on a couple of talk shows, pleading to the

American public to let the courts decide and leave them alone, but it was coming around full circle and was about to bite them all in the ass. There had been a shift in sentiment. The sports channels and magazines were no longer the only media outlets for the story. Now women's publications had come on board.

Initially, Sam had been very angry about the leak. This wasn't the way he liked to win cases. Whoever had released the information hadn't counted on the fact that a person can only be beat up on so much before she fires back. At some point, Stanten had decided just that and began talking more freely to women's magazines and newspapers until a gag order had been issued. But the damage had been done and public perception of Connors was poor. While the vast majority of sports lovers only wanted to be sure none of it would affect Connors' preseason training and time on the field, women's groups had been all over the professional league, home offices, Connors, and the firm. It had also generated enough PR that other women had come forward to accuse Connors of various crimes.

To date, the only confirmed case pending against Connors, besides the Stanten case, was the Carmen Hernandez paternity suit, but there were rumors that other women were preparing to come forward.

Since the backlash against Stanten, Hernandez had gone into hiding and proven difficult to find. Although Sam was certain she would be found, he was running out of time. He wanted to talk to her as soon as he could and find out what kind of lover Connors was. It was possible the Hernandez paternity suit could work in their favor. What he needed most was for her to come forward and say Connors was a tender, passionate lover, not a rapist.

What he didn't need was women's magazines continually making speculations or unofficial polls about Connors' guilt or innocence, and—Sam looked to the magazine once more—connecting him with known, convicted rapists and wife beaters was not helpful.

No, he had to keep Mike focused.

"Mike, before the week is done, we'll see three more just like this. It comes down to this. She's nothing but a lady-in-wait. She hung around way too long in a relationship that clearly wasn't going anywhere, and then she seduced a known playboy and got the boot after he got what he wanted. Keep digging. We'll find more. This lady uses her body as a tool and doesn't like it when the tool isn't treated well. Case closed." He smacked the desk hard with both hands.

"You still hopped up on this idea of going to a dude ranch?" Mike asked.

"Got my spurs on right now," he said and grinned lazily. No, it wasn't something he was wildly excited about, but getting Jeremy Connors out of circulation was essential. "Had to custom order yours. Double wide."

"Nice. Thank you. And I'm supposed to ride?"

"Only on the ones that'll have you."

"Well, I don't see a problem there." Mike smoothed a hand over his belly and did a small hip swivel that made Sam grimace. "Those mares won't know what a stallion is till they lay eyes on me."

"I just, uh, I can't respond to that, Mike. It's wrong on so many levels."

Mike turned on his heel, cackling as he left the office. "I think we both know what's going on here . . . you're just a weensy threatened," he called out over his shoulder.

Sam laughed but as soon as Mike disappeared, he grew serious again, staring at the picture of Jessica Stanten. He rocked back in his chair, his fingers forming a steeple in front of his mouth, and his mind raced.

He had not asked for this case. It had been assigned to him and had come with a price.

Make this problem go away, he had been told, *and you could be looking at a full partnership with the firm.*

It was an offer that hadn't been extended to the others. When he combined it with Mike openly speaking about the possibilities of a partnership with a win from this case, and Ed needing something extraordinary to jumpstart his career after the slump he'd been having, it was the very reason Sam hadn't been able to talk to them about the importance of a not guilty verdict. From the sports networks to the early morning talk shows, the three men had been dubbed the newest legal dream team.

It was one more reason to get away from it all.

While he couldn't prove that it was Mike who had leaked the information about Jessica Stanten, Sam wanted the legal team as far away from a media platform as possible, at least for a little while.

No. He hadn't asked for this case, but he damn sure needed to win it.

He looked at Jessica Stanten's picture again. What made a woman like her, a woman who could otherwise have whatever and whoever she wanted, hook up with the likes of Jeremy Connors?

Sam knew there was no easy answer.

What made a woman like his own mother act the way she did? In some regards, Sam's mother would qualify as a lady-in-wait. Each time she tipped back the bottle she had known what she was doing. She had known that she was abandoning her children, if only for a few hours, each time she had erased her mind. She had known when the doctors told her that her liver was going that she was killing herself and leaving her babies to be orphaned. But she hadn't stopped. Some had said she couldn't stop, but Sam wasn't buying. She could have stopped, but she had chosen not to. She had chosen her bottle over her babies. She had used pain, addiction, and selfishness over the reality of what was to come. She had died, leaving three children behind to fend for themselves.

When women walked into hotel rooms of elite athletes with wild reputations and made themselves available for whatever was to come, they were not victims.

He glared at the picture across the desk. "She is no lady." He called for Lisa to see how the arrangements for the cattle ranch were coming along.

Chapter Three

"Son of a bitch! Where is he?" Mike paced a stretch of carpet back and forth. "This is just beautiful. We're in the middle of nowhere for the sole purpose of saving his ass, and he can't manage to show? Beautiful!" He threw his hands up in typical Mike fashion.

Sam settled back against the wall to watch as he put on a show. There was no sense trying to talk him down when he was like this.

Salt Lake City had been the prearranged meeting place. Lisa had made all the arrangements, including the rendezvous with Jeremy Connors. While the legal team from Jackson, Keller & Whiteman had come directly from Houston, Jeremy had been partying in San Francisco and had promised to catch the next available flight into Salt Lake.

Mike paused his next round of pacing near the suitcase carrousel and eyed each piece of luggage as it circled once more—the same six pieces of luggage for the last thirty minutes. Inexplicitly, theirs were nowhere to be found, which only added fuel to Mike's anger.

It had been a rough couple of days leading up to their excursion, and Mike didn't handle change well. The recent paternity suit and nonstop media blitz had made things difficult, but the latest information that Sheryl Houghton of the receptionist pool was leaking information to the media had been too much. The irony had been she claimed to have done it to pay some bills. Now, Jackson, Keller & Whiteman were going to nail her to the wall, taking everything she ever owned or thought about owning. Trash had to be shredded and hand carried out of the office to be thrown away miles from the office, all phone calls and incoming clients had to be heavily screened, and not one but two different news agencies had been discovered posing as potential clients only to get a chance to nose around the office and talk to low-level employees. It had been the final push Mike had needed to reach the edge.

Sam checked his watch and sighed.

According to their itinerary, a ranch hand named Wade something-or-other was supposed to pick them up and deliver them some two hundred and seventy-five miles away to a ranch called Rainwash.

He looked around again.

No Wade.

No suitcases.

No Jeremy Connors.

"Lisa is going to hear about this," Mike said, muttering and punching numbers on his cell. He seemed determined that someone would be his audience.

"Samuel Spann?" A deep voice echoed in the terminal walls.

Sam and his small group came alive.

A short, stocky man extended a hand toward Sam.

He could be no one other than Wade.

Faded jeans. Worn and still dusty boots. A handshake like a vise grip. His skin on his hand was calloused, thick, and permanently marked by hard labor, dirt, and sweat. His black hair and eyes set against his chiseled face gave him a distinctly Native American look.

"That's right," Sam said and stuck out his own hand. "You Wade?"

"Been standing around for some time," Wade said as he sized up the bunch of lawyers quite thoroughly. "Thought I better walk around a bit." There was the faintest of smiles on his face.

Sam spotted a luggage cart filled with their bags and suitcases and Sam groaned.

Mike strode over. "I'll be damned. He's got our stuff. Good man!" He stuck out a hand and pumped Wade's arm with certain enthusiasm.

"We're just waiting on another person," Ed said, properly introducing himself.

Wade exchanged names and pulled a notebook from his shirt pocket, studying it. "You waiting on Reginald Perry?" he asked and Mike's head jerked up. He had been busily inspecting all the suitcases, making sure all five of his bags had made it on board.

"Perry called you? That prick. What's he doing calling?" Mike asked and shot a look of annoyance toward Sam, who waved a hand at him, trying to quiet him down.

"You say Perry called you? When?" Sam wanted to yell in irritation like Mike, but he wanted details first. He couldn't stand Reginald Perry.

Since Jackson, Keller & Whiteman had taken the Connors case, the guy had been nothing but a thorn in Sam's side. He had convinced himself and Connors that as Jeremy Connors' sports agent, it was essential for him to be part of every move the legal team made. In truth, he was nothing more than a leech, trying to cash in on Jeremy's fame and bad boy image while desperately trying to be seen as a productive and vital member of the team in the eyes of Jeremy. Sam was certain that Perry was a big part of Jeremy's troubles.

"Well, he didn't talk to me. Talked to the boss, Ms. Kat. Said him and his party wouldn't be arriving for another day. Got hung up or something." Wade studied the name one more time on his notebook as he spoke then tucked it back in its pocket for safe keeping.

"Where was he calling from?" Mike demanded but Wade only shrugged.

"Sorry, gentlemen, that's all I can tell ya. I just got the message and wrote down the name. That's it. But I'm sure Ms. Kat can tell you more."

"That's fine," Sam said and managed to force a smile on his face. "I appreciate the message."

The plan had been so simple. *Start fresh. Work under the radar.* Fresh air, good clean fun, relax, and unwind for a few days before getting to work. Hell, at one point, he had actually entertained the notion that they might all learn something new about each other and maybe even come to like Jeremy a little. They could become a team, work as a family. The more he had thought about it, the more he had liked the idea of working the land, doing something besides pushing papers and arguing cases. But the bastard hadn't even been able to get that right. And now, to make matters worse, he had Reginald Perry with him.

"I was starting to think you boys give up on me." Wade smiled slightly.

"No, we're just too stupid to figure out where to stand." Ed examined the cart heaped with bags and suitcases. "Looks like you got it all. I'd like to say you accidentally picked up some that isn't ours but, uh, this is all ours." Ed grinned as he scratched his head.

Wade shrugged, positioning himself behind the cart again. "Don't matter. We've got plenty of room."

It had been a magnificent understatement. The Rainwash Ranch courtesy van was roomy enough but paled compared to the ranch itself. By the time they reached the ranch, the sun had begun to dip behind the mountain, lowering a thick orange curtain over the spectacular scenery in front of them, and whatever concerns or frustrations Sam had been having about Jeremy faded as he took in the view.

Several dogs rushed the van as it entered the compound, alerting everyone to their arrival. To Sam's right, about the length of a football field away, sat a huge barn, complete with hayloft, swinging cable rods for lifting bales, and horse stalls. He could just make out someone moving from stall to stall inside the barn, busily feeding while the horses beckoned him to move more quickly.

Dinner time.

Straight ahead, cows called out. It was a huge herd, too many to count, that had converged over the hill toward the front gate, mooing for their share of grain or hay.

Sam stopped, pulled in a long, slow breath, filling his lungs completely, and took in the smell.

Pure country.

How sweet the air smelled depended on which way the wind shifted.

He'd heard it said many a time by fellow Texans, there was no better smell than horse manure. The jury was still out on that one, but cow dung was something else altogether, and he said as much.

"I'm thinking it's the same thing, Sam," Ed said with an easy laugh. "Both horses and cows eat the same grass, hay, grains, whatever, and process it the same way. And, if my memory of early field trips to Old MacDonald's Farm serves me correctly, it all comes out the same way."

At last, the light banter Sam had imagined when Lisa had first mentioned this place. Complemented by a light breeze moving across the valley, and it was suddenly very nice to be at Rainwash.

As they stepped out of the van and stretched, Wade brought their attention to the main house—a majestic lodge, situated in the center of the complex with intricate details in the woodwork that made it both impressive and inviting. The massive front porch was a masterpiece in and of itself complete with oversized rocking chairs, tables, and decorative ornaments. A man could sit and watch the world from that very porch. In fact, it had been the main house that had caught the attention of Lisa's brother-in-law as well as Sam's when he had checked out the website. That, and the name. Rainwash. The logo on the site had said something to the effect of "wash your troubles away." It was perfect.

Wade called out to a few more men to unload the luggage, and he invited the lawyers to take a look around.

The landscape was breathtaking, and just what Sam needed. Red-dusted mountains set off in the distance, looking much closer than they actually were. Whispers of red, yellow, and blue flowers brushed over the pale green landscape.

And an ear-splitting whistle to jerk his attention to the lone horseman barreling over the hills just beyond the barn

"Look there!" Mike had also spotted the rider and pointed in the direction Sam was watching.

As horse and rider drew closer, the men could see the rider was female, and they moved closer to the round pen that was set apart from the front corral.

She came flying down the side of the slope on a beautiful, muscular palomino that thundered across the grassy slopes, chasing down the cows.

"We've had some coyote troubles," Wade hollered from the van. "We like to bring 'em in at night, particularly the calves."

None of the men spoke as they watched the strong lean rider slightly bow over the horn of the saddle. Her hands were on the reins, urging her horse on, oblivious to all the openmouthed spectators.

She wore a blue, ragged baseball cap pulled so low over her brow that Sam could only see her mouth and the chiseled outline of her jaw.

Her white T-shirt looked like thin cotton, flapping against her body with one sleeve hitched up, maybe caught in a bra strap, revealing a long, tanned sinewy arm. Her jeans were snug, though it could have just been that she was straddling a horse, but it looked good to Sam. She was the precise picture of what he would have imagined a cowgirl to be—except for the feet.

Briefly, he scanned her feet. No cowboy boots, but open-toed sandals. Her white feet were such a contrast to her tanned arms and the rest of her look. As she swung a loop close to the fence line nearest them, he noticed she had purple, glitter nail polish on her well-manicured feet, and he couldn't stop the chuckle that hit him. She was a complete contradiction, and he caught himself looking back toward her face, wondering if she were aware of this fashion oversight, but something else caught his attention. There was a second rider, then a third, and a fourth.

As the riders crested the hill, they fanned out, directing their horses in different directions. He could hear the first rider make a gruff *h'yup* sound, followed by lots of short whistles. The dogs who had greeted them in the courtyard responded, dashing past them and ducking under the fences to join the chase. It was fascinating to watch as each rider, horse, and dog worked in unison, driving the cattle in.

A moment later, Wade joined them at the fence, his elbows propped on the boards. "Yup, there they are. Now watch this, boys, and prepare to be schooled."

Sam heard Mike suppress a surprised laugh.

As they moved closer, the men could see that the second rider couldn't have been more than ten or twelve years old. She was a miniature version of the first rider—blond, lean, and muscular. She rode like the first rider as well, bowed over the saddle, reins drawn up, and in complete control of an animal that outweighed her a hundred times over. She wore a straw cowboy hat with the rims curled up tightly on both sides allowing Sam to see her features more clearly than the first rider. She was pretty, with a small nose covered with freckles, and a face that looked like a little doll. Although she was a child, it was clear she was going to be a very pretty woman.

Wade pointed. "That one is Brooke. First born. Natural born rider, sits nice in a saddle ever since she was a babe."

Suddenly, Brooke turned her head and yelled something over her shoulder to her companion, surprising Sam with her intensity. The command was followed by the same series of short whistles he'd heard before, a slightly higher-pitched version of her mother's. A lone calf had broken ranks and was trying to flee back up the hill into open terrain, but the child was on it.

The third rider brought her charge in successfully and caught Wade's eye. For a moment, she trotted toward the fence and allowed the men to take in the full measure of the cowgirl. Though just a child, there was no doubt exactly who was in charge of the huge animal.

"Hey, girl!" Wade called out.

The child flashed a quick grin in his direction. "Hey, Wade!" Her voice sounded so small.

Sam guessed her to be no more than eight years old. She was tiny. Her legs, arms, and trunk were skinny. Up close, he could see the bluest eyes twinkling over her smile at the older man. Her skin was like porcelain, not nearly so tanned as the other riders, yet it was clear they were related. She had the same features. She wore a cowboy hat like the others complete with jeans, a white T-shirt, and boots.

"Hey, babygirl! Heard you kicked some booty with the barrels." Wade chuckled, owning some joke of his own.

The little girl frowned and sighed heavily. "Wade," she said, her tone clearly disgusted. "I'm *Danni*."

"Awww." Wade hit the fence. "Dang it, but I can't keep you twins straight."

"I've got the cowboy hat," she said, her voice hinting at a whine as she pointed to her hat.

Wade's chuckle let everyone know he knew exactly which sister she was. It seemed to be a joke that never got old for Wade but was obviously wearing on the little one's nerves.

"How's it lookin'?" Wade asked.

The little girl was no longer looking at Wade but was watching for more cows. Her horse paced from side to side, ready to break out at any moment. She coached him, giving a soft *whoa* from time to time.

"Momma's got the first batch. They broke up in four different groups, but I'm looking out for the bull. He's red hot mad." Her voice squeaked with excitement.

Wade laughed and nodded with approval.

He would have said more, but the whistle distracted him. He froze. Sam saw the woman standing up in her stirrups, frantically motioning to the fourth rider as a bull made the crest of the hill. It was enormous. Although it appeared calm, everything seemed to get eerily quiet as he descended toward the barn. For a moment, all the riders seemed to have disappeared.

Somewhere in the distance, a female voice echoed. "He-yup, he-yup! Jacks is comin' up. Danni! Brooke!"

Sam and the others craned their necks as the woman rider came up hard behind him. She was headed right for the bull, and at the last instant, made a sharp turn causing the bull to shift its stance.

"We don't let him come in. That's Ramrod. He can take care of himself out there," Wade said. "He's a big ol' boy and could really damage some of the younger heifers if he mounted them."

There was some kind of verbal exchange between all the riders.

The fourth nodded and picked up the last of the cows and drove them toward the barn.

"My God," Mike said, breathing hard and shaking his head. "They're little girls!"

Wade nodded and smiled like a proud papa.

After a moment, the bull lost interest in the woman and moved toward the herd again, with Danni in its path.

The woman made more noises, turned the horse, and looped behind the bull.

The child seemed to know just what her mother wanted and responded.

Although Sam knew nothing of herding cattle or horses, he knew that he was watching something extraordinary in this silent communication.

A light wind blew across the compound as more people came out to watch.

Sam scanned the crowd. They all looked like they were part of the Rainwash Ranch and appeared completely at ease with the notion of a woman and three little girls bringing in the herd and holding off an enormous bull. It was an honest-to-goodness showdown.

"That one, you've seen, is Danni. A regular cowgirl. Competes, too. That's what I was teasing her about. She's good. And that one—" Wade pointed to the fourth rider but froze.

Sam turned and saw the woman shift in her saddle. Her entire composure changed. She saw something, and Sam felt everyone follow her eyes . . . straight to Danni's twin.

While Danni and Brooke wore cowboy hats, this one was dressed identical to her mother—white T-shirt, jeans, open-toed sandals, and a baseball cap. Unlike her mom, her ball cap was on backward and exposed her entire face. She had porcelain skin, delicate features, full lips, and rosy cheeks. She looked like a Campbell's Soup kid, but her face was intense. She rode her horse hard, charging down the grassy bank some fifty yards behind the bull.

Sam's eyes flicked back toward woman. Pure terror had stolen her composure. The sick look she had on her face quickly turned to anger.

She leaned over her mount, digging her heels into the horse and yelling violently. "Jacks! No!" It was on.

Wade began to yell something and several men were up and over the fence, headed toward the bull before he even finished.

The woman barreled down the hill toward the giant animal and small girl.

The bull had changed its position and snorted, lowering its head. The woman's screams momentarily distracted him, but Ramrod showed only a mild interest in her. He was back to the little girl and her horse, and he was picking up his pace.

Within seconds, the woman was on him. Remarkably, her horse didn't argue.

For a split second, Sam wondered if a bull had ever killed a horse. The horns on the massive head were immense, but the woman and her hoofed partner didn't seem to notice. She urged the horse on, leaving just inches between them as she zigzagged back and forth across the path of the large bull.

"Oh, man!" Mike's disbelief broke the tension where they stood.

Sam had completely forgotten where he was. He realized he had been gripping the boards of the fence so intensely that his fingers ached.

Suddenly, there were horses and riders everywhere. All men. There were too many hoots and whistles to keep track—a plan clearly designed to distract Ramrod who simply stood in one place, snorting and tossing his head. With men yelling and horses closing the circle, Ramrod turned in disgust and headed back toward open terrain.

With the help of horsemen getting everything back under control, Wade turned back, grumbling under his breath, and climbed the fence once more. Once he hopped over, he dusted himself off and looked into the distance where the other twin hung her head.

She knew she was in trouble. Every inch of her body language screamed it.

"And that is Jacks," Wade said and shook his head, sighing. "She's a piss-ripper. A real firecracker. Believes herself to be the best rider out here and daily gives us heart attacks." He blew out another breath.

As he spoke, Jacks gave her horse a nudge and trotted toward the round pen, hoping to lose her mother.

No such luck.

The woman had turned her horse and was on the warpath—for Jacks.

Suddenly, both riders were beside the round pen, completely oblivious to anyone else.

Sam felt his body jump slightly when she spoke.

"What in the hell did you think you were doing?" she asked. There was no missing it. She was seething and looking tall and intimidating on horseback, just inches from where the men stood.

The girl, however, even sitting on a large horse, looked tiny.

"I was just trying to help," the child said, her voice more of a squeak.

The woman wasn't giving an inch. "What have I told you about—"

"Now, Kali, the girl was just trying—" Wade held up his hand as he spoke, as if to calm the woman, but she turned on him, almost shouting.

"Don't go telling me to back off, Wade. She could have gotten herself killed and you know it! That was stupid. Dangerous. *Stupid!*" She leaned forward in her saddle.

Sam watched as a small vein appeared in the side of her neck.

"And you *ever* pull a stunt like that again, you'll never ride again. I swear it, Jaclyn." She looked down at Wade. "And you! Stay out of it!"

Wade threw up his hands in self-defense.

The woman snorted, clicked her tongue at the horse and turned away.

"She don't mean it, Jacks. But Judas, you scared us all."

"I was just—"

Wade waved a hand at her. "Nope! Don't even say it. You can't be tryin' to turn out bulls, Jacks. You just stick to what you do best."

A sharp whistle from the woman brought Jacks' head up. She gave a little nod to Wade and set off, digging her small heels into the sides of her horse.

"And that, gentlemen," Wade said, pointing first to the fading figure of the angry woman and then the three girls. "That is Kali Jorgenson, your head instructor, and three of her very best assistants."

Chapter Four

In 1862, President Lincoln had signed the Homestead Act to encourage more Americans to settle out in the west. Many of those inspired to move, with little else to keep them back, were European immigrants. And Johan Jorgenson was no exception. The great-grandfather, five times over, traveled west with the hope of starting a new life, settling down with his family, and working the land. While he played with the notion of hooking up with a renegade group called the Mormons, Jorgenson created a homestead in eastern Utah, outside today's Canyonlands National Park. Jorgenson, his wife, Ilsa, and their eight sons squatted on over four hundred acres nestled in a breathtaking valley and began to build their cattle. While the family lived in a modest, dirt-floored cabin, Jorgenson and his sons labored for more than four years to build a large guest home and the most extraordinary barn anyone had seen. Jorgenson had it in mind that his land could be the resting place for travelers. The barn was designed to keep stagecoaches, horses, and whatever livestock he deemed necessary in the harsh winters. Jorgenson was a frugal man and harsh businessman but notoriously softhearted when it came to newborn calves.

One hundred years later, Jorgenson's great grandson, Jon, would turn the mammoth barn into a great house. The interior of the post and beam structure was similar to the hull of a ship with high vaulted ceilings lined with an intricate crisscross pattern of rich wooden beams that ran the full height and stretched out to wrap around the spiral staircase and built-in bookshelves.

Wade watched the men's looks of astonishment as they each stepped in and looked around, and he moved across the house to give a proper tour. "It's sixty-eight hunnert square feet, a forty-eight by a hunnert and twenty foot structure. You can see where some of the original stalls were left intact." He pointed toward the old wrought iron posts that might have once served as dividers between stalls and were now encased in a deep, cherry wood to create bookshelves. Wade led them into a fold of the massive barn. "Once upon a time, this was just a dirt floor, but when it was renovated . . . when?" He glanced over his shoulder, looking for a quick answer. "The late 1930s, it was set atop a stone and masonry foundation. Solid." He stomped the floor. "The Jorgensons are big into natural woods," he said and smiled as he gestured around the room.

Oak floors had been laid throughout, neatly decorated with Native American rugs, except for one bear rug in a far corner that looked to be in a designated reading area. The corner was cozy surrounded by bookshelves and featured an overstuffed chair that had seen better days but most likely felt wonderful. While the fabric was very worn, a colorful quilt had been thrown over, adding to the comfortable look. A wrought iron lamp hung low over the chair with a tricolored stained-glass lampshade.

The three of them stood, dancing tiny little circles as they spun from one grand sight to the next, around and around the room, *oohing* and *ahhing*. Rustic yet luxurious, functional yet elaborate, masculine yet a showpiece anyone could appreciate. It really was like being inside Noah's Ark. This was the stuff of pure male fantasy, complete with an enormous fireplace that was large enough to roast an entire pig.

Sam was sure the same scenario occurred each time a newcomer walked in the room.

"That . . ." Wade stepped forward, waving an arm toward the fireplace. ". . . was added with the renovation. There are two more, one upstairs in the game room and a small pit in the kitchen."

All the men simply nodded, mouths hung slightly loose.

Tucked neatly into an overstuffed couch with Native American patterned fabric was Kali Jorgenson. She wore a sleeveless white blouse with a low neckline and buttons up the front. From the way she sat, the weight of the top button folded into her cleavage, exposing rounder, fuller breasts than Sam would have imagined. She sat at an angle, leaning against the arm of the couch with her legs folded up beside her. Her feet were buried between the cushions next to her.

The flames from the fireplace cast a soft light along Kali's profile, making her look incredibly young and soft.

Nope. *That* was the stuff a male fantasy was made of—entering the hunter's lodge with her waiting for his return.

Sam wanted to move over toward her, make a formal introduction and compliment her on her earlier ride but, mercifully, he was interceded by Wade, who began making the introductions to a whole slew of people Sam hadn't even noticed sitting around the room.

"Of course, you know Evan Jorgenson, the oldest of the clan, a decent horseman," he said, drawing chuckles from those who knew better. "A better poker player. Don't let him con you. That's his wife, Gina." He pointed toward a solidly built woman in her late thirties or early forties with a two hands full of potatoes and a broad smile.

She had dark brown skin that was offset beautifully by a peach colored dress, which hugged snugly at her rounded hips. Her long, black hair was pinned up against the back of her neck with at least six inches falling over the clip and dusting the tops of her shoulders.

"And somewhere around here are their two kids, Tessa and Robert, or Robby.

"Over here is Stephen Jorgenson, our on-again, off-again cowhand. When he's not playing big-time CEO, he's even more pathetic than Evan in the saddle."

More boos, this time from Stephen himself.

"His wife—" Wade looked around. "Where is Tammi?"

"David's not feeling good," Stephen answered.

Wade nodded. "You'll see his lovely bride tomorrow. They have a little boy named David who's usually tearing it up around here when he's feeling good." Wade turned back to Stephen. "Everything okay?"

"Yeah, just a little bug."

"Good. And of course, there's Matthew, the baby." Wade grinned shamelessly and Matthew sighed.

Clearly, he was resigned to the baby talk.

Matthew leaned back in his chair and gave an informal 'how do' wave.

A man built like a bull snorted and waved before Wade had time to say, "That there's Tracy."

Tracy was a sharp contrast to everyone else. His complexion was irritated, perhaps by the sun or hay, but his eyes appeared watery, like a man on the verge of something. A sneezing fit or an all-night bender, it was hard to be sure. He had that look about him—slightly wild and unpredictable, but one look told any man, he was stronger than hell.

Between the white scalp peeking out beneath Tracy's thin batch of red hair and the death grip he had on the wide brimmed cowboy hat, Sam was pretty sure this was the only time he allowed his scalp to breath. But what he lacked up top grew freely on his upper lip. Tracy was working on perhaps one of the finest handlebar mustaches Sam had ever seen.

As Sam looked around the room once more, it was easy to see the Jorgenson resemblance. Dirty blond or brown hair with the classic Scandinavian features—straight nose, chiseled features, thin lips, and light eyes. With the exception of Matthew Jorgenson, the lot were long and lean, reaching over six foot three each and every one. Matthew was shorter, thicker, more powerfully built.

While several of the women made their way toward the kitchen, the menfolk, guests, and Kali sat in the great room.

All eyes were on Kali, and it was clear she knew it. She tilted her head to the side, giving a look of amused annoyance as Wade laid out the specifics.

"Kali'll be teaching you the ropes of horsemanship, and she'll be the final judge of whether you make the run to the O-Kay-Doke or not. So be nice to her and listen up. There's no one better," he said and gave a quick wink to

Kali. "Present company excluded."

She leaned back in her chair, a lazy smile on her face.

Classic beauty. Sam had heard the expression used many times but had never been struck by its meaning until that moment. When Sam had first laid eyes on her, her hair had been swept away from her face, allowing him to see her sharp jawline, perfectly straight nose, and full lips, but for dinner, her golden hair fell loose and framed her face. She had a touch of lipstick—light pink and just enough to draw Sam's attention to her mouth. Again. She had an incredible mouth.

She had been holding a wine glass, nursing it while the men spoke. For the most part, she had appeared disinterested but played the part of instructor and hung out with the men.

An hour slipped by easily without talk of sports, Jeremy Connors, or how much this case meant to the careers of all the men, but Sam knew it was too much to ask that it last forever.

* * * *

"Evan tells me you boys are lawyers," Kali said. "What kind of practice do you have?"

There was an awkward moment during which the men exchanged glances.

Samuel Spann shot a look toward Evan that Kali keyed in on right away.

"Uh, criminal." Mike cleared his throat, moving cautiously forward. He turned to peek at Evan as well. "We're clear on this, right?"

Evan nodded. "Yes, this is the perfect place for you," he said and waved toward the window framing the magnificent landscape. "We've got satellite, but we almost never watch any television. We're out of the loop out here, which is just what you want. I got that." Evan shot a look at Sam and Ed.

Kali cocked her head, her interest clearly piqued. Evan knew something about the men he was keeping from Ms. Kat. And from her. She leaned forward. "Criminal? Any particular case you're working on now?"

Evan wrinkled his nose and shot another look toward Sam, and she knew she was on to something.

"We're working on a case right now that is somewhat high profile," Mike said, coughing into a closed fist. "It's why we came here, to unwind a bit and lay out our strategy before—"

Matthew Jorgenson grunted a sound of recognition and sat up in his chair. "You fellas are working that Connors case, aren't you? That's right. Jeremy Connors." He got more excited and waved a finger at his brothers. "You know . . . the safety, busted for raping that girl in Houston. That's your neck of the woods, isn't it?" He was on a roll and didn't need to have his suspicions confirmed or denied. He knew it. He seemed to know almost everything there was to know about the case and seemed keen on sharing it all.

The youngest of the Jorgenson men was also the biggest sports fan. In fact, were it not for Matthew, there probably wouldn't be a game room or wide-screen television at Rainwash Ranch at all.

He glanced back at his sister-in-law and scooted to the edge of his seat, noticeably trying to get her as excited about the details as he was. "C'mon, Kal, you know who Jeremy Connors is, don't you?"

"Who?" she asked and gave an exaggerated shrug.

Matt's mouth fell open. "Oh, come on, Kali. You have to know who Jeremy Connors is. It's all anyone is talking about. He plays for the Boston Rebels. He's—"

"Ahh, a football player," she said, doing little to hide her bored tone. "He was arrested for rape, you say? *Shocking.* Let's see . . . an overpaid, spoiled athlete rapes a young woman, and lemme guess, he doesn't expect to do one day in jail."

"Uh-oh. Here we go."

All eyes shifted toward Tracy as he folded his arms, taking a step away from Kali.

"What? Am I wrong?" She swung her head back toward Mike. "Is your client *not* an overpaid, spoiled athlete?"

Mike's mouth fell into an openmouthed smile. "Is that a trick question?" he asked and Sam chuckled.

As she tried to find out the details surrounding Rainwash's newest visitors, Kali caught a glimpse of Danni and Jacks making their way across the yard and the small crooked smile that crossed Mr. Spann's face when he saw them as well. "No tricks. I'm simply curious. How much does your client make?"

"Well." Mike coughed and cleared his throat self-consciously. "I'm not really at liberty to— "

"Mattie." Kali redirected her attention to her brother-in-law. "How much does this guy make?"

"Like twelve million, not including bonuses and endorsement deals," he said and Tracy blew out a low whistle.

Even Kali's girls perked up as they reached the top step of the porch. "Who makes twelve million?" they asked in unison.

"And this isn't his first brush with the law, is it, Mattie?" Kali asked, ignoring the girls for a moment, focused entirely on Matthew, her own personal sports world informant.

He shook his head with a laugh. "Are you kidding? Jeremy Connors and trouble go hand in hand."

"But he's never done time, right?"

"Mmm, I don't think so." Matthew chewed on a piece of straw, thinking. "No."

Kali turned to face Mike. "So he's overpaid and spoiled, yes? And he's been in trouble with the law. Repeatedly."

"He's got a pretty bad reputation with women," Matthew said and Evan shot him a look.

"Ah, yes. So now he stands accused of raping a woman. I wonder what his defense is. Why would you defend a man like that?"

Mike opened his mouth to speak then stopped. He drew in a deep breath, appearing to choose his words. "We believe there is a very good chance Connors is innocent. And, really, that's all I can say about it. We came here to get away from questions so that we can begin a more thorough, proper analysis of the situation."

What a load of crap. It was the typical nonanswer she had expected, but she bit her tongue and politely nodded, yawned, and let Mattie take over the conversation. They were guests, and the ranch needed all the good business it could get. Matthew didn't care about the legal mumbo jumbo Kali had been digging for, he wanted to know about Jeremy Connors, the man.

Kali had risen, taking a few steps from her chair, when she heard it and stopped in her tracks. "A *what?*" she asked as she turned on her heel.

Evan, Sam, and Ed slunk back in their seats.

Tracy rubbed the back of his neck and looked down at the porch, careful not to let anyone see him smile.

"Lady-in-wait," Mike repeated. His eyes darted toward his partners for a moment.

Kali gave a false laugh. "What in the world is a lady-in-wait?" There was no mistaking the edge to her voice.

Mike gulped and looked at the rest of the men, and Kali waited to see how he would try to get out of this. "It's not a legal term. It's just jargon we use around the office."

"Yes, but what does it mean?"

"It's the girl who marries a guy who used to push her around, the girl who marries a guy knowing he's a playboy and will cheat on her." He shrugged.

Kali's eyes narrowed as she looked around the porch, and she nodded. "Uh-huh, like the girl who willingly walks into a man's bedroom or goes to a bar wearing really suggestive clothing," she said, and Mike nodded. "But it's the man who actually rapes, strangles, mutilates, degrades, destroys, or murders, isn't it?" Kali counted off the offenses on her fingers.

Mike's expression dropped.

"We're in agreement that these women are foolish to put themselves in the various dangerous situations, but in the end, it is the man who rapes, who punches, who stabs, and who violates." She ducked her head slightly so Mike could look her in the eye once more. "Right?"

"Well, no." Mike adjusted in his chair. "But just so we're all on the same page, this has nothing to do with the Connors case. We really do have reason to believe another person, not Connors, mistreated the alleged victim." He looked around the porch as though he wanted the rest of the group to show their support of his argument.

Kali stiffened at the term *alleged*. "You mean lady-in-wait." She folded her arms across her chest.

"What's a lady-in—?"

Kali made a sound that stopped Danni's question in its tracks and scooted the twins out of their seats and inside the house.

"But, for the sake of an argument, let's talk about the kind of women who knowingly, consciously, willingly seduce married men for the sole purpose of getting money, whether it's through a cash payout for services rendered or a paternity suit later on down the road. When these . . . *ladies* get up in the morning, they have set a plan in motion to get money. They are not victims like the ones you were just talking about."

"Because a beautiful woman, perhaps even a scantily clad one, seduces a famous athlete, it makes her a conniving whore?" Kali asked. "Is it not possible that many—not *all*, but some of these women really are just starstruck? Isn't it possible that many have no idea what they are getting themselves into and truly believe because they are so darned cute that the athlete might become so smitten with her that he will sweep her off of her feet?"

"Oh, please." Mike laughed. "No woman is that naïve. Not anymore. They know the score. Someone like—" Mike looked like he was about to choke on his tongue he cut himself off so quickly.

"Like Jeremy Connors," Kali said, finishing the sentence for him. "Yeah, I've heard his name before, but I didn't know who he played for and I didn't really know he had such a bad boy reputation. I just know about him because of these guys." She waved a hand at her brother-in-laws. "They're always talking about him."

Kali watched as her oldest daughter made her way across the compound.

Brooke was always the last to make it to the table because she had to tend to her horse, rub him down, and share some special treats before she would ever consider feeding herself. Although she was an excellent rider, Brooke was always more interested in the grooming aspect of horsemanship than the actual ride. It made her a rare bird indeed.

Kali lowered her voice. "Is it at all possible that a girl like, say, Brooke, ten years from now, would seek out an opportunity to be with a celebrity athlete because she just thought it would be fun to hang out with him, be seen with him?" The idea actually repulsed Kali, but she was trying to make a point. It disgusted her how men thought of women as harlots, sexpots, and play toys but never entertained the idea that these very same females were daughters, sisters, and nieces to other men.

Matthew sat forward in his chair. "She would never do that. Geez!"

Kali smiled and pushed the envelope. "Why? Couldn't it happen just that way? Only when she was brutally raped—"

"Kali!" Tracy jerked his head up, startled. He had been quietly working a piece of wood with his knife. It was his way of keeping an eye on things without having to take part in conversations he didn't like.

Tracy had recently started fussing at her about the things she said. He'd told her before that she had always been outspoken but, since Nicky's death, he thought she spoke too freely of death and destruction, and said she had become fatalistic.

"The point is . . ." Kali said, looking away from Tracy and back to Mike, ". . . we know and love this girl, and we're willing to believe that she would never be able to anticipate what bad things might befall her because she's so young and innocent and naïve. You're willing to accept that, but you are unwilling to accept the same case could be made for this other woman?"

People were such incredible hypocrites. People who professed to be ultrareligious but had no qualms about killing another human being. How many people believed they would be rewarded in heaven by taking lives, that they were doing God's or Allah's or some other higher being's work? But if you were programmed for extreme violence, it's possible you could believe anything that served your own cause.

All men were programmed to be self-serving. For that matter, so were women. Romance novels always had the playboy bedding the virgin, ceremonial wedding dresses must be white, bad boys were exciting, bad girls were whores. It never stopped. And, Kali knew, she was no better than anyone else. She had only been with one man her entire life and vowed to keep it that way. While she was raising three very tough competitors in a male-dominated arena, she was always pressing the point that they should act like ladies—no burping, no spitting, and no cursing.

"But the point is, she—this imaginary victim we're talking about—still sought out a celebrity with questionable intentions. If she was really a good girl, she wouldn't have been there in the first place." He cocked his head at her, smiling patiently. It sounded like a closing argument.

Kali's face flushed angrily, but she swallowed the words on the tip of her tongue. After all, pissing off the paying customer wasn't good form. Instead, she forced the sweetest smile she could muster. "Lady-in-wait, huh?" she said quietly.

All eyes were on her as she eased out of her chair.

Mike shrugged, feeling every bit the winner of the evening's debate.

"I get it." Kali nodded again. "Like a known car thief who gets busted alongside a friend who was the one that stole the car."

"Don't do the crime if you can't do the time," Mike said.

"Or . . . a hunter who suddenly loses his gun and gets mauled by the very bear he intended to kill."

"Well—"

"Or four city-type lawyers who make a living out of making female victims the bad guys until they go off to a dude ranch and get their asses kicked by a female instructor."

"Kali!" Ms. Kat's voice snapped from the kitchen door. She had stepped out to ring the dinner bell just in time to catch that comment. "You get in here right now!"

"I'm just trying to get the terminology. That's all. 'Ladies-in-wait.' " Kali picked up her wine glass and took another sip. There was an unmistakable glint in her eye. "I like it."

Chapter Five

It had only been a few years ago, but it felt like a lifetime ago. Literally.

Kali had awakened before anyone else, rolling over carefully to assess the situation. No one had stirred except Star. He had been snoozing with one eye fixed on her, and the moment he'd seen her shift, he had picked his head up. They had put in many hours on the trails together at that point, but this had been his first overnighter outside.

Kali smiled. Not entirely awake, she squinted, one eye refusing to open, and cooed to him. "Hey, big boy," she whispered.

He nickered back.

She carefully crawled out of the sleeping bag and pulled on her jeans. Another perk to getting up first—no one saw the panties. Careful not to get any sticker burrs or rocks on her feet, she tried stepping into her boots. Her attempt at the right boot was successful, but lack of proper sleep and coffee worked against her on the left, and she found herself hopping around on the hard ground, cursing quietly, and trying not to fall all over people.

Star nickered again.

Once the boots were on, she was off and running. She drew in a deep breath and sighed contently. Her first overnighter completed. Nicky would be so proud.

Nicholas Jorgenson had been the crusader for Rainwash Ranch since its inception. He had been the one who had brought all the families together, gotten the sponsors on board, found the monies, and lined up clientele.

Gingerly, she stepped around sleeping bodies and made her way toward her fourteen-year-old gelding. She wouldn't be able to start the fire or begin the morning coffee until she had given the most beautiful horse she had ever seen a proper good morning.

Star was a chestnut with a matching mane and tail, and a small star marking the middle of his forehead. He lacked the square head of a fine quarter horse and looked more like an aging circus horse. There was nothing unusual about him, except for his mildly swollen left knee, but Kali thought he was perfect.

Nicky had always teased her about Star being a mutt. Though his papers had claimed him a quarter horse, his history had been suspect. He was well trained and well-mannered, yet he had sold for a fraction of what he'd been worth. Nicholas had wanted to look at others, but before he could stop her, Kali had slipped through the panels and stood inside the fenced area.

Instantly, one of the auction attendees had come wagging a finger, telling her she had to get out of the round pen. She hadn't cared. As she had reached her hands up around his neck to see if he was hand shy, Star had tucked his head down and trapped her back between his chest and chin. A horse's hug—the greatest, warmest feeling on earth.

She liked to say Star had chosen her.

Brooke's horse had fetched more than eight thousand dollars, yet Kali had settled on an eight hundred dollar horse. It had pained Nicholas.

Just four days later, Star had begun to stumble and Nicky had started to grumble. "You were had."

But the horse hugs had continued and nothing else mattered.

"I'm not the one competing," she had said again and again, not listening to anything anyone else had to say about her Star.

And when she had seen him with her daughters and the farm animals, she had known it was the seller who had been had. Children and small animals could slip up behind and under him without as much as a snort from Star. He didn't care. In fact, he liked the activity around him. He just loved being part of a herd—be it people, cats, dogs, or horses.

That morning was no different as she reached up for a hug. She felt the warmth of his soft, fuzzy chin as it tucked down over her back. His powerful neck arched over her shoulder, gently pressing her body against his chest. Her face pressed into his shoulder, and she took another long breath. She loved the way he smelled. She raised her arms over her head, blindly feeling for his ears and stroking them softly until she reached the tips, and then let her hands glide down the sides of his face.

"Starman." She turned, kissed his huge jaw, and took another whiff. It wasn't coffee, but it was just as soothing.

She got the fire blazing and coffee brewing just as the first members of the group rose. Rainwash Ranch had eight paying customers riding along as Kali and her brothers-in-law pushed a head of two hundred toward a small town outside Grand Junction, Colorado.

They had come a such long way since Kali had first read about a Texas cow being destroyed after it showed potential signs of a central nervous disorder, otherwise known as mad cow disease, only to be made into pig feed, and she had lost it.

"So, what? Now I can't eat bacon? These people are idiots!" she had roared. "Mother Nature, God, and any other natural force you can think of never intended for cattle, sheep, goats, and pigs to be eating each other!

What in the hell are we doing?"

Despite the scientific knowledge that feeding herbivores other animals wreaked havoc on the health of both animals and of those who ate the animal-fed meat, the practice of putting animal byproducts into grain continued, and it had been more than Kali could stomach.

Fights had ensued between Nicholas and Kali on the subject of feeding their daughters meat. As far as Kali had been concerned, no meat was safe unless it had come from the Jorgensons' ranch, so when he'd approached her with the idea of turning his parents' homestead into a fully functional cattle driving resort ranch, Kali had loved it. Fresh, pesticide-free fruits and vegetables from Ms. Kat's lavish garden, free-range chickens, and grass-fed cattle, and urbanites helping support the land by playing cowboy and feeling good about moving organic cattle.

Nicky had first come up with the brilliant partnership between the Jorgensons and a man named Davis who had opened a ranch based on a movie about city slickers trying their hand at cattle ranching. The O-Kay-Doke Corral had never made a profit but continued to survive, and Davis had sworn the only hitch in his plan was the lack of a partner—a place to move the cattle to and from.

Without a purpose for the cattle drive, what's the point?

Nicholas had been instrumental in everyone's success when he hooked up with the Cattlemen's Association and made heavy connections in the beef industry. The O-Kay-Doke Corral not only had the partner it had needed, but both ends of the cattle drive had a lifeline. Rainwash and O-Kay-Doke Corral had created an alliance that allowed them to serve as chief suppliers to the west coast promoting grass-fed cattle at a time when the use of the term *mad cow* had the beef industry walking on eggshells.

Fifteen months later, there she and Star were, leading their first overnighter together like old pros.

Evan had been prepping the horses while Mattie tended the fire when Kali departed to call Nicholas.

They were the true cowboys in the bunch. Both Evan and Matthew had competed in rodeos since they could remember. In fact, the great joke was Mattie's best ride was a sheep. At age four, he had been entered in the Rustle-Up contest. Whatever animals were cornered and captured by little people became their property. As soon as the cap gun sounded, Mattie had thrown himself atop a sheep and never let go, as the woolly critter had bucked, twisted, and leapt. It had been the beginning of a great career.

Evan was tall, ridiculously lean, and muscular. It was his long stature that ultimately ended his rodeo career. Tall, lanky cowboys have a much harder time staying on the bull than a more compact body. His dark brown hair and hazel eyes reminded Kali most of her husband, Nicholas. Where they differed was how they sat in the saddle.

It hadn't mattered that Nicholas had grown up around horses, he had never been quite comfortable with the equine and, that being the best excuse, spent his entire adulthood in the trenches, studying military history and eventually becoming an officer in the army.

As he had risen in rank, he'd never turned his back on Rainwash, however. In fact, the three other brothers had run the business themselves until they had been able to hire on.

For Ms. Kat it was a lifeline after having lost her husband, Nicky's father and Kali's father-in-law, two years earlier. And while Stephen had announced he was taking a break to get his MBA from UCLA, the timing of everything had been magical for Kali.

The US Army had sent Nicky to different posts and all the moving had become increasingly difficult as the girls grew. When orders had come through that he would be going to Afghanistan, both Nicky and Kali had known it was time for the family to settle at Rainwash. Kali had family in New York and, briefly, there had been discussion of settling the girls there, but what kind of riding could they or would they do in New York? Images of dressage had flashed through Kali's mind, and she'd resisted. Her girls were rough. They were bona fide cowgirls. She had known Rainwash was where the girls needed to be.

"Hey," she said when Nicholas answered the phone.

"Hey!" He sounded surprised. "What time is it?" he asked, though she knew he knew the answer. "You're up early. It's not even five o'clock yet."

"No rest for the weary," she said happily.

"Yeah? How's my best girl?"

She loved that. Four simple words but, always, it melted her heart. It was the way he said it. She was his best girl.

"Me, personally?" She toyed with him. "I slept with a rock in the middle of my back and am wearing two-day-old socks and underwear. Oh, and I haven't brushed my teeth yet. I've got rot breath."

"Sexy."

"That's me to a T. I'm havin' to beat them all off of me."

She had described the group they had with them. Had she known better, she would have memorized each word spoken, every sound he had made. Instead, she had enjoyed teasing him.

The girls had stayed with Ms. Kat, and there was a mixed aroma of fresh air, coffee, and horse, and the day promised to be excellent. In two days, they would be at the O-Kay-Doke Corral with immensely satisfied customers. Much to her delight, Nicky complained about Matthew getting too close to her.

"I'm serious," Nicky said, feigning concern. "That boy has got an eye on you. Damn weasel. I can't trust him and neither should you. Where is he? What's he doing right now?"

Kali laughed and looked over her shoulder.

As if on cue, Mattie looked back at her, giving a chin nod.

"He's putting out the fire. We'll be settin' out soon. Oh, wait, I think he's winking at me."

Nicky said something back but Kali couldn't hear. It was garbled. Finally, she lost connection altogether, but thought herself lucky she had gotten anything. There were pockets in the valley where they could get cellular connections. She'd call him back when they got to Miller's Point.

But it had been Evan who'd caught the next cellular connection.

Out of the corner of her eye, Kali had seen Evan jerk and twist suddenly in his saddle, looking down at his waistband. He had pushed his hat high on his forehead and retrieved the phone, speaking into the receiver as he'd looked around at the greenhorns waving their brand new three hundred dollar Stetsons at the cows in great circular motions to everyone's amusement. Evan had shown a few how to use their hats to urge cows on, and they had liked the results so much they had continued for miles and miles.

But Evan hadn't been smiling.

Kali had seen him bend over in his saddle, covering his other ear with his free hand. He had become rigid and, instantly, Kali had known something was very wrong.

She had whistled to Mattie, pointing to two of the greenhorns she had been watching, and urged Star across the path of the cattle. Head held high, Star had bullied his way through the herd toward Evan. Still too far away to talk, she had tilted her head at him when they made eye contact, as if to say, "What's wrong?"

Fragmented pieces.

It still came to her in fragmented pieces but, amazingly, her brain retained just enough to comprehend the incomprehensible.

In the early hours of that very morning, just minutes after she had spoken to her husband, rebels had driven a jeep loaded with explosives into the compound of the Allied Forces, killing dozens.

Kali, go home.

Maybe it had been while they'd been talking.

Kali, go home.

Nicky had been walking across the compound, on his day off, talking to his wife. He had been standing directly in the path of the jeep as the suicide bombers had smashed through the gates.

Kali, go home.

She had wanted to know if Evan had been talking to Nicky.

It had been the slow, frightened shake of his head—

No. It was Mom.

Ms. Kat.

No one had been able to get in touch with Nicholas.

Kali had jerked on Star's reins and slammed her heels into his sides.

Star had bucked. He'd never expected such behavior from Kali, but he'd shot forward, doing what was asked of him.

The ride had been a blur—both Kali and Star covered in sweat, hearts pounding.

Kali had reached for her phone as they'd ridden, easing Star long enough to see the panel. She had pressed number five and called Nicky.

"Hi. You've reached Nicholas Jorgenson. I can't come to—"

Kali had screamed and slammed her heels into Star again.

As hard as he had tried, as fast as he had run, as much as his own knee must have screamed at him, Star hadn't been able to deliver Kali from her own agony.

That day was forever cemented in Kali's brain.

While the news had covered the story, and it would be footnoted in the history books, the war and life would go on. Nicky's body would never be recovered, but life would go on.

Chapter Six

Jessica Stanten sprinted for the phone, hoping to intercept it before her roommate, but the floor was wet from her dripping body and made it difficult to stay on her feet. She used the walls to keep her balance, pushing off either side to keep herself from falling down.

A male voice echoed through the house. "Bitch!"

Her heart pounded, and she began to cry as she entered the small living room and slammed her hand down on the answering machine.

It was a relic, but she had liked it. Answering machines allowed you to screen calls, listening to whatever the caller had to say. Voice mail offered no such luxuries but now she was questioning the luxury of hearing death threats.

"I'm gonna kill you, bitch. You know you wanted it. You're a whore, a slut, and a bitch. And you're gonna die before you testify. Got that? You're gonna die. I'm gonna—"

She picked up the receiver and slammed it down again then fell back on the couch, sobbing. It would never stop. The phone calls, the threats. Her friends and family would never be safe. She clutched a pillow to her chest and buried her face into it. Who was she kidding? She couldn't fight this. She couldn't fight Jeremy Connors' multimillion-dollar legal team, hundreds of thousands of fans who thought he walked on water, and the professional sports league that did everything possible to leak information about who she was, her past, her friends, and her career all in the name of making her life so unbelievably miserable that she would drop the suit—or to prejudice any possible jury pool so she'd never be able to get justice.

Caroline Peters poked her head out into the hall. "Jess?"

Jess jumped slightly and fought to slow her whole body down.

"Jess?"

"Yeah." Jessica struggled to make her voice even. "Yeah, I'm out here. Sorry. I didn't . . . I didn't mean to wake you."

Caroline walked into the living room, still rubbing her eyes, and leaned against the doorframe. She wore an old T-shirt with their alma mater emblazoned across her chest and faded boxers as her pajamas. She still had her perfect college volleyball player physique: tall—six foot two inches in bare feet—slender and muscular. Caroline Peters was all legs. While Jessica had had to fight to keep her form in shape, Caroline seemed to be genetically blessed.

Caroline had once told her, "That, and the fact that I don't smoke or drink." It had been a direct hit. Jessica had picked up both habits after graduation. She couldn't remember exactly when she had begun smoking. It had been a gradual thing. She had hit the party scene pretty heavily when she'd landed her first job in a sports management firm. One of her functions as a floater had been to see to it that everyone was happy—happy with their service with MacIntire Sports, Inc. and with their agents. She had socialized with clients, but she hadn't had any clients of her own—yet. She had learned more about skiing, golf, and auto racing than she ever thought possible and could talk the talk with just about anyone, but the thing that had surprised her most had been discovering just how many professional athletes drank and smoked.

If only the public knew.

She had had certain low expectations of professional athletes and their behavior, and for the most part, she'd been right, but even she had been unpleasantly surprised by the behavior of many of America's little darlings —Olympians. They were spoiled prima donnas. They were hyperaware of being consistently compared to other athletes on the rise or already putting in better times and scores, and would have raging fits if their promotional posters were placed too close to an opponent's. Even athletes who were on the same team went to great lengths to distance themselves in the eyes of sponsors and the public. It was insane, but she had loved it. She had been good at it. She'd played best friend, nursemaid, and secretary, girl Friday, and—yes—sometimes a major tease to get what was needed for the firm. Whatever had made the athlete happy made the bosses happy. But she had never, never offered sexual favors to anyone. Certainly, no one at her office had told her to seek out Jeremy Connors.

Jeremy Connors had been her idea. No one had put her up to it. Since he had entered the NFL two years ago, Jeremy had been with another firm based out of Los Angeles. Jessica was sure it was why Jeremy had signed with them. He'd mingled with Hollywood types, gone to world premieres, and attended black tie affairs. It had been rumored that Jeremy had toyed with the idea of acting, but there had been problems with his firm and— specifically—with his agent, the infamous Reginald Perry. Perry, as everyone called him, apparently had spent more and more time with his precious Hollywood "It" girl and managed to let not one but two deals go south for Jeremy. The biggest one had been the McDonald's commercials. Although the restaurant chain was certainly happy not to be associated with

Jeremy and his legal problems at the moment, it had been a burn at the time. It was meant to be a series of commercials involving Jeremy with a bunch of school kids and would have been great for Jeremy's image as well as the sale of his merchandise on his personal website. His marketability from the commercials could have proven a big draw at the box office, but Perry hadn't been available for his client and the deal had gone to another player.

The second blunder had been a squabble over a television script with a scene specifically written for Jeremy. Perry had been so busy playing the big-time agent, resembling a stage mother gone mad, that it had resulted in the exasperated producers and writers removing Jeremy from the show entirely. Not even the great Jeremy had been worth all the hassle, and, with the flick of a pen, his acting aspirations vanished.

Word had gotten out that Jeremy was unhappy with his agent and contemplating leaving the firm, so when Jessica had learned he would be in the Houston area, she'd decided to pounce. Landing Jeremy as a client could have put her on the map, not just with MacIntire Sports, Inc., but also given her the leverage in the sports management community to strike out on her own. For years, she and Caroline had talked about creating a sports agency to represent outstanding collegiate and professional women in sports but, quite frankly, female athletes couldn't bring in the big bucks that someone like a Jeremy Connors guaranteed.

Jessica had found out what hotel Jeremy was staying in and tracked the team's activity, making sure she was in the hotel's bar an hour before the team returned. She had wanted to talk to various bartenders, waitresses, and bellhops to find out the inside scoop—who he was with and what kind of person he was. She'd confirmed Reginald Perry was nowhere in sight. She had known what a playboy Jeremy was—no surprises there—but she had hoped to use that as bait to lure him into a conversation about his future. She had learned long ago that men were suckers for long legs, short skirts, the stroke of an ego, and some booze. That combination had usually gotten her whatever she wanted. She hadn't counted on the team losing, however. She hadn't counted on his rage. And she'd never considered her ability, or inability, to get out of a perilous situation.

She wasn't a complete idiot. She had shared the athletes' dorm for four years at college in Texas, where football players were gods and everyone else fell short, and had turned the players down so often while she and Caroline had roomed together that word got around she and Caroline were gay. They had to be, right? It was the only explanation for their lack of interest in the finest of the male species. She had seen how young women would find excuses to visit the ball players' rooms only to leave upset because they'd felt used and tossed to the side. She'd heard about a female student being raped by an athlete, only to have it completely hushed up by the school. There were always division conferences and national championships that far outweighed the personal safety of individual students. The happy result for the school was that those females usually went away, never to be heard from again. It was disgusting and embarrassing. And it was dangerous. A select number of girls behaving like idiots indirectly gave license to the ball players to treat all females the same way.

Jessica had long ago concluded that life was like sports. How you play, how you carry yourself, and how you interact with an opponent dictates the outcome. It had been for that reason that she had truly believed she could handle Jeremy. He was another horny, dumb jock looking for a score, the limelight, and a multimillion-dollar contract to affirm his power.

They had discussed the possibility of someone recognizing her and mentioning it to Perry. She'd wanted to be sensitive about not putting him in an awkward situation with Perry, or worse, breach of contract, so she had agreed to go to his room to talk freely about his agent and his future.

Turned out Jeremy had had no intention of leaving Perry.

He played nice in the lobby, the elevator, and the hallway leading to his room, but the moment the door closed behind her, he didn't even pretend to be civil. He didn't offer her a drink or attempt to hide behind shoptalk. He turned on his heel, pinned her against the closed door, and pushed his body against hers, and she smelled whiskey or something heavy on his breath.

His voice was thick and dangerous, but she still believed she could handle it. She was right next to the door and she told herself that if things got out of hand, she'd push him back, open the door, and flee.

Simple.

But it hadn't been simple at all.

He talked about her body, every inch of it, until she was extremely uncomfortable and on the verge of frightened. His comments were meant to be compliments, but each statement sounded more like a threat. Each time he looked over her body, the hair stood up on the back of her neck.

He smiled eerily and told her what he was going to do to her.

She struggled with her composure, trying desperately to turn the conversation back to Perry, when the reality of the situation hit her. This wasn't just some story gone wildly out of control—everything she'd heard about Jeremy was true.

He kissed her neck, but when she tried to push him away, all hope of talking her way out of this was lost.

"What? You don't want it, bitch?"

Just like that.

It startled her. She couldn't remember being called that name before, certainly not in that manner.

How many times had she read about a woman who had been date raped and then blamed herself for sending mixed signals? She wanted to make sure he understood her fully. She had been very honest about what her interest in him was. She had been straightforward about why she was willing to come to his room.

She tilted her chin upward. "No."

Now, with the threat of physical danger very real, she gave one hard push against his chest so that she could have just enough room to move to the side of the door and escape.

He didn't budge, not the tiniest fraction of an inch. "Yeah, you want it. You know you do," he said and pinned her against the door with his left forearm. It was a sudden, brutal move, and the pain was instantaneous.

She blinked in shock and gasped for breath.

"Wearin' this little itty bitty thing, tryin' to . . ." He seemed lost in his own world, mumbling to himself. He ran his right hand down her body, pressing hard, until he reached the hemline of her dress.

She felt him tug on the material. It was all so sudden. There was a rush of air on her skin as he twisted her dress up and said things she couldn't really even understand. He didn't make any sense, but then none of this did.

This wasn't happening. This just couldn't be happening.

But it was. The pain was intense. For a brief moment, the pressure on her collarbone was released, and she tried to scream.

Then the world exploded.

He had moved his left forearm back just far enough to throw a solid elbow strike across her face.

The elbow strike was one of the most powerful and effective throws in close quarters. Her brain was so scrambled and stunned that she couldn't think of the counter to the action, only numbly recall the name of the technique from self-defense class and recognize the ridiculousness of her timing.

She tasted blood in her mouth—warm, rusty iron, sickening. She felt dizzy.

"Little whore. You want Big Daddy to teach you some lessons." He was practically hissing in her ear.

She tried to scream again, but he placed his left hand over her face. Her lips felt as though they were ripping apart, the pressure was so intense. She squeezed her eyes shut and he chuckled.

"That's right, baby," he said.

He loved it. She could tell. He knew she was scared, but he smiled at her as if he was flattered by some compliment she'd given him. She had believed she was in control of the situation, that she might regain control of the situation, but that notion completely left her.

She was lightheaded and felt her body falling as he tossed her across the room, onto the bed, and landed heavily on her. His hands were everywhere. She felt him rip the remainder of her dress off.

He squeezed her, nearly choked the life out of her, and plunged inside her. He called her the most horrible names, slapped, and pinched her. He violated her in the cruelest way, grunting like a rutting pig.

She was crying, and he loved it.

He hated her. He hated her in such a way that paralyzed her. She was numb and confused.

How could he hate her so violently when he didn't even know her? What had she done?

Bitch. Whore. Slut.

Then he was done. Minutes after the assault began, he was done with her. She felt his heartbeat racing against her chest, the pulse of his body, and she held her breath.

This didn't happen. It didn't happen.

Jessica didn't dare move, speak, or even breathe. She closed her eyes once more and the tears burned trails down her cheeks. She waited until he rolled off her and listened until it sounded as though he was headed for the bathroom before she shifted her head slightly to one side. She ached. She watched the back of him carefully. It didn't matter that she had almost nothing covering her naked body—she had to get out.

Rape.

It didn't matter that people always said you should yell "fire" rather than rape. She would scream at the top of her lungs, but then he turned, smiled, and she felt her heart sink.

"So, Perry sent you?" he said, looking down at his own body. He stroked his chest, and angled his body so the light hit in different directions.

Jessica felt her mouth drop open as if she no longer controlled it. Was this some kind of game?

"No." Her voice sounded funny to her. Very far away. Disembodied. "Perry didn't send me." She managed to rise slightly and gathered her nerve. "You attacked an innocent woman."

It was a foolish thing to say.

He froze in mid-stroke. He never lifted his chin, but his gaze came up, settling on her face. He looked partially amused. Completely insane. "Oh, there's nothing innocent about you," he said and moved back toward the bed.

All her senses tingled so loud they were a steady hum. *Now, now, now! Run, scream, fight, spit, cuss, do whatever you have to do to get away!*

She scrambled backward, putting the length of the bed between them and, for a moment, he stopped.

He looked puzzled, then enthralled. "Damn, but you've got some long legs. Maybe you need to come wrap them around Big Daddy," he said as he crawled across the bed.

She rolled off the edge of the mattress and ran, hoping to skirt around him and make it to the door.

He was too fast. He caught her wrist and pulled her down sharply to the ground. Another blink and she was on the floor, face down, with Jeremy on top.

"You're a good one," he whispered as she fought.

She could tell by the tone of his voice that he had plans for more and, as tired and hurt as she was, she knew she would have to fight her way out.

She twisted sideways, trapped under his body and legs, and punched at his face. He was drunk, and he didn't see it coming. It threw him back enough to enable her to scramble free and deliver another kick that knocked him flat on his back. She was up, headed for the door. Then the world tumbled and turned. She wasn't sure if she'd fallen or had been hit, but suddenly, violently, she was on the floor again. Her head slammed into something hard.

A desk? A dresser?

She was blinded with pain as the room went dark.

He was talking to her again, saying something vile.

She began to cry. There was no way out. This wasn't a dream. It was real. Her blood, her pain, her terror . . . all very real. She couldn't stand. She tried to crawl for the door and hoped he would feel sorry for her. She had never played the helpless routine but, dammit, she was helpless. She prayed, in the midst of his insane rage, he would have pity on her and let her crawl out the door.

He laughed.

Let him laugh. *Just please let me go.*

She felt his foot in the center of her back. She had nothing to fight with and her arms and legs slipped on the floor, spread out, and the grunt was forced out of her as she hit the floor. "Please, don't hurt me. Just let me go." Her own voice frightened her. She didn't even recognize it. "I won't tell anyone. I swear, I won't say a word."

A loud explosion of sound assaulted her ears as she heard a short bark of laughter erupt from him.

The memory of those dorm days and the girls with their hurt feelings and injured pride came back to her. Suddenly, she was sure Jeremy had probably raped many college girls only to graduate from a school that had knowingly covered up his heinous crimes while his victims had been forced —through shame, fear, or devastation—to withdraw from the university and possibly find some small, no-name college where they could try to start over or perhaps quit school altogether.

He nudged her side, forcing her to roll over.

She looked up, ready to plead, but his face was expressionless. He was disconnected, distracted even. Slowly, she pushed her body into a sitting position. Was it possible he had taken pity on her, that he had considered his own actions and realized he had made a big mistake? She covered herself and tried sliding with her back to the wall toward the door.

He watched her, his head cocked to one side as though he was intrigued and curious.

Maybe, if he was like a lot of the athletes she had known, he was thinking about calling his lawyer, agent, or coach.

He smiled. "Where are you going, baby?"

She shook her head. She wanted to vomit. The notion of screaming for help was no longer with her. She was terrified of what the punishment would be next time. She wanted to fall to pieces, beg for mercy. She shook uncontrollably and realized she was babbling under her breath. "Nowhere. Nowhere. Not going anywhere."

He stooped down, pulling her up and against his body. He was incredibly strong and fearsome. Fighting him off wasn't an option and it was that thought alone that completely crippled her. Never in her life had she felt so weak or helpless. Never in her life had she been forced to realize that she had absolutely no chance of getting herself out of a bad situation. She had been an athlete most of her life and brought up in a home that taught her she could be and do whatever she wanted. The world was hers for the taking. Now, someone was taking her—without her will, without her consent, and there wasn't a damn thing she could do about it.

Help me!

His eyes changed. He was no longer distracted. "You change your mind, baby? You don't wanna play anymore?" He leered at her, pulled a fistful of her hair up to his nose, and inhaled deeply as he ran his face across her neck and chest.

She had tried to speak, but her voice was lost, and when he had grabbed her by the hair and pulled her to the bed, laughing and talking of more playtime, her legs had completely given out, but it hadn't mattered to him. He'd been perfectly content to drag her.

Jessica had lost track of all time. In the darkened room, lying on her back, with her eyes squeezed shut, and enduring the greatest of humiliations and agony, she had done the only thing she'd been able to—she'd let go. She had let go of herself, of time, of everything.

* * * *

Jessica rocked back and forth on the couch, her face covered with a pillow, sobbing.

Caroline sat down next to her friend and placed her hand on Jessica's back.

Initially, Jessica had been in shock. She hadn't spoken, eaten, or slept. She had been distant. Detached. Bruised and battered. And, in the beginning, uncertain she would step forward to prosecute Jeremy for what he had done to her, but the hospital staff, the police, and her family had all been determined to see justice done. As loved ones had rallied behind her, the old Jess had emerged. As each bruise had healed, she had become angrier. Jessica's training had taken over and the athlete within her surfaced, dragged out by her fighting spirit. She wanted to see Jeremy go down.

That had been before the death threats, the verbal assaults, and the destruction to personal property. It had been well before Jeremy's legal team let the press know all about his accuser—Jessica Stanten. That one little cue and Jeremy's popularity had trashed the rape shield law as the media and public did the rest. Websites had popped up with open chats about what Jessica *really* was—she was out for money, she was out for fame, and she was just a whore and got what was coming to her. It had been atrocious, and now . . .

"It's never going to stop, is it?" Jess cried behind her hands. She took great gulps of breath. She was crying so hard she couldn't get enough air. "It's just never going to stop. They'll find me wherever I am. This will go on for the rest of my life. And . . . no one is safe around me. They know where I am, Caroline. They know I'm here. You're not safe as long as I'm here."

She fell back against the couch and Caroline caught her, wrapping her friend up tightly in her arms and shushed her. "They got a phone number. So what? We'll change it. Don't let them do this to you, Jess. Don't let them beat you down. You've been down once . . . never again. You are better than this. Stronger than this. You can do this, Jess, and I'll be with you the entire time. But you can't let them do this to you."

The phone rang again and both women jumped.

Caroline started to let go of Jessica, hoping to catch the phone before the message could be heard, but Jessica trapped her arms, holding on tighter than ever. She squeezed her eyes shut, bracing herself for the next voice. She prayed that it would be her mom, saying something soothing and sweet. She hoped to hear from her brother and Nana.

"Yo, bitch! You like the big boys? I got somethin' for ya, you want it that bad? I got something for ya. Come outside and I'll make you . . ."

Caroline jerked her arm away from Jessica and catapulted her body over the back of the couch. She pounced on the phone. "Listen, dick wad, I don't know who you think you're calling but I've got a tracer on this phone and nothing would please me more than for you to share your little goodies with a cellmate for the rest of your life. Call again, ass, and I will personally see to it you become someone's bitch." She slammed down the phone and huffed out loud. Her whole body vibrated.

She looked over at Jessica and, together, they both smiled nervously.

"Wow," Jessica whispered. "Your mother would be proud."

"Where do you think I learned to talk like that?"

For the first time in a very long time, Jess tilted her head back and laughed.

Chapter Seven

They heard the music before their feet hit the floor, and Mike groaned audibly.

"What the hell is that?"

But he knew. They all did. Tracy had warned them.

"I believe that would be the mistress," Ed said and let out a groan as he rolled out of bed. "What time is it?" Still rubbing his eyes, he sat in a heap on the edge of his small bunk.

"Tracy said she cracks the whip at five thirty on the dot," Sam said from under his covers. "Which means we've got about thirty minutes to grab something to eat."

Although still groggy, they all remembered Tracy's warning about Kali Jorgenson.

"I'm protesting." Mike pulled the covers over his head, rolling to one side. "What's she going to do? Drag me out of bed?" He snorted.

"I don't know about you guys," Sam said, flinging the covers back and rising like a zombie from the comfortable recesses of his warm sheets. "I saw what she has her three little girls doing." He pulled on his jeans and squinted in the still darkened room, searching for his boots. "I'll admit it, I'm more than a little worried about that 'kicking our asses' comment." He found the boots and guided them on. "What is that?" He tilted his head, listening. "Michael Jackson?" The corners of his mouth curled upward. "She's listening to Michael Jackson."

"It's—" Ed was second behind Sam, pulling on his last boot. " 'Bad.' It's Jackson's 'Bad.' "

Ed and Sam finished dressing, each smiling at the absurdity. Only Mike didn't smile.

"What kind of person wakes up at five in the morning and blares Michael Jackson? Doesn't she know how irritating that is?" Mike fell in line behind the others as they made their way to the door of their bunkhouse.

A rush of sweet and cool air hit them as soon as Sam pulled the door open, followed by the resounding, "I'm bad! Who's bad?" thump-da-dump of Mr. Jackson. To their left, a thick smoke rose from the chimney of the main house that drew them closer. Ms. Kat's cooking was definitely worth getting up for.

If the Jorgenson females saw their new charges, they gave no sign of it and continued working their horses in the round pen. Kali stood at the edge, watching as her girls moved the horses around various barrels, and Sam stopped to watch. Specifically, he watched Kali.

She wore faded jeans, boots, and a T-shirt. Her hair was pulled into a ponytail that she'd slipped through the back tab of her baseball cap. Her hair looked silky and Sam imagined how it felt. With every breeze, wisps of it picked up and tumbled around the back of her hat. With her back to him, he had a perfect view of her hindquarters, and while it was something to admire, he remained fixated on her T-shirt. It was of a size that was better suited for her daughter, Brooke, but he had no complaints. It was navy blue and fit her frame snugly, resting just above her hips, but when she moved from side to side, as she periodically did to illustrate something to her daughters, or raised her arms, several inches of flesh was exposed. Each time, Sam felt his breath catch in his throat. Her jeans rode low in a style that, in his view, either looked fabulous or ridiculous on a woman. Once upon a time, women had tiny waistlines but Fat America now had fat waistlines and someone forgot to tell the clothes designers. Or, more importantly, consumers. But Kali had missed out on the fast food and coffee house consumption and looked incredible. Her body was lean and muscular. She was soft and strong at the same time. Sam was transfixed.

Jacks broke from the pattern in an attempt to pass her sister. For whatever reason, this angered Kali, who left her post and waved her arm at horse and rider, driving them back. She stepped into the middle of the corral, completely oblivious to the possibility of being trampled at any moment.

She walked up to Jacks' horse and grabbed the reins close to its mouth, motioning backward to Brooke at the same time.

Brooke had been sitting so quietly, Sam had almost missed her. Both she and her horse hugged the far railing, waiting and watching. On cue, Brooke gave a little kick to the horse and they trotted forward. As per her mother's instructions, she did the crazy eight pattern, weaving her horse in and out of the barrels behind Danni—something that Jacks had been expected to do but failed.

Sam watched Kali nodding with big, enthusiastic dips and imagined her cheers. "Yes, that's what I'm talking about."

The music roared in the background.

"She's not much fun to listen to," Mike said, interrupting Sam's thoughts, "but she's fun to look at."

Sam pushed past and headed toward the main house.

As Mike joined Sam, Jacks lifted her chin and said something to her mother, and all four Jorgenson females looked at the men.

Mike and Sam's steps both faltered as the slow smile swept across Kali's face. It was on.

Horse Care 101 began immediately. While they ate breakfast, Kali began with the basic rules of horses—how to walk around a horse in the corral, in the stables, in the barn. Body language, voice command, proper attire. The lists were endless. Kali promised to repeat everything over and over as there was no way anyone could remember everything, but she promised it would sink in as they began riding.

Sam, Ed, and Mike never said a word. They sat, eating possibly the best eggs, grits, hash browns, homemade jam and biscuits ever consumed, while Kali assigned the horses. The Jorgenson brothers—Evan, Stephen, and Matthew, along with Tracy, would be joining them on the drive.

As they continued packing away Ms. Kat's delicious cooking, Kali explained how she based the rider and horse matches on the personality of each—an interesting statement considering the limited contact she'd had with the men.

Ed broke their silence with a shot at Mike. "So . . . guess that means you'll be riding the jackass."

Even Kali laughed and Mike shook his head good-naturedly. The man had always been able to take a joke.

"Seriously, how did you assess our personalities? I mean, how did you figure what kind of horses to give us? I'm stronger than a damned bull." Mike flashed a huge grin.

Tracy snorted. "Three guys from the big city, soft hands, never ridden, not seriously, anyway. Pasty white skin indicatin' you might get sun poisonin' long before you could beat the heat. And your boots are so shiny I have to wear shades—" Tracy pointed toward both Mike and Ed's feet. He winked across the table to Ms. Kat and Matt. "I don't think she's judging you on the brute strength of a cowboy."

Sam felt as if he was under a microscope. It was true he was no cowboy, but he was no pansy either. As dedicated as he was the courtroom, he was also committed to working out. It kept him from going insane. He had been studying Hapkido, a Japanese fighting style of martial arts, for over four years. He was a former All-American football player. A powerhouse. In fact, until that moment, he had always been told he was intimidating, both in size and posture. He looked down at his hands. He wouldn't have called them soft.

"I wouldn't call 'em soft." Everything Sam had thought, Mike said. Loudly. He protested vehemently in the way only Mike could. He had center stage, making lawyer jokes while postulating his position as a real man's man. The entire room was laughing, including the twins who had entered through the back door and were giggling at the funny city slicker.

"Ed Slader is quiet and reserved, content to sit back and watch his buddies make asses of themselves." Kali tossed a smile toward Ed.

"Oh, Kali!" Ms. Kat tried to cover her amusement behind a stern look, but her laugh lines framed twinkling eyes.

"But he's always thinking. Very clever. And if you give him too much time on his hands, he'll get in trouble. Do you get bored easily, Mr. Slader?" She tilted her head.

"Oh, did she nail you! Yes! Yes! Mr. Attention Deficit Disorder." Mike clapped his hands as he roared over the others.

"Well, now, I wouldn't say—" Ed's grin gave way to the truth.

"I gave him Choo Choo."

"Choo Choo?!" Ed looked crushed.

Howls of laughter filled the room from everyone, even the Jorgensons who knew the horse. What self-respecting man rode a horse named Choo Choo?

"Choo Choo is intense. He always wants to know what is over the next hill or the next ridge. He will push you, Mr. Slader, so you will have to stay on your toes. You will not and cannot be bored with Choo Choo. But the two of you should have a very good time together—you'll be my adventure boys." She smiled at him in such a way, almost flirting, that suddenly made Choo Choo sound more than acceptable.

Ed sat back looking particularly smug and satisfied while Mike and Sam glanced at each other with similar little boy pouts poking out their bottom lips.

It was clear Kali was quite charming. Even as she put each man under the microscope, dissecting them individually, and exposing their weaknesses, she made sure to identify their strengths. *Tear 'em down, build 'em up.* It was a tactic the lawyers were familiar with and had used often in court.

"He's a quarter horse. Good size. Chestnut with a black mane and tail. Yes, I can see you on him." Ms. Kat nodded, comparing the man to the horse.

Ed was, as Ms. Kat had noted, a good size. Just over six feet tall, he was solidly built, an athlete in college who still played the weekend warrior in a racquetball league. His dark hair and olive skin was something he got from his mother's side of the family—the Sicilian bunch, as he put it.

"Mr. Spann is quiet, brooding, always questioning, more stubborn."

Another hoot escaped Mike, who had forgotten his own analysis was coming up.

Sam shot a look at Mike then turned back to Kali. As ridiculous as it was, he thoroughly enjoyed the fact that she had given him thought. Never mind that she had done the exact same things to the others. He was intrigued to know what she thought of him. He raised his eyebrows, smiled, and waited.

So far, so good.

"Strong, athletic, good endurance. Quiet," she said again. Her eyes crinkled at the edges as she squinted and scrutinized every detail. "But not shy. Maybe a bit of a clown when he's in more comfortable surroundings," she said and Mike and Ed lit up. Again, she had nailed it. "I gave him

Lightning."

"Oh, dear," Ms. Kat uttered.

Even Tracy questioned that one. "I don't know, Kal. Maybe not Lightning."

Suddenly, Sam was a little worried.

"No, really. I've been working with him. He's ready and he needs a big, strong rider. He'll respond. This'll be good."

"Uh, who . . . which one is Lightning?" Sam asked.

"No, I think he's okay," Matthew said.

Everyone talked over or around Sam, paying him no mind.

"I was on him the other . . . Tuesday last. He did okay. Still tries to hop around at first but he settles in nicely." Matthew stroked his chin. "That's a good choice. Sam here's a big guy. He'll do good."

"Um, hopping around? Like bucking?" Sam looked around.

"I'd put him on Duchess or Redwing. He's a pretty big guy. I'd give 'em a bigger horse. Hell, he might wear ol' Lightning out. He's a lot of body to be carryin' around." Tracy poked a sideways finger at Sam.

Mike and Ed grinned as Sam struggled to be heard. "Look, I don't mind a challenge but I don't think—"

"But don't you think Redwing would be better?" Ms. Kat asked. "He's big, solid, but requires a strong hand. He'd be perfect."

Kali shook her head. "No, I'm saving Redwing for Mr. Waters."

At last, Mike was quiet.

"Redwing is a big ol' teddy bear in the right hands." Kali's smile faded somewhat as she leveled a hard stare at Mike. One eyebrow rose ever so slightly and Sam was struck by the look of sarcasm across her face and how incredibly pretty she was. "But he's all talk, he bluffs, tries to make the others in the herd think he's more than he is."

"Now, see here!" Mike stood, a big goofy grin on his face. He rolled with the joke but leveled a hard stare right back at Kali.

She didn't miss it. "He's strong, intelligent, and can back up his bluffs when he's pushed."

Mike puffed up, enjoying the last bit of information.

"You must never underestimate Redwing . . . something I am keenly aware of with Mr. Waters." With that, Kali temporarily turned the men over to Tracy, whistling at the girls to follow her and ready the horses. "Don't get used to it," she said over her shoulder as they headed back outside. "First time, the honor's mine. After today, you'll be tacking your own." And she was gone.

"An annoyin' little twerp, to be sure," Tracy said quietly, drawing appreciative grins from the Jorgenson clan. He patted down his shirt pockets and retrieved a cigar, sliding it under his nose and considering Kali. "She'll give ya hell every time," he said.

"Say, I bet that's a lot fun to be around." Mike chuckled out loud, but Tracy was quick to put him in his place.

"Naw, she shoots straight from the hip. I like that. Not enough people do it, and Kali's good people. A might bossy. She'll not only tell ya how to put your boots on, she'll be tellin' you why you need to the entire time. She does act like she's got all the answers but she's usually right." Tracy shot a look toward Sam, Ed, and Mike. "You learn to listen to her and you'll be just fine."

"The girls are the same way, cut from the same cloth," Matthew said. "Sassy little things. And, again, they know what they're talking about. Little farts are too smart for their own good. You boys would be wise to say as little as possible around them, listen up, and learn."

As the men spoke, Ms. Kat began to clear away the plates, nodding with each statement. Unquestionably, Kali and her daughters were the best.

"Especially Jacks," Evan said and the Jorgenson clan all chuckled. "She'll give ya the what for if you don't do as you're told."

"There's three sides to Kali Jorgenson, and they come in the form of her girls," Matthew confided. "She's Mother Earth, loving, sweet, caring. That's Brooke. She's also extremely intelligent, always watching and observing people, putting them under a microscope to figure out how they tick. That's Danni. And she's a damn bulldog. Headstrong, willful, won't take no for an answer, it's her way or the highway. That's one hundred percent Jacks."

Tracy had leaned back in his chair, sliding the cigar between his fingers. Ms. Kat wagged a finger at him and he sighed. "Let's not forget, they're a lot like their daddy, too."

There was a chorus of nods. Then, silence.

Finally, Mike who spoke up. "Who's their father?"

They'd stayed longer than anyone had intended but the talk had been good in many ways. It had distracted the legal team once more from the Connors case. It had connected the men to the Jorgensons and hired hands. But it had also offered some insights into Kali.

Matthew and Stephen pieced together the story of Nicholas and the attack on his military compound, but Evan never spoke. He carried a thoughtful expression on his face as he stared at his lap, occasionally nodding at something another brother had said.

Somehow the story of a brother lost only made the main house seem all the more inviting. The interior had been designed and decorated with much consideration and warmth, but there was more. There was something that emitted from the walls, the table, the family members themselves that made a body feel at home and in place.

"Kali never cried." Matthew remembered the first days. "Well, she did that first day. Damn near killed her horse, too, but after that, not a peep. She never cried, complained, or backed away from anything. She picked up the slack for the kids."

"It changed her, though," Stephen said quietly.

Again, Evan nodded.

"She doesn't talk so much or laugh so much, but she's coming back, bit by bit, I think. She's a rock, I tell ya what. Never cries."

"Never cries," Ms. Kat said then sniffed. "You boys better scoot on out. She'll be waitin' on you."

Chapter Eight

Jeremy stretched out on the bed of his luxury suite, flipping channels with the remote control. He was torn between some sports channel's early morning breakdown on the rookies to watch and an old episode of *The Honeymooners*.

God love Ralph Kramden.

Jeremy smiled unconsciously at the television screen. It was a nice distraction from his last argument with Perry.

What a pain in the ass!

The whole thing had been a ruse. Perry had been going on and on about some premiere they needed to attend. It had been typical Reginald Perry, and Jeremy was about through with him. It had been a premiere all right—for some low budget, nobody-ever-heard-of-it film with B-rated actors. There were a few models, one of whom he'd scored with. Otherwise, it had been a complete waste of his time. He couldn't even remember what the film had been called much less what it had been about. What he did remember caused him to shift his hips.

What was her name?

Leslie?

Lori?

"Hey, baby." A voice sounded from the bathroom.

"Yeah?"

"What are we going to do today?" a young woman called back just as Jeremy flipped back to the rookie roll call.

"Well." He turned up the volume a tiny bit. The sportscasters were talking about return players. Jeremy knew he'd be mentioned. He was all anyone was talking about, after all. "Don't know about you, but I've got a plane to catch."

"What?" She stepped out from the bathroom, a tiny towel wrapped about her amazing body.

He smiled. Her hair was still wet from the shower and her skin glistened against the sunlight streaming through the bay window. He patted the bed and she smiled coyly and shook her head.

What was her name?

"I thought—" She formed her pretty little lips into a perfect pout.

"I told you, baby doll. I have business. As it is, I'm already late. My lawyers are probably cussing me to hell and back. C'mere." He patted the bed again, with a little more determination.

The towel didn't quite cover her entire body, leaving a wide slit forming at the top of her thigh and narrowing as it trailed up to her breasts. He was getting a hard-on just looking at her.

Oh, but he had been a good boy. He'd whispered sweet little nothings in her ear, nibbled her neck, and massaged her back. He'd kissed her all over her body, careful not to put a hair out of place or rough her up in any way. He had been the perfect gentleman. Just as Perry had instructed.

She was one of the . . .

Laurel! That was it.

"Laurel, sweetie, come here." He cooed and she giggled, exposing a thick, juicy thigh. "Don't make me come after you."

She was the perfect Hollywood actress wannabe. She was tall, lean, platinum and overly tanned. Her teeth couldn't possibly get any whiter. She was perfect eye candy. Nothing you'd want for more than a night but fun to have while you had it.

He inched off the bed, ready to drag her back when he saw himself on television and froze. He grabbed the remote and turned up the volume.

"Hey, don't you—"

"Shhh, dammit!" He waved his hand frantically.

". . . and Boston's bad boy just can't get enough. With a new paternity suit and a rape case pending, Jeremy Connors has been doing anything but settling down. In the last two weeks, he's been bar hopping in at least ten major cities and just last night was spotted attending the movie premiere of *Feline Fantasia* in San Francisco." The commentator barely suppressed a smile.

"What's that about?" The coanchors broke into a laugh.

"No one knows, Dan, but some insiders believe all this traveling is causing major rifts with his legal team, and he may be on the outs, leaving many more to wonder if Boston's bad boy has sold out to an image."

"Daryl, any word from the Rebels?"

"Coach Smyth refuses to comment, stating he doesn't want anything to distract from the team's efforts for a championship this year, but one has to wonder how much the team can block out."

Jeremy felt his throat tighten. They were laughing at him, making a joke of the situation. He felt the rising need to whip the remote right through the television but he was entranced. He wanted to hear more, see more of what they had to say about Jeremy Connors.

"That's right, Daryl. The press coverage has been enormous, but there's been almost no word from Connors' camp."

"Only from his agent, Reginald Perry, who insists he's continuing with his training, is in excellent shape, and ready to return to the field."

They wrapped the segment with a picture of him leaving the premiere, an arm draped over Laurel, and the parting comment from Dan the Man. "I don't know. I didn't get to do that kind of training when I was playing."

More chuckles.

Dammit. They were laughing at him. There was no mention of his previous records. There was no talk of his returning to dominate the field, tear up the lines, and crush the opposing team. Nothing. It was just crap about him jet-setting from one city to another. All Perry's ideas.

He fumed and felt the rage building inside. He picked up the phone and dialed Perry's room, drumming his fingers impatiently on the desk until Reginald picked it up.

"Hello?"

"Yo, Perry. Man, this is bullshit!" Jeremy yelled into the phone.

"Whoa, whoa. What's going on?"

Jeremy heard the sleep in Perry's voice and knew he didn't fully comprehend anything.

"Wake up, man. I am seriously pissed. I'm watching this report, and I'm a freaking joke."

"Oh, baby," Laurel said and walked over to him. She tried to sit next to him on the bed and comfort him but he gave her a hard shove, nearly toppling her over the edge of the mattress. She spun and caught herself before she actually fell to the floor but lost her towel in the process.

Jeremy couldn't have cared less.

"Hey!" she protested, and he waved a finger at her.

"Shut up!"

She jumped and his eyes flashed as he watched her reach for the towel.

"Jeremy, settle down." Perry's voice was meant to be relaxing, but Jeremy only found it patronizing and felt his blood boiling.

What could a little shit like Perry know about image and records and position within a football team? Nothing.

"No, man," he said.

"Jeremy. Is she still there? Is Laurel still there?"

"Listen to me, Perry. You got to fix this. You got to fix this fast. I'm not gonna sit here and watch them make fun of me on ESPN. That's bullshit!" His voice rose, as did the pounding in his head.

"They weren't making fun, Jeremy. No one is making fun of you, are you kidding? You're the man. You're it!" Perry sounded more awake, more clear, more sure of what he was saying.

"And what's this about my legal team getting sick of me? You know about that? You know something I don't know, Perry? 'Cause, I swear, man, if you're—"

"Jeremy, wait. Wait, wait . . . hey, cool down, man. This is ridiculous. No, we're leaving today, aren't we? We're going to see them today."

Jeremy saw Laurel cross her arms over her bare chest and cock a hip to one side before stomping into the bathroom, and he rolled his eyes.

Women.

* * * *

Speaking of bullshit!

She'd had her big premiere, and this was supposed to be just the beginning. She didn't need this load of crap.

She threw the towel on the countertop and packed her makeup bag into her purse. It was regrettable that she would be leaving the hotel wearing what she had been seen in the night before, but she was leaving. If nothing else, she could say she dumped him. He'd proven to be nothing but a bore.

When she stepped out, Jeremy peeked up and patted the bed. She hesitated then spied her dress on the floor.

"Hey, c'mere."

"Screw you," she said, tilting her chin up and shaking her dress in a vain attempt to pop out the wrinkles.

He stiffened, a strange smile playing across his lips. "Oh, getting saucy, eh? Little Miss Hollywood too good for the football player." He moved toward her, and she liked the notion that she held her ground and teased him right back.

"What football player? You're just a bona fide playboy now."

She choked on her own giggle.

She never saw him move, but he was there, grabbing her by the neck and throwing her against the bed. Her hips slammed against the box springs and she groaned with pain.

"Is that funny?" His voice sounded peculiar.

She started to call out but he was on her, jerking her toward the headboard. She squeaked and clawed at his hands. She had no sooner gotten a hold of his hands than he released her only to flip her on her stomach.

"I don't think that was funny," he said, his voice hissing against her hair. He landed on top of her and pushed her body deeply into the mattress.

It was difficult to breath, but she managed to say she was sorry. She managed to say she was only kidding and that it was a bad joke, but he never heard her. She squeezed her eyes shut and kept repeating that she hadn't meant anything by it as he pawed at her.

"Hey, open up!" The voice and pounding at the door sounded urgent.

"Go away!" Jeremy called over his shoulder, shoving a free hand between her legs.

Laurel tried to wiggle her hands down toward her privates, to protect herself, but his weight was too immense.

"Jeremy, it's me—Perry. Open up. We're late. We gotta get moving."

"I swear, Perry! Go away!" He gave her another shove.

She would have yelled had she been able, but her voice was muffled in the blankets and pillows.

Perry pounded again.

It was clear that he was not going to go away, and Jeremy relented. As he stood, releasing her from his grip and weight, he slapped her on the ass. "Just kidding, baby."

While Laurel grabbed every blessed breath she could, her skin crawled. The way he'd said it. If she wasn't sure of anything else, she knew that Reginald Perry had just saved her ass.

Jeremy strode to the door and flung it open as Laurel scrambled off the bed and managed to dress herself despite her shaking hands.

Perry walked in and halted. He stared at her unapologetically as she struggled to cover her body as quickly as possible.

She just wanted to get the hell out of there. She wanted to thank Perry for saving her but wasn't about to stop to do that. She couldn't breathe. She wanted to get out of the room, out of the hotel, and as far away from Jeremy Connors as possible.

"Uh, everything okay here?" Perry took one last lingering look at her body before he glanced around the room.

She didn't make direct eye contact.

"Well, you broke up a little morning romp." Jeremy's voice was light and cheery. "Other than that, yeah. What's up?"

"Laurel, honey," Perry said. "What's the matter?"

She was sure he meant his tone to sound soothing, but she found it and him repulsive.

"What's the matter?" She almost laughed. "Your *boy* here tried to rape me."

"What?" Perry appeared shocked, looking from Laurel to Jeremy and back to Laurel again.

She only rolled her eyes at him. "No. You both were—"

Laurel looked at Jeremy kicked back and propped up on an elbow on the bed. He looked as innocent as a child merely channel surfing for a cartoon, and suddenly Laurel knew . . . all the stories she had heard in the news were true.

As stunned as she had been by his sudden change in personality, she was also eager to get out as quickly as possible.

As she shifted and grabbed her bag, Perry placed a hand on hers, and smiled. "Let me walk you to the elevator," he said, reaching for his wallet.

Chapter Nine

"You should have kept your big, fat mouth shut." Sam groaned as they made their way back to the main house for dinner.

They were sore from top to bottom—particularly the bottom.

Brooke, Danni, and Jacks suddenly became miniature adults. From the moment the men had left the main house that morning, the prestigious legal team from Jackson, Keller & Whiteman had been in trouble. The rules of getting into and out of the saddle, how to turn, and how to hold the reins were endless. The only thing more painful than watching Kali and her junior hit squad maneuver horses like play toys was what the day's activities had done to their egos.

"What?" Mike asked, but he knew exactly what Sam was talking about. Once again, he had let his ego get in the way. He hadn't been able to stand the fact that Kali had taken complete charge of the show while Tracy and Wade had simply stood by.

"You couldn't stand it, could you?" Sam winced as they climbed the stairs to the main porch.

The only thing that carried Sam and the others through their pain was the magnificent smell that filled the compound. The lure of Ms. Kat's cooking was indeed greater than being saddle sore.

"What the hell were you thinking, challenging a twelve-year-old?" Ed asked and then let out a grunt as he took his first step on the stairs.

As the lessons had worn on, Mike had soured. While Kali had overseen the whole show, Danni had given instructions to Sam, and Jacks worked with Ed, leaving Mike to Brooke, and Mike hadn't been able to stand the idea of being instructed by a little girl. He'd had to challenge her.

Kali hadn't missed a thing. She had seen what was happening and had quickly, happily, taken up the challenge of pitting girl against man. It had been a contest that included putting away the horses and cleaning out stalls. While the girls had moved with great proficiency, the men had been in agony. They'd only been halfway through when Sam saw the girls skip off, their horses completely cared for.

As the men made it to the top of the steps, both Sam and Ed leaned heavily on the porch support beams that led to the front door.

Sam sighed long and hard. "Maybe if we stand out here long enough, they'll get the hint and serve dinner outside. Shit, I can't take another step. I can't even—"

The door opened.

Brooke smiled sweetly, cocking her head to the side. "You can come in."

There was no mistaking the giggles behind her voice, and Sam noticed her head tilted the same way her mother's did when she was having fun with someone. Sam knew that Brooke had seen more than her share of soft city folks learning the hard lessons of first day riding. Every one of the girls probably giggled themselves to sleep each night. He stuck his chest out, took one last deep breath, and held on to it as he picked up his foot and stepped into the house with nary a whimper.

"You do okay today?" Wade asked with a grin.

No doubt he was also well aware of the condition of their backsides.

Wade led the men past the kitchen to the dining room.

A half wall separated the stove and oven from the couch by the fireplace. Standing on the other side was Ms. Kat.

She smiled as the men entered and quickly wiped her hands on her apron. "Good, good. You're here. I imagine you boys are hungry. I know Wade is," she said and shot him a look of mock irritation then waved her hand over the solid oak table loaded down with the most glorious assortment of roast beef, potatoes, rolls, salad, corn on the cob, green bean casserole, some kind of pudding, and fruit. The men felt as though they were seated at Thanksgiving dinner, but as they would soon learn, each meal was an event.

"So how did it go today?" asked Ms. Kat as she found her way to her seat. As she did, all the cowhands rose to their feet, catching the newcomers off guard. Mike and Sam were less graceful than the others, floundering to push the heavy oak chairs back.

Ms. Kat waved a hand at everyone. "Sit, sit."

"It went well," Evan told Ms. Kat. "Danni worked with Sam, right?" He looked to Sam for confirmation.

Sam froze. He had been staring into a bowl of gravy, licking his lips, and couldn't seem to come up with any words beyond *food*.

"You can call her Danielle, though she might do unspeakable things to you in your sleep if you call her that."

Danni giggled. It had become pretty clear early on that no one but her mother called her Danielle.

"I wouldn't dream of it." Sam smiled directly at Danni. "I have a healthy respect for what she can do in the saddle."

"As you should," Wade said, passing a tray of biscuits around. "This here is a state champion, maybe a national contender one day in her age group for cutting." Wade squinted at the new men. "You'll understand this soon enough but she and her horse work together as a team to move cattle left, right, wherever she wants. It's a dying art but essential to what we do here."

Danni looked even tinier sitting in the large chair rather than her saddle. If he hadn't seen it with his own eyes, Sam would have never believed such a little person could control a horse, let alone a herd of cattle like she had.

As Wade spoke, Brooke and Kali joined the others at the table, mumbling something to Ms. Kat as they passed.

Ms. Kat chuckled loudly and patted Kali's arm.

Kali moved gracefully behind Sam and the other men, finding a seat near Tracy at the end of the table. She smelled good. A light, floral scent.

Sam shook his head slightly and cleared his throat as he tried to focus.

"Jacks had Mr. Slader." Evan turned to Ed for a moment. "Now, she actually has a different birth name, but if I was to say it out loud, terrible things would happen to me. Whatever it is you think Danni might do to you, Jacks will triple it just for *thinking* about what her real name is . . . which I'm not. I'm not even thinking about your real name." He suddenly turned to Jacks, suppressing a smile.

Jacks grinned. "That's right," she said, straightening in her chair and nodding once, hard, as though punctuating her point.

"Jacks is also a champion rider. She does barrel racing, and, boys, wait 'til you see her ride. I mean, really ride. What you saw today . . . child's play."

Ed groaned.

Finally, Evan turned to Mike. He regaled the entire table with Brooke's encounter with Mike but never took his eyes off Mike as he spoke. "Brooke showed Mr. Mike how to ride, including how to properly mount and dismount and muck out a stall. Brooke," he said with a slow smile, "is one for detail. And if it's not done properly, she will do it again and again until it's gotten right. But I guess you've figured that one out for yourself, eh, Mike?"

As Evan spoke, Brooke blushed.

"She keeps everyone in line, the smartest one in the family, though that ain't saying much," he said with a wink.

"I beg your pardon?" Ms. Kat spoke up, ending whatever joke Evan hoped to continue.

"Present company always excluded, Ms. Kat." He coughed in his hand and a light shade of pink tinged his cheeks as more laughs erupted around the table.

Ms. Kat smirked and nodded, checking that everyone had full plates. "I don't know how you boys start a meal but around here, but we always give thanks." She gave thanks to good health, good weather, good folks, and good eats.

Another mealtime hour slipped by easily without talk of sports, Jeremy Connors, or how much this case meant to the career of all the men. Danni and Wade told their version of the first day on horseback, and while it was all in good spirit, gibes were sent back and forth. No one was safe. The conversation was light, the feeling extremely warm.

Sam decided this was indeed a home.

Kali never said a word, but the tilt of her head or the wink of an eye encouraged Wade, Evan, and the twins all the more. Throughout the meal, there were glances exchanged between Kali and her daughters, and Sam was entranced. It was the way she held her wine glass, the way she sat, the way she wrinkled her nose when she laughed. He could easily have watched her for the duration of the meal but, eventually, it had to come to an end. All good things always did. This was no different.

"Well, boys," Wade said and his tone suddenly ended the light-hearted jokes. "The only thing longer and harder than today will come tomorrow. You best get some sleep."

* * * *

Danni had been working the cattle for almost an hour, driving them back and forth. Both Ed and Sam watched her from the front porch of the main house. She was just a speck out there on the wide-open land.

"It's amazing how someone so little has so much control," Ed said.

Tracy sat on his horse with a stopwatch timing Danni as she picked just one cow from the herd, separated it out, and moved the beast to her liking. Horse and girl moved in unison as the one cow frantically tried to make its way back to the herd. The object, as near as Ed and Sam could make out, was to keep that from happening. It was fascinating to watch the horse zigzag back and forth, cutting hard to the left or right, blocking the heifer from her family.

"Thus the name cutting," Ed said and Sam nodded.

Every thirty seconds to a minute, Tracy would hold up a hand signaling Danni. She and her horse would release the trapped cow, turn, and start the process all over again, selecting yet another unwilling participant in their game.

Matthew stepped out onto the porch. "She gets judged on the fight." It was as though Matthew had read their minds because even after all their observing, they still hadn't figured out the finer points of judging this particular contest. "See, like that little one there," he said and pointed toward Danni's current cow.

The young cow was paralyzed with fear and confusion. Rather than darting back and forth, trying to get around the horse as the others had done, it simply stood still, looking pathetic.

"She'll get nothin' from that, so she needs to dump that real fast and select another friskier one."

Danni did just that. She picked up another young cow, desperate to get back as it bellowed and mooed, frantically racing from one side to the other as it attempted to dodge the horse.

Maybe it was testament to the time Sam had put in to his own horse, but it was pure poetry. The horse moved effortlessly, anticipating most of the calf's moves, and danced back and forth.

"She's only got so much time on the clock to show the judges what she's made of and really show off Fancy."

Fancy was Danni's mare—coal black with white stockings and a white blaze down her nose.

"She's a beautiful horse," Sam said and Matthew nodded.

"She is that. And multitalented. It's a shame to see her just doing one event. She's amazing with the barrels, but Danni won't do it."

When Matt's voice seemed to turn a bit wistful, both Ed and Sam glanced at each other. There was something else there, but both men were conditioned to wait out a witness. More confessions came from silence than the most well thought out interrogation.

Matthew delivered. "Not since her daddy died. She won't do it. We're not really sure why. Jacks hasn't got a problem with it. But Nick, you know, her dad, he really wanted them girls to barrel race. It's like she can't do it without him. I used to think she was just scared, but it's more than that."

"Scared?" Sam asked.

All three men continued to stare at the little girl. Although her arms were tiny and thin hanging from the sleeves of her T-shirt and her small face was sweet under the brim of her cowboy hat, she was in complete control of the horse and cattle. She didn't appear to have a timid bone in her body.

"Barrel racing ain't for the fainthearted." Matthew lifted his chin toward the pen closest to the house. Jacks and Kali were inside taking a few practice runs before the day was to begin with the men. "Now, Mocha is a different story. She was born to do barrels and nothing but."

They watched Jacks wrestle with the reins as Kali shook her head.

Sam got a good, long look at Kali. This morning she wore her standard jeans, but she had black riding boots and a black sleeveless top. No hat. Rather than the normal ponytail, her hair was down and the bangs pulled back with a clip. Sam studied her profile. She looked like a teenager.

"Mocha is a seven-year-old mare, all piss and vinegar. She hasn't quite bonded the same way with her rider as Fancy has. A good horse'll look after you, take care of you. Fancy is real partial to Danni. Mocha don't have the same feelings for Jacks . . ." He scratched his head and took one step down from the porch. "That's nobody's fault but Jacks'. She's reckless. The exact opposite of Danni. She'd ride Mocha straight into a brick wall to win a race, and Mocha knows it, so they fight."

"Shouldn't they be in school or something?" Sam asked.

Matthew shook his head. "Homeschooled. They could go to school. I know the other kids around these parts go. It's like an hour bus ride, but Kali likes to keep them close." He inspected his cowboy hat still held in his hand, dusting off dirt that was permanently embedded in the fabric. "If you haven't noticed," he said with a smile, "she's a bit of a control freak."

Mike walked by, chuckling.

Ed and Matthew fell in step behind him and all three continued chatting as they made their way toward the barn.

Sam had been staring at Kali. Again. He frowned, hoping that Matthew hadn't seen, but if the sideways glance Matthew had just thrown his way was anything to go by, Sam was busted. Maybe it was because she barely knew he existed that intrigued him so much about her. Women generally liked Sam Spann. They usually sought him out, flirted with him, and managed to find a way to get information about him. Not Kali. She could not have cared less.

"You boys got like five minutes before Kali will be done. Go on ahead and get your horses out." Matthew called over his shoulder, and he hustled to open the back pasture, leaving the lawyers to their own devices.

After three days, they had become more confident, or, as Mike had pointed out, "You kidding me? These horses won't make a move sideways without Kali's say so." It was for that reason alone that they had the confidence to deal with the large animals. It was clear that she was the boss. Most of the horses had been trained by Kali, and each one of them responded to her voice.

"No!" Kali's voice echoed through the barn doors.

One by one, the men and their horses lined up outside the pen, quietly watching Jacks, Mocha, and Kali.

Kali sent Mocha and Jacks trotting to the far left of the corral while she stepped back, checked her stopwatch, and then threw a hand up.

Jacks jammed her heels into the side of Mocha and they were off. Ten hard strides in, Mocha turned left and headed for the first barrel.

The turn was smooth, they cleared the barrel, and Jacks pumped her legs as hard as she could, urging the horse on.

Mocha dug and strained against the earth, making each step explosive. It was a credit to the horse how quickly they were able to get going in such a small area. They were flying right for Sam and the men, but all eyes were on the barrel in front of them. The turn was last minute.

Sam had witnessed Mocha and Jacks make this same run dozens of times, but this time she slipped. The back left side of the horse tucked under. It was like watching a train wreck in slow motion.

Jacks knew she was in jeopardy with the first off step. She tried to counter the barrel, pulling Mocha's reins to the right, hoping to give her some balance but it was too late. The heavy animal was in full skid. Jacks went over Mocha's head and slammed into the iron fence with a heavy thud. Jacks crumpled like a rag doll.

Mike started. "Shit!"

Everyone moved forward at the same time, everyone but mother and daughter.

Kali grabbed Mocha, catching her high on the reins, near the bit.

"Ow!" Jacks' little voice echoed in the ring, but she stood, holding her shoulder, and looked at her mother.

All eyes turned to Kali.

Kali didn't move. No tears, no "Oh, my poor baby." Mother and daughter simply stared at each other for a moment.

"You know what you did?" Kali asked coolly.

"No." Jacks started to cry then straightened her back, threw her chin up a notch, and stopped the tears with a swipe of her hand. "Yes. I went too soon," she said.

Kali nodded and turned to give Mocha a quick once-over, checking for any injuries. "Again."

"Shit!" Mike mumbled on a hard exhale.

Sam was pretty sure he'd been holding his breath the whole time.

Kali leaned against the fence. "Mocha knows what she's doing, Jacks. She's been doing this longer than you."

"I know!" Jacks hollered over her now-injured shoulder, giving it a quick roll as she did.

"Yeah? Then act like it. Give her the lead. Let her take the rounds. You go after her once you've cleared the barrel, you got that?"

"I know, I know!" Jacks practically screamed.

"Excuse me?" Kali stomped forward, kicking up dust as she crossed the pen.

Sam peeked at Jacks, who licked her lips nervously.

As Kali approached horse and rider, she flicked a wave at Jacks, motioning her to get off Mocha.

Jacks didn't hesitate.

Somewhere Sam heard Matt's voice. "Showtime."

Kali never put her foot in the stirrup. With an almost effortless hop, she pulled herself up on the saddle and gave a quick shot to Mocha's ribs. For all the lessons spent on making sure the stirrups were properly measured to one's leg length and making sure the reins were even in the hand, Kali didn't give a millisecond's notice to anything. She was gone. Bowed over the saddle, just as he had seen her that first day, she and Mocha raced toward the first barrel. It was flawless.

As she rounded the barrel, she opened up, tapping Mocha, but she looked over at her daughter. "I'm letting her go," she yelled, not even watching the barrel coming up.

Another smooth semicircle around the fifty-gallon drum, and they were off again, headed toward the last barrel at the other end of the pen. Once they made that barrel, Kali let out a big yelp and kicked Mocha for the first time.

Mocha doubled the speed she'd had with her first rider.

As they approached Jacks, still moving at a pretty fast clip, Kali threw a leg over the saddle. Mocha slowed, creating a cloud of dust around them, and Kali jumped to the ground.

Jacks crossed her arms and sulked.

Kali walked off, never looking back, and resumed her place at the second barrel. *"That's* what I'm talking about. Mocha knows what she's supposed to do."

Mocha stood, head held high, while Jacks climbed back on. She fidgeted with her hat. "Sorry."

"Damn," Ed whispered, and everyone nodded in unison.

That had been poetry in motion.

Kali threw up her hand and Jacks was off.

They made the left barrel cleanly. Jacks and Mocha steamrolled to the second barrel, charging forward.

"You're pulled back! Let go, let go!" Kali yelled, but Jacks was already trying to steer, and Mocha was fighting her.

Another skid.

Jacks dropped the reins and wrapped her arms around the horse's neck, fighting to stay in the saddle, while Mocha slid back and forth, looking as though she would come right through the fence.

All the men backed up.

It was ugly, but they made the semicircle.

Jacks was disgusted and grabbed the reins, jerking them back.

Mocha came to a short stop and snorted.

"This stinks!" she shrieked.

"Hey! You don't stop. You never stop. I don't care if you come in dead last. You finish the cycle!" Kali, hands on her hips, looked down at the ground and spat.

"Momma's mad." A small voice piped up right beside Sam.

He looked over to see Brooke perched on her horse.

Brooke gave a little nod. "She spits when she's mad."

Sam chuckled and he looked back at Kali walking across the pen toward the second barrel.

"You're going to clear this, Jaclyn. When I yell at you, let Mocha take the lead. Got it?"

"Yes, ma'am."

"When I yell again, you urge her on. It's that simple."

It took three more tries before Mocha was allowed to clear the barrels, and it was sweet.

All the men broke into applause—something that Kali didn't like. She shot a look over toward them but the damage was done.

Jacks strutted forward, blowing kisses to her adoring fans.

"Too bad nationals doesn't give you six tries," Kali said as Jacks trotted by.

"Momma!" Jacks' feelings were hurt.

"Momma nothin'," Kali said with a shrug. "Cool her down then get on in to Ms. Kat. She's waiting on you." She dusted her pants and looked to her next class. "Sorry, fellas. That took a little longer—"

"She's not going to take it out on us, is she?" Sam stage-whispered to Brooke.

Every person had their own comfort zone level but to see someone sitting cross-legged on a horse, adjusting her shoes just wasn't right. Brooke had put on her socks and boots while sitting on her horse, watching her little sister nearly break her neck. Just an everyday affair.

For Sam, this whole thing had been a frustrating and demeaning experience. He had been a gifted athlete all his life but, suddenly, he was struggling just to stay seated. Muscles ached in places he didn't even know he had muscles. Fortunately, he wasn't the only one. Mike had made sure everyone was keenly aware of his discomfort—all of it—and all of the locations of discomfort as well. It hadn't stopped Sam from feeling so awkward about being coached by a woman who could ride like the wind and spit while looking cute.

Damn her.

"Gentlemen," Kali said. "You saw what happened with Jacks. As good a rider as she is, her horse—all these horses—know what to do. If you get in a tight spot, let them run it. Matthew, Tracy, and I will always be on hand. Just remember, don't panic, hold on, and let the horse do what he or she is supposed to do. So, without further ado . . . Mr. Slader."

Ed had the great misfortune of being closest to her, and he flinched at his name.

"You saw the pattern Jacks ran." It wasn't a question.

Ed's face fell. "Like Jacks?" he asked.

Nervous laughter filled the little arena.

One by one, the pathetic horsemen took their position. Each man trotted to the first barrel, tentatively circling it, but once Mike had the first barrel under his belt, he decided to open up.

Redwing snorted and jerked his head up, startled at the feel of the man's feet digging into his sides. A half step later, he decided to take the fat man for a ride.

Within fifteen feet, Mike was leaned so far back in his saddle he was practically lying flat on the horse's rump and pulling hard on the reins.

Redwing fought back against the sharp pain of the bit, twisting his head from side to side.

"Whoa! Whoa! Shit, shit, shit!" Mike cried out.

As suddenly as it had begun, Redwing stopped short at the second barrel, throwing Mike off balance.

Everyone watched as, almost in slow motion, he pitched forward, grasping at Redwing's neck.

Redwing stood perfectly still as Mike wrapped his arms around the horse's massive neck, but momentum kept his body sliding lower and lower until Mike's toes reached and tapped the dirt underneath him, then his feet, and finally, he was planted firmly on the ground once more and bear hugging the horse standing in front of him.

There was a moment's pause while everyone digested what they had just witnessed, during which Redwing lowered his head and Mike stumbled backward.

Always the diplomat, Ed rocked his head back and howled with laughter. He was not the only one. Even Kali couldn't stop the snicker.

"Yes, here we are, ladies and gentlemen . . . the dream team." Ed laughed out loud.

Without meaning to, Ed had reminded them why they were really there, and the laughter subsided. There was something about Rainwash that had made it easy to forget what they faced.

"Let's hope you're better lawyers than cowboys," Tracy said and winked.

Mike never missed a beat. "This, good sir, is defective equipment. There's a major liability here. You see how he just stopped, trying to kill me. You'll hear from my lawyers." As he spoke, he clambered around the horse and tried to get his boot back in a stirrup.

Alexandra Allred

Chapter Ten

Brooke fell in line with Sam as the group left the pen.

Lightning had sensed that something was different about today's ride, and he jerked his head up and down, fighting the reins.

"Don't let him do that," Brooke said, cautioning Sam about his horse. "Loosen the slack and he won't fight it so much. You fight all day like that, and it'll kill your hands." She reached across her own saddle and patted Lightning on the side. "Plus, it'll hurt his mouth."

"I didn't think he'd notice." Sam breathed heavily. "I swear, I think your mother hates me," he said, giving a final jerk to the reins.

Brooke frowned. "Mom likes to test people. Take it as a compliment."

"I'm not so sure about that. I'd be more flattered if I didn't have a horse that was trying to kill me."

Brooke giggled. "Lightning would never try to kill anyone. He's just a big puppy. Do you know dogs?"

Sam raised his eyebrows at her. "Dogs I know. This is no big dog."

"No. A puppy," she said and giggled again.

As they talked, Kali led the group outside the main gate and toward the mountains in the distance. The scenery was truly breathtaking. Sam had heard the expression *God's country* many times over but hadn't been able to appreciate it until he'd come to Rainwash.

The moment was disrupted by Lightning when he crow hopped—a term he had learned while attempting to ride the blasted animal—and seemed to signal he was either about to take off in a full gallop or buck off his rider. Maybe both.

"He's not paying attention to you," Brooke said helpfully.

Sam tried to pull back on the reins and get the horse in line, but Lightning had other plans.

"He knows he's got you," Brooke said. "He's that way. He knows you're getting upset so he's going to push you. Wait." She trotted forward just enough to lean out and catch Lightning's reins. "Whoa," she said, bringing Lightning and Sam to a halt. "Mr. Spann, if you'll stay put." She swung a leg over and landed between the two horses. "You need to stop acting up, Light," Brooke said as she stroked his neck. She gave Sam a nod. "Maybe it would help if you rode Mouse for a few minutes, Mr. Spann. I can work with Lightning for a little bit. He'll settle back down."

Sam didn't hesitate. He was happy to be away from the wild, young horse.

Lightning tried to walk off on Brooke while she was stepping into the saddle, but she barked at him, pulling on the rein while she had only one foot in a stirrup. Lightning reared a little, but Brooke was too fast and swung around into the saddle. Once in place, she gave him a sharp kick to the ribs and steered him to the back of the line.

Sam heard her working his gait, making him canter, then trot, and then walk.

Mouse made Sam feel like a new man. Suddenly, he was very tall and in control. At least, this was how Mouse let him feel. Mouse responded to the lightest touch, but, as Kali had said again and again, it wasn't necessary because Mouse knew what was expected of him and followed the trail. Sam took a deep breath, embracing the moment. He saw Mike trotting behind Kali and wrestling with Redwing, just as Sam had been with Lightning, only Redwing was very aware of Kali and settled back each time she turned on him. Sam smiled. Mike had become Kali's pet.

Ed was behind Mike and absorbing everything Utah had to offer. He was relaxed, with one hand resting on his lap, his cowboy hat pushed back, and looking around, occasionally pointing to something for Tracy to see. Tracy, who no doubt had seen it all twenty times before, nodded accommodatingly. As funny as it had seemed at the time, Choo Choo had been an excellent selection for Ed. The two got along famously. Why Kali had decided to give Sam a horse like Lightning remained a mystery. They were like oil and water.

"Ke-yup!"

Sam heard the pounding of hooves and turned to see Lightning coming alongside them. He was a good-looking horse, no doubt. With Brooke on his back, he had his head high, mane flying. With each step, he brought his legs up unusually high—regal, elegant, and ready to break into a full gallop at any given second. His eyes were almost wild with excitement.

"It's the wind," Brooke said as she settled Lightning into a pace next to Mouse.

Mouse drew a breath so deep that Sam felt his legs bow out. The horse huffed loudly and Brooke laughed.

"I'm sorry, boy. Lightning was being a brat. Next break," she said, an unmistakable promise to her tone, and Mouse shook his head, as though he understood.

The little girl was a marvel. Just like her mother. Sam opened his mouth to say as much, but thought better of it. Brooke had probably been told over and over how amazing she was with horses. Her personality was much like Mouse's. Calm, cool, sweet. Instead, he asked about school.

"I'm supposed to be in the sixth grade," she said with a shrug. "I tested out, though, so I'm in the eighth right now. I'll be starting ninth pretty soon."

"You're kidding?"

"No. I excel in biology, math . . . you know, all the science stuff that will help me get into veterinary school. That's what I want to do."

"But don't you miss going to school with friends? Going to parties or hanging out?" he asked.

"At first, I was really lonely. I missed my friends, but Momma takes us into town on weekends and we see everyone so it's not like I'm missing anything really. I couldn't spend the night with people or anything until weekends anyway," she said and grinned. "Now it's even cooler because everyone always wants to come here to Rainwash and go riding and stuff. When the bungalows are empty, we get to have our own rooms. It's really cool."

"I could see that. You might have to be careful of who wants to be your friend just because you've got the coolest house in town." Sam chuckled, but Brooke shot him a serious look.

"Oh, I already know it. That's why I kind of stay with the same friends. A couple of times we've had some girls over and all they want to do is ride or go swimming. They don't really care that much about me. Momma is pretty picky about who gets to come here."

Sam looked toward the front of the line. They were ascending a steep slope and Kali reached back and gave a warning shot to Redwing, who had begun to give Mike a hard time.

"Momma" liked to run the show all right.

"Besides, we wouldn't be able to travel like we do if it weren't for our schedule. We can take school pretty much anywhere."

A gust of wind carried over the ridge of the hill and Lightning bolted to one side. The move was so sudden it took both Sam and Brooke by surprise, but Brooke had composure, and in the blink of an eye, had Lightning back on track, prancing around again, and eyeballing everything suspiciously.

"They're flight animals," Brooke calmly explained.

Had it been him, Sam knew he would have been eating dirt. He nodded.

"They can't help it. Did you know they can hear things five hundred feet away? That's why their ears are able to make almost complete rotations. They act like sonar. And their eyesight is excellent. They have almost three hundred sixty degree vision, except right in front of their noses and back by their rumps. But wind does two things, it blocks out proper sound so they can't really judge how close or far away something is—"

A swirl of leaves whipped up miniature tornadoes, causing Lightning to rear back. Even Mouse jumped a little, but he managed to stay on course. This time, Lightning did bolt. Brooke hung on, letting him take a few long strides before she turned him back. His nostrils were flared and he looked wilder than ever.

"And, it makes them really jumpy," Brooke said and she leaned forward, giving Lightning a strong pat. "It's okay, boy. It was nothing but a big ol' bad bunch of leaves." She spoke in a baby voice that seemed to settle the massive animal.

Sam watched in amazement. "I'm just glad you were on him and not me. I don't know why your mom gave me that horse. I'm much happier on Mouse. He's great." He gave Mouse a good sound pat as he'd seen Brooke do but passed on the baby talk.

"She's got a plan. I don't know what it is, but if she gave you this horse . . ." Brooke looked toward her mom at the front of the line. "Oh, we should probably switch back before she gets mad at me."

Sam cringed internally. Again, he saw Mike fighting with Redwing.

"You shouldn't be worried, Mr. Spann. She knows what she's doing. She's the best there is."

"Never makes a mistake?" He raised his eyebrows at her, feigning suspicion. Brooke was a cute kid.

"Nope."

"Never lost a customer to a runaway horse?"

"No!" The idea of it seemed to strike her particularly funny as she doubled over Lightning's neck in a fit of giggles.

"Never mismatched a horse and rider?"

"Never." The unstoppable giggles only further confirmed she was highly entertained by his uncertainty.

"She walk on water?" Sam winked at her.

"I've never seen her try."

Sam laughed. "Touché."

"She smokes," Brooke said and shrugged. "That's the only thing she does wrong, but we let her do it."

"We?"

"Me, Danni, and Jacks. We know she does it. She sneaks out at night to have a smoke. She started doing it after Daddy died, so we let her because she needs it. I mean, she doesn't need the smoking. Yuck. But she needs to have something like that, I guess, 'cause she never cried."

Sam was fascinated.

"She cried when she first heard about it, I guess. We all did," she said. "But I never saw her. Danni, Jacks, and me have never seen her cry. She keeps . . . she thinks she keeps us happier and stronger if she never gets upset."

"She never gets mad?" Sam had seen Kali get mad himself.

"Oh!" Brooke laughed, rolling her eyes. "She gets mad. Boy, does she ever! She gets upset like that, but you won't ever see her cry."

They rode in silence, and Sam watched the back of Kali. Composed. Strong. In control.

"Does it work?" Sam asked. Brooke frowned and he saw her confusion. "To keep you and your sisters feeling happier and stronger, I mean."

Brooke stared straight ahead. Maybe she was looking at her mother.

Sam studied her profile. She was a miniature Kali. Already she had beautifully chiseled cheekbones.

She pushed out her lower lip, thinking. "Yeah," she said with a slow nod then a small laugh. "Yeah, I guess it does." She pulled Lightning to a stop and tilted her head at Sam, smiling. "We have to trade again," she said, almost a little too sympathetically for Sam's liking, but she followed it with another giggle.

Sam sighed and threw a leg over the saddle horn, dismounting from Mouse. "You think this is funny? My entire ego is in the hands of a young . . . what? How old are you?"

"Twelve." She smiled.

"Fabulous. I think I have a pair of shoes older than you." He walked tentatively around to Lightning's side. "Whoa, boy. It's just me. Your lord and master."

Brooke laughed again. She stood in front of Lightning, holding his reins up high with one hand and stroking the horse's powerful jaw with the other. "He's riding smoothly now," she promised "The wind's died down. He'll be fine. But you have to let him know you're the boss."

"Blah, blah, blah," Sam muttered, and Brooke giggled once more. As he stepped into the stirrup, Lightning swung out his rump, and Sam's heart jumped.

This was insanity. He needed to be working on his argument. He needed to be talking to the detectives. He needed to know more about Carmen Hernandez. He needed to know more about Jessica Stanten's personal background, her sexual partners, and her drinking habits. Hell, he needed to be talking to Jeremy Connors. It had been too long and there was no telling what else Jeremy had gotten into.

Brooke's short stint had done wonders for Lightning's disposition. Other than a few sideways trots, Lightning behaved himself and Sam relaxed as he listened to Brooke explain life on the ranch in Utah. He'd never considered himself a kid person, but he enjoyed her company. She was bright, articulate, and inquisitive. Several times she had tried to learn more about his client, Jeremy Connors, and what he was being charged with. True to form, Sam artfully dodged and deflected the questions, putting the spotlight back on the girl and her passion for animals.

"Momma says it'll save me. She says it's important to have a passion. If you have a passion for something it'll save you from being bored or unhappy. If you have a passion for something you will always have something to work for, somewhere to share it and love it." Brooke leaned forward again, patting Mouse. She looked up. "Do you like animals, Mr.

Spann?"

"Yeah, I guess you could say that." He shrugged. He had never owned a pet, but he liked them all the same. Truth be told, he'd never really understood some of the women in his office. They were nutty about their dogs and cats. But he was wise enough to understand there was a strong bond between most pet owners and their four-legged friends that couldn't be questioned.

She nodded. "Good. Momma says there's a special place in hell for people who abuse animals."

"What about your mom?" Sam asked. "What's her passion?"

Brooke looked off into the distance then a slow smile spread across her face. "This." She spread out her hand in front of them.

Sam turned to look and drew in a sharp breath. He hadn't even noticed how much the sun had gone down. Between Lightning and the engaging Brooke, Sam had already gotten what he'd paid for—he was swept away.

Kali stopped the group as they all stood atop the small mountain they had climbed.

He looked around. Was it actually a mountain? He was from Houston. What did he know about mountains? But it was certainly too large, too long, too steep to call a hill.

The horizon as far as the eye could see was washed in bright yellow. Above it was a deeper, more orange yellow. It made the mountains in the distance look red and fireball orange. Between the two mountains appeared to be some kind of lake acting as a mirror and reflected the brilliant yellow back up to the sky.

Sam tilted his head back and saw a swirl of colors he had never seen before—reds with streaks of blue, orange, and pink.

"Wow, this is amazing!" Ed said.

Sam was no romantic, but this was the stuff of songs and stories.

Suddenly, a cell phone rang, startling everyone.

"What the hell?" Ed snapped.

Kali smiled sheepishly, pointing to the phone on her belt. She fumbled with the dial pad.

"Yup, God's country and also one of the best places around here to get reception," Tracy said. He gave a little yip to his horse, leading the pack back down. "Must be a sign we need to get back to the homestead. Let's hope it's not God callin'."

As Tracy circled his horse back toward the trail, Redwing flattened his ears at Lightning. Before anyone could react, Redwing reached out and nipped at Lightning who jerked his head back.

Brooke lunged sideways and pulled back on Lightning's reins.

"No! Bad horse!" Mike wrestled with the reins, throwing a "sorry!" over his shoulder to Sam.

"Bad horse? Holy hell! What's your problem?" Sam asked. The question appeared to be directed at Mike, Redwing, and Lightning.

"If you want to get him to respect you, you have to correct him!" Brooke told Sam.

Sam raised his eyebrows. She looked like a little adult. Her tone was scolding.

She gave a swift tug and chastised Lightning through gritted teeth. "Knock it off!"

Kali was off to the side with one hand covering an ear. She shook her head as she listened to someone on the other end of the phone call.

Lightning settled once all the horses had passed, allowing Sam to look down one final time at the scene before them. He leaned back in his saddle, grateful for a quiet Lightning, and breathed it all in. He understood.

"This is a great passion," he said. "It's so . . . just wow. This is gorgeous." He gave a small nod to Brooke.

"Not for long," Kali said, frowning. She and Star stopped a few feet away. With her baseball cap pushed back she looked like the picture of healthy living. Beautiful. She sighed deeply, took one last look at the sunset, and then turned to Sam. "You've got company."

Chapter Eleven

Sam's heart fell as soon as he saw Jeremy and his posse standing near the corral.

He hated the entire concept of a posse—grown men, following another grown man around simply because he had money and could catch a damn ball.

Unconsciously, Sam pulled back on the reins, slowing Lightning even more while Mike charged ahead.

As he closed in, Sam saw Jeremy say something to one of his cronies, and the four-man posse laughed.

Sam cringed. This was exactly the kind of thing Sam had tried to talk to Jeremy about. Moving around with other players, all with suspect reputations, was not the way to go.

Roderick Bouche, a New Orleans native, was one of the hardest-hitting offensive linesmen in the game. At almost six foot six inches, tipping the scales at over three hundred and fifty pounds, Bouche was an entertaining yet volatile player known for vicious tackles, late hits, in-your-face celebration dances on the field, and DUIs and run-ins with local police departments wherever he went. As a young black man, he managed to fulfill every negative stereotype there was for African-Americans.

The funny thing was that Jeremy was cut from the same cloth, but as a blue-eyed, white kid from the Midwest, he approached legal troubles in a different manner. Jeremy *expected* to be rescued from trouble. He had been told he was a star since his high school days, and when his college had fallen under intense NCAA scrutiny for recruiting violations, drug use, and criminal behavior by players, Jeremy had walked away clean. He had been their golden boy. Some fifteen players and boosters had been leveled at the expense of keeping Jeremy happy and clean.

Bouche, on the other hand, believed he could do whatever he felt like, and if caught, point out that if he were white, he wouldn't be questioned.

Both felt they were entitled. Neither had any concept of responsibility or accountability. They played life like they played the game, leaving carnage everywhere and never had anyone tried to teach them otherwise.

Mike deceived the group by sliding gracefully from his horse when he reached them and drew a round of cheers from the football players.

Despite himself, Sam smiled. Mike would never be able to repeat that performance.

Redwing stood, snorting impatiently to be put away and fed, but Mike didn't notice. He plowed through the group of men to get to Jeremy, probably questioning his sudden appearance.

Sam sighed so heavily that Brooke leaned forward to study his face. He knew Mike had called an impromptu meeting in the bunkhouse, not wanting to discuss anything out in the open. Mike, the cowboy, was forgotten. Although he still wore his Stetson, it was just an oversight. The lawyer was back.

After his own clumsy dismount, Ed was hot on Mike's heels, and Garret Jackson, a Jeremy wannabe, lumbered close behind.

Jackson was nowhere close to Jeremy's skill level, but they had been roommates in college. Jeremy had been a first-round draft pick whereas Garret Jackson had been one of the last chosen at all, but the two shared a history. From the outside, the relationship appeared lopsided. Jackson was a nobody in the world of sports, and Sam was sure it was one of the reasons the man clung to Jeremy. He was his ticket to all the things he would otherwise miss. In exchange, Jackson had become Jeremy's high-five guy. He laughed at everything and followed his buddy into the depths of hell without question. Those might have been qualities to admire if they were soldiers in war, but they were a bunch of party boys, and their conquests were always young women.

As Sam and Brooke entered the main gates of Rainwash, he watched the last member of the party disappear into the bunkhouse, Jeremy's weasel of an agent, Reginald Perry.

It was all slipping away—no, it was being pulled away. Sam wasn't ready to be sucked back into the strain and drain of Jeremy's legal woes. He wasn't ready to see Mike and Ed go into autopilot, spinning the case for the sake of the media. Sam was surrounded by possibly the most glorious sunset he would ever see, and he wasn't ready to shut that out. He slowed Lightning to a snail's pace next to Brooke as he focused on the little girl's chatter.

"That's good," she said. "Keep him steady, make him wait . . . that's good." She giggled. "Look at him. It's killing him. That's very good, Mr. Spann. See?" She gave a happy little nod. "You're going to make him respect you if you test him like this. He has to learn to listen to you."

Mouse drew a deep breath and snorted but never changed his pace.

"Oh, you big baby," she said and patted him. "You'll get your yummies."

Sam and Brooke tethered their horses, groomed them, and turned them out while the feed was prepared.

Lightning began bucking and kicking inside the corral. He was frisky with the cool air on his back.

As the sun fully set, Sam realized how suddenly the temperature dropped. Evenings were quite cool in the mountains unlike the sweltering humidity of Houston.

"Well." Sam sighed. "No time like the present." With all the horses curried and put away, there was nothing else to delay the inevitable.

"You're coming to dinner, right?" Brooke asked.

Sam nodded. He noticed Kali was still in the barn, partially hidden behind her horse as she inspected Star's feet. As she reached for another hoof, giving it a little tug, he had to admire her arms. Lean and cut, she had rounded shoulders with a clear definition into her bicep. As she reached and flexed, he made out the indentation of her triceps.

He knew dozens of women who paid top dollar to get arms like that. They spent countless hours in the gym with personal trainers and kickboxing classes for something Kali probably never thought about.

There they were, the two of them. It never occurred to her that Star could crush her leg, and it never occurred to Star that he could or might do such a thing. They were incredibly at ease and peace with each other.

She was talking to herself, or Star—Sam wasn't sure which—and patting Star's leg when she looked up and made eye contact with Sam.

He wanted to wave or smile, but he was frozen by her stare. He tried to read her expression. Sam knew no one had expected the additional customers, but wasn't that a good thing? More business equals more money. Most likely, it was that one of the men was Jeremy Connors. While she was neatly tucked away from the rest of the world, she had already made her very strong opinions on the matter well known.

With the last hoof inspected, she wiped her hands, gave Star a quick kiss, and led him back to his own stall.

Sam watched a moment longer, and, with great trepidation, faced the inevitable.

As his hand fell on the giant door handle, he heard Mike's voice. Sam sighed and rested his head against the heavy wood, inhaling his last bit of peace.

"Well, hell, Jeremy! Can you not stay out of trouble? What is it with you?"

Sam could tell from the way his voice carried that Mike was pacing—a typical Mike response to a bad situation.

Sam reluctantly gripped the iron doorknob and pushed the door open.

"I don't know wha—"

All eyes turned to Sam.

He hesitated, wanting to assess the situation, and noted first thing that Garret Jackson had planted himself on Sam's bed—shoes and all. Roderick Bouche stood against the wall, sandwiched between two large, heavy dressers in typical Bouche modus operandi—be present, watchful, but out of the line of fire. Ed was on his own bed, sitting forward, head in his hands. Jeremy sat at the small table, legs sprawled out in front of him, looking very much like a teenager getting read the riot act by an irate parent —smug, contrite, and not the least bit sorry about anything. Sam took a step inside, eyeing Perry.

Perry was always trying to match Mike's moves and gestures. While Mike found it amusing, it was grating to Sam. Perry was a punk who postulated and puffed up for athletes who bought into that load of crap. He fancied himself a master of characters, studying people around him. He had seen Mike in the courtroom and had seen how Mike worked a jury. He believed he could work that same magic on his clients.

Ed raised his head, his fingers raking through his hair and along his face as he locked eyes with Sam.

Sam looked back to Mike. "What?" He braced himself.

Mike had been ready to explode out of his shoes and was obviously just waiting for Sam to ask. "Man! You just wouldn't believe." He threw his hands up in the air. "Dumbass," he said, gesturing toward Jeremy.

"Hey!"

"Hey, nothin'." Mike never took his eyes from Sam's. "He got into a fight. Put a guy in the hospital." Mike began to pace again, rubbing his head. "I can't believe this. I mean, hey, I'm thrilled that you're so confident in our abilities to defend you that you—"

"What was I supposed to do?" Jeremy asked. "The asshole was pickin' a fight with me. Wasn't he?" Jeremy turned around, looking for verification. "I'm minding my own business—"

"At a bar?" Ed asked.

Jeremy hesitated, wrinkling his forehead. "Yeah, so?"

"Shit," Ed muttered under his breath.

Jeremy shot him a look of irritation then turned back toward Mike and Sam. "*Anyway,* I'm just doin' my own thing, ya know?" He smiled the wolf smile Sam had come to know all too well. "And this little shit comes up and starts on me, you know, saying I'm a rapist, that I'm ruining things for the team, you know, causing too much distraction and shit like that."

"I thought we talked about you not going to bars. We talked about you keeping a low profile. What happened to all that? What happened to you not getting into trouble?" Between Ed's tone and body language with folded hands and bowed head, Sam couldn't tell if Ed was asking, pleading, or praying.

"Man!" Jeremy rolled his head, letting it fall back so that he faced Roderick upside down. The two smiled at each other, causing Mike to pace again, muttering under his breath.

Ed said nothing.

Just moments ago, Ed had finally relaxed on Choo Choo. The memory of it burned in Sam's brain, and he repressed a deep-throated chuckle at the memory of Ed chastising his horse, *"Bad horse. Bad Choo Choo."* It had been the most relaxed Ed had been in months—maybe longer—yet, in minutes it had all been undone by Jeremy who couldn't have cared less. Sam studied his body language. He was relaxed, legs outstretched, arms hanging off to the side as though he were sitting in the locker room with the team reviewing last week's plays. He was confident, cocky.

"Darius Smith." Sam spoke to no one in particular.

Silence filled the room and no one moved.

"I'm sorry." Mike stopped, looking bewildered. "What?"

"Darius Smith. You remember him?" He looked first to Mike then Ed. He knew Ed remembered him.

"Basketball player." Ed nodded and Mike turned to look at him.

"Yeah, I know the name. What the hell does he have to do with—"

"Top of his game. I bet you remember him?" Sam stared at Jeremy. "Middle of the season, he's partying at a topless joint, has one too many for the road and plows over two guys in the road." He turned to Ed. "They were stopped to change a tire, right?"

"No. They had stopped to help out some other guy, remember?"

Sam nodded. "That's right."

Jeremy's eyelids dropped. He offered a lazy smile. "Man, what does this —"

"Two really nice guys stop in the middle of the night to help out a family, and Smith is drunk, runs over them, and drags the one kid almost fifty feet. The son of a bitch never hit the brakes, just keeps on plowing through. He drives home and parks his car in the garage.

"But he doesn't call the police or anything like that. Oh, no. He sits on it. Doesn't say a word until he realizes the police have been on all the local radio and TV stations. Witnesses have described his car and he knows there is no way he can take his car anywhere for repairs. So what does he do? He calls the team manager." Sam stepped fully into the room, moving more freely as his anger rose.

Mike's mouth dropped open.

Jeremy just looked bored.

"Once it's revealed it was Darius, everyone goes nuts. The strip joint suddenly can't remember when or if he was there because, see, they don't want to be liable for sending him off drunk. The team starts making noise that he was going to be traded anyway. Suddenly, no one wants to touch the guy. But still, you know, he's Darius Smith." Sam spread his hands out as if he was the ringmaster announcing his star performer at this twisted circus. "*The* Darius Smith. So, when the police come to get him, they don't handcuff him, they don't throw him in a cell . . . no, they treat him like a celebrity coming to visit the station. It's just like Darius expected it to be. Kill two people. What the hell? No one cares. He's Darius Smith."

"You got a point to all this?" Jeremy asked.

"Yeah. I got a point. The evidence is just too overwhelming, even for an idiot like Darius Smith, and he's indicted, but he's rich so . . . what the hell? He posts bond and remains a free man while every possible argument can be made, dragged out, questioned. But he's so unbelievably full of himself, he can't be bothered to make payments to the bail bondsman and gets himself throw in jail—for good, this time." Sam laughed and shook his head. "Honest to God, he thinks after all this . . . I mean, a gift has been handed to this guy. There was brain matter in his car. Blood all over his effin' car, but he can't be bothered to make payments to keep his sorry ass out of jail." Sam waved a finger at Ed. "You remember who was representing him?"

"Yeah, Calloway." Ed chuckled.

Sam forced a laugh for effect.

"Yo, man."

Even as Perry stepped forward, Sam ground his back teeth. He hated that man—*Yo, man?*

"What does this have to do with our problem? I don't give two shits about Darius Smith. He's a has-been."

"The only reason he's a *has-been*, as you say, is because he's in prison, and if you're paying attention and have any real interest in your client, you would note that this has *everything* to do with Jeremy." Sam took a deep breath and silently counted to ten.

"Darius came to us first," Sam said, waving a finger back and forth between himself and Ed. "We passed. Calloway didn't have the same good judgment. From the get-go, it was a disaster. There was no way for Calloway to win. Plus, the guy was an ass." Sam brought his gaze back to Jeremy and leveled a hard stare. "*You* are Darius Smith."

"Say what?" Jeremy's eyes flew open. He started to stand, but Perry was quick to put a hand on his shoulder, holding him back. It was the typical bravado he expected. As if to say, *hold me back*, and Jeremy wrestled with himself to stay seated.

Sam was unimpressed. "I'm done." Sam looked at Mike, who stood speechless. "I mean it, Mike. I'm not going to get sucked down by some dumbass athlete who can't get his act together long enough to stay out of prison." Sam turned on his heel and was out the door.

That felt great. He felt his heart pounding and was quite sure he also felt at least one set of eyes burning into his back.

Was he bluffing? They would all be asking themselves that. Only Ed really knew. As closely as Mike and Sam had worked on this case, it was Ed who knew Sam best.

Just keep walking, Sam. Keep walking.

Chapter Twelve

Sam knew the good feeling was fleeting, that Mike would come find him, talk him down, and attempt to bring him back into the fold. Mike would point out that they had a job to do. They had a potential partnership with Jackson, Keller & Whiteman to consider.

A partnership.

Sam lost a step.

Mike had no idea. He had worked just as hard as Sam on this case. Maybe harder.

Sam looked back toward the bunkhouse. Mike was probably patting Jeremy on the shoulders, promising the spoiled brat that he would make Sam come to his senses. For Mike, this case meant the possibility of a partnership, but the higher powers hadn't been looking at Mike. Only Sam. He wasn't sure how Mike would handle that. He wasn't sure if Mike should have to handle it. While it was certainly true Sam had turned in numbers that Mike couldn't touch, including all kinds of new clientele, Mike had busted his ass on this case.

Sam was drawn toward the center of the compound and the bench wedged neatly between two overgrown trees. Both trees bowed out into a giant V, making a nice backboard for Sam to lean against. Tucked against the tree trunk, Sam felt partially hidden. This was the kind of place a man could get lost in his own thoughts. Truly lost, allowed to swim in fantasies, dreams of the future, the possibilities of what might have been or could be. He rocked back and forth against the tree trunk, finding just the right spot. After riding a horse for so long, it was nice to have the back support. He closed his eyes and waited for the inevitable.

Sam had fantasized about dumping Jeremy as a client but knew the reality was he would see the case through to the end for the sake of his career. Until his brief stay at Rainwash, making partner had been his one goal. Things had changed. Here, surrounded by horses and people he barely knew, he'd realized just how tired he was of Jeremy Connors and his attitude. He was sick of the posse mentality and the tortured hours wondering what had really transpired between Jeremy and Jessica Stanten. Samuel Spann hadn't gotten where he was by wondering about the innocence or guilt of his client. He had always taken the word of his client at face value. No questions asked.

No, he had convinced himself that Ms. Stanten was a woman of low moral standing. Just another groupie wanting to get into the pants of a big star with hopes of being the one who got the ring. Women always made the best victims in court, but as Sam had seen time and time again, they were just pre-victims—ladies-in-wait—ready to cry foul and sue when things didn't go as planned. Watching disgruntled wives, who'd had nothing before they married their billionaire husbands, suddenly unable to live without a forty million dollar settlement and a monthly allowance of thirty-six thousand dollars had been enough to turn Sam off women altogether.

It was the music that pulled Sam off his train of thought. Something young. Pop music. He couldn't identify the singer but knew it was some new, flash-in-the-pan fifteen-year-old singer with the latest, greatest hit.

The lace curtains fluttered in the window of the largest bunkhouse, drawing Sam's attention. Kali and her daughters leapt around in their little house, dancing. The images were fleeting. It looked as though one of the twins was jumping on a bed. Kali was twirling around and around with the other twin, periodically letting Brooke cut in. It was the mashed potato then the bunny hop, and the swim. All the greats from the 1950s and 60s, and Sam couldn't stop his chuckle.

He decided it had to be Jacks on the bed—just like her mom's freestyle wild windmill swim around the room, she was wild with no inhibitions. Her hair was flying as she swung her head from side to side. Brooke and Danni, while still dancing, were a little more controlled. All four were laughing with periodic whoops.

"Ahem."

Sam jumped and turned to see Tracy leaning against the tree behind him. "Oh, hey! I was just, uh . . . j-j-just sitting here."

Tracy raised his eyebrows and glanced toward Kali's bunkhouse before smiling. "It's worth a gander," he said. He drew a deep breath then motioned for Sam to slide over and took a seat.

The two men watched the girls dance a moment longer. Both Danni and Jacks were on the bed. It had to be Jacks who was bent over slightly, spanking herself as though she were whipping a horse.

Tracy laughed out loud. "That would be Jacks."

"I figured." Sam smiled.

The song ended, and they could hear the girls' voices. Kali was telling them to wait while she picked another song. Jacks was in rare form, still spanking herself and leaping wildly about with Brooke yelling, "That's not dancing! That's not dancing!"

"I've known Kali since she and Nicky got married," Tracy said. His voice was somber, quiet.

Kali found another song, this time something Sam thought he recognized, though it was still pop music.

"You should have seen her then." Tracy shook his head and smiled. "She was so sweet and silly. You could see it in her eyes. She was wild. A lot like Jacks. Everything was an adventure. Everything was new and excitin'. Even after she had her babies. You know, a lot of women change the instant they have a baby, but Kali still had that zest for adventure. Everything she wanted to see and do, she wanted for her babies as well. It was just the way she was. So much energy."

"I don't know," Sam said with a chuckle as he watched the images in the window. "She still has more energy than most men, most people I know." He couldn't imagine anyone working harder than Kali.

"No, not like that—an energy, like, something . . . a force that came out of her. It just exuded from her body. She could walk in a room and everything would light up. You just never knew what she was going to do or say. You could just break into a grin lookin' at her. She just had this raw energy." Tracy held his hands out, as though trying to put them on something to illustrate what he was talking about.

Sam understood. It was the same kind of energy Jacks had. She was a child with so much everything that she barely seemed in control of herself.

"The day Nicky was killed changed her. I mean, of course, it changed her. It changed us all. You remember where you were, what you were doing when you found out. For a lot of the world, hearing about another bombing or more troops lost was just news, ya know? But it was like a national disaster to us," he said, drawing a deep breath. He studied the ground for a moment. "But ya move on or at least you learn to cope. Not Kali. She didn't recover. It sounds clichéd, but a piece of her died that day."

Sam hummed in agreement. How many times had he heard a sound bite from the news of another bombing in Afghanistan or Iraq and it had barely triggered a response from him? It wasn't that he didn't care. It was just . . . what?

A predictably sad occurrence.

"They were set to move to New York, Kali and Nicky. She was excited about it. Just how she was about everything then. In fact . . ." He chuckled. ". . . it was Kali that got Rainwash going. She got on this whole free-range, all organic kick. You know, all our animals are free-range, and all our produce is organic, chemical-free."

"You have produce?" Sam asked. It didn't really matter. He really only wanted to hear more about Kali, but this last statement had surprised him.

Tracy nodded. He looked surprised as well. "Yeah, man, what do you think that big ol' thing is past the main house? It's our garden. Don't ever let Ms. Kat hear you say something like that. It's her pride and joy. We can all kinds of veggies and fruits here but sell at the market as well." He shook his head and waved his hands as if dismissing his tangent. "Then, just like that, she was cemented. Couldn't move. Nicky's body was never recovered and Kali wouldn't go to New York. She couldn't move literally and figuratively. She just stayed here. That's why the girls are homeschooled. She got Ms. Kat to do most of the teaching."

Sam felt wrong, somehow, watching Kali in a rare, carefree moment after Tracy's story. It wasn't who she was anymore. Instead, he sat next to the older man and stared at the ground waiting for anything else he could discover about this enigma called Kali.

"I think she did it on purpose, getting Ms. Kat to teach, that is," Tracy said. "That way, she didn't really have to talk. She would do whatever she needed to do to stay busy and far away from anyone. She mended fences, hauled hay, repaired woodwork, walked the property line, cared for the livestock, whatever it took. She kept busy enough to come in just for dinner and to tuck in her babies.

"The horses," Tracy said and lifted his chin toward the barn. "Them and that damned Star are what brought her around. Slowly, but surely."

Sam didn't understand. "What's wrong with Star?"

"He's an old horse. Not as foot-sure as I'd like, but she won't give up on him. He's got a bum leg . . . got no business working cattle, but I ain't gonna look a gift horse in the mouth." Tracy grinned. "Star, Fancy, Mocha, Mouse . . . they all got Kali to traveling, you know, to local shows while the girls competed. Still do. As they get better and better, Kali's got to travel farther and farther. It's another reason we all encourage their training as much as we do. It's still in a safety net, something Kali is comfortable with, but it gets her out and about."

Michael Jackson's "Thriller" blared from the room.

Tracy looked up and smiled again.

Kali had her hands over her head, like a monster, chasing after the girls. Squeals and screams could be heard above the music. Briefly, both Brooke and Kali disappeared from sight. Kali had laid a full body tackle on Brooke, and they both fell on the bed. Jacks appeared on another piece of furniture. Wild dancing ensued, causing both men to laugh quietly.

"Then, every now and then, there's this—glimmers of the old Kali poking through. It gives us all hope." Tracy looked alarmed and turned toward Sam. "But we don't ever let on that we know about this—"

Sam shook his head. He wouldn't say a word.

"You know, she rides those girls pretty hard. She has great expectations from them. Their grades, their riding—"

"I just can't believe how disciplined they are," Sam said. "I mean, I don't really know kids, but most kids today are kind of fat and lazy . . . these girls are amazing."

"Well, I tell ya, Kali is structured, if nothing else. She's got those kids set so they will have a variety of skills. Even when she was going through losing Nicky, she didn't sit back and cry."

A door opened, and both Tracy and Sam turned to the left to see Mike and Jeremy emerge from their bunkhouse.

Sam swore under his breath.

"Well, that's my cue," Tracy said and stood, straightening out his pant legs. He cleared his throat and adjusted his belt buckle. "There's something else you should know about Kali."

"What's that?" Sam asked, eyes still on Mike and Jeremy. He saw Perry lurking in the doorjamb. No doubt he had been told by Mike to hang back, but he just had to watch.

"She doesn't like surprises," Tracy said. "It's why she didn't take kindly to those fellas of yours suddenly showing up. She just don't like change very much."

Sam looked away from the walking irritation headed his way and fully focused on Tracy once more. "Noted," he said, giving a polite nod.

"Well, I need to go rest my jaw. I think I just said more than I have in a month," he said with a wry smile.

As Tracy walked off, Sam cut his eyes back toward Kali's place. He wanted her to stop dancing. He didn't want anyone else to see her through the window. He felt a wave of protectiveness wash over him concerning her and her girls. He sighed and moved forward, meeting Mike and Jeremy halfway.

Jeremy spoke first. "Look, man. I'm sorry. I just . . . it's a defense mechanism. You know, trouble's all I've ever been in . . . you know, petty stuff. Harmless barroom brawls. Just like this thing that just happened. The guy came at me. I should have walked away, I know it. But I just couldn't. And I'm sorry. I don't mean to act like I don't care. The truth is, I'm scared shitless. You know, I didn't do it. I didn't do what she says I did but, still, I'm scared, man. That's why I'm here. That's why I came here. I just knew I had to listen to you, get away from everyone. It's the only way I guess I can stay out of trouble."

Mike was nodding happily and silently going over all the points he and Jeremy had discussed.

Sam smiled slowly. If nothing else, Mike had just proved Jeremy could be coached, although Sam didn't believe a word. Jeremy hadn't come because he wanted to stay out of trouble. He'd come because he wanted to stay out of jail.

"Come on, man. Don't give up on me now," Jeremy said.

Sam raked his fingers through his hair and studied Jeremy's face then Mike's. In the distance, he could still hear the music playing. Another Michael Jackson song, and he smiled briefly. "Okay." He nodded at the two men in front of him. "But no more games. No more trouble. No more controversy. You do as you're told. When we tell you what to do, what to wear, what to say, how to act, you do it."

Jeremy nodded enthusiastically as Sam spoke.

Sam leveled a finger at the man, and Jeremy looked like an enormous child being chastised. "Or I walk. No second chances. And let me tell ya something. It won't bode well to lose your legal team at the twelfth hour."

Jeremy was a like a bobblehead doll—his head bouncing up and down. "You got it," he said, sticking out a hand to Sam.

Reluctantly, Sam took it.

"Woo-hoo!"

The sound of a female's voice instantly lightened the mood. Forgotten was the apology. Sam saw it in Connors' eyes.

Son of a bitch!

* * * *

Sam watched him warily. He'd seen lot of men like Jeremy. Always needed to be the biggest, strongest, and toughest in the room. Certainly, Jeremy, Roderick, and Garret had the size, but Garret was a butterball and Roderick, while strong, had been trained exclusively for a brief hand-to-hand combat with a possible sprint to take a man down. Sam watched for a moment longer and saw that Jeremy had made the mistake of dismissing Wade and Matthew, based solely on their height. A mistake, to be sure. Any one of the Jorgenson boys could whip all their asses, and although Wade and Tracy weren't relatives, they also showed the signs of living the cowboy life. Even Tracy, some twenty years older than the other men, was not a man to reckon with. Jeremy knew it, too.

Jeremy had engaged in a conversation with Tracy and Evan, asking them about the renovation of the main house, but he really didn't care. The only thing Jeremy cared about was how much the Jorgenson men cared about football.

These boys had grown up testing their strength and grit against two-ton animals with horns. Each and every one had busted broncos and had the air kicked out of them by some large animal. They enjoyed watching football but to live and breathe the game was, in their minds, a giant waste of time. They were gracious and cordial to their guests, but by no means starstruck.

Matthew was another story. He was tickled pink to have *the* Jeremy Connors in his home, and Roderick Bouche wasn't anything to sneeze at. Sam heard Matthew talking to Garret and Roderick near the table.

Roderick was pleased to be properly recognized for his talents and happily talked shop with Matthew while Garret tried desperately to get something of value into the conversation.

All talk subsided with the entrance of Gina with her children.

"Daddy!" Tessa ran toward Evan, jumping into his arms.

With his daughter on his hip, Evan made the introductions to the new men in the house and Tessa beamed.

Sam put her at about six years old, and the spitting image of her mother.

Little Robby toddled in behind her, trying but failing to keep in step with his big sister.

Gina rushed past, barely giving anyone a nod as she hurried into the kitchen. "Hi, hi!" She waved. "Oh, Ms. Kat, I'm sorry. We were a little crazy." She disappeared into the kitchen area, not to be seen again until dinner was served.

Sam heard another voice with Ms. Kat and assumed it was Stephen's wife, Tammi. Sam ducked away from the cluster of men standing at the stone fireplace and stepped into the kitchen. "Ladies," he said, causing everyone to stop. "May I help?" He smiled.

"Absolutely not!" Ms. Kat feigned shock and horror. "I won't have you in here, Mr. Spann. You can just plant yourself at the table and dinner'll be ready in less than ten minutes."

He nodded, giving an extra-long look to Tammi. "You must be . . . Tammi? I'm Sam Spann."

"Yes, Mr. Spann. I've been watching you. You're coming along nicely with Lightning," she said, startling Sam.

He couldn't recall ever seeing her outside and wondered how often she watched from the main house. He felt his face redden. "I'm afraid that's not entirely true," Sam said with a weak smile. "Lightning's just been a little more tolerant of me, but it's nice of you to say so. Maybe you can put in a good word for me down at the barn, bribe him with a carrot or something."

"Don't listen to him, Tam." Sam heard a familiar voice behind him. "He's doing very well. Lightning's grudgingly giving in because Mr. Spann is making him."

Kali.

Sam turned quickly and found her beside him. She looked lovely in a flower print dress, buttoned up the front with a wide scooped neck, and a pretty necklace. He considered it for a moment. Turquoise. Her hair was pulled back with two clips, and with several pieces of straw caught in its waves, it looked a little messy but messy in the very best way.

He reached forward but she stepped back, startled. Sam pulled his hand back. "I'm sorry . . . it's—" He pointed. "You've got hay or something in your hair." He waved a finger at her head and she smiled, embarrassed.

"Oh, yeah. I fed before I came in. Star needed a little extra TLC."

"Oh, for heaven's sakes," Ms. Kat bellowed above the clanking of pans. "You jumped like he was going to electrocute you, Kali."

Sam was pleased to see Kali flush. It was an unusual sight and utterly enjoyable. For a moment, she looked unsure of what to say. It was a moment he couldn't let pass. "Now, there's something you don't see very often: Kali at a loss for words." The lawyer in him came out and so did his confidence as he spoke. "I assure you, Ms. Jorgenson, I only had hay on my mind."

Her expression softened.

She was standing closer to him than he had ever remembered. Standing so close, looking up at him, she looked incredibly vulnerable. Her eyes were far bluer than he remembered. Creamy skin, soft, full lips, soulful eyes . . . hers was a face a man could get lost in.

"You could take this." Suddenly a warm, heavy plate of stacked corn on the cob was thrust against his chest.

He stepped back, not wanting to look away from Kali, but she had already turned to help. He spun and nearly tripped over Jacks.

Arms folded across her chest, one foot kicked out to the side, she was studying him.

He was uncertain as to how he should respond.

Her face was tilted down, just slightly, but her eyes were cut up toward him. She was deadly serious.

"Dinnertime," he said cheerily.

She only stared.

Mercifully, Brooke bellowed, "Dinner!" causing a scramble for the table.

They were twenty-two in total at the table. While it was a little tight with so many large bodies, the table was easily built for such a crowd. The women created a chain, passing down the food to the table and, already, Jeremy and crew were making noises. Biscuits, gravy, roast beef, several kinds of vegetables in heavy butter, Ms. Kat's special salad, which consisted of bacon, sweet pickles, lettuce and some kind of sweet sauce. There were even pecan and apple pies for dessert. Every night was a feast and this night was no different.

Sam found himself a seat at the far end of the table, sandwiched between Tracy and Jacks. While Tracy was busily talking to Jeremy, who sat across from him, Sam felt the increasing scrutiny of Jacks. "I feel like a bug under a microscope," he said at last.

Jacks didn't smile.

"Boy, you're a tough crowd."

More silence.

Sam reached for the potatoes. Carbohydrates were a staple of life out here, and he said as much to Jacks.

Nothing.

"You know, there are people who refuse to eat any bread, pasta or potatoes so they can lose weight."

For a moment, Jacks loosened her grip and eyed the heaping bowl of potatoes.

Danni leaned forward in her seat from the other side of the table. "Are you kidding me?" Her eyes were wide with disbelief.

"Oh, yeah. Mike—Mr. Waters, there—went two months with just eating meat." Sam pointed at Mike, who glanced up from his buttered corn on the cob and frowned.

"Why would he do that?" she asked, loudly.

"To lose weight." Sam was busily trying to throw Jacks off her game . . . only Danni bit.

"Why did you do it, Mr. Waters? Did you lose weight?" Danni leaned forward again, looking down the table to Mike. Her voice caught almost everyone's attention.

"Thank you, Sam. Yes, I did it to lose weight, and I lost about thirty pounds, thank you very much." What he failed to mention was that as soon as he opened his mouth to eat a piece of bread, twenty pounds came right back.

"Well, we like to think we work you hard enough that you can eat whatever suits you and you'll still get in the shape of your life," Ms. Kat said proudly.

Briefly, there was talk of diets and fitness, of organic foods and healthy nutrition, but Sam was still very much aware of Jacks right beside him.

"Are you mad at me or something?" he asked. He pushed his plate away, set an elbow on the table, and turned to look down at her. She didn't shy away. Jacks was an incredibly confident, strong-willed kid. He liked her.

"I know you like my mom," she said flatly.

"Yeah, she's very nice," he said, keeping his tone as monotone as hers. She'd be a hell of a poker player when she got older.

"That's not what I mean. You *like* like her."

They spoke very softly so that no one else could hear, but Danni had scooted forward in her chair, ducked her head down, and watched them like television show, fascinated.

"Jacks, I don't even know your mom." He tried a laugh. It was ridiculous for her to think he liked her—no, that he *liked* liked her. He felt like he was in junior high again. "I mean, yes, she is beautiful, but I don't even know her." He gave her a shrug as if to seal the deal.

"I may only be ten, but I know stuff." She picked up a fork and took her first bite. She looked to her mother to find that Kali had been watching them.

Kali's eyebrows were tugged together. There was a slight tilt to her head. Clearly, she knew something was going on and wondered what.

Jacks gave a wave with her fork, looked back to her plate, and spoke in a tone so low only Sam could hear. "I know what I know. And I know something else, too." She took a bite. She waited.

She would make a hell of a poker player. Sam sighed, looked across the table at Danni then back to Jacks. He had to ask, "What?"

"You're not my dad."

Chapter Thirteen

"We've got one day, gentlemen!" Kali announced as she walked between the men and their horses.

The day's drill was to move cattle effectively from one side of the pen to the other, and it was Danni's day to show off her skills and, generally, make the men feel horrible. Together, Danni and Fancy singled out cows and moved the herd back and forth without as much as a moo. She made it seem so easy, so effortless.

While little Danni Jorgenson did it within sixty seconds, Kali just asked the men to move the herd without a time limit. She just wanted to see them use their voices and possess an ability to direct their horses—horses who already knew what was expected of them and were ready to move the herd without any instruction at all.

Sam had volunteered to go first. He knew it would be ugly so he wanted it over and done with.

Unfortunately, Lightning joined his rider in his enthusiasm, and Kali had no sooner said, "Okay, have at it," than Lightning was bolting forward, throwing Sam off balance. He shifted in his saddle, trying to get properly situated when Lightning picked out his cow. If it hadn't been so frustrating, it could have been amusing, but as Lightning dodged back and forth, singling out a cow, Sam fought to get position. He felt his leg muscles fighting gravity, trying to keep himself upright.

"Wait, wait—" Kali said and stepped in.

Sam heard the chuckles.

"What are you doing?" she asked.

As she walked up to the side of Lightning, she pushed her faded blue baseball cap back and looked up at him. Same face, same eyes, yet a totally different look than the previous night. Now she was Kali the instructor. In the kitchen, Sam had felt certain feelings, some primal need to take care of her, but, sitting atop Lightning, he felt like a jackass. He was clumsy and awkward.

Kali shook her head. "You're fighting him too much," she said. "Remember what we said about rope reins?"

He nodded, like a scolded schoolboy. All Kali's horses were trained to respond to the feel of the reins against their necks. If Sam wanted to turn his horse left, he needed to make the reins touch on the right side of Lightning's neck. Instead, he kept yanking on the left side.

She lowered her voice. "Look, you're going to have a more difficult time staying in your saddle if you don't sit right. You're very muscular—top heavy," she said and, for a moment, Sam felt a surge of pride. She had noticed. "Every time you lean forward and Light moves, it throws you off. You've got to find your center, sit upright . . ." She demonstrated, sitting on an imaginary horse, legs bowed out, back straight, chest sticking out.

Somewhere, someone made a noise. Sam blocked it out. He wanted to do well. As much as he'd once thought he wanted to be able to make a respectable cowboy, he really wanted to impress Kali, but in the end, Kali was most impressed with Lightning.

Once Sam and Lightning had successfully moved the small herd to the other side of the pen, Kali flew to the horse, patting him heartily and stroking his mane. "Oh, big boy. Who's a big boy? Oh, what a grand fellow you are!" It wasn't until Roderick pointed out a man had to be a horse to get the right kind of love that Kali caught herself. She praised Sam for how he sat in the saddle and handled the reins, but it was evident that she was most proud of her young horse.

It hadn't mattered. Sam was simply relieved to be done. He happily trotted Lightning over to the far end of the corral and halted to watch the next round of riders. Mike rode next then Ed.

Outside of the corral, leaning against the fence, stood Tracy, Matthew, Wade, Roderick, Jeremy, Perry, and Garret.

Had Sam been worried about blocking Jeremy from his mind, Mike took care of that right quick. From the moment Mike stepped forward, there was a mishap.

Redwing was feeling particularly frisky. Unlike Lightning, Redwing stood stock-still waiting for Mike to pick out his cow. It didn't matter that Mike had, in fact, picked out a cow.

He even called it out loud. "That one." He pointed. "That little heifer right there. Black and white."

Redwing didn't move.

"That one." Mike pointed again and Wade snickered.

"Mr. Waters," Kali said, rubbing her left temple. "Redwing needs actual direction, not description."

More snickers.

Mike banged his heels against Redwing's sides.

Nothing.

He did it again, and Redwing turned around and looked at him. "Oh, hell!

He's getting pissed!"

"He's just testing you," Tracy called out, trying to give encouragement. "Lean forward a bit and give him a kick. Let him feel you moving forward —"

Mike did as instructed and Redwing turned to glare.

Roderick and Jeremy began laughing. Roderick was talking trash—the kind of talk his teammates and sports networks loved. While he was incredibly obnoxious, he was funny.

Sam saw all the men suppress smiles as Roderick talked on.

"I'm not kidding. He's going to bite me. I can see him looking at me. He doesn't want to move." Mike sounded a bit panicked.

"That's what he wants you to think," Kali said as she stepped in.

As soon as her foot stirred the dust, Redwing raised his head as if he knew the one in charge was moving in, and he knew he was in trouble.

"Again," Kali said. "Let him know you want to move forward."

Again, Mike slammed his heels into the sides of Redwing, and the horse jerked forward, catching Mike off balance. He never had a chance, rolling backward off the saddle. He landed with a heavy thump as Redwing charged ahead for the black and white heifer.

Panic ensued among the herd and they rushed forward, swarming either side of Redwing.

Kali yelled for Mike to get up.

For a moment, he appeared disoriented from the fall, but as he lifted his head and saw the oncoming cattle, he became light on his feet, running toward the fence near Tracy.

Five or six cows had the same idea, which caused Mike to turn and run the distance of the corral. Fists drawn up, head tipped back, legs pumping, Mike gave it everything he had.

Roderick jumped on the fence and pounded the crossbar as he cheered Mike's touchdown sprint, the earth shaking and rocking behind him, and Redwing bringing up the rear. "Go, go, go!" Roderick's eyes were alive with delight.

But as Mike got to the far end, nearest the water trough, he slipped in the mud.

Kali stepped into the back of the herd, grabbed hold of Redwing, and hoisted herself onto his back. With the smallest gesture, she moved the herd back to the other side, giving Redwing the command to hold the herd steady.

Tracy and Wade were already up and over the top bar headed for Mike.

"Oh, man! You okay?" Wade shouted, but there was no missing the humor in his voice.

Even Tracy couldn't contain his laughter.

Jeremy was less diplomatic. "Hoo-wee! That was the funniest thing I have ever seen!" He was pounding on Roderick, who was doubled over.

Sam tossed a glance at Ed who was doing everything possible not to laugh—head scratches, chin rubs, ear tugs, stares up to the skies, but Mike's loud and violent cursing made it almost impossible.

"Son of a . . . I'll be a motherfu—"

"Man! I've never seen anything like that." Roderick continued to heckle him.

Sam looked over to Kali. She had pulled her cap down low and dropped her chin to her chest. She was turned in the saddle, one leg hitched up, hooked over the horn, so that she could look back at Mike. Only, she wasn't looking. Her arms were folded and there was a gentle shake in her shoulders. Sam's grin broadened.

As Tracy and Wade led Mike back to the center of the corral, Kali slid off the back of Redwing.

"You wanna tell him what he did wrong?" Tracy asked. His voice was a tad shaky, as he fought back against any humor.

Kali just shook her head, still looking down to the ground. She couldn't look at Mike. She said something softly, something that Tracy and Wade understood and Tracy nodded, taking over the lesson.

Wade covered his mouth and turned away, hoping Mike wouldn't see.

"I'm sure as hell glad everyone thinks that was so damned funny!" Mike only made things worse and Sam watched Kali drop her head even lower.

She hurried her pace to get out of the corral. Although she never outright laughed, it was the most amused Sam had ever seen Kali.

She slipped easily between the fencing and patted Matthew as she passed, pausing just long enough to say something to him as well.

He chuckled and nodded.

For Kali, the lesson was done. She walked back to the barn, leaving nothing but smiles in her wake, and Sam felt a certain growing affection for the woman who never showed emotion.

"Ya'll think it's funny that I almost broke my damn neck! And got crushed by a wild stampede!"

Howls of laughter.

Sam felt a deep chuckle brewing in his chest.

"Let's try this again," Tracy said, still struggling for composure. "I'm gonna break it down for ya, Mike, real easy."

Sam listened intently as Tracy explained how Mike had lost control of his horse.

Mike argued, calling Redwing the "horse from hell," and Tracy stopped midsentence as he looked toward the barn.

Sam turned in his saddle to see what had caught the man's attention. He had been laughing and having a wonderful time, but as he turned, he understood the scowl on Tracy's face.

Heading through the barn doors, not ten paces behind Kali, was Jeremy Connors.

* * * *

Kali sighed heavily, wiping a tear from her cheek. She couldn't recall a time, at least not recently, that she had fought so hard not to smile. It had reminded her of the day when she and her sisters got the giggles in church. Her head had throbbed for several minutes after a good finger-flicking from her father seated in the pew behind them. There was a kind of warming of the heart that came with those kinds of moments. Boredom, problems, sickness . . . everything washed away in those moments, and the image of Mike, the puffed-up, know-it-all lawyer, toppling over Redwing and fleeing for his life, would stick with her for some time.

Kali grinned as she walked through the quiet barn. Most of the horses were out, except Star, Duchess, and Daphne. She heard Tracy's voice echo across the compound and through the barn, but it felt miles away. There was something about the barn that brought comfort and distance from the world.

Star stomped in his stall and Kali called out to him. "I know," she said.

He hadn't seen her, but he knew the sound of her walk, the way her boot hit the ground, and her smell. He understood that she worked with other horses, and was tolerant most times, but he expected frequent one-on-one sessions to make up for sharing her.

She headed into the tack room to grab Star's bucket from his shelf.

Periodically, the Rainwash Ranch did rescue work with the Mustang Roundup crew, an organization that helped keep the proper balance of wild mustangs and burros, and worked with wild horses until they were deemed adoptable. Tracy, Matthew, and Kali had worked with the horses in the past, and sadly, some had been in horrible condition. Mange, mites, fleas, and the threat of various equine diseases were always an issue at Rainwash when a new horse was brought in. The twins had decided that each horse having his or her own shelf not only kept all the horses straight but free from contaminating one another as well.

Kali reached the tack room and found various brushes and bottles mixed up on the shelves. Matthew and Tracy weren't quite as on board with being organized and orderly as everyone else, and she constantly had to straighten up after them.

She muttered to herself and pulled on the memory of Mike, spread-eagled in the mud, as she organized the brushes.

"A woman's work . . . isn't that what they say?"

Kali jumped and her heart pounded against her chest. She spun around to find Jeremy Connors with his hands anchored to the top of the doorjamb, his arms pressed to either side, filling the doorway.

He leaned in slightly, showing the width of his chest. He was the size of Evan but with an extra hundred pounds of solid muscle.

Kali forced a smile. "You scared me!"

Jeremy smirked and there was an awkward second of silence before Kali turned back to the shelves, straightening the different boxes.

"Is there something I can do for you, Mr. Connors?" she asked, trying to be cordial but too busy for idle chitchat.

"I just wanted to talk to you. I haven't really gotten the chance to introduce myself, you know, get to know you."

With her back still turned to him, Kali made a face. She knew that somewhere there were women who found him charming and attractive, but she saw through his little act. She heard the way his tone changed when he talked to a woman. It wasn't sweet or engaging. It was patronizing and offensive. It was manipulative. Jeremy wanted something, and she had a pretty good idea what.

"I'm one of the head instructors." She shrugged, careful not to turn around as she shifted through more boxes, sorted through combs and brushes, and began rearranging the now well-organized shelves. "Been training for years but started trail rides and cattle drives about four years ago. I like it." She'd run out of things to shuffle and turned to face him. He had stepped inside the small room and took up . . . everything. She gasped involuntarily. She was sure he thought his lips curled into a charming smile, but all Kali saw was a mocking sneer.

"Sorry, didn't mean to startle you."

Yes, you did, you bastard.

"Just what is it you needed?" Kali asked as she forced another smile and gave a little wave with her hands, indicating her need for Jeremy to back up.

He raised his eyebrows and looked around, confused.

Kali kept flicking her hands, using the same gesture and patience she gave the larger horses that tried to crowd the feed room when the gate was left open. Just like the horses, Kali was wary of the danger involved.

Star nickered again and stomped his feet impatiently.

Kali cut her eyes cut toward his stall then back to Jeremy. "Sorry, I need to move out."

"Oh, hey, I just wanted to say 'hi' and, you know, see if I could lend a helping hand." He stepped back just enough to leave a gap to open space, but not enough for Kali to squeeze by without touching him.

Although she found it very annoying—another power play—she pretended not to notice. She made sure her voice was extra sweet, enthusiastic and clueless. "Well, that's great. I'll remember that for this evening. After dinner, the guys are going to be moving in more hay bales. I know they would love to have you and your buddies help."

She moved quickly toward Star's large, handsome face hanging over the paddock door.

He raised his head as soon as he saw her, nostrils flaring with delight.

She quickly threw the outside safety latch, releasing the door and stepped into his stall. An instant feeling of security washed over her. His large, solid body was her safety net.

Jeremy made the mistake of trying to follow Kali, and Star stretched out his long neck, ears slightly flattened. He pushed against Jeremy, giving a hard blow from his nose.

She loved that look. It brought her an enormous amount of satisfaction to see him turn ugly and mean while protecting her and defending his turf. "Don't worry, Star," Kali said more to Jeremy than her horse. "He won't come in here." She looked across to Jeremy. "He's very territorial of this area and me, Mr. Connors. I recommend stepping back just a little." She gave Star a long, hard rub across his back and underbelly.

"You're good with animals," Jeremy said. Kali gave a semi-friendly nod as she continued to rub Star down. "Must get lonely, though."

She stiffened. "Hardly." She tried to laugh. "I'd much rather spend my time with Star than just about anybody, excluding my kids, of course."

"No man?" he asked, giving what Kali was sure to be his most disarming smile.

In truth, he was a very handsome man. She understood how such a man could sway young women. He was muscular, handsome, successful.

"No man," she said and kept working on Star.

"But, obviously, there was at some point. Your girls—"

"Once. Not anymore."

"I can't imagine a man letting you go," he said.

Arrogant, crass, stupid.

"Sometimes life has other plans," she said, and managed a shrug as she felt her throat closing up.

"You're not wearing a ring."

She froze for a moment and stared at her hand.

No. She wasn't wearing the ring, but what he couldn't know was that she had never worn the ring. Working with leather and ropes all day, the ring had torn up her hands so she had worn it around her neck on a chain. She had stopped wearing the chain long ago.

"Nope. No ring," was all she said.

Star stomped a foot. All this talk distracted Kali from properly grooming and hugging him.

"I just can't believe you're the mother of three children. Most women . . ."

Kali started to grind her teeth.

"I mean—" He laughed. His voice was husky.

Kali moved around Star, hiding herself behind the huge animal.

"Damn, I hope you don't mind me saying so, but you are fine."

Go away! Go away!

"I bet you don't talk that way to Tracy," Kali said. She would love to watch him try, though.

"I like the name, just not the way he fills out his pants."

Kali rolled her eyes as she bent down behind Star.

"Not that I'm lookin' at his ass or anything."

Go away! Go away!

"But you—"

Kali wanted to scream.

"Kali!"

Mattie!

"You in there?" Matthew called out from the barn doors.

Kali moved toward the front of Star, ducking underneath him. Her back rubbed against his neck, and he dropped his nose down on top of her, slowing her up. She let him get in a silent hug and calm her at the same time.

"Kali? Hey, she in there?"

"Right here." Jeremy stepped back, pointing toward the stall.

"Kal, Tracy wants you. We're about done out here. You coming?"

Thank you, Mattie.

"Yup, be right out. Just brushing Star down." When Matthew turned to go, she felt the lump jump back in her throat. "Hey, Mattie?"

"Yeah?"

"Come here, would ya? I want you to take a look at something." She stepped out of the stall, far too close to Jeremy, but she locked eyes with Matthew as he hustled down the barn aisle with a look of concern.

"What is it? Star?"

She nodded and the two of them stepped into the stall.

Mattie was one of the few Star tolerated in his stall. In fact, for the brief period that Kali's world had fallen apart, it had been Matthew who cared for Star.

Kali led Matthew toward the back of Star and pointed.

"What do you think of that? Think it's a schnook?"

Matthew leaned in, squinted, and then turned to Kali. "A what?"

"Right there." She took his hand, pressed it lightly against Star's flank, and repeated the word, giving a hard squeeze to Matt's fingers. "Isn't that what Tracy was talking about at that last horsemanship meeting?"

Matthew looked at Kali closely then stiffened. He hemmed and hawed and rubbed his hand on Star's belly. "You know . . . I just don't know. I'd have to see it in the light. Could be. Better ask Tracy."

Jeremy hadn't moved, watching and listening to everything.

Go away!

"You think you ought to ride him?" Matthew was still playing up the schnook thing.

Kali nodded and struggled not sprint out of the barn. "Yeah, I think so, but I'd better ask all the same. Hand me the headstall, would ya?"

As Kali led Star out of the barn smiling, Matthew discussed the dangers of schnooks with Jeremy.

"Schnooks can be really tricky. Could take a horse out for weeks . . ."

Chapter Fourteen

Tracy had read the expressions on the men at the dinner table. There had been polite banter back and forth but almost no talk of the next day. Each man held his own ideas, own reservations about the cattle drive, and Tracy understood. He'd seen it in the faces of many men many times before. The lawyers were anxious about their own performance and whether they could really handle the long haul. It was one thing to ride for half a day. It was quite another to ride for four solid days without the luxury of electricity, running water, and a soft bed. Thus, the invite.

"You've earned it," Tracy said, smiling around the table. "Let's go check out the game room." He led the group up the stairs.

They had all been aware that there was an upstairs, but because it was never addressed, no one had thought much about it.

"What is this? Oak?" Mike asked.

From the moment Tracy led the small group around the corner of heavy, built-in shelving, the men had been in awe. An enormous tree acted as the base for the spiral staircase they were to take. Its base was as thick as five men put together. Around it, spikes had been driven in to support the stairs. It was breathtaking.

"Redwood." Tracy headed up the stairs. As a man who had been asked that same question a hundred times over, he still appreciated the beauty of the tree and artistry of the design. He reached over the inside railing, trailing a hand along the polished wood. "It was just one of a bunch felled in the fires of 1968. A lot of the wood you see here is redwood, but this little beaut was so solid, Jorgenson turned it into this. Nice, eh?"

* * * *

Jeremy and Mike, the first two to reach the top, stopped in their tracks and took it all in.

Ed, Roderick, Garret, and Perry peered over their shoulders and peeked between the railings to the stairs as they came up, leaving Sam for verbal leftovers.

"This is unbelievable." Roderick laughed. "I've seen a lot of places . . . a lot of places, and I ain't ever seen anything like this. This is amazing." More utterances of praise filled the staircase until Sam pushed against them.

While the upstairs had been turned into a modern-day game room, complete with a fully stocked bar, two pool tables, deep-seated leather chairs, chess games—all natural wood—and a gigantic wide-screen television, a sense of the past and old man Jorgenson's eye for detail was strong.

The heavy ceiling-mounted hay track brought the old hayloft to life. Hanging from the track were wrought-iron lamps with tinted windows and candle-like lightbulbs giving the hardwood floors a rich glow. All the woodwork, the pictures, the leather and fabrics, all matched perfectly. There were a few signs of a feminine touch in the vases of wildflowers at either end of the bar and placed on the old-fashioned clothing trunks that served as side tables. At the far end of the giant room were two swings hanging from the rafters with small, patterned throw pillows scattered across the backs. Everything was polished and the smell of leather filled the senses with history, tradition, and pride. The room was alive with ghosts of traveling cowboys and stagecoach hands.

"Now, this is what I'm talkin' about." Jeremy pounded his chest and looked around the room at all the men. "This is a man's room."

Tracy smiled and moved behind the bar, ready to play barkeep.

Jeremy waggled a finger at Tracy. "Ah, my good man. A round of the house's best ale for everyone present."

Cheers went up.

Sam understood why Jeremy was so popular for a flicker of a moment. Throughout the evening, he had told hilarious stories from the gridiron and the locker room. While Roderick and Garret knew most of the stories, they had still roared with laughter along with everyone else. Eventually, their laughter had drawn the other men in the house and even Wade and the Jorgenson brothers had become part of the knee-slapping good times.

Jeremy's wit was sharp and quick, and while his observations were incredibly humorous, they were absolutely right on. The way people dressed, walked, or talked. What they wanted, how they got what they were after, why games were won, how men were beaten, and why coaches were canned. It all left Sam wondering about his client. Jeremy was full of bluster and bull, but his insight was honest and real. Maybe his version of the Jessica Stanten case was legitimate. Sam wanted to believe in his client. For the sake of Jackson, Keller & Whiteman, he wanted a credible client. These were big stakes, and it would be nice to have a client Sam could bet money and a career on.

But as the bottles emptied, Sam began to reconsider.

Talk turned to women—specifically, Kali Jorgenson. Suddenly, the most popular guy in the room was under scrutiny, and Jeremy knew it.

Sam watched as Jeremy worked the room.

"So what did happen to her husband?" he asked Matt.

Matthew dutifully gave what few details they knew about Nicholas Jorgenson's mission in Afghanistan and the suicide bombers, and brushed on the fact that Nicky had been able to talk to Kali before it all happened.

"She ever dated since then?" Jeremy asked turning to Wade as the two played a game of pool.

Wade stiffened. "Never had a notion." His tone was flat. "Besides, I'd feel sorry for the poor bastard who tried. Evan, Stephen, and Mattie ain't gonna like anyone who comes sniffin' around Kali, much less me or Tracy, but them girls are hard core. Any man who tried to get to Kali would have to get past the girls first." He gave a laugh, though it held no humor. "And I just don't see that happening."

Before the evening was done, Jeremy had tried to talk to everyone who knew anything about Kali. While he also talked about the horses, the beautiful reconstruction of the barn-turned-main house, the ranch, and the ongoing trials of his own life, but Sam had seen through to his main objective, and it gave him some worry. He had nursed the same beer for half the evening and kept careful check on Jeremy's various conversations.

He finally finished off his beer and decided it was time to turn in.

It bothered him that a man of Jeremy's reputation had such deep interest in Kali. It bothered him that Jeremy bothered him so greatly. It bothered him even more that he had seen Jeremy follow Kali into the barn.

* * * *

Kali lit her cigarette and watched the tobacco burn against the paper, admiring the colors. The orange and red cherry was mesmerizing against the black canvas of the outdoors.

She slid down against the trunk of the tree, taking in a deep breath. She loved it here. This was her home.

There had been a time when that wouldn't have been the case. A time when there had been no Duchess, Mouse, Fancy, Mocha, or Redwing, and she had to wonder how Star would have survived in New York. Jacks and Danni wouldn't have competed in rodeos but equestrian events—perhaps something Brooke would have liked.

She raised her cigarette and studied the glow of it in her hand again. It was hard for her to imagine her wild twins in something so proper and poised as equestrian, but had Nicky lived, they would have been in New York, and this place would have been run by Tracy and the boys. Instead, she was part of the working crew.

She flipped her hands over and watched as the smoke swirled between her fingers and across her palms. They were calloused and rough, her nails kept short and without any nail polish. She had decided long ago that polish was pointless. Every time she tried a new color, they were chipped and mangled in half a day.

She loved the demanding work and the sense of accomplishment she had driving and delivering free-range cattle. She could honestly say she contributed to the world and was teaching her children the values of hard, honest work, but how different things would have been . . .

She missed Nicky so much. At first, it had been his smell and touch. She had missed the way his early morning beard rubbed and burned against her face. She had missed the way he pulled on the covers, forcing her to roll against him for warmth. She had missed their lovemaking and his kisses. The way he liked to kiss along her jaw and down the back of her neck. He'd always told her it was his favorite part of her body.

Lately though, she just missed *him*.

* * * *

He watched her from the shadows of the barn as she enjoyed a rare moment by herself. He had wanted to be alone with her since he'd first seen her, but there was always someone around.

There was something very intriguing about a woman who held such little interest in him—or any other man, for that matter. She didn't operate like other women. There was no interest in money, lavish gifts, finer clothing, expensive manicures, or hairstyles. She was a ponytail, baseball cap-wearing gal with little to no makeup, and she was gorgeous. She was tough, no-nonsense, and yet, there was something very vulnerable about her.

In her role as instructor, she was in complete control, but up close, when she had looked into his eyes, the roles had shifted. He had felt it instantly, and it had excited him in a way he hadn't expected. It had taken everything in him not to reach forward and pull her into him. She wanted and needed a man to take care of her needs—emotionally and physically. She wanted to be handled. She wanted to be caressed and kissed. That was why she had looked at him the way she had. Not too long. She wasn't that way. She wasn't aggressive the way many women—too many women, in his opinion —were today. She had looked just long enough to reveal herself and her needs. She had looked long enough to let him know she wanted him.

But there were always too many people, too many distractions, and he couldn't act on it.

From the moment he'd seen her walking across the compound, he had frozen. She wore a tiny spaghetti-strapped shirt that stopped at her waist and, when she moved, flashed bits of bare flesh just above her jeans.

He held his breath.

There were hundreds, if not thousands, of women who would wear this kind of outfit for the sole purpose of being seen. Yet, here she was, dressed strictly for comfort, in the middle of the night when no one would see her.

He pressed close to the interior wall, peering out through the crack between the barn and the swinging door. He watched as she lit up and slid down the side of a tree, in a most provocative pose. Only Kali could do this to a man. He wet his lips.

He knew she would smell of something slightly sweet, floral. She would be warm, soft, and yet strong. He imagined how she would look up at him. Suddenly, he ached.

She had been looking at her cigarette, tapping it with her finger, occasionally knocking its ashes to the ground, when she let her head fall back against the side of the tree and her features were lost in its shadow, leaving him only a silhouette to gaze upon. So strong, so gentle, so tough, so soft.

He wanted her, and he would find a way to be alone with her—at any cost.

Chapter Fifteen

Tammi and David watched the early morning activities. Tammi could feel the heightened emotions in the air. The lawyers were nervous. Evan and Matthew, as always, were anxious. Tracy was mad as a hornet, cursing at every man, woman and horse who crossed his path and, much to Tammi's amusement, Kali was always calm and quiet. It was the good cop/bad cop routine. While Tracy hollered, cursed and swore, Kali went quietly about her business, disappearing to another place. Tammi had seen the routine time and again, always wondering about where it was Kali went.

Ms. Kat had once said each cattle drive began with such promise. Tammi had always been struck by that statement. It must have been how Kali felt each time she set out on one. The people with whom she worked were so excited. The horses sensed the new adventure as food, water, and supplies were packed in the wagon. It was full of promise for a smooth run and good times for the paying clients, but it held something else for Kali. Tammi couldn't help but wonder if Kali relived a happier time when she couldn't wait to shove off and recount a successful run to Nicky when he called to check in.

But this cattle drive was not a typical one. Tammi leaned forward slightly when she caught sight of Kali. She was dressed in her typical attire—worn blue jeans, black boots, white cotton T-shirt with the sleeves rolled up, tucked into her bra straps, and her hair pulled through the back strap of the faded blue baseball cap that Nicky had given her the day he left for Afghanistan. Kali usually wore the ball cap low over her brow, but today it was pushed up high, exposing her face.

She stood toe-to-toe with Evan. It was an unusual sight. While no one ever questioned Kali's round-up abilities, no one ever questioned Evan's authority. Clearly, something was very wrong. Kali's hands were on her hips, her chin was raised, and she was giving Evan grief about something. Evan wasn't backing down.

"What's going on?" Gina stepped out onto the porch, already watching the events unfold between her husband and Kali.

"I don't know. Kali's fired up about something," Tammi said.

"Huh. I wonder what's up." She took a seat beside Tammi and David and together they watched the show.

"No. I won't!" Kali's voice was suddenly very clear.

Tracy and Matthew, who had been rechecking the saddles for each horse, both stopped and looked over their horses toward Kali and Evan before glancing back at each other.

The lawyers had not emerged from their bunkhouse, but Tammi was sure this would surely bring them out.

"Hey! Don't—" Evan chased after Kali as she stormed toward the house. He caught her arm a few steps from the porch.

Tammi and Gina found themselves with front row seats.

"Kal, look, I don't like it either, but this is good business. These guys are big names." Evan tried to appeal to her but she shook her head.

"No. Dammit, Evan." Kali pulled her cap off and rubbed the sides of her face. Her movements were jagged and rough. Tammi could see she was highly agitated. She paced a little, even locking eyes with Tammi before she turned back to her brother-in-law. "No!"

Evan looked down at the ground and kicked the dirt. He, too, was extremely uncomfortable. "Sorry, Kal. It's already done."

Kali jerked her head up. "What?"

"I said—geez, Kal, this is good business. I don't see why you can't see that."

"I don't want them coming along. I can't stand them. I . . . what horses am I going to put them with? Shit, Evan. That one guy? Bouche. He'd break the back of any good trail horse we've got. I'm not putting that chuck wagon of beef on one of our horses."

Evan stifled a laugh but Kali only got more agitated.

"And Garret Jackson is just a big tub of lard. I don't want that ox on my horses. He'll kill 'em. No, Evan!"

"Kali, these guys are paying top dollar—"

"To kill our horses?" Kali asked and turned, facing the porch, and spread her hands out toward Gina and Tammi. If she was hoping for support, she didn't give anyone time to respond. "Nope, nope. Not going to do it."

"Am I the only one seeing this?" Evan also turned to the porch.

Gina instantly threw up her hands in the universal "leave me out of this" pose.

"Jeremy Connors is practically a household name right now," he said but Kali threw a palm out, stopping him cold.

"I don't trust the guy. He's a snake."

"I appreciate that, Kali. Actually, I agree with you. But when word gets out that he was here during his trial preparations for relaxation and peace, it could be huge for us."

"So he's already here. We can say he's been a guest, but we don't have to let them go on the drive," she shot back.

Tammi saw the lawyers and athletes emerge from their bunkhouses and head straight toward Kali and Evan. Tracy fell in behind them.

It was last call for drinks, bathroom breaks, or whatever urbanites needed to do before setting off into the sunset.

Feebly, Gina tried to warn Evan and Kali of the oncoming traffic as they continued their argument. Only when Mike, Jeremy, and Perry were practically on top of them did Gina loudly clear her throat. Although it was very apparent to everyone what she had done, it was better than having wealthy clients overhear Kali refer to them as lard asses.

* * * *

Tracy slowed his pace as he drew nearer and scanned Kali, Evan, Gina, and Tammi's faces.

Tammi gave him a chin nod toward the men and Tracy sighed.

Kali did not like change. He should have figured she would be upset by the announcement that the new group would be traveling with them. More than the fact that these men had missed out on vital lessons on safety and cattle and horse maintenance, Kali didn't like last minute changes. He pulled back and planted himself a few feet back from the pack, and let Evan do all the talking.

He knew what she was thinking. She didn't like this particular group of men. Tracy couldn't blame her for that, but Evan was right. Money was tight and they didn't exactly have a waiting list. They needed these clients, and they needed whatever referrals this group might give.

Kali was digging in, though, with her jaw set and arms planted firmly on her hips.

"Everything okay?" asked Mike.

Kali continued to glare at Evan, and Mike was forced to look to Evan for answers.

"Just a small disagreement about who's gonna ride what horse." Like Kali, Evan didn't break eye contact.

"Whoa!" Roderick laughed from the back of the pack. "You better not be including me in that group." He muscled his way toward the front, looking from Perry and Mike to Kali and Evan. "Ain't no way I'm riding one of those things," he said and jabbed a finger toward the corral.

"Is that what you're talkin' about?" asked Garret. "To hell with that. No, I'm here for the good food, pool, hot tub, and the bar." He looked around the compound. "Although you could stand to use a few more women around here."

Roderick laughed.

"No offense." Garret looked up at the porch toward Gina and Tammi.

"Oh, hey!" Gina waved a hand. "None taken by me. As for my fellow sisters around the world—"

Tammi laughed, leaving Garret bewildered.

"Yo, man," Roderick said to Perry. "I'm here for moral support. I am not getting on a horse. You cowpokes can do that. Not me. I'm staying put." He looked to Wade as he climbed the stairs toward the kitchen. "Wade, man, you said there was some action going on in some little town around here."

Wade turned and nodded, glancing toward Evan.

Evan shook his head, raising his voice as he spoke. "You don't want to ride, that's fine, but we don't run a chauffeur service. Wade'll be tied up with work around here. We expect our guests to stay at Rainwash. You stay here, we'll do everything possible to make your stay relaxing. Head out into town and get in some kind of bar fight, and you're on your own."

Roderick and Evan stared at one another for a second longer.

Then, with a dramatic shrug, Roderick smiled. "That's cool."

"There you go." Evan lowered his voice toward Kali. "Two less to worry about." Evan excused himself and trotted up the stairs, urging Wade into the kitchen. Tracy knew Evan was warning Wade to keep an eye on the new guests. This was the part of the cattle drive Evan had never liked—leaving Gina and the kids alone with strangers. It was part of the business, and if there were any big problems, they could call on their neighbor. Tyler McWilliams was fifteen miles away, but he was always willing to lend a hand.

Tracy gave a quiet cough, catching Kali's attention as she watched Evan disappear. "You want to decide what horses I turn out?" he asked.

Kali looked past him toward all the horses.

He had brought out Daphne, Duchess, Duncan, and Scotty before heading over to see what all the fuss was about.

She pulled down her baseball cap and stared at the ground for a moment.

Tracy knew that Kali was stuck. She didn't like what was happening, but recognized she had no choice in the matter.

She looked up, not addressing anyone but Tracy. "Yeah, we'll put Mr. Connors on Duchess, and Mr. Perry on Duncan." Without another word, she turned on her heel and jogged up the stairs.

"Right." Tracy motioned the men toward him. "Let's go check out your horses. You guys have missed some important lessons so let's see if I can't give you some quick pointers before we shove off." He took a step back then nodded to the lawyers. "You guys need to take care of any last minute things . . . do it now." He turned and walked toward the horses with Jeremy and Perry.

"Good luck!" Gina whispered and she and Tammi laughed out loud.

* * * *

Jeremy wasn't an idiot. While he'd never claimed to be a horseman, he knew his way around horses. He was a Nebraska farm boy and had done the whole small town thing—riding horses down Main Street for their pathetic Fourth of July parades and Homecoming, entering a few races as a young teenager, and riding to impress the girls. In fact, it hadn't been so long ago that he had rented two horses in the Bahamas for that girl.

What was her name?

Of course, those nags had been so broken down they'd stumbled along the sand in a comatose state.

He had seen the look on Tracy's face when Kali had named off the horses. The horse named Duncan was completely still, head dropped, blinking lazily in the early morning sun. Duchess, on the other hand, was a large horse that stamped her hooves impatiently and periodically flattened her ears at any horse that looked at her sideways.

Jeremy smiled.

Kali had purposefully put him with a difficult horse just to bust his rocks. Maybe she wanted to test him or see if she could scare him away from the cattle drive, but she had miscalculated. She didn't know who she was dealing with. Jeremy loved the challenge. She would see just what kind of a man he was. He found himself more intrigued with little Ms. Jorgenson than ever before. Typically, women hunted him down, begged hotel clerks for his room number, mailed him panties, and promised him amazing feats of acrobatics behind closed doors. No one had ever tried to get him bucked off a horse before.

He ran his hands over Duchess while Tracy spoke to Perry about Duncan. "He's a bit stubborn," Tracy was saying. "You'll have to keep on him to stay with the group. First mile or so, he'll give ya hell, trying to turn around and come back. He's a barn baby. Give him any slack and he'll come running home, with or without you. Ya can't let him do it."

So that was it—she didn't want Perry around but hoped to test Jeremy.

"You wouldn't try to toss me, would ya, girl?" Jeremy spoke gently to the mare. She was a beauty.

"Don't let her push you around." Tracy had made his way over, leaving an ashen-faced Perry to measure up against Duncan.

Duncan remained amazingly unimpressed.

"I think I can handle her," Jeremy retorted.

"You have much riding experience?" Tracy asked, running a hand over the mare's rump.

"A little."

"Then you know never to underestimate your horse," Tracy said flatly. "There are two kinds of riders—those open to any help an instructor can offer and those who measure their self-worth by how well they handle a horse."

For a moment, the two men looked at each other.

Jeremy nodded. He didn't like being lectured.

"She can be a bit of handful around other horses. She likes to take the lead, but with a firm hand, you can keep her in line. She'll figure out who is in charge."

"Sounds like you're describing Kali." Jeremy laughed.

Tracy scowled. "Yeah, right. I'm sure you'll be okay."

Jeremy watched as Tracy walked away. He had misjudged the old man. Jeremy thought he was a man's man, but he was in Kali's pocket like the others. "It's a firm hand," Jeremy muttered to Duchess.

She shook her head, tossing her mane, and Jeremy was mildly amused.

Noise from the house caught his attention. The Jorgensons all piled out of the house for the big send-off. Ms. Kat handed over a last minute basket of goodies, prompting her youngest son to lean in to kiss her cheek. While Evan said his goodbyes to his wife and kids, Kali eased down the stairs, Lady Cool again with her cap pulled low, and her shirt loose and billowing out around the waistline of her jeans. It was funny that so much of her was covered, yet there was a way she moved . . . the combination of a jock and lady walk that warned, *Don't you dare mess with me or I'll stomp the snot out of you!*

He smiled.

As she passed her own bunkhouse, her daughters ran out. There were hugs from the twins, but the older one was, from what it looked like, begging to come along. Kali shook her head, giving hugs but also small swats to the oldest's behind, letting her know she needed to stop begging.

That little girl was going to grow up to look just like her momma. While the twins were too skinny to tell, the older girl already had a shapely build. It wouldn't be too much longer before she was driving all the boys in town crazy with her rounded little bottom—just like her momma. Although the girl's hair was far longer, he could tell it was thick and full-bodied. Jeremy suddenly found himself wondering about Kali's hair. Personally, he liked his women with long hair, but Kali's shoulder-length hair suited her.

Wade and Stephen untied the reins and handed them over to the greenhorns, but Jeremy continued to watch Kali with her daughters until Ms. Kat clambered down the stairs and shooed the girls away so that Kali was able to reach her horse.

"But you promised," the older girl called after her mother.

"Next time," Kali shouted over her shoulder. With one effortless motion, Kali threw a leg over her horse, turned him around, and trotted toward her girls.

"That's what you said last time," the girl cried.

"I know. I'm sorry, but you can't go on this one. This one . . . I just don't want you to go on this one. It isn't right. Next one, baby. I promise."

The girl crossed her arms over her chest, huffed, and turned toward the house.

Jeremy was intrigued. What was it Kali would be doing on this trip that she didn't want her daughter around for? It was a deliciously interesting question indeed.

Chapter Sixteen

Although they had taken several long practice rides before, this morning the sounds of cattle moving along and the constant yips and whistles of his fellow cowboys made him feel like a kid again, waking to an unexpected snowstorm.

Lightning was excited as well, and Sam wondered if this was his first cattle drive, too. The horse seemed friskier than usual, and while he was behaving very nicely, there was an extra spring to his stride.

They had been on the trail for several hours, and Sam had noticed that despite Tracy hanging close by, Duchess was giving Jeremy quite a battle.

Atta girl!

He couldn't stop the smile from teasing the corners of his lips every time he heard Jeremy fight Tracy's attempts to help.

Matthew had taken the lead with Mike. It was a position Mike enjoyed. He played scout, calling back any new sightings of wolf tracks. It was a bunch of nonsense, Sam was sure, but it kept Mike excited and alert.

Sam had fallen near the back of the herd, to the far right, looking for and dreading any stragglers.

Ahead of him, Kali and Ed were discussing something interesting. While she wasn't talking, she was listening intently. With his hat pulled down low, Sam was able to sit back into his saddle and admire her backside without worry of being caught.

It was a great thing, the female form, particularly this female form. Her shoulders were strong and broad, making a nice gentle curve down to her small waist. Then, as if a perfectly drawn picture, her hips swelled from beneath the beltline. Her bottom was rounded in the saddle with her legs melding into the side of her horse. Even her head, fitted into the ball cap, was perfectly shaped with its small, blond ponytail swishing back and forth and matching the horse's gait.

Behind him, Evan was working with Perry, trying to encourage him along despite his horse's effort at every chance to turn around and run home. "The horse can sense how his rider is feeling by the way he sits or holds the reins."

As Sam continued to watch Kali's form, he found himself readjusting his legs, hands, shoulders, and rear end in ways Evan suggested.

A sharp yell came from the rear of the Rainwash crew.

Sam turned to see it came from the man driving the chuck wagon.

"Kal," Evan called forward. "Can you see to Buddy?"

With a quick nod, Kali doubled back toward Buddy, the driver, without so much as a smile to Sam. She was all business, trotting by in one smooth motion.

Sam let Lightning fall back a little more until she started to pass back by. "He's a good horse."

She hesitated, letting Star fall in step with Lightning.

Lightning lifted his head for a moment, uncertain about his new walking buddy.

"Just hold him steady," Kali said. "Yes, he's my baby. He's a great horse. Bum knee and all."

"Hoo-wee!"

"There she goes!"

"Go on, boy!"

Sam and Kali looked up to see Jeremy on the run. One of the young heifers had bolted from the herd, disappearing down a ravine with Jeremy hot on her tail. Matthew had doubled back, was right behind Jeremy, and hollering the entire time.

With a kick of the heels, Kali cut Star across the herd, making her way toward Jeremy. She, too, disappeared for several minutes.

More whooping and then, as quickly as they had dipped out sight, they were back, cow and all.

Dammit.

Sam hated to admit it, but he was jealous. He could see Kali already engaged in conversation with Mike and Ed. No doubt discussing the amazing athletic feats of Jeremy, and Jeremy's already disproportionately large head was getting bigger with every word.

Sam settled back into his saddle and sulked.

Eventually, they arrived at a frequent stopping point. Sam noticed a fire pit surrounded by rocks blackened by the smoke of many fires. Part of the camp area had been cleared, making it easier to pitch tents. The herd huddled down the hill in a small enclosure that looked as though it had once been a riverbed, but dried up long ago. As soon as the riders' feet hit the ground, they groaned. The city dwellers were in agony after hours in the saddle while the cowhands never missed a stride.

Evan handed out instructions while Sam was still trying to find his legs.

Mike and Ed were sent in search of firewood.

"Don't turn over any rocks or reach into bushes," Evan warned. "This part of the country is full of snakes."

"Buddy Mann, this is the crew." Matthew hefted himself into the wagon, introduced the clients to Buddy, and began handing items out.

In no time, each man had his own assignments, caring for horses and assembling tents.

By the time the last tent was pitched, Mike and Ed had accumulated an impressive pile of firewood.

"Oh, man," Mike said, unfolding a chair and falling back into it. "Somehow I don't think the cowboys of the old west had folding chairs, but I don't give a rat's ass. I'm so effing tired." He let his head fall back and groaned loudly.

Matthew carefully placed the other chairs around the campfire.

One by one, each man took his seat.

Sam had to hand it to the Rainwash staff. They had the routine down perfectly. The campfire and chairs were angled so that the men could sit overlooking the herd below and watch the sunset.

"Buddy? How's it coming?" Matthew asked.

" 'Bout ready now. Give me another twenty minutes!" Buddy yelled back without stopping his work.

Kali made her way toward the men and dropped into a chair. She used her left foot to step on the heel of her right boot, slowly tugging her foot out, and then reversed the process. She leaned forward, pulled off each sock, and wiggled her well-manicured toes.

No one spoke but each one of the men watched her grin grow larger with every move.

"Evan?" Buddy asked.

Immediately, Matthew was up and moving toward him. "He's at Radio Rock. What'cha need?"

"What's Radio Rock?" Ed asked while continuing to watch Kali.

She removed her hat, slid the hair band out, and let her head fall back as she raked her fingers through her hair. Framed and softened by her thick mane, her face took on a new look. "Radio Rock? It's just what we call it." She scrunched up her nose. "I'm not sure how that name came. Anyway, it's one of the few places you can actually get phone reception. I called earlier to make sure the girls were okay, and Gina needed to ask Evan a question." She shrugged. "He's just checking in."

"Wait." Perry leaned forward. "You can get reception out here?"

"Soup's on!"

Buddy's spread rivaled the home cooking of Ms. Kat—grilled and glazed chicken, vegetables and peaches, bread, and sweetened tea.

"Oh, man! This is amazing!" Ed cried out while others simply nodded, mouths too full to talk.

As the last of the plates were cleaned and the sun buried itself behind the mountains in the distance, Evan brought out a guitar. Music was the perfect dessert for such a feast. Buddy joined in with a fiddle, playing songs that surely brought out ghosts from the past throughout the plains.

Sam closed his eyes and imagined a happier, simpler time.

* * * *

Kali slipped out of her sleeping bag and moved gingerly across the tent, careful not to wake her brothers-in-law. She hated this part of old west living and was thankful she hadn't lived during those times. It must have been horrible having to deal with that time of the month while traveling across country.

She felt Evan stir when she moved the flap of the tent. He was awake but he let her go. She knew that he would not sleep again until she returned. Silently, she slipped into her sandals and grabbed a flashlight and her emergency bag with its tiny shovel.

There was nothing romantic about this. Besides the major inconvenience, her biggest fear was being bitten in the ass by a snake. Try telling that one to the boys.

As she found a spot far enough away from the site, she pulled out everything she needed then turned off the light. The moon cast just enough light for her to do what she needed to do in private, while watching out for predators.

* * * *

He couldn't sleep and lying in the tent next to the other men wasn't helping. Ed snored like a freight train.

He stepped out to poke at the dead fire, maybe turn a still-burning ember, and then he saw her. Actually, he saw a beam of light first but instantly recognized her frame. Unmistakably Kali.

He watched her and wondered and wanted her.

She was always in control of everything. He might have believed she was truly that naïve, but then he had seen the way she teased and tormented at the campsite. She had known she'd had an audience. The way she played up taking off her boots, stroking her feet, and playing with her hair. It was a giant tease, but she was in the protective envelope provided by her brothers-in-law. Even the way she ate, licking her fingers and rolling her eyes. She lavished praise upon Buddy, but the effect had been for everyone else. He was sure that, given the chance, every man in the group would have been all over her, and she wanted it.

Just as he decided he would go to her, she turned out her light. Although he could still see her, her image was vague.

He watched for the strike of the match to give him the perfect excuse to join her, but she squatted down instead, and he waited.

Oddly, this was just another vulnerability and he loved it. Even the great Kali Jorgenson succumbed to the call of nature.

Since they had met, it had been a test which one could get the upper hand. Clearly, Kali was in charge when it came to horsemanship, working around the barn, or pulling ranch duties. She always had to be the best. He had established himself as well, however, and he had very little time with her— too little time to play games.

She stood, flipping on her flashlight, and was so intent on getting her small bag together she didn't see him until her light beam shone on his feet. She gasped and jumped back.

His heart jumped and he smiled.

"Oh! Oh, crap!" She fell back, her hand flew to her chest, dropping both her bag and flashlight, and she fumbled to pick them up, still cursing under her breath.

"Sorry," he said. He thoroughly enjoyed watching her fumble.

"Geez, Louise! What in the hell are you doing out here? Why aren't you asleep? Crap! What are you doing sneaking around?"

"I'm really sorry." He leaned forward to touch her, assure her, but she jerked back. "I just wanted to make sure you were okay," he said in low tones.

"How did you . . . what are you doing up?" she asked again.

"Couldn't sleep." He shrugged. "I saw you walking around up here, and thought I better, you know, check to see that you were okay."

"I'm fine." Her voice was composed and in control. She was back. She walked back toward the tents and brushed past him.

He started to reach out, to grab her, hold her . . . plant a kiss on her that would melt her down. He could feel the urge building up inside him.

"Kal?" Evan stuck his head out of the tent. Although his voice was just a whisper, it carried along the small canyon and riverbed.

"Coming." She turned back to look at Jeremy. "You need to get to sleep. Tomorrow is another day of hard riding, and you want to stay sharp."

He tensed up and couldn't help wondering how things would have gone had it not been for a brother-in-law.

Chapter Seventeen

Morning had come quickly. Only a small tin coffee pot bore evidence of there having been a meal at all. Chairs, tents, tables, and gear had all been put away, and within moments, Matthew had all the horses saddled and ready to go.

"Where's Kali?" Mike had asked.

"We've got a heifer missing. Pregnant. Kal went off to find her, bring her back." Evan looked at his watch. "We'll give her about twenty more minutes."

"That cow is dumber than dirt," Matthew said. "She wanders a lot. Kali will find her."

But it was almost thirty minutes before Kali and Star returned. No cow.

As soon as they saw her both Evan and Matthew dropped what they were doing and made their way to her.

"You couldn't find her?" Evan asked, already preparing himself for a search.

"No, I found her," Kali said with a heavy sigh, shaking her head. "I'm not sure what got her." She nodded, thinking out loud. "Most likely wild dogs. Some of the prints were pretty small, nothing wolflike." She sighed again, and it was clear she was disturbed by what she had seen.

"Damn!" Tracy kicked at some dirt.

Evan swept his hat from his head, scratching it. "I didn't hear a thing," he said in wonderment.

Kali shrugged.

"Damn!" Tracy muttered, walking back to his horse.

As Matthew pointed out later on, it was part of the harsh reality of country living. "We'll have to keep a sharper eye out for the pack," Matthew said as they loaded up. "They'll stick with us now, travel the whole damned way just for a shot at a second cow."

Sam wasn't sure what was eating Kali. She had been so friendly and social the night before, but today she held back next to Buddy and the chuck wagon. Buddy made a light lunch of simple sandwiches to hold them until the next watering hole, and whether she wanted to or not, Kali handed Sam his.

Sam took full advantage of the opportunity to engage Kali in a conversation. He asked about the cow and what it would mean when they reached the O-Kay-Doke Corral.

"We lose money," she said flatly, inspecting her sandwich before shaking her head and passing to Sam. "You want it?"

He nodded. "You sure?" He waved it at her again.

"No. I can't get the picture of that cow out of my mind. You know, it's funny. I live out here, see animals get killed a lot. Too much. But that's just the part of me that will never be a country girl, I guess. I can't get over it. No one, not even a cow, should die that way. Scared, alone in the dark. Total ambush."

They rode for a few minutes in silence, and much to Sam's happiness, she showed no sign of pulling away. Star was in perfect step with Lightning.

"People question the intelligence of dogs but let me tell you, it's spooky to watch them take down a large animal. They communicate, send out signals, and are able to work as a team to take down a prey. She—the cow —never had a chance."

"That Tracy . . . it's an unusual name for a guy, don't you think? Not something you would expect for him." It was random, but Sam was willing to talk about anything as long as Kali stayed.

"I don't know," she said, straightening up. "It's kind of fitting. Like 'A Boy Named Sue.' "

"What?"

"You know, 'A Boy Named Sue.' The Johnny Cash song?"

"I'm not familiar with that one," Sam said with a smile. Truth be told, he was familiar with very few of Johnny Cash's songs.

Kali turned in her saddle, reared back, and looked down her nose at him under the bill of her cap. "How can you be a Texan and not know that song?"

"Not all Texans listen to country music and ride horses, you know."

"At least, not very well." She smiled and looked straight ahead again.

Sam grunted, grabbed his chest, and rubbed. "That hurt."

Kali's smile broadened.

"But . . ." Sam didn't care one bit about the name, truth be told, but it was safe ground, which was where he liked to be with Kali Jorgenson. ". . . isn't it an unusual name? Maybe that's why he's so rough and tumble?"

"Well, if you knew the song we were talking about, you'd know that the father of the boy named his son Sue because, with a name like Sue, he knew his boy would have to be tough." She shrugged. "Maybe Tracy's daddy had the same idea."

Again, they rode on for a few moments.

"You've got gender issues, don't you?"

"What?" Sam couldn't contain the laugh.

"First my horse, then Tracy. I think you've got serious gender issues."

"Now, that's a new one."

"You've got women issues," Kali said and Sam stared, slack-jawed.

"I don't have issues with women!" He'd been accused of many things over the years but never that. Womanizer. Playboy. Emotionally empty. Afraid to commit. Never a woman hater.

"Sure you do. You take the sides of known rapists—"

"Now, wait a second. First of all—"

She wasn't interested in a response. "You defend monsters and persecute women based on the fact that they are women. What was it you call them? *Ladies-in-wait?*" She gave a hard shot to Star's ribs and bolted away, making her way to the front of her herd.

Sam was left stumbling over his own thoughts and didn't see her again until much later—when all hell broke loose.

* * * *

She wasn't surprised this was happening, and yet, she couldn't believe it. She squeezed her eyes shut, trying to block it out. It was the only way she would survive. She had to survive. Now, more than ever, she had to survive. She couldn't die this way. She wouldn't die this way.

He struck her again.

She gasped then began to cry, and her assailant loved it. He made disgusting, guttural noises as she cried. She didn't care. She'd give him anything he wanted at this point.

"Bitch!"

His last blow had been so powerful it had knocked her against the wall where she stayed, crumpled, on her side. She stayed still, praying that he would go away. But she knew he wouldn't. The bastard had stalked her for weeks, promising to punish her, and now he was making good on his threats.

"You know you wanted it." His voice was filled with hate. He pulled at her clothes, dragging her up the wall.

She cried out in agony. He threw her to the floor, and she felt something give in her face, then warmth. Searing pain shot through her head and she suddenly tasted blood. Lots of it. She tried to raise her hand but he grabbed her wrist, wrenching it behind her. She cried out in more pain.

No.

She wasn't trying to fight. She just wanted to touch her face. Her nose was broken, she was sure of it.

It hurts so much.

She tried to focus through the blinding pain. "No, I—" She tried to speak but she choked on her own blood.

"Shut up, bitch. Shut your mouth! You asked for this. You did." He ripped at her clothes again, swearing at her and randomly hitting her when the fabric didn't give.

She thought she felt a knee in her spine and stabbing pain ran up and down the back of her legs.

"You asked for all of this!" The man spat the words against the side of her head.

She smelled alcohol on his breath. It smelled thick, musty . . . stale—beer.

"You miserable little bitch . . ." He shoved her against the wall. ". . . and now you're going to . . ." He pushed again, and it felt as though her bones were giving way to the sheetrock. He had managed to tear her jeans and underwear from her body, but her mind had begun to pull away from the situation.

She had gone numb to all but the pain in her nose and living through this. She knew he was going to rape her, sodomize her . . . possibly butcher her. The threats had been so horribly graphic that she had every reason to believe he intended to follow through on it all.

She used to think of herself as a strong woman. She had worked out, taken kickboxing classes, even broken a board once. She had deluded herself into thinking she could hold her own. But she couldn't. She couldn't even protect herself in her own home. She had turned over recorded messages to the police to no avail, given the letters to the attorneys, and turned over photographs of the vile things written on her doors, car, and places of work. Fellow coworkers had even given statements about what they had seen and heard. But there was no hiding and no protection.

She groaned again. What home? She had no home. This was Caroline's home. What if Caroline walked in and found her dead, or worse, was attacked as well?

Ironically, there had been a point in which she'd been ready to drop the suit, but the threats had kept coming. Women's groups had gotten involved, family members had stepped forward, and it had become an "us" against "them" situation. It was when threats had come against her family that she had refused to back away because Connors and every athlete like him and all their filthy lawyers would continue this abuse. This attack was the handiwork of his lawyers.

So much had happened. So much was happening.

The news reports had been relentless trying to find Jessica. Jeremy had been in some kind of bar fight and police wanted to speak to him, as they put it, "for a witness's account of what happened." Plus, there was the whole mess with Carmen Hernandez, some barmaid in Chicago, who suddenly wasn't so sure Jeremy was the father, yet she was driving a brand new car and had quit her job as a waitress. Everything had started unraveling around Jessica.

So Caroline had promised to take her to a new movie.

That's why she opened the door. Sometimes Caroline knocked when her hands were full, like she used to in college, and Jessica hadn't been thinking. She had just been looking at the different movie times. The knock had been so familiar.

Then there he was.

It hadn't even fully registered that it wasn't Caroline when the first punch landed. She had crumpled like a doll. When she'd come to, he was calling her whore and slut and bitch and worse.

"Bitch!" he spat out again.

She focused on pulling her thoughts out of the darkness, and recognized the sound she heard . . . the front door had opened.

No! Run. Oh, please, run! Run!

She wanted to scream but couldn't. She tried to turn her head but was unable. Instead, she lay there, paralyzed, listening.

"Hey, what's goin—" It was Caroline's voice. "What? Oh!" She screamed, and Jessica felt the weight of her assailant shove off her.

She heard heavy footsteps and the sounds of Caroline struggling.

A thud.

A slap.

Muffled screams.

Please. Not Caroline. This isn't her fault. She can't be hurt. Don't let her be hurt.

Jessica rolled away from the wall. It was difficult to see, but she saw movement coming toward her. She blinked and wiped the blood from her face. She tried so hard to understand what was being said, what was happening.

"Please . . . don't." Caroline's voice sounded so far away.

Jessica gathered her strength and began to rise. "Stop!" Her vision was seriously impaired. She couldn't see anything, but she could sense Caroline wrestling with the assailant in the entranceway. Again, she heard a hard slap followed by a thud.

"You son of a bitch," Caroline's voice was ragged, her breathing hard, and Jessica was sure she was fighting back.

She got on her hands and knees and began crawling toward her friend, sliding her hands in front of her along the baseboards. "Leave her alone," Jessica said. She wanted to yell but it was just a dulled whisper. She coughed, squeezed her eyes shut and tried again. "Leave . . . leave her alone!" She couldn't let anything happen to Caroline. She could never live with herself if something happened to Caroline.

"You bastard!" Caroline screamed.

But the man was striking back.

Jessica heard her friend groaning, but Caroline was strong. And angry. She continued to fight.

Yes. Fight him! Just long enough to get to a phone, call for help, open the front door. Anything to get attention.

She crawled on, ignoring the pain, the blood, the throbbing. She was just at his feet.

He swore violently and she heard his footfalls thud hard on the floor.

Jessica never really saw it coming, but it didn't surprise her.

* * * *

Travis Dilmont was pleased with himself. He'd done his research, and of all his most recent cases, this one was going to be especially useful on his résumé.

Carmen Hernandez came from a traditional Latino family—big, proud, centered around the parents. They were Catholics and mighty unhappy about the recent news of their youngest daughter's pregnancy, but it couldn't be helped. The Hernandez family really didn't want the national attention, but the media has gone into a frenzy. It was the Carmen and Jeremy story. Where and how they met. Magazines and television shows featured pictures of the small bar where Carmen had worked, the small house she was raised in, the neighborhood where she grew up. The family didn't like being the butt of the late-night talk show jokes, and they wanted to distance themselves as much as possible from the Connors case. Dilmont had the solution.

He'd played it cool and made his pitch to the entire family "since this is a sensitive family matter that involves everyone."

The papa had liked that.

They signed an agreement to never speak of Jeremy Connors again and drop any suggestion that Jeremy was the father. In exchange, Jackson, Keller & Whiteman would make out three annual checks that if, invested properly, could set mother and child up very comfortably.

It had been an easy sale and, as Dilmont stepped out into the street, leaving the Hernandez home, he reached into his pocket, pulled out his phone, and punched Reginald Perry's number first. After all, Perry had just as much invested in this case as the lawyers . . . maybe more.

Chapter Eighteen

As they pushed the cattle through the next ravine, Sam grilled Tracy for an explanation for Kali's cold shoulder.

"I'd say she has it in for me," Sam said and shook his head.

"Naw, that isn't it. She's just testin' you, that's all. For those of us who know her, I can tell you, that's a sign of affection."

Sam laughed.

"Well, it's the same way she drives those kids. Hell, she don't give 'em a break. Always pushin' and proddin' 'em as hard as she can."

"Except Brooke." That had slipped out before Sam had really considered it.

"Now, it's funny you should say that." Tracy stared hard at Sam. "That's pretty astute. Yup, you're exactly right on, Mister. She's not hard on Brooke 'cause Brooke won't stand for it." Tracy chuckled. "That Brooke, I declare. She's something else. She's more like a momma to Kali some days. But, no, she won't stand for it. Years ago, Kali started pushing Brooke, and Brooke just threw a leg over to one side, jumped off the horse, and wouldn't get back on for weeks."

"Why? Why does she push so hard?" Sam asked.

"Well, now that depends on who you ask. Ask Kali about it, and she's liable to tell you it's because the girls need focus. After their daddy died, things kind of fell apart. Suddenly, they didn't know where they were going to live, go to school, nothing. Horses and family—those have been the constants in their lives. So Kali poured them into the family business and ridin'. She'd tell you that Jacks is reckless and needs to be able to compete to learn self-discipline and control. Danni is the opposite, real tentative. She doesn't believe in her abilities, but Jacks thinks she's invincible. Kali's been tryin' to get Danni into barrel racin' because it would send her to the edge, make her trust the horse and her own skill. Cuttin' comes too easily for Danni. She needs to challenge herself."

"And what do you think? The rest of the family?" Sam asked.

"You want the standard answer or the gospel truth?" Tracy asked as he reached into his shirt pocket and pulled out a can of snuff. He stretched it out toward Sam who shook his head.

"No, thanks. The truth would be refreshing. I don't get a lot of that in my line of work."

Tracy chuckled. "I bet not." He spat off to the side and turned to watch Sam, almost as if he was studying him. "Kali flipped out after Nicky was killed."

Sam nodded solemnly.

"Nooo!" It was Kali.

Tracy jerked upright in his saddle while Sam spun in his trying to decipher just what had happened.

A roaring sound seemed to erupt from everywhere, and the cows scattered in all directions.

Sam heard someone else yell then he saw it. It appeared out of nowhere— a helicopter. With it came a dust storm so fierce it blinded everyone. Sam doubled over Lightning, trying to find some cover from the dust while fighting to stay on, and Lightning bucked and reared.

"Mike!" Matthew yelled.

There was a horrific noise—loud and pounding that echoed through the canyon.

"I got him, I got him." It was Evan's voice.

But there were more shouts that Sam couldn't make out in the confusion.

"He's gone, he's gone!" It was Ed. "Mike!"

"Hey!"

"What in the hell is going on?"

"Go! Go! Get the hell out of here!" Sam heard Tracy yelling at a helicopter.

Shit! A helicopter out here, in the middle of nowhere, coming up like a Black Hawk or something.

"Jeremy, go, go!" Matthew was screaming so as to be heard over the helicopter.

There was a loud metallic banging noise.

Horses fled.

Sam couldn't tell who was where, only that Lightning had lit out, flying across the rough terrain, and he held on for dear life. His heart was pounding. If Lightning slipped, fell, stumbled, or turned suddenly, Sam was done for. He had no control, no posture, no grip. Nothing.

"Whoa!" He pulled the reins against Lightning's massive neck. "Whoa, boy!" He heard the fear in his own voice. "Whoa, big boy. Whoa!" He felt Lightning's pace slow, and Sam sat up a little straighter and pulled back.

Slowly, Lightning began to respond. He was sweating. His nostrils were huge, snorting and panting.

Sam tightened the reins a bit more and talked to him, trying to mimic

Matthew, Evan, Kali, and Tracy's voices and words.

He realized that the rumbling had ended, and he turned around in his saddle.

Nothing.

Each time he turned, he heard the sounds of the saddle leather stretching and giving. It was an incredibly lonely sound.

"Hello?" He called out.

Lightning stamped, ears still swiveling.

"Oh, man." Sam exhaled.

He and Lightning made a small circle.

Nothing.

His heart pounded. Had it really been a helicopter? Sam's mind was reeling, trying to come up with some kind of explanation while he squelched a feeling of growing panic.

He sat a moment longer, and not knowing what else to do, turned Lightning back in the direction they'd come. Not four steps into this new plan, he saw dust up ahead. He could just make out the distant whistles. His heart leapt.

A gentle tap sent Lightning forward.

Suddenly, Sam wasn't nearly as afraid of the speed at which Lightning carried them as he was of what he might find up ahead. He stood slightly in the stirrups, wanting to see more, but terrified of what it might be.

Matthew was the first person Sam saw. He was standing high in his saddle making a circle motion with his hand.

"Good, yes! Good man!" he yelled when he spotted Sam. It was a genuinely happy greeting from a man who had no time for social niceties. He pointed down the far ravine. "We've lost a few," he said.

Sam nodded. He'd seen them scatter. He licked his lips, looking around for more clouds of dust.

"There!" He pointed to their far right. They were small specks.

Matthew shook his head. "That's Tracy. He's got Ed. We're missing Mike."

Sam's heart sank. Briefly, Sam thought Matthew had been talking about the cows . . .

"Kali's gone west scouting Jeremy and Perry." He sighed. "You stick with me."

Sam followed as Matthew's horse took off. His mind was numb. He remembered Evan and asked about him.

"Don't worry about him," Matthew said. "He knows this terrain like the back of his hand. He's gone after the bulk of the herd." Matthew sounded calm and then he exploded. "Dammit! What the hell was that?" He shook his head and looked at Sam with wide eyes and a slack jaw. "We've got cows all over the . . ." He drew in a sharp breath and slowly exhaled.

Sam could tell he was trying to control his temper, but Matthew was shaking. Not once had he questioned his safety with these guys . . . until now. It had all been a game.

Sam's heart fell.

The helicopter. Paparazzi. Jeremy Connors.

Unbelievable!

The question wasn't *if* a helicopter had buzzed them because of Jeremy, the real question, was *how?* Jeremy had sworn that no one, not even his coaches, knew where he was—only his legal team and Perry.

Reginald Perry.

After almost an hour, a bloody Ed showed up with a handful of cows.

Sam's mouth dropped open as he looked at his friend. "Ed?"

"Now, don't get excited." Tracy held a hand up. He was incredibly calm. "Buddy, you got that first aid kit? Ed here needs some bandages."

The side of Ed's face and hands were mangled. He looked as though he had done a header over his horse, and he was in a state of shock—quiet and miserable.

"You boys know enough to keep these cows close to home," Tracy said. "Spread out. You'll be fine."

"Wait." Ed straightened in his seat, looking almost scared. "Where are you going?"

"To find the others," Tracy said as he turned his horse and took off.

Ed swore under his breath, and Buddy began assuring them how competent everyone was.

Sam scowled. If it really was Perry, how was he going to tell Ed?

The crew came back in waves. Evan drove most of the herd back by himself, and for a fleeting moment, it seemed like the day was saved.

Tracy came in next at an alarming speed, and red flags went up instantly.

He barely acknowledged the return of Evan and the herd. "Buddy, we got Perry. He's got a broken arm, and it ain't pretty. We need to put him in the back of the wagon and try to brace him." He turned to the others and cut straight to the point. "Sorry, boys. Change of plans. We're closer to home than to the O-Kay-Doke. We're turning back. Ed could stand to see a doctor, and Perry's going to need immediate medical care."

"Wait," Sam said. "Why not a helicopter?" It seemed reasonable. But it only agitated Evan.

"We don't have helicopters, only the *assholes* have 'copters," he practically screamed. "Only assholes, crackpots, and renegade cowboys have 'copters!"

"We could get us a 'copter," Buddy said quietly. "But by the time we got word out and got it here, we'd lose half a day." Buddy climbed in the back of his wagon.

Evan followed Tracy to meet Matthew as he led Perry's horse.

Even at a distance, they could all see the seriousness of his injuries. Perry was only semiconscious, moaning loudly, and his already pale skin had turned an ashen color, slightly blue due to blood loss if his heavily stained shirt was anything to go by.

As they rode closer, the reason for that loss became very clear. A bone jutted out from Perry's shirt.

"Oh, Lord," Ed exclaimed.

"No sound effects." Evan hushed him, and Ed looked away as Sam helped shift Perry into the wagon.

Whatever thoughts Sam had been having about the man just moments before were gone. He felt only pity.

By the time they had Perry strapped down inside the wagon, he had passed out.

No one spoke.

Matthew gave a nod to Tracy. "You'll find Kali."

"You know it," Tracy said with a firm nod. He folded one hand over the other, watching the men. "Go on, then. You need to get Perry help fast."

"Wait! Look!" Ed pointed to the dust off in the distance.

A horse appeared.

Sam squinted, trying to make out which horse it was.

"It's Duchess," Matthew called.

Jeremy's horse, but no Jeremy.

A silence fell over the group.

"I'll call ahead." Evan's voice was grave. "We're going to need more help." He rode hard toward Radio Rock so he could call for a medical unit to meet them at Rainwash.

Matthew directed the remaining men, asking Sam and Ed to fan out and watch the herd. Behind them, somewhere, was Kali, Jeremy, and Mike.

It was stupid, almost foolish, but Sam couldn't help himself. He locked eyes with Tracy. "You'll find her?"

Tracy smiled and gave one sure bob of his head. "If she don't find me first."

* * * *

For all Tracy knew, Kali had broken something, too. He winced. Kali would have handled this the same way, though. He couldn't keep Perry here, hoping to find Kali. He had to believe in her. Tracy headed toward Gallows Creek. It was one of the places he, Matthew, and Evan hadn't touched, but if Kali were in trouble and could move, she might have headed that way. Gallows Creek sometimes got telephone reception and it was good for low cover and water for the horses.

* * * *

Kali hung on by a thread.

They were separated from the group with less than an hour of good daylight left. The cattle was scattered, she only had two horses, one of which was lame, Mike was in bad shape, slipping in and out of consciousness, and Kali felt the pressure building.

She worked hard to block out the impulse to lay all the blame at his feet. It wasn't Jeremy's fault. Who could have prepared for this? She still wasn't sure exactly what had happened. A helicopter? Had it been a bunch of young, stupid cowboys hunting wild dogs and coyotes again? They'd had a problem with ranchers hiring them in the past, but why would they come up on an obvious cattle drive?

Unless they had just been trying to cause trouble . . .

She looked down at Mike and his shoulder. She couldn't be sure if it was broken, but she had been too afraid to move it. There was a chance it was just out of its socket. The pain was apparently unbearable. Even unconscious, he hadn't stopped moaning.

The noise had panicked every animal in a five-mile radius. She wasn't sure they'd ever get the entire herd back. She had seen Ed falling sideways as Choo Choo tore out headed for the large rocks then a dust cloud had swallowed them both, but when she'd spotted Mike fly by on Redwing, hollering about his stirrups, she had given chase only to have Star stumble and fall. She'd flown over his neck and head, and everything had slowed down. She remembered consciously working through the next millisecond and thinking, *"Crap, this is really going to hurt."*

She moved slightly and gasped with pain. Her own knee was swollen to the size of a softball. She kept telling herself it wasn't serious—maybe a sprain.

The ground had come at her so fast—a flash of brown, tufts of grass, rocks. Then, just as suddenly, the world had stopped while she'd stared at the sky and listened to her own breath.

Poor Star had looked so guilty when she'd finally managed to get vertical again. The two of them must have looked a sight—filthy, ragged, and worse for wear—as they'd both come limping around the bend of jagged rocks to find Duchess.

Only Duchess.

Kali's only question had been where was Jeremy?

She'd tried calling out to Duchess, but the horse had been in full flight and stopping for nothing. Duchess knew where to go so Kali hadn't been too concerned about her, but she had to find Jeremy. Whatever hopes she'd had of flying off to the rescue had been dashed with Star's first step. Just when Kali had thought things could not get worse, she'd felt a pang of relief as Jeremy had climbed over the ridge and waved at her.

Jeremy had wrung the last ounce of relief out of her as, since his rescue, he had twisted every bit of the situation to his advantage to make disgusting come-ons.

She had to get them out of here and fast!

Chapter Nineteen

"Ms. Kat! Oh, geez! Ms. Kat." Tammi ran across the game room. From the second floor, she saw into the kitchen perfectly. "Ms. Kat!"

"Heaven's sakes, what?" Ms. Kat stepped back from the chicken frying on the stovetop.

Brooke and the twins had been working on homework, and all three looked up at their aunt leaning over the railing.

"You better come see this!"

Everyone knew what a grand request that was since Ms. Kat had declared long ago that she and her knees were no longer interested in anything going on upstairs. The last time that statement had been used was a lifetime ago—Nicky's lifetime. They had all gathered around the giant screen to watch the attack on the US compound in Afghanistan. The images had been horrifying. It was just another reason she never watched television.

Brooke rose to her feet. "What is it?"

"Just you mind your own business, missy," Ms. Kat said. "You finish your work. I'll check it in a minute."

Gina arrived just as Ms. Kat reached the game room, and they both joined Tammi in front of the television.

"Where has Jeremy been hiding? Just where you would expect . . . on a dude ranch. CNN correspondent . . ."

Images of the cattle drive, cows scattering wildly, flashed on the screen. It had been difficult to see anything clearly but there were clips of Matthew, Evan, Tracy, Jeremy, some of the lawyers, and Buddy's wagon. It looked like something out of a movie. Clearly, they had been taken by surprise, and it was complete and utter chaos.

The news showed the footage over and over and over as they reported Jeremy was staying at the Rainwash Ranch and was expected to reach the O-Kay-Doke Corral outside Miller's Point, Colorado, within the next few days.

The phone rang and Gina pounced. "Evan?" She practically screamed into the receiver.

Both Tammi and Ms. Kat were on their feet and moving toward Gina.

"Evan, you won't . . . what's wrong?"

"Oh, dear Lord!" Ms. Kat's hand flew to her chest.

They stared anxiously at Gina's face, watching for clues as she frowned at the floor then gasped and rolled her eyes toward the ceiling.

Tammi couldn't stand it any longer. "What? *What?*"

Gina put her hand over the receiver. "It's just what we saw. All the horses panicked. Reginald Perry has a broken arm, and one of the other lawyers is pretty banged up. They've turned back. Evan's radioed ahead for medi— yes . . . and Tyler is going out to meet them." She nodded as she spoke, listening as she relayed the information.

"Oh, dear Lord," Ms. Kat said again and grabbed Tammi's hand.

"What is it?" Brooke called from below.

"Yes . . . I will. I know. Yes, honey, I know. I will. Me, too. I love you, baby." Gina hung up and stared at the phone for a moment, looking as though she was screwing her courage on, then her face scrunched up and she burst into tears.

"Gina!" Ms. Kat snapped. "You must tell me now . . ."

"Duchess came back without a rider. Jeremy. And . . ." Gina looked at Ms. Kat, took a deep breath, sniffling and hiccupping the whole time, and then said it. "And Kali is missing."

"What?" one of the twins asked from downstairs.

"Nothing!" all three women shouted. They stared at each other. Tammi's eyes welled up, but Ms. Kat shook her head defiantly.

"This is nonsense! Utter nonsense. No one knows the area better than Kali. She's fine." Ms. Kat reached over and patted Gina's arm. "I won't hear any more of this. She is fine. Just fine. No woman is stronger than Kali."

"It's back on," Tammi said in a hushed tone.

Their mouths dropped open as a reporter from Miller's Point interviewed Patrick Davis, founder of the O-Kay-Doke Corral.

Davis proudly told the world how Jeremy and his dream team were coming to powwow at his esteemed establishment.

Ms. Kat raged. "Of all the stupid, bone-headed—"

While the newscast gave a brief background for that one human being on the planet unfamiliar with the Jeremy Connors case, they showed the footage again.

They saw Kali, just a glimpse, and then she was gone. Both Tammi and Gina fought tears as they watched.

"I just spoke to Reginald Perry, Jeremy Connors' publicist, not an hour ago. He called me from a midway point, something we call Radio Rock." Davis chuckled.

Gina scoffed. "That little weasel freak."

"I'll be damned. This was just another publicity stunt."

The three women sat in stunned silence as the news feed led to another story, but not before the smiling reporter had promised more updates on the missing superstar and his legal dream team.

"What's going on?" Jacks stood at the foot of the stairwell.

"Nothing. Do your work," Ms. Kat said in an unusually calm voice. "I'll be there in a minute."

"We'll have reporters coming out of our ears," Tammi whispered.

"Oh, this is terrible." Gina started pacing.

Ms. Kat stood, straightening her clothing and putting on her game face. "We have bigger problems than that," she said, reminding the other two of the girls waiting downstairs. "Where's Kali?"

* * * *

"Are you completely insane?" Kali slapped Jeremy's hand away.

He just smiled. His eyes danced in the light of the fire. They looked full of mischief and humor, though not the kind of humor Kali appreciated. He was like a small child bent on wicked ways, except he was incredibly large and powerful.

Kali should have known it was coming, but due to the circumstances, she hadn't believed it possible.

Jeremy had helped her work her way to Gallows Creek. It had not been a complete waste of time as both Redwing and Star were able to drink, but she'd gotten no reception. She had even goaded Jeremy into climbing on top of some rocks for a higher point but still nothing.

Even with her company, Kali had a terrible feeling of loneliness—one that brought her back to the night she'd lost Nicky.

It was difficult to explain why her initial reaction had been to run. She'd wanted and needed something, and it hadn't been anywhere in the main house—not with Ms. Kat wailing in grief at the loss of a son or the constant prattle of the television. Gina had become obsessed with watching the news day and night while Kali had needed the land and Star, her one constant. She'd needed to grieve in her own way. She'd run because nothing else had made sense, not even her girls. She had known that there was no way to put on a brave face for her girls in the hours that had followed the attack.

Star had been confused by her erratic behavior as she wept and screamed and kicked at the dirt and beat the ground with dirty, bloodied fists, but he hadn't left her. He'd never left her. He'd stood, stoically watching and calmly waiting for her to come to her senses.

Cold, exhausted, and sitting in the dark, she'd realized that Brooke, Danielle, and Jaclyn were her solid ground. With that, Kali had stood, dusted herself off, and resolved never to cry again.

Beside her, Jeremy was babbling on about living in the country and the kind of woman he hoped to settle down with, and Kali only half listened.

"Like you," he said, his voice low and thick.

She felt Jeremy's finger trace along her arm and jumped.

"Easy." He chuckled. "I understand. You're scared and—"

She leaned out from the waist, feeling a twinge in her knee, but making it very clear that she didn't wish to be touched, and he held his hands as if surrendering.

"You looked like you were going to cry."

She forced a laugh. "I was not going to cry."

"Fine."

"Fine."

The fire crackled and they both stared into its mesmerizing flames.

Please, someone come!

Jeremy leaned in and brushed the hair from her face. "You're very pretty."

"Hey!" She jerked back.

"What? That's so wrong? You are. And you know it." He moved in again, rubbing the back of his hand against her cheek.

She knocked his hand away again and glared, but he didn't care. It hit her that this was part of the game he enjoyed. She started to get up, ignoring the stabbing pain in her leg, but he looped an arm through hers and around her waist. He dragged her back and she yelled. "I'm not kidding, Jeremy. Knock it off. Now." Her voice echoed through the darkness. She looked at Mike.

Nothing.

Fabulous.

"I'm not kidding either. You could drive a man insane. I've been around a lot of pretty women—"

"Yes, about that," Kali said. "Let's not forget it's the reason you are here. Okay? On behalf of your lawyers who are trying to save your sorry ass, hands off. The fewer females you mangle, the better."

Jeremy obviously found her amusing as he tilted his head back and laughed. "I think there are some on my team who would agree that you are a man tease."

"A what?" She was aghast. "Who?"

"Oh, there are others." He smiled, scooting over to get closer. "I've seen the way a certain person looks at you. You know, Kali, it's okay to be desirable. It's okay to turn a man on." He slid his fingers over her body again, and she gave him a hard shove, trying to rise to her feet but her knee rebelled. Not that it mattered anyway. Jeremy was far too quick, pulling her back against him.

She felt the heat rising in her face. This stupid pig was partially responsible for Star's stumble, and he intended to sit right next to his own lawyer in a rape case, for crying out loud, and maul her? She struck fast and hard and caught him off guard.

His face snapped to one side and he held it there for an extra pointed two count.

She felt her heart beat a little faster.

He turned to face her. He was smiling. "I've seen you at night, when you think you're alone."

His voice startled her—it was the same man, same expression, but his voice sounded completely different.

"I've seen you in your skimpy little shorts. I've seen your legs. Long, lean, muscular. I've seen your sweet, round ass. I've seen how you sit, the way you move your legs, how you let them fall apart."

Oh, shit.

Her heart was pounding out of her chest. She was in the middle of nowhere with a crazy man.

"But I know you know men are watching. Maybe me, maybe someone else. But I've seen the way you put your head back, how you want it—" He pulled her back, no longer pretending to care if it hurt her leg.

She cried out then, all composure gone. She screamed. It terrified her. She had never heard that sound come out of her mouth before. She had never feared another human being before.

Mike made a strange snorting sound and his eyes flashed open, and hope flared as she thought he might be awake, but his eyes rolled back and he went back to sleep.

Jeremy smiled at Kali. "How long has it been since you've had a real man?"

The thoughts that flashed though her mind . . . she held her tongue. It would only get her in more trouble with a man like Jeremy. He was truly dangerous, and anything she said, any challenge or threat to his manhood, could set him off. She just stared at him, but that was equally damaging as she realized he perceived everything she did or said as a come-on. "Look, Mr. Connors. It isn't perso—"

"*Mr.* Connors?"

Kali gulped and tried reason. "I'm just not interested in any man. Can't you understand and respect that?"

He wasn't listening. He laughed and rocked forward, moving toward her like a giant cat. It was that voice. There was something very disturbing about the change in his voice, as though he had an alter ego.

"I mean it," she said, her voice more of a shout. "Get back. Just get back." Her voice squeaked, which upset her greatly. She was always composed, always in control. It was an image she worked very hard for and relied on, but deep down, she knew she couldn't stop him from hurting her. He was too strong. Panic flooded her emotions, and she fought hard not to shake.

He kept moving toward her, and she fell back on her elbows.

"Don't—"

He kept coming.

She lashed out. If he was going to hurt her, she was going to hurt him.

He dodged her punch and knocked her to the ground, landing on top of her. He was too heavy to push away.

She felt his hands on her breasts, and she stared at the sky, the surreal absurdity clicking as she realized she recognized the Little Dipper. She couldn't believe this was happening and with one last effort, she screamed louder than she ever had in her entire life.

"Oh, Kali, you smell so sweet," he said and nuzzled the side of her neck.

She grunted, trying with all her strength to shove him off her. It didn't even faze him. A new fight ignited in her as she felt Jeremy's leg slide between hers. For a few moments, she had held him off, and she heard him grunt then laugh as he fought to pry her legs apart.

"You are a wild cat," he said as if it was a compliment.

He wants a wild cat . . .

She lashed out at him, trying to scratch his face.

He caught her arm and laughed again.

Her heart was about to pound out of her rib cage, and Jeremy was playing a game. She held her breath, ready to draw her good leg up and kick the crap out of him as soon as he moved enough to give her freedom.

She never saw it coming.

She heard a thud followed by a grunt. Then . . . air. She felt suddenly light and realized the weight of Jeremy had been torn away from her. She gasped.

Tracy stood over her, larger than life and staring at Jeremy who was crumpled to the side, holding his stomach, wheezing to catch his breath. "You sorry son of a bitch! I got no idea what was going on and don't want to, but I'll tell ya this: you ever lay a hand on that woman, as much as a hair on her head, and I swear to you, by God, I will blow your brains out. I will kill ya just as soon as look at ya." He spat at the ground.

Jeremy grunted and rolled over to a seated position.

"We clear?"

"Just a misunderstanding," Jeremy said, nodding.

Tracy turned toward Kali.

She flushed. Never was she so happy to see someone and so embarrassed at the same time. She shook and struggled to regain her composure.

Tracy turned away again and stooped over Mike, inspecting his injury while Jeremy stood, explaining what he knew.

Kali blinked—it was as though nothing had happened.

Within minutes, Tracy had concluded the shoulder was out of its socket.

"No time like the present," he said, instructing Jeremy to get Mike in an upright position. "An old cowboy trick," he said over his shoulder.

Mike gasped, then yelled, but the almost sudden relief washed over his face.

Jeremy was back on Duchess with Mike riding Redwing, leaving Kali to ride sidesaddle with Tracy as he regaled Mike and Jeremy with his stories of being a cowboy "when cowboys were cowboys." She held Star's lead and watched as he carefully picked his way behind them.

Kali was in a daze and confused by her own emotions. She had been attacked. Actually attacked. Jeremy had admitted that he watched her. She swallowed. It was very disturbing.

Her head throbbed as Tracy told jokes. She tightened up the reins, holding Star close, watching her marvelous old friend. She decided this had to be his way of handling things. Tracy was a good ol' boy. Maybe he was just dealing with a difficult issue in the good ol' boy way—the cowboy way.

She glanced at Jeremy. He was smiling at her.

Chapter Twenty

Roderick had been leaning against the bar, grinning widely, thankful for the One Ton Saloon and all its inhabitants. He was sipping some kind of concoction the bartender whipped up and watching Garret make an ass of himself when someone had called out his name.

They had found the One Ton through Wade. He'd brought them the day before and made them promise not to get drunk or engage in any bar fights.

Roderick had one-upped that promise with one of his own—neither he nor Garret would admit to being friends with Jeremy Connors, and if someone asked them what brought them to this tiny little town, they would simply say they were passing through, taking in the sights of America.

"No scenes, man. We'll just blend in."

A funny statement indeed from a large black man in the middle of white bread America, but the people had been cool, making idle chitchat about sports.

The bartender—Sanders was his name—knew Roderick and Garret were ball players, but he had sensed Roderick didn't feel like talking about it, so he kept the conversation neutral and tried out new drinks on him.

"Finally," he yelled for the five customers inside the dingy, all-wood saloon. "I got someone who'll try something besides a damned beer!" Sanders blew out a halfhearted whistle. "These guys," he said, shaking his head as a man and two women, all wearing muscle shirts, entered the bar. "They enter all the local arm-wrestling events. That one there . . ." He pointed to the blond woman, about six feet tall and solidly built. "She's the midwest champion." He raised his eyebrows, smiling and taunting the two men. "Gotta say, she beats the men, too. Never seen her lose."

"Oh, yeah?" Garret spun around on his stool. "How much says I can win?"

Roderick was already shaking his head. "Man, don't be wrestling some chick. That's embarrassing."

"If you can, and that's a big 'if,' I'd say it's worth free beer for the rest of the day," Sanders said and leaned against the bar, smiling.

"Garret, don't even tell me—"

"He's sayin' a woman can't be beat in arm wrestling." Garret spread his hands out and pushed back from the bar.

Roderick scoffed. "Man, he's not sayin' anything. Sit down."

"No, maybe your friend here is right. Maybe you shouldn't bother." Sanders' voice dripped with sarcasm.

Garret eyed Roderick. He couldn't stand it.

"What are you going to do, challenge her?" Roderick asked incredulously.

"No, I will," Sanders spoke up. "Hey, Mel. I got a guy here who says he can take you."

There was a shushing noise among the small gathering.

The large woman named Mel turned on her heel. She had been inspecting a cue stick when Sanders called out, and she cocked her head to the side, looking the men over. "Oh, yeah? Which one?"

"This one. Bet the house a free tab."

There were some whoops around the room.

Roderick dropped his head and turned back toward the bar. "Shit!" he spoke into his beer.

The entire bar got involved. A table was cleared, and Garret blustered his way toward it. "Shit, man! I throw men twice her size around for a living. It's what I'm paid to do. I just don't want to hurt anyone, you see? But, hey, free beer is free beer." He laughed at his own joke.

Roderick squinted up at Sanders. "She's going to win, isn't she?"

"I'm betting on it," Sanders said, and his grin widened. "You taking odds?"

"On him?" Roderick chuckled. "Naw." He swung around to watch Garret make a complete ass of himself.

As he rolled up a sleeve, he blathered on about what he did for a living and that this was just part of the training.

Man, shut up!

She whipped him soundly, and he complained that he hadn't been ready. It was met with howls of laughter.

As they went for round two—as if Garret hadn't embarrassed and humiliated himself enough—Sanders called out. "Hey, Bouche, that's you, right?"

Roderick looked up and saw a man sitting at the edge of the bar, near the front door and just beneath a television mounted high on the wall.

He nodded toward the television. "That you?"

Oh, shit.

"Hey, turn that up," he said, waving at Sanders.

There he was, a picture of Roderick and Garret identified them as traveling companions of Jeremy Connors, and both were wanted for questioning in the death of Jessica Stanten.

Oh, shit!

"Jessica Stanten and her roommate, Caroline Peters, were rushed to a local hospital today after being discovered by a neighbor. Stanten was pronounced dead on arrival, and Ms. Peters has been listed in critical condition after both were violently beaten and raped."

Roderick felt the heat rise on the back of his neck.

Beaten . . . to death?

". . . Connors' legal team is now facing questions as the key witness against Connors is brutally murdered. This, only days after Carmen Hernandez, the woman claiming Connors fathered her unborn child, withdrew her paternity suit. Yet the legal dream team is nowhere to be found. Connors and his teammates Roderick Bouche and Garret Jackson are missing, leaving police with many questions. Coming up, we caught up with Connors' publicist, and you'll never guess where he is or what he's been up to."

Even as the segment broke away for a commercial break, Roderick continued to stare at the television.

"I thought that was you," the man at the end of the bar said. "I heard Emmit say the Rainwash had some celebrities or something. That's you. Well, I guess we know it couldn't have been you who killed her. You were here. Right?"

Roderick tore himself from the television and nearly choked. "Yeah, you just remember that!" He stumbled to his feet and turned just in time to see Mel slam the back of Garret's hand to the table.

The crowd erupted in applause, and Garret dropped his head.

He stood and was saying something inane when Roderick yelled at him.

"Pay up, my man!" Mel said. "Pay up! You lost!" Her voice was drowned out as Sanders turned the volume on the television up even further.

As the stampede footage played out again, Wade entered the bar.

"Wade!"

He nodded politely and signaled for Roderick and Garret. "Something's come up," he said, but Roderick pointed to the television.

"We know."

Wade looked up to see the image of cattle scattering. A glimpse of Evan and Matthew could be seen through dust and mayhem. "Oh, man," he said and turned on his heel, not waiting for Roderick or Garret.

* * * *

It was long past suppertime, yet Ms. Kat hadn't even bothered with dinner, and Brooke grew increasingly worried about what the adults were discussing. Every time she'd asked, Ms. Kat had told her to continue with her assignment. That made no sense. She was already weeks ahead of her schedule as it was.

"There's something on TV they don't want us to see," Brooke whispered to her sisters. Brooke leaned her chin into her palm as she rested her elbow on the table. Whatever was going on, the answer was on the television. She was sure of it.

Her mind flashed back to the day Daddy had died, the television, pictures of the explosions and other people celebrating in the streets, and the distress of her family. But what had it all meant? Finally, when Momma disappeared, it had been Uncle Matthew who'd told her—Daddy wasn't coming home.

Once again, people were upset, and it seemed to be about Momma.

Had something happened to Momma, too?

Finding the answer to that question was what drove her plan. She sent Jacks to Aunt Gina's cabin.

Jacks had been all too eager for an adventure, but when she returned, she was no longer smiling.

"What?" Brooke whispered.

Jacks walked right up to Brooke, stood perfectly straight, like a robot, and opened her mouth, but nothing came out.

Brooke saw Jacks' mouth tremble and she felt sick.

"I didn't . . . I don't know exactly what happened, but I-I-I saw it. I saw it on the TV." Jacks stammered as she tried to explain what she saw to her sisters.

"What?" Brooke grabbed her hand and yanked it. She wanted to slap her, shake her, and make her say what she saw.

"It's Momma. Uncle Mattie and Evan and Tracy. They . . . they were on TV, and the cows just went crazy. Everyone was running different places."

Brooke blinked. She didn't understand. That was ridiculous. Cows just don't go crazy. And even if they did, Uncle Matthew and the rest knew how to settle the cows down and rope them in.

"And Mr. Connors murdered someone. The police are looking for him." Jacks shook her head. "Someone is missing."

"Mr. Connors murdered someone?" Danni asked. She almost choked on the words.

"What? Who?" Brooke shook her sister by her shoulders. "Who's missing?"

"I don't know." Jacks started to cry.

Brooke wasn't sure what Jacks had seen, but someone was missing and Momma was in danger. "We have to go find her," Brooke said, decisively.

Danni and Jacks looked at each other.

"She's in trouble. She needs us," Brooke said and both Danni and Jacks were up. Without question, they were ready to follow Brooke. "We'll go out the kitchen. Danni, go get our boots. Jacks, let's go get the horses ready."

As they crept out of the kitchen, Brooke gathered up as many apples, bagels, and energy bars as she could inside her shirt.

"Yeah," Jacks said. "We can find her better than anyone."

The adventure was on. Only this was no game.

* * * *

All they could do now was wait. And pray.

Ms. Kat called down to the girls who had been sitting so patiently, waiting for their dinner. When she got no response, Tammi went to the railing to check on them.

"They're not there," Tammi said.

Gina, who had been playing with the babies, suddenly looked up. "What do you mean, they're not there?"

She looked out over the house and called out to the girls. No answer. All three women looked at each other.

"What now?" Ms. Kat headed for the stairway, but Tammi slid passed her, racing down the spiral staircase.

Ms. Kat was only halfway down when Tammi found the note. "Oh, no!"

Gina looked over the railing. "What?"

"It's a note. Oh, no, no, no. It's a note from Brooke. The girls. They left a note . . ." She stopped trying to explain and just began reading the note. " 'We've gone to find Momma. Don't worry. We'll be back soon. Ms. Kat, we'll be good. We love you.' "

Ms. Kat hit the landing running. She snatched the note from Tammi's hands and reread it, moaning all the while. "Oh, Lord. My babies are out in the dark, all alone. Oh, Lord!"

Alexandra Allred

Chapter Twenty-One

Together, the three girls saddled up and headed out the front gate easily
enough. It was dark outside, but Momma had gotten them up many
mornings when there had been no light. The winter months were always
darker, and although it was quite warm, they convinced themselves this was
just another February morning, just like before a competition.

Brooke hadn't been scared about riding in the dark or leaving home
without telling Ms. Kat. She knew the terrain, and since she had packed one
of the mobile phones, she would call Ms. Kat as soon as they reached
Radio Rock. Ms. Kat would be mad, for sure, but Brooke couldn't think
about that. No, what she was scared about was not finding their mom. She
didn't know what her little sisters would do if they couldn't find Momma.

She watched the back of Jacks as they began the steady climb toward
Radio Rock. It wasn't that Jacks was a better rider, but Mocha was
probably the best choice for the lead. Fancy and Mouse were more than
happy to follow along in the dark.

The horses kept swinging their heads from side to side, constantly
looking around. This was a bad hour for a horse to be outside and they all
knew it.

It had been a last minute grab, and Brooke hadn't liked it, but she hadn't
argued too much when Jacks brought along her Marlin .22—the rifle Daddy
had given Brooke when she was eight years old. It had been a tradition
among the Jorgensons even though Momma hadn't liked it. He had just
begun teaching her how to shoot it when he left for Afghanistan. Brooke
had never touched it again, but Jacks had been fascinated with it and always
begging Uncle Matthew or Uncle Stephen to teach her how to use it. It
hadn't seemed like a bad idea to have some kind of protection in the dark.

They didn't speak. Each girl knew the way to Radio Rock, as did their
horses, so they walked, each lost in her own thoughts and hopes of finding
their mom.

* * * *

"This is Wade," he answered his phone on the first ring.

He had been driving like a wild man toward the ranch, not listening to Garret as he tried to defend his friend. In truth, he didn't care one whit about Jeremy. Maybe it was a publicity stunt. Maybe it wasn't. He cared that Kali was missing. Paying customers were hurt, cows were scattered, money was lost, but most pressing was Kali. He couldn't believe it.

"The girls are gone," Gina said.

No pretense, no "how's it going?" Nothing but more heartache.

"What?" His brain was on overload. Hell, he didn't understand anything at this point. "The girls?"

"Brooke, Jacks, and Danni," Gina yelled. Her voice was panicked. "They left a note, Wade. They've gone. They've gone to find Kali!"

Wade quickly tried to reassure her then broke the connection and pressed the accelerator.

"What is it?" Garret asked.

"Shut up," Wade said, ending any further conversations until they got to the ranch.

Wade did a tailspin in the compound, jumped out, and headed toward the main house. He left Garret and Roderick sitting in the truck, clueless. He left the lights on with the engine running.

Tammi was at the edge of the porch looking down at him before he made it up the first few steps.

They stared at each other, silent, each hoping the other had news.

"You hear anything?" Wade gave first.

"No!" She was crying. "They're gone. Horses, boots, gear, water bottles. They just packed up and left!"

"How long?" Wade felt panic growing inside him as well but fought hard against it. If he rode hard, he could catch them and paddle their little butts.

"We . . . we don't know exactly. An hour?" She swayed a little. "We tried to call Evan, but they've passed Radio Rock. There's no contact. They're out there alone."

Wade broke into a run, headed for the barn. His mind was racing.
Which horse? Who would Tracy pick?

All his personal favorites were gone so, without wasting any more time, he pulled the tack for Daphne. She'd been a rescue horse—solid and strong but a little spooked around other horses. He didn't know how she would handle the dark, alone, but he'd find out soon enough.

Roderick and Garret stepped out of the truck and watched Wade as he galloped out the front gate and into the darkness as Tammi glared at them from behind.

* * * *

Danni pulled Fancy to a stop and turned her head. "What was that?"

"The wind," Jacks said, almost in a growl, and frowned at Brooke.

Brooke didn't say a word, but the truth was she'd been hearing it as well.

When she'd first heard it, she had looked to her sisters and watched their reactions. They either hadn't heard or hadn't thought it was anything to worry about, but she'd noticed Mocha had heard and raised her nose high in the air, taking in the smells.

Somewhere, there was trouble.

When Jacks stiffened, Brooke knew her sister had heard it, too, and they all stopped.

"It's dark outside, so you're hearing things." Brooke kept trying to convince everyone, most of all herself, that it really was just something simple . . . like the wind.

Fancy jerked her head up just as Mouse tossed his head to the side and did a little half step as he looked. Something had him spooked and Brooke was done pretending.

"I told you," whispered Danni. "Something is out there."

"Mocha feels it," Jacks said as she carefully reached for her rifle.

"Maybe it's Momma," Danni said hopefully.

Brooke sighed. "Momma doesn't scare the horses." She looked around and leaned closer to Mouse. "It's something else."

Without another word, the girls pulled their horses in a little closer.

Brooke cocked her head to one side then the other. She tried to remember everything that Tracy had taught her about tracking and animals. She knew this one. In fact, as soon the idea hit her she almost spoke out loud, proud of herself for remembering.

This was an animal noise.

Coyotes talked to each other. When they worked in packs, they yipped. It was part of their clever hunting abilities. Just three or four coyotes could sound like dozens. This wasn't coyotes. Wild dogs tended to be more abrasive, growling as they moved forward or alongside a prey, but the wolf worked silently. They had a whole form of communication with each other that required little to no noise.

This was a wolf. Brooke knew it.

There it was again. To her right, about the distance of the crazy eight pattern which was about fifty feet.

Wolves.

"Jacks," she said calmly.

"I know it," Jacks said.

Her voice sounded so calm and quiet, and Brooke knew their mother would be proud of how bravely Jacks was behaving.

"I don't know what to do." It was an unheard of confession coming from Jacks.

In the darkness, Brooke peered at her sister.

They had pulled the horses side by side, putting Danni and Fancy in the middle.

"I'm getting really scared," Danni said, her voice a whine.

"If I shoot, I could scare them off, but I might spook the horses," Jacks said, and Brooke knew that Jacks was trying to remember all the safety lessons Uncle Matthew had given them.

You never shoot in the dark or unless you have a clear shot. You never know what you're shooting at unless you can see it.

"If they bolt, one of us could fall," Jacks said.

Brooke shook her head. "We're not going to fall."

"But a wolf will eat whatever falls," Jacks said.

"Wolves don't attack people," Brooke pointed out.

"Maybe you should jump off and become friends," Jacks said, and Brooke could tell her little sister was frustrated but scared.

"Let's just go faster!" Danni ignored her siblings and urged her horse on. "We could canter a little faster and maybe they'll give up." Without another word, she gave a little kick, and Fancy started to move recklessly fast into the dark.

"Wait!" Jacks called out and Danni slowed down.

"What?" Brooke had always loved wolves so much, and she wished they knew that right now. She had wolf poster and wolf folders and a wolf blanket. She had always been interested in them and felt bad for the way they were treated. But here they were in the dark by themselves, with wolves moving all around them, no doubt, and everyone knew wolves didn't hunt alone. For the first time, she doubted this quest to find their mother. It was stupid to be out in the dark, and very frightening.

The horses stirred, making it increasingly difficult to hold them. As flight animals, their instincts were taking over, and Brooke knew if she and her sisters were left on their own in the dark, in the midst of panic, they would be in serious danger.

Mouse was moving around so much he was agitating the others.

The sound grew louder, heavier.

Whatever it was, it was big.

They turned their horses to face it, not wanting to be attacked from behind. Mouse, Fancy, and Mocha were almost wild with fear. The girls struggled to keep them steady, and Brooke leaned over to help hold Mocha while Jacks leveled her gun.

"Whoa." Brooke tried to keep her voice calm. Her heart was pounding so hard she was sure the wolves could hear it. They could probably smell fear, too.

Certainly Mouse could, but she rubbed her neck and steadied the horse as Jacks took aim.

Brooke held her breath as Jacks slowed her own, squinted one eye closed, and gently laid her finger on the trigger.

* * * *

To help him track the girls, Wade had taken one of his glow sticks on a string. He often joked that he would have been a hero in the old west with his glow sticks. Tonight, he had gotten lucky and was able to pick up fairly fresh tracks with the help of his party lights. The girls were traveling tight, walking the horses side by side. He was glad to see it, but he still couldn't wait to get his hands on them.

He couldn't remember the last time he had felt this scared and helpless. They were the closest things he'd ever had to a daughter or niece. He'd known them since they were babies.

They had been so brave after Nicky had been killed. At first, he had thought they hadn't really understood what had happened, but as he'd talked to them he realized that they knew their daddy was never coming back. Each one of them had talked about being brave for Ms. Kat and Momma. In their own way, they had given everyone at Rainwash Ranch strength during those difficult times.

It was good that Evan and the group had passed Radio Rock. They would have split from that point with the injured heading down to where Dr. Thom would have people waiting for them there. The rest would head back to the ranch and, most likely, run into the girls on the way. Assuming the girls stayed on course and didn't get lost in the dark.

He lowered his glow stick again and studied the ground. He looked into the darkness. Straight ahead, somewhere, they were up there. He gave Daphne a solid kick and quickened his pace. He wanted to catch them before too long and bring them back to Ms. Kat, who was slowly losing her mind.

As he neared the top of the hill, he heard something. In the dark, Daphne's senses were heightened and it gave her an extra spring to her step that he didn't particularly care for. When they reached the highest point, she tried to turn. He had to fight to keep her in line and had begun to say something when he saw it.

A shadow . . . no, shadows.

"Whoa." He pulled Daphne sharply to the side. The horse tried to bolt, and for a moment, he was lost. He hadn't expected them to be standing there. He hadn't expected the gunfire.

Chapter Twenty-Two

"So what are we looking at?" asked Detective Regan Phillips. He looked to his young, new partner as they walked down the corridor. "Please tell me something good."

The twenty-year veteran had spent what felt like a lifetime working homicide in Shreveport, Louisiana. The outward appearance of the neat, trim man was a ruse. While Phillips was well respected among his peers, his methods were sloppy and unorthodox. He didn't bother with notes. It was all in his head. His partner, however, was the opposite, obsessively taking notes about everything.

Detective Patrick Krane peered up from his notepad. "Doc's in with her now."

"What about Caroline Peters?" he asked.

"Got a man on the door and two in the hallway. We're checking anyone and everyone going in and out, including any calls," Krane said and shrugged. He was trying to get every detail down in his notes just as he remembered it.

Phillips studied him for a moment. Krane had been on the force just five years, only recently making detective. This was the third homicide of his short career but promised to be the most high profile. The media was behind them at every turn, asking questions and demanding answers, and camping out near the station in the hopes they would get the scoop on Jeremy Connors and his women.

It had bothered Phillips that that was all these women were in the grand twenty-four-hour news day scheme of things—mere players in Jeremy Connors' game of life. It was all about Jeremy Connors. That was the reason Phillips hadn't bothered to take notes. He had already learned more than he ever wanted to know about Jessica Stanton through the newspapers. He didn't want to recall facts about the woman from his own notes.

It was ridiculous how many conversations he'd had about the woman who had accused Connors of assault and rape. It was all anyone talked about. Caroline Peters, however, was a different story. He knew almost nothing about her.

"What about her condition?" Phillips asked patiently. He wanted to hear that she was awake and ready to talk. He was in desperate need of information.

Krane looked up. "We'll be lucky if she ever wakes up," he said. "She's bad, Phillips. Bad. Even if she does wake up, I don't know if she's ever gonna be the same. I know I'm not holding my breath for an eyewitness account."

Phillips sighed.

A door pushed opened and Marlena Hendricks poked her head out. "You ready?"

She was a short, fiery redhead with freckles and a plunging neckline. Phillips never bored of her. It was funny to him that she'd chosen this line of work, but he couldn't imagine her doing anything else. She was a damned fine coroner.

"What have you got?" Phillips followed Hendricks back into the room.

Krane caught the door and hovered. He looked a little squeamish, and he referred back to his notes while the grown-ups talked.

Phillips suppressed a smile, cocking his head at Hendricks in a gesture to continue.

"Well, no name, if that's what you're hoping for."

"Initials, maybe? I'm not picky."

"How about this . . . it wasn't Connors." Phillips looked deflated and Hendricks gave a halfhearted smile. "Sorry." She moved around the body and listed the details she had found. "There are a few things. First, your guy is Caucasian with brown hair. This was the work of one person. I mean, there could have been someone watching, I suppose, but only one maniac had a hand in this."

Phillips and Hendricks studied the body together.

Stanten looked as if she'd been tortured. Phillips had seen her picture many times in the last few months on the news, and she had been stunning. This woman was battered and bruised. She looked broken, fragile, and the word came to him again, *tortured*. Not so much in the body, although it was easy to see she had been put through hell.

He winced.

There was something in her face. She had been through an emotional hell as well. In a very short span, she had lived in five different places, lost her job, sold her car, and changed her cell phone number countless times in an attempt to get away from the public glare.

It bothered him. It bothered him a lot.

"Her attacker was close to her height, maybe six foot one or two. See, here," Hendricks said and moved around the table, pulling back the sheet to expose several stab wounds. "From the angle of these wounds we can estimate his height."

Phillips nodded. He was inclined to take her word for it. Instead of looking at the wounds, he found himself looking at the young woman's face again.

"And she put up a hell of a fight," Hendricks said.

"Atta girl," he whispered.

"I wouldn't be surprised if your guy has a few marks himself. She may have gotten one or two good hits or punches off. From her bruising, I can tell you that they wrestled quite a bit. That may have been when the roommate walked in."

"What about semen?" Phillips asked, hoping to hear something more concrete about DNA.

"No. Our boy didn't use his own instrument," she said flatly.

Krane looked up from his notepad. There was an awkward moment.

"Come again?" Phillips asked. "I thought she was raped. Right?" He glanced over his shoulder. "Wasn't she raped?"

Krane fumbled, scrambling through his notes.

"Well, in a manner of speaking. She was sodomized. Violently." Hendricks looked from one man to the other. "The damage that was inflicted . . . this was an act of extreme anger." She shook her head and moved away from the table. "But . . ." She caught Phillips' eye. ". . . you didn't hear that from me."

He gave her a little nod.

Phillips and Krane watched as Dr. Hendricks methodically filed away materials. She labeled and tagged each piece of clothing and scraping.

"So who?" Phillips asked finally.

"Well, if I were a betting woman, I'd say a fanatical sports fan."

"Well, then, what's that, Krane? Huh? About two, three or four million?" Phillips took another hard look at Jessica Stanten. "Poor dumb kid," he muttered.

"Dumb?" Hendricks appeared shocked. "Am I missing something? Wasn't she the unwilling victim?"

"Yeah, but she sought him out." Phillips shoved his hands in his pockets.

Stanten's hair had been neatly pulled back from her face and combed out. Hendricks was thorough. She had probably checked Stanten's entire head of hair for evidence.

"The killer? How do y—"

"I don't know who killed her, who did this to her." He shrugged. "Least, not yet. I meant everything, all the gossip rags and hate mail and the lawsuit."

Krane nodded.

"You read the sports, Doc? Jessica Stanten has been living in a nightmare —on the run really, ever since she accused Jeremy Connors of rape. I can't imagine why she would hook up with him in the first place," Phillips said.

"Sure you're not suggesting she asked for it?"

"He's a bad man, Doc. She knew that going in," Phillips said matter-of-factly.

"So, because she heard rumors that he loved to rough women up, she had this one coming?" Hendricks placed her hands on her hips and scowled.

"Uh, I don't think it's right to talk like this right over her, you know?" Krane spoke up.

"Oh, no. If she's still hovering about, I'd like her to know there are those of us who are still fighting for her. We don't believe a woman should be murdered, much less raped, simply because she had a moment of poor judgment." Hendricks wagged a finger at Phillips. "And that's all it was. I *do* read the reports. She went to his hotel thinking she could get him to sign on with her agency. She didn't go to get raped."

"Hey!" Phillips raised his hands to the sky. "I'm with you, remember?"

"I wonder."

"Hey, now, that's not fair. Listen! Of course, this shouldn't have happened to her. It shouldn't happen to anyone. I was simply stating my frustrations. A young woman with a promising career approaches a famous athlete with a bad boy reputation in hopes of landing him as a client. We don't really know what was said or promised between the two."

Hendricks opened her mouth to protest, but he waved her off.

"But we do know she was beaten and raped. We know that for sure. We know that we have witnesses who saw her state after she left his room and the rape kit from the hospital. Unfortunately, we also know she may have had relations with other men, or another ma—"

"Her *boyfriend*," Hendricks said.

"Ex." Krane examined his notes. As Phillips did the recount, Krane flipped through his notes. "Ex-boyfriend." He looked up to see Hendricks glare and smiled meekly. "It's what it says here," he said, tapping his notebook.

"Ah, so the slut had sex with a man she once loved and may have been talking about reconciling with," Hendricks said and slammed an instrument down on the tray.

"Marlena!" Phillips was shocked.

"Isn't that what you're implying? Because she was with another man, a man she had once known and loved, before she went to visit Connors, she was a slut? Or could it be she had two items of business, one was personal and one was strictly business that turned violent?"

"See, you're trying to pin me down, Marlena, but that's not what I am saying at all. For whatever reasons, as you just suggested, she met Jeremy. For that, I said, and affectionately, I might add, 'Poor, dumb kid,' because I sincerely believe she really didn't know what she was getting herself into. The guy just lost the Super Bowl and was a ticking time bomb. That's not to say he wouldn't have attacked her had his team won.

"I read the kid's bio. *Sports Illustrated* did a big spread on him a couple of years ago when he went pro. He also has those two books on him.

One . . ." He turned, snapping his fingers at Krane. "What was it called?"

"*Jeremy Connors: Up Close and Personal*," Krane answered.

"No, that's the unofficial biography. Although, that's a goody," he said and turned back to Marlena Hendricks. "The author goes back and interviews kids, teachers, and coaches from his high school days in Hodunk, Nebraska, or wherever he's from. There are stories about rape even in high school, but no charges were ever filed. He raped the Homecoming Queen, allegedly, and there are stories about abuse of animals. He supposedly did things to animals on dares—shot his own dog in the head, drowned the hunting dog of a rival coach. Dog was supposed to be some kind of hunting champion and Jeremy got it in a burlap bag with a cement block and threw it in a pond."

"Nice," Hendricks sighed, staring up at the ceiling.

"He shot out the tires of all the security trucks at his college," Krane said "He's got a thing with guns and knives."

"Yet no one thought this might be the beginning of a serial killer?" Hendricks asked.

"Well, now, technically, he hasn't killed anyone yet."

"He's killed animals and raped people, but it's okay to sign this ticking time bomb to a multimillion dollar contract and put him above the law because he can make money for the team owner and the league?" She sighed heavily for dramatic effect.

"All hearsay, for now," Phillips reminded her.

As sad as it was to say, the strongest case yet against Connors had been Stanten. With her dead and Connors hundreds of miles away when the murder was committed, the case was unraveling before their eyes. Still, it bothered Phillips. Connors had conveniently allowed himself to be captured on film for the entire world to see while the murder had taken place.

"But I thought there had been some other case against Connors as well?" Hendricks scowled.

"Lawsuit for battery. Assault and battery," Krane spoke up again. "Case was dropped when the jury overturned it, saying he just looked like a nice guy and that they thought it was a case of someone trying to make money off of him."

Hendricks groaned.

"Actually, it was a pretty solid case. There were a handful of witnesses, but they were all young and drunk." Phillips shrugged. "Such is the life of the rich and famous. Now, the interesting book was the one he actually participated in—"

"*The Undisputed King*," Krane called out.

"Yeah, don't you just love it? That's the title. He talks about how people are always wanting things from him. It's disturbing because you can see how he thinks. I mean, he really believes he is owed whatever he wants, and that we're here—most of us anyway—are here to serve. You almost can't blame the guy," Phillips said.

Hendricks balked. "What?"

"I said, *almost*. You have to read it, Doc. He's been handed everything since he was a kid. I don't think he would know how to respond to someone telling him no to something."

"Like women." She looked back at Stanten lying on the slab. "Probably the one thing that's been served up to him more than anything else is women, so when one actually has the audacity to say no or reject him in any way, he goes off."

"Well, now that's just the thing about the witnesses from the high school rape of, oh, what was her name?" Phillips thumped the side of his head. "The entire school knew that Connors had done something to this girl. I gathered coaches, the school principal, local sheriff and parents were involved, but no charges were ever filed. But it was a small school and the kids talked. The girl wound up going away, finishing up school somewhere else and kind of dropped out of contact with everyone. Whatever was done or said, she remained silent while Connors went on to brag about it. In the book, he talks about women throwing themselves at him and wanting some kind of commitment, but he is unable because he doesn't know if they love him for him or his fame and fortune. It's such horseshit. But he's living his own lie and it justifies everything."

They all studied Jessica Stanten for another moment.

"So how are you going to tie this to Connors?" she asked.

"For now, I'm not sure we can." He turned to look at Krane. "The rape took place in Houston. This is Shreveport. And this is a murder. Two different crimes by two different people."

Dr. Hendricks pulled off her latex gloves with a loud snap. "So, in the meantime, he continues to do whatever the hell he wants, beating and raping women." She started to walk out with Phillips and Krane. "I need a cup of coffee." She sighed. "I just pray there aren't any women out there where he is now."

"Well, at least there isn't a whole lot of damage he can do to a bunch of cows," Krane said humorlessly.

Hendricks frowned. "Don't underestimate the undisputed king."

Chapter Twenty-Three

As soon as they reached Radio Rock, Kali flipped open her phone. It had been the one thing keeping her sane and focused on something other than what had happened earlier that night. She hoped for two things when she called—the sweet voices of her babies and information from Ms. Kat. What had the helicopter been about? What was the status report on Reginald Perry and Ed Slader? Where was Evan and what was the latest report on the cows?

Gina answered the phone before the first ring even registered on Kali's end. Her voice sounded panicked then surprised when she realized who she was speaking to.

"Oh, Kali, thank goodness. It's Kali!" she screamed away from the mouthpiece and Kali heard a commotion in the background. "Are you okay? Is everything okay?"

"Yeah, we're okay." Kali rubbed her head. She felt dull and listless. "Mike was injured, dislocated shoulder, but Tracy put it back. He's going to need some medical care. We've got Jeremy with us. He's fine." She could barely make out the outline of Tracy's face in the dark.

Mike sagged heavily in his saddle.

"We're gonna bed down for the night. We can't go any farther," she said. "But—"

"Kali, have you seen Wade?" Gina asked.

Kali raised her eyebrows. "Wade?"

"Wade?" Tracy looked out into the darkness. "He out here?"

Kali feared there had been another accident. "Did Buddy and Matthew make it to—"

"No, no," Gina said impatiently. "They made it fine. Dr. Thom was there and took care of everyone quickly. Mr. Perry is going to be okay. He's in surgery up at County. Everything is going to be fine. Look, you haven't seen or heard anything of Wade?"

There was a strange pause and Kali could hear voices in the background, instructing Gina what to say. "It's pitch black out here, Gina. We can't see our own hands in front of our faces! What's going on?" Kali felt a tightening in her chest.

"It's just crazy around here. That's all. Just crazy. Hey, let me talk to Tracy." Kali didn't like it, but she didn't hesitate. She handed the phone to Tracy. "It's Gina. She wants to talk to you. Something's wrong."

Kali tried to stay busy while being all too aware of just how little Tracy said while he listened to Gina.

She slid carefully from Toby's back, trying to land on her good leg. The landing jarred her knee, and Kali cursed before hobbling toward Star. She wanted to check his leg, feel his knee, and make sure he was okay. She knew that Star didn't like being out so late and this had been particularly hard on him. She hoped that Mike would be all right to stop. The horses needed it.

Kali felt Star's face in the darkness, running her hands over his forehead and down his nose to the soft, velvety tip.

He gave his friendly growl, his lips and chin quivering as he talked quietly to her.

She kissed the side of his face, tasting the salt on his hide, and she promised him a cortisone shot when they got home. It would bring new life to his knee again. Maybe for her as well.

"We need to go," Tracy suddenly announced in the dark.

"Tracy, everyone is exhausted. Including the horses. We need to give them a break," she said, but he was already making moves to leave.

"We need to keep on. They need us at home."

"Is everything okay at the house?" she asked. Something nagged at her, yet she was so numb and muddled she couldn't imagine anything else happening.

"Everything at the house is fine, but we need to get going."

Kali laughed in exhaustion. "Toby is not going to make it with the two of us riding him. You know it, Tracy. He needs a break."

"Fine. You're right. I'll walk and lead him while you ride. You can't walk, and Star can't carry you," he said.

Before she could protest, Kali jumped when she felt Jeremy step beside her, breathing against her neck.

"I need to walk a little and stretch my legs," Jeremy said. His voice seemed unnaturally loud in the dark. "I'll lead Duchess while you ride. That way, Tracy can scout ahead if he needs."

Kali wanted to scream. To her astonishment, Tracy agreed. He seemed too distracted or preoccupied to care that Jeremy was standing next to her. It was dark, but Kali was sure he was leering. He wasn't even touching her, but she could feel his hands on her. She shuddered. "I can—"

"Kali!" Tracy snapped. "We've got no time for your tomfoolery or constant backtalk. We need to go."

Kali tried to swallow the lump caused by Tracy's words while not choking on the scream when Jeremy lifted her off her feet and placed her in the saddle. Kali hated it. He picked her up as though she was a child without any say, but she was helpless—emotionally and physically.

She wondered if she was losing her mind. She had always believed Tracy had her back, no matter what, but it was as if he'd forgotten exactly what he'd seen just hours before. It made her feel slightly sick.

She squeezed her eyes shut and fought back her emotions and the memories—Jeremy on top of her, smiling at her, loving the fact that she couldn't fight him.

She furrowed her brow as she petted Duchess. She could feel Jeremy looking at her, thinking about her, and she went rigid. This man had tried to violate her, shake her from her world, and take everything from her.

A quiet rage began to well up inside her.

Nicky never would have stood for that. It didn't matter how large or powerful Jeremy thought he was. Nicholas Jorgenson would have whipped him. He would have beaten his ass for touching her.

She missed him so much.

Jeremy whistled as they moved through the dark.

The prick was enjoying himself. She wanted nothing more than to kick his head off his shoulders.

It had been a very long time since she had ached for Nicky the way she had tonight. When Jacks turned her head in a certain way or Brooke said something particular or Danni would smile that lazy smile of hers . . . they were so much like him in so many ways. When she saw Nicky in his girls, she was reminded of him in the best of ways, but riding on Duchess, being led by a man who had almost ripped her clothes off, not far behind Tracy, who could not have cared less, she wanted Nicky.

She looked down at her hands, at her nails biting half moons into her palms, and she tried to loosen her grip but couldn't. The memory of what happened paralyzed her. It consumed her. The fact that she wasn't powerful enough to bring him to his knees, that she was vulnerable . . . she wasn't ready to accept it.

Kali was numb. The whole day—the helicopter, the stampede, the attack, it was all starting to feel surreal. What Jeremy had done was unforgivable, but what Tracy had done hurt worse.

As light began to filter in against the blackened sky, she watched the back of his figure. Tracy Sommers had always been one of the bravest men she'd known. Loyal, faithful, honest, and not afraid to speak his mind—he had never been one to back away from a confrontation, but after everything they had been through together, Tracy had taken the side of Jeremy over Kali. More than anything, Kali felt betrayed.

* * * *

He remembered a time he had gone dancing with Sarah. She had worn a thin white, cotton dress with tiny blue flowers sewn around the hem and the neckline. He had made a few remarks about the flowers, and they had laughed because they had both known he wasn't talking about the dress at all but her beautiful neckline.

He couldn't remember the song that played, not that he had even been aware of it at the time. He had wanted to scoop her up in his arms and run out the back door with her, but he hadn't. He had held her hand properly, holding her close but not too close, and tried to talk about the room filled with people, the dance, and her dress with tiny blue flowers.

She had smelled so sweet, and when they turned, he had felt her hair—a kind of reddish color he'd never found the right description for but knew it to be the prettiest color he had ever seen—brush over his hand and wrist. It was heaven.

Sarah had been the only gal for him.

He had been on the rodeo circuit for much of his life and had had many conquests. It was a fact he had once been proud of until he'd met Sarah.

Because she had been so tender, so sweet, so loving, he'd often wondered if he had done those others wrong in some way or if he had been wronged himself. He hadn't known how strong the love of a good woman could make a man feel. Or be.

They'd had plans—she'd let him finish out the season, and then they would settle down. With an engagement ring on her finger, he had been committed. Completely. He had loved her so much that when she had talked about how her kitchen would look, or how many children she wanted, it hadn't scared him. It had filled him up.

One trip to the doctor had changed all that.

Tracy rubbed his eyes. They burned from dust, sand, and lack of sleep. They burned from the feeling of sudden moisture mixing in, and as much as he tried to fight it, as strong as he was, he couldn't stop the tears. He had loved Sarah so much.

It was something he had always wanted to say to Kali but couldn't. Or wouldn't. He understood what it was like to have a life mapped out, to have plans and hopes and dreams only to have it all taken away. But when Sarah had been diagnosed with cancer, they had been given some time to grieve together. Kali wasn't given any time, and honestly, Tracy couldn't decide which was worse. So he had never spoken of Sarah. It had been so long ago.

He had gone back to his old ways, busting wild horses by day and dogging women at night. It had been a way to forget. Or heal. Actually, his reasons didn't matter because the end result had been the same. There would never be another Sarah.

Tracy thought about that particular night and his face flushed. They had been dancing when he'd spotted some of his buddies from the circuit. He had given them a wave and, when the song was over, led Sarah by the hand toward the bar. Together, they had stood talking. Compliments had been given to Sarah in the off-handed way he had expected.

What's a beauty like you doing with this old dog?

She's pretty . . . too bad she can't see.

He had been a good sport about it all because it was true—Sarah was too good to be true.

When Burleson had asked to dance with Sarah, he hadn't objected. Burleson was a good sort, and Tracy had known him for years so he'd hung back, talking to the guys about this and that.

As he recalled, Toby White had strutted in with a girl who just about every man in the bar had been with. White thought he had the Virgin Mary on his arm. And they had all laughed.

He had looked for Sarah but couldn't find her. Both Burleson and Sarah were gone from the dance floor. At first, he hadn't worried as he scanned the crowd. Then panic had set in.

There was this thing they did. There wasn't a name for it and he couldn't explain when, why, or how it had started, but when one of the guys had a pretty little gal, you did whatever you could to get her with you. You'd take her around the corner and kiss and love on her and whisper whatever sweet nothings came to mind to get her to forget the other guy.

Sarah was different. Sarah was off-limits.

He had cursed and asked anyone and everyone if they had seen Burleson when Jimmy Cabeen made a joke about Burleson stealing away with her. Tracy had punched him full in the face, knocking the little bastard out. He had been in full panic and headed for the back door.

Tracy had thrown the door open to find Sarah pinned against a pickup truck. Her body had been arched back in an uncomfortable manner, her face turned to the side, eyes closed as she tried to push against Burleson, and Tracy exploded.

Even as Tracy walked along with his horse, almost thirty years later, he could see Burleson's face when he'd thrown him to the side. He still remembered the look on her face. She had been so happy and relieved to see Tracy. She had just reached a point of desperation, that point when she'd known she couldn't hold him off any longer, and her mind had been racing, trying to escape.

He couldn't imagine not being able to fight against Burleson because he had pounded him harder than he'd ever ridden any animal or fought another man. When he was pulled from Burleson's cowering body, he had wanted to beat every man there until he'd seen Sarah crying against the truck. And from that moment on, he had clung to her like a faithful hound dog. He had quit the circuit and never thought much about riding again until she died. During that time, he had heard that Burleson had retired after some of the damage Tracy Sommers had done to him. Tracy hadn't cared and never bothered to find out about the injuries.

He thought about Kali. She had had that look, and it had startled him. In truth, it shook him in his boots. He had never seen that look on Kali's face before—almost desperate, looking for an escape. When she had looked up, she was so thankful he had come, and it made Tracy sick to his stomach at the memory.

He had thought about killing Jeremy. He was a big ol' boy, but Tracy knew he could have whooped up on the boy in a manner he had never experienced, even on the gridiron. Fact was, Tracy hadn't even entertained the idea of using his fists. Jeremy simply wasn't worth it. Tracy had felt an itch in his hand to lift his rifle and blow the prick's head off. Only maturity and reason had stopped him, but he couldn't stop thinking about the expression on Kali's face. He never wanted to see that again.

As he walked, his heart still beat with rage, and he wondered what Jeremy's motive had been. Of course, Kali was gorgeous. Any man could see that. But, out there, with Mike injured and all hell breaking loose, Tracy couldn't help but wonder if there had been some bet between Jeremy and his football buddies. He could imagine the conversation as he had partaken in similar ones so many times himself.

He felt a twinge of guilt.

Seeing Kali on the ground, so vulnerable and presumably part of some game, Tracy had felt more disgusted than mad. He could barely look at her. It was a funny place he was in. He was sorry as hell he had seen what he saw but eternally grateful he showed up when he had.

Then there was the phone call about the girls.

God, help us.

He had bitten Kali's head off in his quest to press on. He had seen the look of surprise and hurt on her face and feelings of Sarah rushed to the surface. He wanted to hold her and tell her he was sorry, but that just wasn't something one did with Kali Jorgenson, so he'd hollered at her to keep her going instead. He couldn't tell her what he knew about the girls. He couldn't say anything. All he could do was move forward. The sooner they got to Rainwash Ranch, the sooner they could start to mend things and get rid of Jeremy Connors.

Chapter Twenty-Four

Casey Dillon slammed down the phone and flopped back in her chair, forgetting the hard clip in her hair. She winced and jerked it out. "Shit!" Casey swept her bangs out of her eyes, and using her fingertips, pulled her skin tight. She looked at Luther Monroe.

The pressure made her lips and eyes stretch, and Luther smiled.

"Shit, shit, shit!"

"Troubles?" He raised an eyebrow at Casey, taking a seat across from her.

Casey dropped her head to the desk with a hard thud. Her hair sprawled out, her hands flailed, and she sighed.

Luther never said a word.

When she looked up again, he smiled, and she snarled, which only made his smile broaden.

There were many who misunderstood her relationship with Luther. He'd even been accused of having a thing for the assistant prosecuting attorney when in actuality, he was happily married.

A tall, slightly heavy man, Luther Monroe was one of only a handful of black attorneys in Houston's legal system. A former football player, he stood out more for his appearance than his legal prowess, but it was no secret he was determined to change that.

When Casey heard he'd drawn the Connors case with her, she had been excited. She knew his reputation and hoped he was new enough that he might not yet know of her own reputation as the Ice Queen. *Ice Queen* was just one of her many names, but Luther hadn't appeared to care.

Fact was, Casey had no time or interest in the men of Houston, hence the nickname. The Ice Queen was rumored to be a man-hater, a lesbian, bisexual, even asexual. Luther never questioned any of it. Instead, he'd taken her into his home and his family had basically adopted Casey. Luther's wife had often fed them during all-night sessions and never appeared threatened or concerned about the long hours her husband kept with Casey. She adored his children, and for the first time in years, she'd had a place for go for the holidays.

It had been during one such visit that Casey had broken her own cardinal rule and shared some brief, but factually to the point back history with Luther and his wife, Vanessa. A drunk driver had crossed the median and killed her brother right in front of her. Casey and her family had later learned it has been his fourth drunk driving offense, and the second time he had killed a person. His initial murder had been pled down to involuntary manslaughter, and he'd served only minimal time as a first time offender.

The nation had not yet started cracking down on drunk drivers. After he'd killed Joe, David Mifflin had been convicted but served only seven years.

Luther and Vanessa had been appalled by the light sentence, but Casey had simply shrugged. As she had spoken about the laws and Mifflin's parole hearings, Luther had connected the dots—Joe's death was the basis for Casey's compulsion for detail and obsession with the law. At the tender age of nine, the law had failed her, and she had resolved to make it work for others.

She knew exact dates, times, places, and kept everything neatly filed in her brain. She was methodical, precise, and orderly. Some might have called it obsessive compulsive, but she called it preparedness. Nothing had prepared Casey for the Connors case, however.

Everything was falling apart, and Luther only laughed as Casey flung herself back down on her desk.

Their star witness was dead—murdered. There were no leads. Jeremy Connors had the world as his alibi. Carmen Hernandez was suddenly very quiet and very wealthy, and no one else was talking.

Jackson, Keller & Whiteman hadn't wasted any time filing a motion to dismiss. As speculation continued to swirl around Jessica Stanten's character, it was becoming increasingly clear that Connors was going to walk.

She kept her body slumped over but rested her chin on the desk so she could look up at Luther and sighed. "That was homicide in Shreveport, a Detective Regan Phillips. We've got nothing. The roommate, Caroline Peters, is conscious but can't help." Casey sighed again and sat back in her chair. "Whatever description she's given of the assailant, it's a far cry from Connors. Medium build, husky, chubby—*maybe*—brown hair, tanned or possibly Hispanic." She looked up at the ceiling and studied the pattern as she fought slamming her head back down on her desk. "We've got nothing."

"No mention of Connors during the attack?" Luther asked.

"Nope."

"No possible friendship between the attacker and Connors?"

"Not that anyone knows about."

"DNA?"

"At the moment . . . unknown. But certainly not Connors', which is all I care about." Casey looked back at Luther and clasped her hands together. "I can't believe this is happening. I just talked to her." She thought she might cry.

That poor girl had been through so much—more than most could even imagine, much less endure, but Jessica had repeatedly told her the only thing keeping her going and reasonably sane were Casey's reassurances that they would show the world what a horrible monster Jeremy Connors was and clear Jessica's name. More importantly, illustrate why celebrities and athletes should not get away with murder—literally and figuratively.

Initially, Casey had taken the case because she'd wanted to right a wrong. Like Jessica, she had been sick of watching celebrities get preferential treatment within the legal system. She was sick of watching moms on welfare get twenty years for unknowingly carrying drugs for some boyfriend while the rich and famous got slaps on the wrists for heinous crimes. She had been more than willing to go after Jeremy Connors before she'd known much about him, but as she had delved into his personal life and read his own words about his upbringing and slam dunks against women, she had been repulsed and infuriated. He was a monster of his own making, and one she was all too happy to bring down.

Sportscasters glorified Connors' actions in their reports. Magazines wrote articles praising his female conquests. Teammates and coaches honored his behavior calling him a role model and a hero.

A *hero*?

Not a person who saved lives or fought for our country but someone who played football. That was their hero, and they were willing to forgo morality to preserve the bottom line image they had of Jeremy Connors.

Casey was a good judge of character, and she had believed Jessica from the beginning . . . even when the ex-boyfriend had come into play. She had looked into Jessica's eyes and watched her struggle for composure when she talked about the night in the hotel room. When Jessica talked about how Connors had ripped off her clothing and thrown her against the bed and floor, Casey had looked away. The pain had been too raw, too real. And when Jessica repeated what Connors had said, the names he'd called her, Casey had felt the heat rise in her cheeks and tamped her initial, emotional want for revenge back down. She had wanted more for Jessica. She wanted to make things right. She wanted justice.

Casey rubbed her head and thought about her last meeting with Jessica.

"How do they keep finding me?"

The tears had poured down Jessica's cheeks, and Casey could tell she had been crying for some time. Although she was still lovely, Jessica had changed physically. She'd looked tired and drawn.

"Do you want to stop?" Casey wouldn't have blamed Jessica after all the scrutiny.

"No, I can't! That's what they want me to do, but I didn't do anything wrong. I didn't do anything wrong!"

Casey and Luther had discussed Jessica's need for some kind of apology and worried that if Connors stepped forward to say he was sorry, she might have dropped the case, but his ego was too huge and his lawyers were too cocky to give in that easily.

That prick, Mike Waters, from Jackson, Keller & Whiteman had twice *accidentally* used Jessica's name in the press when they had identified her previous workplace and the name of her ex-boyfriend. After that, any jackass with a computer and Internet access had been able to track her down. It had been terrifying, and the prosecutor's office had considered plea bargains as well as putting Jessica in a safe house.

"I don't want anything that belongs to him," Jessica had said. "I want him in jail. I want him to never be able to do this to another woman. You weren't there, Casey. You didn't see his face. He is sick. He enjoyed it. He . . . he loved doing what he did to me. He's done it before, and he'll do it again."

Those words had haunted Casey.

Now Jessica Stanten was dead, and even though there was no evidence linking Jeremy Connors to her death, he'd had a hand in it. Casey had to prove it.

"So what now?" Luther's deep voice broke her train of thought and she looked back at him.

"He's done it before, and he'll do it again," she said.

Luther looked puzzled then his face smoothed, and he understood, nodding in agreement.

"So . . . we just have to find someone else."

Luther shook his head. "Won't happen. You saw the hell that Jessica went through. What other woman will come forward now?"

The lawyers at Jackson, Keller & Whiteman had done a fine job of locking this one up. They had made sure that everyone watched the hell of going against a celebrity like Jeremy Connors unfold every night in their very own living rooms. Luther was right. No woman would subject herself to the kind of torture Jessica Stanten had endured.

The phone rang.

"Casey Dillon."

"Ms. Dillon, Detective Phillips again. Hey, listen. I just thought of this . . . I'm sure you've already seen it and dealt with it, but we found the website where Jeremy Connors talked about Jessica Stanten."

"Uh, what website?" she asked, reaching for a pen. She was already well aware of the various websites complaining about Jessica Stanten. Still, anything was worth looking into. Especially if it was new.

"It was on her computer when we found her."

Casey froze, staring at Luther. "What computer? Jessica's?" Casey asked, and Luther searched her face.

"Yeah, right there in her apartment. We don't know if she was on it or if the attacker logged on. Can't tell yet, but it's looking like he responded to the web . . . some kind of chat room."

There was a break in the dialogue, and Casey heard a muffled voice in the background.

"I'm not too savvy on this kind of stuff . . . all new to me, but my partner tells me there are chat rooms and boards where you can post messages."

"Yes," she said amazed that he could still be this *un*-savvy.

"There was a message posted. 'The bitch is dead.' That posted within an hour of her attack."

"What?" Casey sprung forward in her seat. Her heart sank.

"I thought I'd contact you, just in case . . . doesn't sound like you knew?"

"No! Didn't have a clue. What . . . what is the website again?" She jotted it down and repeated it twice to make sure she had it right.

Luther came around the corner of her desk, rolled her chair to the side, and logged on her laptop as she continued speaking with Phillips.

"Who's the host?" she asked.

Phillips repeated the question to his partner. "It's a sports fan website but we're looking into who the webmaster is."

Casey knew that he was simply relaying information, not at all sure of what he was saying. Luther nudged her and her face fell.

There was a picture of what was supposed to be Jessica Stanten, spread-eagled, a miniskirt hiked over her hips, ankles bound in some manner to what appeared to be the legs of the table she was bent over. It didn't matter that it was a body double. The image was revolting.

Casey squeezed her eyes shut, the first two words of the caption burned in her mind.

DING DONG.

She knew the rest without looking—*the bitch is dead*.

She turned in her chair, putting her back to the image, her computer, and Luther as her voice turned cold. "The minute you find the webmaster, you let me know."

There was a certain undeniable irony that Jessica Stanten, a former national athlete and fierce competitor who had committed her life to sports, was being portrayed in such a horrible manner by athlete wannabes—pathetic, pissant, fat-bellied weekend warriors who had never gone beyond their local high school in sports and lived vicariously through the acts of others who were willing to make sport of a fine athlete just because she was a woman who dared to be raped by a superstar.

All Casey could think about was the sound of Jessica's voice. *"I didn't do anything wrong. I didn't do anything wrong."*

She felt sick.

No sooner had Casey stood up than Luther took her chair. He was transfixed.

She heard him clicking on various links and investigating every aspect of the site. She couldn't do it. She knew she would have to reach a point where she could look at the picture objectively and professionally . . . just not yet.

"You okay?" Luther asked.

"No. And I'm not gonna be for a long time, Luth." She reached for her gym bag, careful not to look at the monitor, and as she left the small office, she whispered to Luther. "If it's the last thing I ever do, he's going down. Mark my words, Luther. I will bring him down." And she was gone.

Chapter Twenty-Five

After the last twenty-four hours, it was laughable that Sam had ever honestly believed they could escape the drama of the Connors case.

He watched Kali work a young stallion from the front porch of the main house. Axel was a recent rescue horse from the great Utah plains. He was completely wild and unwilling to be touched in any way, but there was Kali, using Mouse to move him nice and easy around the pen. It was a painstakingly slow process that didn't seem to faze Kali.

Over and over, they worked the same drill so that Axel would understand what was being asked of him. Sam would have thrown his hands up long ago, but Kali kept after it. She was amazing. Simply amazing.

Until that morning, if someone had asked Sam who held the Jorgenson family together, he would have bet money on Ms. Kat. She was the matriarch of the clan, after all, but ever since Kali had stopped talking, the entire ranch had been flipped upside down.

Everyone was miserable.

Wade tiptoed around Kali even though he was the one who had been shot at. The general feeling was that he was afraid he reminded her of what had almost happened, so he was in hiding.

Jacks had recovered quickly from the notion that she had almost shot Uncle Wade's head off, but children were like that.

It had been Kali's final say on the rodeo that had devastated everyone. No rodeo. The very thing the twins had worked so hard for, the reason for music blaring from the loudspeakers so early in the mornings, the plans and late-night talks about winning championships were all gone, for this year anyway. Evan and Stephen had pleaded with Kali to reconsider. The girls were sorry and realized how dangerous their decision had been, but no amount of pleading or begging would change Kali's mind.

She was a solitary figure, working the horses, in her own world, while the rest of the household held its collective breath.

Since their return to Rainwash, she ate her meals in her room, kept to herself, and continued to limp around, daring anyone to suggest that she stop. She told them she loved them, kissed them good night, gave them a daily list of chores, but said little else in the form of instruction. Otherwise, she remained in the barn.

Sam wondered if she even knew or cared that the group would be leaving soon. But then, why would she? They had only brought chaos with them.

Whatever fantasy Sam had deluded himself with had been pulled away when the wheels of the Jeremy Connors case were set in a new motion.

Sam had left explicit instructions that they should only be contacted in case of emergency. Only Lisa and family members had known about Rainwash—at least, until Perry had pulled his pea-brained stunt. So when a lone FedEx truck had ambled onto the ranch, Sam's heart had fallen.

They had returned to the ranch just in time to learn that prosecuting attorney Casey Dillon had filed new charges, including evading the police and making the whereabouts of Jessica Stanten known. She alleged that not only had the firm of Jackson, Keller & Whiteman leaked details after a gag order, but that Samuel Spann and Mike Waters specifically had willfully and purposefully endangered Jessica Stanten's life, and their disclosure of information had directly contributed to her death. There had also been an inference that the Connors camp was responsible for the "Kill Jessica" website. The district attorney's office charged that Jackson, Keller & Whiteman were responsible as well.

"Do you like your job as a lawyer?"

Sam turned to see Jacks settled into an oversized rocking chair next to him on the porch. He looked back out at the pen and Kali, and smiled. "Yes."

"But you don't like Mr. Connors."

He saw her turn toward him out of the corner of his eye and would have laughed, but he knew that she was perfectly serious. She had been paying attention.

"Well, I'm not paid to like someone," he said as he faced her. Her eyes were wide and innocent, full of wonder, and as blue as the open skies. "I'm paid to do my job."

"Momma says that when you work with someone you have to have respect. Without respect, you're not really working together. Axel makes her mad, but she respects him so that way he won't hurt her. Do you think Mr. Connors would hurt you?"

He pursed his lips and gave an exaggerated look of concern to show he was really thinking about that question. It was a good question. "Well, I guess I never really thought about it like that," he said. It was the only answer he could give because, truth was, he knew Jeremy could hurt him—not physically but certainly professionally.

"You should pretend that Mr. Connors is a wild mustang," she said with a little smile.

It struck Sam that he would miss more than just Kali when they pulled out. He would miss the girls. He had never considered himself to be kid-friendly, but he liked these girls. They were different from most kids he had been around.

"How is Mr. Waters?" she asked, not waiting for the answer. "Momma says he's coming back tomorrow. She said his shoulder got separated from his body." She shivered.

"Yes." Sam rocked back in his chair and turned his gaze back on Kali.

She had drawn even with the mustang as Mouse trotted next to him, rounding out bigger and bigger circles in the pen. The young horse seemed to be settling in, though his ears moved back and forth as he watched everything. Kali was careful never to lean to one side or move suddenly. Her body was calm yet board stiff. Only her head moved, and Sam imagined she was talking to the young stallion.

"He's coming back tomorrow, just in time for us to pack up and go." Sam furrowed his brow. He hadn't meant to sound quite so sad. He peeked at Jacks and wondered if Kali knew they were leaving.

"Yeah, Momma said you were leaving."

Sam turned his attention completely on Jacks for the first time.

She had settled back into her chair, pulling her legs up against her chest, and watched her mother work the horse before sighing heavily.

"I'm sorry about your competition," Sam said.

She shrugged, but he saw the sadness in her motion.

"It was my fault," she said nonchalantly.

Sam knew better.

A light breeze carried over the porch, refreshing him, and reawakening his feelings about the ranch. He felt a tug at his heart. It was amazing to him that he felt so emotionally tied to any one place, particularly one he had been to for such a brief period of time.

He rocked back and looked up at the overhang's crossbeams. "Gorgeous." He admired the texture of the wood, its pattern, and the design.

"Mom?" Jacks turned toward Sam, squinting and shielding part of her face against the bright clouds before leveling a hard stare.

He looked back. "Um, no. I was talking about this . . . the porch, the house." A slow smile spread over his face. "But your mom is also gorgeous."

"I knew you liked her," Jacks said flatly. It wasn't an accusation. It was what it was.

"I seem to recall you telling me to back off," Sam squinted back at her. "And you weren't very nice about it."

"Yeah." She turned to watch her mother again.

Kali had turned Mouse away from the mustang and headed toward the gate.

To Sam's surprise, the mustang followed, and he wondered if Kali knew that would happen.

Evan was leaning on the gate telling Kali something, and she turned, spotting him, but the wild horse was uncertain about getting any closer and stopped in the middle of the pen, watching both her and Mouse.

"Not that it really matters because I'm leaving tomorrow, but why? Why didn't you want me talking to your mom? Don't you like me?"

"Not really."

Sam laughed and almost choked. He hadn't expected such candor and turned to admire the girl. If only more people were like Jacks Jorgenson. "What did I ever do to you?" he joked.

"Well, it's not you. It's what you do."

"A lawyer?" he asked, leaning forward slightly.

"Defending Mr. Connors. He's a bad man," Jacks said, still watching her mother.

"Ah, that would come from your mom. She doesn't care for Jeremy too much." He nodded. A mother filling her child with ideas was to be expected.

Kali had dipped her head, looking back at the stallion, coaxing him forward. Her silky ponytail had flipped forward, resting on her collarbone.

"No, not Momma. She doesn't talk about it. Especially after what he did to her."

Sam turned to her again. "Who did what? What are you talking about?"

But Jacks shrugged, tilting her chin up in a manner he had seen before.

He would never get any information out of her and his mind was reeling. *Did what?* He thought about Ms. Kat's sudden visit to their room the day before. Sam and Ed had agreed that, under the circumstances, they needed to leave and regroup back at the office, but her polite suggestion had shocked them both. Learning that Perry, the little ass, had been behind the helicopter fiasco had been an embarrassment, and they had assured Ms. Kat that he would be paying for any damages. They had just assumed Ms. Kat's request was more about preventing the media from swarming their peaceful town and ranch. It hadn't occurred to him until that moment that there might be another reason she wanted them to leave.

He tried to play along with Jacks. "Oh, that. Yeah, I guess that's why your grandmother asked us to leave."

"Yeah." Jacks continued to rock in her chair.

The side door opened, and Danni stepped on the porch. She sighed when she saw her sister.

"Didn't you hear me calling?" she asked.

Jacks turned toward her, shaking her head. "I was watching Momma."

Danni eyed Sam suspiciously.

"She's working that new mustang, Axel."

Danni looked toward the corral.

While Jacks wore jeans, boots, and a button-down shirt with the sleeves rolled up, Danni wore a little tank top with a horse across the front, jean cut-offs, flip-flops, and a baseball cap.

Sam smiled at the "girl power" embroidery on the bill. "And we were talking about what happened with your mom . . . you know, between her and Mr. Connors." Sam tried to sound casual.

Danni glanced nervously toward Jacks, and Jacks frowned. "We weren't talking about it." She leaned forward in her chair, and he felt her blue eyes boring holes into him. "We're not supposed to know anything about it, so you can't say."

"Right." He glanced from Jacks to Danni. "Well, I know how I know, but how do you guys know about it?"

"Danni overheard Tracy telling Ms. Kat. He was super mad." Jacks turned to Danni for conformation.

Danni nodded, still watching Sam cautiously.

"He's just lucky Tracy didn't kill him. He would've, you know?" Jacks gave a hard nod.

Sam pushed out his lower lip, as though he were considering that possibility. He could see that it was important to the girls that he know Tracy was a stand-up guy.

"That's why I said you should treat Mr. Connors like a wild mustang 'cause if you don't watch him, he'll stomp and kick the heck out of you. He's mean and underhanded," Jacks said, giving Sam fair warning, but Danni frowned.

"No way can you compare him to a horse. Horses are like a million times better than him!"

Sam nodded thoughtfully. "Well, Jer . . . Mr. Connors shouldn't have done what he did. We'll be talking to him about it."

Kali had hopped down from Mouse, removing his bridle and saddle, and slipped between the bars to stand outside the pen with Evan and Stephen. The trio had presumably been discussing the mustang when Evan and Kali turned and headed toward the main house. Stephen had been left with stalling Mouse.

Sam licked his lips and felt the conversation slipping away from him.

"I don't think you're supposed to do that." Danni looked toward her mother as Kali narrowed the gap between herself and the girls. "No one is supposed to know."

"Then how am I supposed to take care of things?" Sam wondered out loud. He was genuinely curious.

"Duh." Jacks rolled her eyes. "You're supposed to get him out of here before he does it again, like, to Aunt Gina or Aunt Tammi." Jacks turned to her sister and both girls giggled. "Can you imagine if Mr. Connors attacked Aunt Gina? Uncle Evan would kill him for sure."

Danni nodded. "I hate him." She linked her arm with her sister, pulled her up, and they hurried inside still laughing about Uncle Evan.

As Kali's foot hit the first step of the porch, Sam's mouth still hung open. *Attacked?*

Kali nodded politely. "Mr. Spann," she said, limping past the slack-jawed, blinking blob that once was him and into the house.

* * * *

Lunch came and went with Ms. Kat's marvelous cooking and nary a word from Kali. She periodically made eye contact but nothing like he had seen on the trail. He wanted more. He wanted to hear her laugh, see her smile, and listen to the silly banter between Kali and her brothers-in-law. It seemed so little to ask and yet it appeared to be too much. He had scoffed at the notion of love at first sight for most of his adult life, but he had been completely smitten with Kali from the moment she appeared on horseback.

He knew he had to get back to Houston to face more unpleasant business from Casey Dillon, but they could not leave until Dr. Thom had brought Mike back to the ranch. It was a small town mentality that Sam appreciated and hoped would give him the time he needed to find out what had happened between Jeremy and Kali.

Jeremy had only shrugged at the helicopter incident, saying he knew nothing about it, and that was that. No deep apologies for Perry's actions. No sense of responsibility or ownership for his part. Instead, he'd spent most of his time with Roderick and Garret up in the game room. This was all just another speed bump for Jeremy. Nothing more.

After making polite noises about helping clean and being shooed out of the way, Sam made his way toward the game room. As soon as his hand hit the iron railing, he heard them. Sam climbed the giant tree trunk staircase and the steady thump and bump of the bass beat grew louder and felt as if it was coming out his chest. He stepped onto the landing and found Roderick kicked back on the large leather sofa and watching the wide-screen television. He had managed to find a raunchy music video station and was talking appreciatively to the screen full of bikini-clad women with wide hips and even larger breasts dancing around men singing rap.

Sam groaned—correction, that wasn't singing. It was robbery is what it was. The men were attempting to rap along with an old classic they had obviously bought the rights to so that they could rewrite the chorus, chiming together about sex and more sex.

While Roderick's head bobbed and weaved to the music as though it was creative genius, Garret leaned forward in his seat sighing and moaning at the gyrating women. No one seemed to care that the group had no real talent and couldn't have written an original tune to save their careers.

Jeremy was more interested in Sam, however, and as Sam stepped forward, he leaned against the bar and grinned. "Oh, good. The cavalry."

Several months ago, Jeremy had obviously heard someone make a *here comes the cavalry* comment and thought it terribly clever so he'd started with his own.

As always, Sam gave a half nod and a polite smile. "Yep, that's me."

"Drink?" Jeremy waggled a bottle in front of Sam.

"Sure, why not?"

Jeremy's eyebrows seemed to jump to life as they popped halfway up his forehead . "I didn't think you drank." He dug a beer out of the counter refrigerator and popped open the lid. "Least not while you're on a case."

"Well, I'm in between, you could say." Sam took a pull off the bottle and slid onto an oversized bar stool. He leaned back into the arms and sighed. The beer tasted good.

Jeremy nodded and they drank in silence a few moments longer.

"You know, we're in full damage control right now," Sam said.

Jeremy looked around the room. "Right now?" He tried to grin and make light of the situation.

Sam didn't smile. "I've got people right now trying to figure out our next move, Jeremy. Shit." Sam shook his head. "This isn't funny."

The room pulsated with Roderick's music, and Jeremy absentmindedly bobbed his head as Sam watched him, trying to recall just how he had become involved with him. The case had seemed so simple in the beginning, but every week something more unpleasant about the man's character, or lack thereof, had come across his desk. Paternity suits, sexual harassment, barroom brawls, street fights, punching fans, spouting off to the press, flipping off cameramen. It had seemed never ending, but Perry had been Sam's biggest pain.

The pasty, little ass had been trouble and vying for some kind of authority with Jeremy against the legal team from the start. The full-time staff Jackson, Keller & Whiteman had assigned to Jeremy was nothing more than a threat in Perry's eyes. It had been Perry who devised all the publicity stunts that caused more headaches for the defense. But the helicopter incident had been too much. Sam was inclined to believe Jeremy's innocence in this case, but Perry had to go—at least, until the case was over.

Sam took another long pull off the bottle and said as much. Jeremy shifted his attention back to Sam, and the two studied each other.

Finally, Jeremy relented with a slow nod. "Sure, chief. Whatever you say."

"It's just that I don't like being blindsided."

"I got that. No problem. He's gone." He snapped his fingers to illustrate how easily Perry could be replaced.

Sam nodded and cleared his throat, slipping into his professional voice. "And I need to know what happened between you and Kali Jorgenson."

Jeremy gave a look of mock innocence. It was meant to be cute, like everything else Jeremy did when it came to women and his little 'indiscretions,' as he put it.

Sam could feel his jaw set.

"What's to tell?" Jeremy eyes twinkled.

Sam swallowed and thought about punching his face in. He'd probably get the crap beat out of him by Jeremy and his buddies after the first punch, but it would be worth it. "I don't like surprises, and yet, that's all I seem to get with you. No more, you hear? No more or I walk."

Jeremy chuckled and Sam exploded.

"I mean it!" He stood.

Behind him, the music suddenly stopped, and he could tell that both Roderick and Garret had turned to watch the other show.

"I don't see what you're getting so uptight about. It's over, man. I mean, isn't it? Isn't it pretty much a done deal, you know, with her . . . being killed? No witness, no complaint, no case, right?" Jeremy shot a look over Sam's shoulder to his buddies and then back to Sam. "What?" He set his drink down.

Sam wasn't sure what he had expected from Jeremy, but he wasn't prepared for the callous remarks regarding Jessica's brutal death. While Sam may be defending Jeremy in this case, he had hated hearing what had happened to Ms. Stanten.

He shook his head. "No. It's not over."

Garret and Roderick pitched in, offering their own brilliant vocabulary, and Sam was astounded. They had really believed with the death of Stanten it would be like old times again.

Sam raked his fingers through his hair and half-turned, squaring off with the three men. "The DA's office is still prosecuting, Jeremy. This isn't over."

Jeremy's entire demeanor changed. "That bitch!" he spat. He paced back and forth behind the bar.

"Excuse me?" Sam almost laughed. He couldn't believe the level of denial. "You're blaming *her* for being murdered?"

"No! It's that other—Casey . . . what's her name? Dillon? Yeah. Casey Dillon. I knew she was a bitch the second I saw her. Little tight ass, snot-nosed bitch, thinkin' she's better than—"

"It's a total setup, man," Garret said. "It's bullshit. That chick's dead. There's no reas—"

"Little whore!" Jeremy was fuming as if the news was some kind of terrible shock.

Sam was bewildered. "So, what? You thought this was it? We'd just go home, no more questions, no more legal worries?" Sam had to laugh at their ignorance. And arrogance. This was how it had always worked for them in high school, college, and throughout their professional careers. So why would this time be any different?

Roderick and Garret spoke in unison about their distaste for Dillon while Jeremy opened a new drink and tipped it back, silently digesting the news.

Finally, he whispered, "Shit."

"No more surprises. No more publicity stunts. No more fights or problems until all this is over, *capisce?*"

"Yeah, yeah." Jeremy nodded.

"So . . . Kali Jorgenson?" Sam leveled a hard stare at Jeremy.

There was no amusement as Jeremy simply shrugged then sighed. "She —" He glanced toward the stairs. "She's not my type."

There was a flicker of something in Jeremy's expression that made Sam check over his shoulder, and he saw Tracy moving across the room.

Chapter Twenty-Six

He scanned the chat room—all kinds of theories about everything. It was the last comment, however, that caught his eye. She wanted Jeremy herself, but she knew he would never have her. Casey Dillon was a good-looking woman, but was she Jeremy Connors material? His fingers glided along the keyboard as he poured out his feelings. The words came easily and quickly. There was so much that he felt, so much that he wanted to share, and his fingers simply could not keep up with his brain.

Everything about her irritated him. She was a cold-hearted bitch who hadn't had a real man, probably any man, and couldn't deal with Jeremy's reputation. The idea of a man sweeping women off their feet, breezing in and out of different towns, able to have any woman he wanted, offended women like the Ice Queen.

He huffed. Even her nickname confirmed what a coldhearted, vindictive bitch she was.

He wanted to know everything about her—work hours, jogging routes, shopping routines . . . everything. He needed to know every detail about the little bitch so he could slowly crucify her, just as she was trying to do to Jeremy.

He examined the picture that had been taken by the photographer he hired for the website. It had been taken while she was jogging through a local park. She wore a half ponytail. The rest of her hair was too short to hold and fanned out around her neck. Her lips were pulled tight, and he could see the look of determination and concentration on her face.

He smiled. It would be so easy to come up behind her while she ran. She was completely focused on her exercise routine. That and the headphones she wore made her the perfect target.

She wore oversized men's shorts that made her legs look even scrawnier than they probably were. He studied her foot—heel down first. She ran heel-to-toe. A long-distance runner.

He looked at the small tank top that revealed her belly button and imagined how she might argue her clothing decision—it was hot outside or sleeves restricted movement. What he saw was an opportunity for her to show off her arms, abs, and tits—such as they were. Women never casually threw something on. Each and every piece of clothing they adorned served a purpose, and it was all for men. Since the Medieval times, women wiggled their hips, exposed their breasts, flirted, and smiled all for the sole purpose of a man. So what if a man took full advantage and took what was offered to him?

His fingers flew over the keyboard again. Woman was meant for man, and any woman who adorned herself, offered herself in suggestive ways to entice a man, was subject to his wants and needs.

Women like Dillon clomped around the courtroom, demanding respect and equality yet claimed foul when they were mistreated. They gave up everything for love and attention then cried rape when they didn't get it. It was absurd. Feminists loved Dillon. Men hated her. But it was just an act with little Miss Dillon.

He smiled, leaned back, and his finger lingered over the enter button. He was ready to launch the picture that said it all. For all the fans of the website and loyal defenders of the Jeremy cause, this was the image that said it all about Casey Dillon.

There were two pictures, actually, but it was the one of her seated that most interested him. The first had been taken through what he knew to be her bedroom window as she had been entertaining. Casey Dillon was a seductress in a small black teddy. She stood with a slight arch to her back, her hands pulling her hair up and off her neck, and giving delicious curves to her body. The lace cut high on her long legs, exposing more round, voluptuous hips than he would have given her credit for.

His smiled widened. He bet she smelled sweet.

Whatever the rumors about the Ice Queen had once been, this would dispel them. She was no lesbian. She was no man-hater. She might have issues with certain men, but her needs were just like any other woman's.

But it was the picture of her sitting on the edge of the bed, legs apart, back arched, head back, looking up at her partner that said it all. She wanted it. She wanted it bad.

He pushed send.

She wanted it. And he was going to see to it that she got it.

* * * *

He felt time slipping away but had no power to stop it. It was an empty, hollow feeling that he wasn't familiar or comfortable with. While Ed talked about getting home to friends, family, and the matters of the office, Sam was saddened at the prospect of leaving. What else was he but a lawyer, though? He had no steady companion, no kids, no pets, no social obligations. Twice he had gone back home to his parents, reaffirming the expression, "You can't go home." It's true when the one parent is a drunk and the other is angry and in denial. You can't go home.

He walked out toward the barn, wanting to say goodbye, but when he reached Lightning's stall, he paused. Can one really say goodbye to a horse that never wanted to be ridden in the first place? He felt a debt of gratitude toward the horse. Lightning had made his stay challenging, a little frightening and worrisome, but always fun. As far as horses go, he decided, Lightning was a good one.

Sam wandered around the giant barn taking in the smells and, for the first time, appreciating the satisfying aroma that could only be identified once you had worked with and enjoyed the company of a good horse.

He patted Star when he got to his stall. He hadn't ever heard the full story about Star, but Sam knew there was a special bond between the horse and his rider and his mind drifted toward Kali.

He sighed.

Kali Jorgenson was the thing Sam would miss most. He felt like there was so much more to learn about her and felt some impending sense of dread leaving her. It was insane and certainly nothing he could express to his bunkmates. She was different, special, and unlike any woman he had ever met.

Sam doubled back toward the training pen. The wild mustang's shadowy figure was there with his head dropped slightly and probably dozing. Axel exhausted himself throughout the days, fighting against every human and horse he came in contact with, but Kali had already made huge progress with him.

As Sam moved a little closer, Axel lifted his head slightly but stood his ground. Sam watched as his huge nostrils expanded and retracted, and his ears twitched and turned, honing in.

Kali.

Under the cover of night, the man and animal watched the woman who was both their dream and their angel as she moved gracefully across the compound toward her tree. She settled onto the bench wedged in the oak and leaned against the massive trunk. As she tilted her head back, looking up into the thick forest of leaves, she pushed a cigarette between her lips and let it hang for a moment before lighting it.

Initially, Sam thought Axel had moved because he'd stepped close, but he realized Axel had sensed Kali. The horse shifted toward the center of the pen, wanting to get a better look at Kali, and Sam withdrew into the mouth of the barn, not wishing to be detected. She never looked.

Her head was down, and Sam recognized the pose. By day, she was Super Woman—strong, opinionated, independent, and infuriatingly confrontational, but by night, in the quiet times, she appeared small, vulnerable, and extremely sad. As usual, her feet were drawn up to her chest, knees together with one arm wrapped around her legs, making her look even smaller. The arm that hugged her legs was also the hand that held the cigarette. Her other arm, her right arm, was used occasionally to stroke her arm, wipe the dust or flies near her face. He watched closely and Sam realized she wasn't waving off flies, she was wiping tears. He studied the glow of the cigarette, and it came to him.

Axel stomped his hoof impatiently, demanding to be seen.

Kali jerked upright. She spotted Axel first and a slight smile touched her lips, and then she saw Sam, and as quickly as it had appeared, it was gone.

Dammit!

Sheepishly, Sam stepped away from the barn and gave a half wave as he moved toward her. This wasn't how he'd pictured his last night at Rainwash going at all.

Axel stamped again.

Yeah. Thanks, buddy.

"I was just, uh, looking around. Taking a last look before shoving off," he said, wincing internally.

Kali bobbed her head once in acknowledgement and watched him carefully.

It was clear that she didn't want company, and it vexed him that he cared so much for someone he knew so little about, yet he was committed. Despite the reservations, he couldn't stop his thoughts and he wanted—no, *needed* just a little bit more of her time.

He decided to speak briefly then leave her to her own. "This place is addictive," he said when he finally reached her. He stopped right beside her.

"Thinking about becoming a rancher, Mr. Spann?" She smiled halfheartedly as she focused on her cigarette, clearly avoiding eye contact.

He studied her—her frame, her hair, her face. She was lovely. It didn't matter what she wore, how she wore it, what time of day it was. She was lovely. He chuckled softly. She would be appalled by that assessment. She was, by her own admission, an overgrown tomboy. *Lovely* was not in her repertoire.

"Maybe. It has its appeal. Where can I sign up to get a stretch of land and homestead just like this one?" he asked, and she laughed. A quiet, lonely kind of laugh.

"Oh, if I had a nickel for every time I've heard that." She dragged her fingers through her hair, looking off in the distance. "Sorry, Mr. Spann. This is a one-of-a-kind."

"True, indeed. I suspect that has a lot to do with the people." While his mouth made small talk, his mind was on other things. Even beneath an oversized shirt, he marveled at the curve of her hips and thighs. Her petite feet poked out from the frayed cuffs of her jeans, and he smiled. The flesh around her heels was callused and rough, no doubt from the combination of hours and hours inside work boots and walking barefoot around the compound. There was very little froufrou about her.

Froufrou, a word he hadn't even known existed until Danni and Jacks explained it meant being a girlie-girl obsessed with the perfect hair, makeup, and outfits.

"I'm not a froufrou girl," Danni had argued.

He had smiled. There had never been any doubt. None of the girls were *froufrou*, and that included their mother. Yet, standing next to Kali, Sam had to smile again. On each perfectly manicured toe was one bright pink flamingo.

"I, uh, like the flamingos." Sam grinned, and Kali curled her toes instinctively.

"Oh, those girls—" she said with a laugh. "I'm their guinea pig." She flipped her hair to the side and twisted to examine her own feet. Again, no eye contact. No smoking.

He continued to watch her—entranced. "Really? It's hard to imagine one of the twins playing with makeup." He moved closer to inspect her toes.

"First of all, nail polish isn't makeup. Let's be clear on that right now," she said and her playful tone did wonders for his soul. It was an instant shot of adrenaline. "Second, I'll have you know that Danni did this. She's pretty good. Personally, I wouldn't have gone for the flamingos, but she'd used everything else, so it was the bird or little flags." She shrugged. "We're saving those for the Fourth of July."

Sam laughed.

She was so damned cute. Sam had logged too many hours in the courtroom not to notice how nervous and uncomfortable she was as she played with her toes. He watched her a moment longer, enjoying her uneasiness. It wasn't often he got to see her so vulnerable.

Axel had made his way over to the railing nearest the gate and nuzzled it, purposefully making noises in the night. The young mustang seemed sure Kali was there to see him.

It was time for him to go. He knew it, but he needed to say it—to know. "You don't smoke."

"What?" She gave a small laugh, never looking up.

"You . . ." He pointed toward the cigarette she held so carefully in her hand. "You don't actually smoke, do you?"

It had been her routine the entire time he had been at Rainwash, and he never questioned it. Brooke had even confirmed the bad habit. But, on this last night, he had finally realized what had been puzzling about Kali and her smoking tree—she didn't smoke.

She looked up at him, and his world shifted. While it was clear she had regained much of her composure during their conversation, he saw the tear stains on her cheeks and the glistening in her eyes. He felt as though he'd been gut punched.

Her blue eyes had changed to a deep sapphire, and Sam wasn't sure if it was from the crying or the moonlight.

He opened his mouth to speak but had no words. She looked so unbelievably sad and vulnerable. And drop-dead, breathtakingly beautiful.

He wanted to pull her into his arms. Instead, he stood stock-still. Speechless. Helpless. In contrast, he was having an entire debate inside his own head. He wanted to say he was sorry. But for what? For watching her? For Jeremy? For disturbing her quiet? She looked so pained it nearly destroyed him.

She forced a smile and examined the cigarette she had been holding then leaned forward and smashed it into the ground.

He watched as she stood, shoved her hands in her back pockets, and rolled her shoulders back. He couldn't stop his eyes from dropping quickly down as her chest naturally poked out. Intellectually, he knew it was a position of posturing and power.

Kali lifted her chin in that way he had seen when she went toe-to-toe with Tracy or one of the brothers-in-law, but standing so close, her eyes burning a blue he had never seen, and trying so hard to look tough when she looked so fragile, he had to physically restrain himself from touching her.

"You got me," she said and walked off.

Chapter Twenty-Seven

As promised, Mike arrived by way of Dr. Thom's beat-up '67 Chevy truck with instructions for travel and the medications he required.

The Jorgensons were old hands at injuries and the embarrassment that usually followed, so they ribbed him in a way that Mike could appreciate. While Stephen and Matthew gave a hearty round of name-calling and fake punches to Mike's arm, Wade and Evan loaded everyone up.

Wade was set to take the lawyers back to the airport with Evan driving the second truck hauling the unusually quiet Jeremy and his posse. Reginald Perry was still recovering at the Methodist Hospital outside Salt Lake City. While Gina, Tammi, and the kids were all on hand for the final goodbyes, Ms. Kat and Tracy were noticeably absent, but it was not seeing Kali that was the most devastating.

Sam would have to settle for the mini-Kalis.

"Hey," he called out to Danni and smiled. Hands in her back pockets, chest poked out, and head cocked to the side, she was the spitting image of her momma. "I hear you're running out of pedicure stuff." He floundered for a moment, at a loss for the proper terminology. "You know, those little sticker things you put on toes and fingernails."

Danni's eyebrows lifted. She was clearly not even a little embarrassed that he'd discovered there was a froufrou side to her.

"When I get back home, I'm going to send you all kinds of different, uh, stickers and . . . stuff."

"Really?" she asked and clasped her hands together, giving a little hop.

Sam laughed. "You bet." He looked toward Jacks. "What do you like? Flamingos?"

Jacks rolled her eyes.

Brooke stepped forward, eyeing her little sisters with some annoyance. "We don't need anything, Mr. Spann."

Sam nodded patiently.

"We're just glad you liked it here."

"No, I want some more—"

Brooke pushed Danni and glared as her little sister muttered and stomped toward her twin.

"Thank you, Brooke. I appreciate that, but I really want to send you something. What can I send you?" As soon as he asked, he knew. "How about some books?"

Sam saw her glance sideways and smiled.

She cleared her throat and flicked her hair back, trying her best to look grown up. "You don't have to do that, Mr. Spann."

"Uh-huh. What do you like? Fiction? History?"

"Okay, let's get going," Evan's voice boomed across the compound. "We've got planes to catch. Everyone say your goodbyes!"

There was a sudden scuttle of people loading into various vehicles, while proper farewells and good-hearted gibes were sent back and forth.

As Sam rolled down the passenger window, he caught sight of Brooke's sweet face.

"Fiction," she whispered and looked sheepishly about.

As they pulled away, Sam decided he would have to do some serious research into what little girls considered good fiction. Particularly, very bright, inquisitive little girls. Brooke read Shakespeare, for hell's sake. He had to be very careful.

As they moved past the bunkhouses and training pen, Sam felt an ache. Axel stood alone in the pen, waiting for his morning lessons from Kali.

Where was she?

They rolled beyond the barn, and Sam saw Star, Redwing, Lightning, and Choo Choo out in the distance.

Mike and Ed scooted around the seats, arching their necks to look as well.

"Bye, Redwing!" Mike grinned and waved. "Thanks for the ride!"

Once they were through the main gate, Sam settled back and stared, unseeing, out the window. He felt weighted down. He blinked and focused on the terrain as they picked up speed.

Truly, it was a magical place—part mountainous, part desert, and with so much more to explore. While Sam suspected no place called Eagle Rock or Radio Rock would ever be found on a map, the Jorgensons had had names for each plateau, every canyon, and every creek bed.

But that wasn't it. It was something much deeper, something about the Jorgensons. It was the sense of family that he had never known as a child or as an adult. He could only imagine what the holidays would be like at Rainwash, and he felt envy.

He'd had a similar feeling when he had first come on board at Jackson, Keller & Whiteman. He had the office and nameplate but hadn't been a member of the team for months. He still remembered that feeling of desperation to win and prove himself worthy, to belong.

He bounced his leg impatiently. This went much deeper than that. It was a feeling of belonging to the Jorgensons' clan. It was everything rolled together. It was the lay of the land, the smell of Ms. Kat's cooking, the teamwork and camaraderie, and the peaceful manner in which everyone existed. It was the horses. It was the hard work ethic, an extraordinary main house, and the entire throwback to a history now lost.

All of it in glaring opposition to the way he lived, but the strangest thing was, until his visit to Rainwash, he had been okay with that. His biggest concern had been how to let Mike know the Connors case was a clincher for his promotion, not Mike's. He hadn't cared about Jeremy's guilt or innocence. Kali had changed everything. It was cliché and nauseating, but it was no less true. For the first time, he wanted to be with one person for the rest of his life, and not a froufrou girl either.

He rocked his head back and closed his eyes.

"What the hell?"

He heard Wade's voice, and Sam opened his eyes to see all the men in the truck looking out the back window.

Wade slowed the truck, waving his hand outside the truck to slow Evan down. "What is she doing now?" Wade sounded exasperated as he looked into the rearview mirror.

Heavy hooves pounded alongside them as they slowed to a stop, and Sam's heart leapt. He saw Kali riding alongside them. Like the others, he leaned to the side for a better view from his window.

She was bent over, riding bareback—baseball cap turned backward, jeans, a plain white T-shirt, and flip-flops. She looked flawless, moving in unison with her horse.

"What do you think you're doing? Are you crazy?" Wade chastised her.

Sam blinked and the vision of Kali on Star morphed into the reality of Jacks on Mocha, smiling and cutting her eyes toward Sam.

"Well?" Wade waved a hand at her, trying to speed her along so they could move again. "What is it?"

"I want . . . I mean, I like lip gloss." She bit her lip. "Watermelon-flavored lip gloss." Jacks fidgeted uncomfortably on Mocha's back.

"What!?" Wade sputtered. "Girl! Does your mother know you came tearing out here like someone broke a leg?"

"Well, *he* asked." She frowned at Wade then peeked at Sam who smiled and gave her a reassuring nod.

"Watermelon-flavored lip gloss. Got it." Sam pretended to write it down and Jacks' shoulders relaxed as she sighed.

She grinned. "I mean . . . that's just, ya know, if you wanted to know or something. That's all." She scowled, looking as serious as she could with her twinkling blue eyes.

"Jacks, get the hell out of here!" Wade roared at her.

Evan tapped the horn behind them, eager to stick to their schedule. They had a long drive ahead of them.

Without another word, Jacks turned her baseball cap forward, pulling the bill down low like Sam had seen Kali do so often, and steered Mocha away from the trucks.

Wade chuckled to himself. "I'll be damned. Watermelon-flavored lip gloss for Ms. Jaclyn Jorgenson. Who would have thought?"

* * * *

Kali watched with a heavy heart as Sam Spann pulled away from Rainwash. It was bad form not to say goodbye to a paying guest, but she couldn't bring herself to stand before that particular group. It had been difficult since their arrival, but last night had tipped the scales.

Sam saw through her.

He had been right. She didn't smoke. She never had smoked. She just hadn't wanted her girls to see her cry. They had been through so much, particularly Brooke. The ruse had worked perfectly well before Sam Spann had come along.

The bombing of Nicky's compound had been as close to hell as she hoped ever to come, but as implausible as it was, the aftermath had been worse. The real hell was being left behind. The real hell had been trying to explain to three little girls where Daddy was and why complete strangers had done what they had. The real hell had been the stories that came out each day about a new victim and what a really, truly nice person he or she was, and ignoring it. She cared but she'd had to shut it off at some point, so that's what she did. She'd turned it off—the television, the newspaper reports, the conversations, the speculations, everything, and that including crying.

Rainwash didn't allow smoking in closed quarters, so a guest had taken to smoking out by the oak late at night. Kali had discovered and joined him. Upon her return to the cabin, Brooke had revealed herself. While the child had tried to hint at the dangers of smoking, she was too respectful to outright lecture her mother.

For the remainder of the man's visit, Kali had spoken with him at night, staying out long after the man had retired to his own room. Kali had finally been alone—alone with her feelings about Nicky, the ranch, the girls' lives —and while Kali held a lit cigarette in her hand, Brooke had never come out.

Nothing had gone like it was supposed to. She was supposed to have been in New York, resenting the hell out of Nicky for uprooting her and the girls while loving the hell out of him. Instead, she was where she had always wanted to be but without Nicky.

It wasn't bittersweet. Just bitter.

Through it all, she suspected that Tracy understood her best. Although they'd never once had a conversation about her feelings, she'd always known he knew.

Perhaps that had been why his behavior with Jeremy Connors had been so painful. She'd believed there was a special bond between them, but he had turned a cheek, joking and talking with Jeremy afterward, like nothing had happened.

It had become a point of contention between Mattie and Kali. Mattie argued that he didn't care about the person, he just wanted to see the game, but Kali had been unable to separate the two. She could not and would not separate what happened with Jeremy the man versus Jeremy the high profile, paying guest.

From the small window of her cabin, she saw the men leaving. She watched Sam as he spoke to Brooke. She hadn't quite decided how Sam factored into everything, but it was more than coincidence that just when she'd considered leaving Rainwash, he had appeared.

She could not ignore the fact that her older daughter needed more social outlets than she could provide from here. Entertaining well-to-do people who wanted to drive cattle for fun didn't offer the kind of friendship Brooke needed. Initially, Kali had kidded herself into believing the rodeo circuit and occasional trips into town were enough, but even Danni and Jacks had outgrown their little world. They needed to explore in ways that didn't involve trail rides and cowboys. They needed to experience recess with other kids, sitting in a packed gymnasium, and passing notes in class. Lately, Jacks had been infatuated with the notion of a food fight. It was something she had seen on television and was thoroughly convinced that she was missing all kinds of cafeteria fun.

More than that, Kali had finally decided she was ready to see the world outside Rainwash.

Then along came Sam Spann.

From the beginning, she had tried not to notice his powerful build and strong features. He was gorgeous and she had felt guilty for comparing him to Nicky, but there had been something very charming about him. He was clumsy on a horse, and she'd seen that, as a former athlete, it pained him greatly to be so awkward at something.

She liked the way he looked at her. It unnerved her, but it also excited her. There was just something about him. He liked her children and appreciated what she did. He wasn't intimidated by her, and she was certain he could give her a run for her money. It was one of the things she had always loved about Nicky. He never lost his cool, but he never backed down.

Sam's arrival had brought Jeremy Connors, and Jeremy, in her mind, represented two very large problems. First, Jeremy proved that the world was a dangerous place and it was best to stay put at Rainwash. Kali had been living like a turtle and just when she'd gotten the courage to stick her head out . . . *wham*! She was in hiding again. As much as she hated Jeremy Connors for taking her sense of freedom, she was secretly relieved. Was she really ready to leave Rainwash?

Second was Sam himself. What kind of man could represent someone like Jeremy? And what was wrong with her for thinking of him the way she did? She recalled the evening he had stepped close to examine her necklace. His nearness had taken her breath away, and she'd cursed herself and promised it would never happen again. Yet each night she found herself wanting to be alone with him, if nothing else to talk about Lightning and how he might be better handled. She liked the way he smelled, the shape of his large hands, the slight curl in his hair. She liked how early his five o'clock shadow came.

She was losing her mind. She had only known him a few days, but it felt like months. When he'd called her out on the cigarettes, she had felt so exposed. He saw through her in a way no one else had, but he had left to defend a man who had almost raped her. What could she say to him? She was better off at Rainwash. At least she was safe here.

She closed the blinds, stepped away from the window, and fell back onto her bed, staring up at the ceiling. It was better to let him go and not think about him again. Besides, she had the Jorgensons to think of. How could she possibly allow herself to think of Sam in the presence of Nicky's family? There was nothing for him at Rainwash that he couldn't have seventeen times over in Houston.

But she was lonely, and, in the words of Brooke, *"Sam Spann's totally hot."*

Chapter Twenty-Eight

Luther Monroe leaned silently against the wall, watching as Caroline Peters sobbed uncontrollably into her pillow. Following the advice his wife had given him, he had been careful not to make eye contact with the young woman. After being brutally attacked and watching her friend be murdered inches away in their home, there wasn't anything he could say to her to make her feel better, but Casey had wanted him to be present when she spoke to Ms. Peters. So he hung back, avoided making any eye contact, and prayed he wasn't somehow compounding her agony.

Luther had to give her credit.

Three times, Casey had asked Caroline to describe what happened and how it happened. Twice she had stopped to ask if it was too much, but Caroline remained determined.

"It has to be done," the young woman kept repeating.

Luther took another peek when she put her head back down. It sickened him. Caroline Peters had been a former national athlete, tall, strong, accomplished, and all he saw now was a battered woman with a shattered pelvis, dislocated shoulder, mangled face, and a real possibility of never getting pregnant—if that was something she had wanted. He wondered about that. Maybe she wanted kids, maybe she didn't, but all she cared about at the moment was helping the prosecution.

It was sad, really. It was obvious she wanted desperately to give Luther and Casey something new, something damaging to Connors, but she had nothing. Just an enormous amount of guilt and grief.

Her description of the assailant in no way matched Connors or any of his known associates. There were no useable fingerprints, no semen, no names, no viable leads. It was the reason Casey had insisted on Luther coming along. She had met with Caroline Peters twice since the attack and come up empty-handed. As much as Caroline wanted to give something useful, Casey wanted to have it and had hoped Luther might detect something she had missed.

* * * *

As Caroline buried her face into her pillow, Casey looked at Luther. He shrugged, and Casey sighed.

She assured Ms. Peters they would get Connors for what he'd done to Jessica and promised to let her know if anything else came up. Casey stood, called out to Caroline's mother waiting in the hallway, and excused herself with well wishes.

"I hate that," she said once she and Luther stepped outside.

"Storm's coming," Luther mused.

Casey studied the sky. "I hope not. I was going to run later."

"Casey, you need to give yourself a break. Come over to the house tonight." Luther fished the cars keys out of his pocket. "Oh! I forgot, I was supposed to ask you over yesterday." He rolled his eyes. "Vanessa really wants to see you."

"Luth, I wouldn't be good company." She wagged a finger at the car, urging him to unlock it so they could get going. "I just . . . I just can't think of anything else . . ."

"I know it, Casey." He waited until they were both inside. "You're brain dead. You need to take a step back, get a fresh perspective on everything. You need to take a break from all this, and clear your mind."

"That's why I go running. It clears the mind."

"Okay," Luther shook his head, starting the car. "But if Nessa asks, you turned us down, and I asked yesterday."

Casey smirked, nodding. "Right. I'll be sure to know nothing about a dinner invitation and will act deeply wounded that I wasn't invited." She had gotten good at holding nonsense conversations while her mind reeled.

There has to be something. There has to be someone.

She'd had a man look into Jeremy Connors' high school escapades since, according to his own autobiography, there was some little girl who had followed him around and whom he'd treated poorly.

"I want to know what *poorly* means," Casey had told her detective.

She had also tried to find any reports of rape or assault at Connors' alma mater but, so far, had turned up nothing.

Casey Dillon knew from personal experience and recent cases that the typical American college campus was a hotbed for crimes committed against women. According to a study of "The Sexual Victimization of College Women," Casey was most interested in the "unwanted completed penetration by force or threat of force." Together, she and Luther had analyzed and reanalyzed that particular study. Because many of the young victims felt guilt or confusion about what was actually rape, they did not report things that happened to them, encouraging scholastic thugs to continue with fraternity house rapes, mind-erasing date-rape pills, and stalking. It was what allowed people like Jeremy Connors to walk. Again.

"Oh, damn."

Luther's voice broke Casey's line of thought. She looked over to see him studying the rearview mirror. "What?"

"We've got company again."

Casey jerked then caught herself. As much as she wanted to turn around, she knew she couldn't. She reached for her phone and called Detective Phillips as Luther drove on.

"Where to?" Luther asked. "We don't want to go to the hotel, do we?"

They hadn't been in Shreveport more than a few hours before they had picked up their first tail, but Casey shook her head. "Phillips. Casey Dillon. We've got a tail."

"You're a long way from home to be making so many friends so quickly. Okay, where are you? I'll send out a car right now." Phillips spoke to his partner, rustling the phone on his shoulder. "Krane. Not now, later. Yep, it's her. They got another tail. Okay, give it to me."

"Luther, can you read the plates?" She tried to appear to be having just an ordinary conversation with her partner.

"I'll do you one better." Luther lifted his chin toward the oncoming intersection. "We're at Lexington and Charter. There's a cop right there at the corner. Get him to—"

Phillips was already on it and calling in the location.

Casey hung up and tried to relax into her seat as her mind raced on. This wasn't the work of Jackson, Keller & Whiteman. It just didn't have that feel. This smelled of private detective, but who?

"Now what?" Luther asked.

"We sit back and wait for the Shreveport police to pull that sucker over," she said, tapping nervously at the window. "Who could it be? This isn't Spann's style," she muttered out loud, eyeing her side mirror as the blue lights flashed.

Gotcha!

She spun around. "Pull over, Luth! Pull over!"

Another twenty minutes passed before Phillips came to Luther's door with answers. "I don't know who you've pissed off, but it's either someone with a lot of money or someone with nothing else to do," he said, ducking down so that he could see Casey as well.

"Come again?" She raised her eyebrows. She never cared for cute lead-ins.

"This guy is clean. We've got nothing on him. He's been employed to photograph you." He handed over a card for both Luther and Casey to inspect.

"Me?"

"Looks legit," Luther said, passing the card to Casey.

She read the raised lettering.

Wesley Spenser.

President.

Shutterbugger, Inc.

"Who employed him?" Luther asked Phillips.

"For a brief and shining moment, Mr. Spenser claimed he didn't need to share that information, and that it was classified."

Luther played along. "Uh-huh."

"So, of course, we would need to bring him downtown, possibly confiscate his camera—"

"Uh-huh."

"The name Wilson Burrell mean anything to you guys?"

Luther and Casey looked at one another.

"Guy says this Burrell fellow paid by check, in advance, all legit. Says it is for a website, and that you're a public figure, so it's—"

"Yeah, yeah." Casey waved a hand at him. "Wilson Burrell," she mumbled. "We know that name, don't we, Luther?" Casey focused on Detective Phillips again. "We've come across the name, but to be honest, we never knew who he was or how he was connected."

"And we still don't," Luther said.

"I don't want to state the obvious, but you've gotta find Burrell. And, uh, Ms. Dillon . . ." Phillips patted the side of the car. ". . . you know you've been tagged in some pretty raunchy websites, don't you?"

She sighed and nodded.

He shrugged. "I don't know who this Burrell creep is or what his beef is with you, but you need to find him before he—well, he's already found you."

She nodded again and put on her best game face, not even batting an eyelash.

In truth, however, his words frightened her. Detective Phillips was rather rough around the edges, but he was good. With Jessica neatly out of the way, only Casey posed a threat to Jeremy Connors. But who was Wilson Burrell and why did he care so much about Connors?

* * * *

That little bitch had no idea what she was into. She was so drunk with power that she didn't even realize how much danger she was putting herself in. So she had discovered one of his photographers. It didn't matter. There was no way in hell she would ever find him or figure out his part.

She jogged by, and he visualized running alongside her, maybe even making light conversation until she rounded the curve, just beyond the trees and . . . pop! He'd blow her head off and keep right on jogging. A silencer and no one would be the wiser.

It had been his own little fantasy, but when the kid started making noises about killing her, he knew he had to pull back. The kid was a ticking time bomb and too easily manipulated.

Finding Devon Buckley had been easy. He had been just one of hundreds logging on to complain about the Connors case when it first broke. He had begun to collect names and exchange e-mails with some of the more volatile Connors supporters. Devon had been among them. He was fourteen years old, on the verge of flunking out of school, a huge Connors fan, and dealing with the sudden death of his old man, also a big Jeremy Connors fan. He was sure that was why the kid was so damned protective of Jeremy. Buckley Sr. had protested loudly about Connors' innocence before he'd died, and the kid had latched on and taken up the cause for his old man. Devon had been one of the few morons who had celebrated Jessica Stanten's death publicly via the Internet.

He had e-mailed Devon, told him to cool his remarks, and the kid had listened. But in his grief and with Stanten dead and gone, Devon transferred all his hate to a single person—Casey Dillon. Devon's words of hatred and venom had provided many a late-night laugh. The kid could cuss.

Still, his latest description of what he wanted to do to Dillon had been unsettling. Not because he gave a damn about the woman—and on a personal note, he was quite curious to see if the kid was up to what he claimed he would do to her—but killing a prosecuting attorney in one of the highest profile cases of the decade was not a wise decision. It wouldn't take the heat off the Connors case. It wouldn't fix the damage that had been done to him. No, sadly, she had to be allowed to try her case.

He needed to log on again, talk the kid down, and make him see that Casey Dillon had to do what she was trained to do in the interest of Jeremy Connors. The longer the case dragged on, the more it harmed Connors' chances of playing in the upcoming season. Surely even Devon Buckley, young and impulsive as he was, could understand that.

* * * *

He rolled over, pulling her with him, and easily set her on his hips.

She groaned and rolled her head back.

She had changed, he noted with some discontent. Three kids and a fat belly later, she was nothing like the Ashley Williams he had kicked it with. Man, she had been something then, and he'd been like a rutting buck. Partially clothed from practice or a game, in the locker rooms, under the bleachers, or in the back of his truck, it hadn't mattered. She had been there and willing.

Jeremy smiled as she bucked and wriggled.

He remembered the time he had bent Ashley over the seat of his truck. With the door wide open and her feet dangling, he had whispered that no one could see. He wanted her. He needed her. He had kissed her.

That was all it had taken—sweet talk and tender kisses, and she'd peeled off her shirt and bra. Damn, but it had been hard not to smile, knowing that behind him, standing on the benches on tiptoes, half the team craned their necks to see Ashley Williams' incredible body. With all the guys watching, he had performed. Without knowing it, so had she! It had been beautiful.

Only when Jeremy had been sure the guys had had enough had he hiked her dress up, pulled down her panties, and spread out her thighs wide so they could see everything. He had said some things he couldn't remember now, but it had gotten her going. Before he was done, she had practically been grinding the seat, begging him, which was something he did remember as Ashley begged him again.

"Oh, don't stop," she moaned. "Oh, don't stop." He adjusted her once more, pushing her forward, and her eyes flew open. Fear then carnal lust glazed over her face. Her eyes rolled as she rocked back and forth.

"Yeah, baby," he said, cooing at her. "Take it all."

All those years ago, she had groaned so loudly, it was entirely possible the team would have known about it anyway. That was something else about Ashley he remembered enjoying. She had always been a loud one.

There she'd been, begging for more when he had pulled her back and given his teammates the show of a lifetime. It had gotten his rocks off like never before. All the guys watched as he screwed Ashley Williams so hard the entire truck rocked, and she had moaned and gasped and screamed. It had just made him go harder and faster until he was almost in a frenzy. It had sapped him of all his strength.

When a charley horse grabbed him, he'd let her fall against the truck seat, and she had heard them. She had seen their faces in the window and pleaded with Jeremy to take her home. She had cried that he hurt her and asked how could he have let the others see, but by the time they had reached her house, he had settled her down. Some sweet kisses on her tear-stained cheeks, a rub here, squeeze there, and he'd reassured her that they had only seen because she had been groaning so loudly. She had sniffled and whimpered like a wounded little kitten but she'd come back. She always came back.

Just like now—she was married, three kids, and this time, she was the one looking for trouble. He scanned her body. It wasn't the same Ashley Williams, but he appreciated her enthusiasm.

Jeremy had made arrangements to have her where he wanted her, and then casually bumped into her while visiting his old high school. Using his old charm, he had talked her into having lunch with him—for old time's sake. He had paid for her childcare and had taken her to the fanciest restaurant in town. They'd hit the hotel bar and, eventually, made their way to his room. It had hardly taken any effort at all.

She had brushed quickly over talk of her husband, Bobby Nelson, saying only that he didn't make nearly enough money and that they had probably gotten married too early. Of course, Ashley had never planned on being Mrs. Bobby Nelson, but she had gotten herself knocked up, and being in a small town and all, marrying had simply been the right thing to do. It hadn't been like Ashley was ever going to go to college. Being a momma had been inevitable.

He told her how sorry he was that he'd gone off to college, leaving her behind, but he had missed her and thought about her. He had confided that he was glad she wasn't all that happily married because he still had a thing for her. He paid her some money, swearing that it wasn't like a prostitute kind of thing but that he had lots of money, and he just wanted her to have something nice for herself.

There was nothing sweeter than her reply, "Well, all right. If that's what you want." She shrugged.

"There's something else," he said, and he told her about his ongoing memory about her and his pickup all those years ago.

"I'm not that same little girl," Ashley said with a chuckle.

"No, you're not," he said in a husky voice that left no doubt what he meant. He cocked one eyebrow and admired her body. He wanted her to feel desirable—something he was sure she hadn't felt in a very long time.

She blushed, waving a dismissive hand at him.

"You drive me crazy, Ashley. You always have. You're my weakness." He almost laughed listening to himself talk, yet she bought it all. She was so desperate for the attention, desperate for those high school days when she had been hot property.

"What do you want from me?" she asked coyly, but they both knew and she succumbed.

He flipped her over on her stomach and, standing over her, raised her hips with several pillows. The shot was perfect. He looked at his own reflection in the mirror. He could see his entire body and the still shapely backside of Ashley Williams Nelson.

He squatted down slightly and, placing one hand on her back, asked, "You ready?"

Just like old times, he wasn't gentle. She squealed at first and tried to crawl forward, but he leaned close and grabbed a shoulder, holding her in place. Again, he glanced at the mirror. The image set his stomach on fire. He released her shoulder and trapped her hips with both hands, pulling her back. "Am I hurting you?"

She gasped a shaky "No."

She was lying and he loved it. He knew it hurt but he didn't care. She was trying to endure whatever the big man gave her, and he was capturing it all on the video camera that sat out in the open, bold as could be.

He leaned forward to whisper in her ear and told her what he wanted to hear her say. Just like old times.

"I want you!" she cried.

He watched himself in the mirror, like a rutting buck, giving her everything he had, shaking the entire bed, slamming her against him. He closed his eyes, imagined how it was all those years ago, and how Mike Waters and the guys would see this video and how she begged for every inch of him.

Chapter Twenty-Nine

As promised, Sam had sent each of the girls a gift and had, much to his surprise, loved doing so. The book had been easy. He had simply walked into a bookstore and asked what all the twelve-year-old girls were reading. It was a mystery series about owls, and he bought all four. Even the flamingo press-ons had been relatively easy to find. He had also gotten palm trees, panda bears, and, as the be-all and end-all, two packets of horses. The watermelon-flavored lip gloss, however, had been more of a challenge. He'd finally found a company that produced every imaginable flavor so he'd bought several of each of the melon flavors and a couple of berry ones as well. He had sent it all Federal Express because he knew from personal experience how much the girls had liked having the truck come up to the main house. Regular mail went to town and no farther.

Then he waited. He hoped for a phone call or a thank-you note from the girls. Given their manners, he was sure to get one or the other, and the waiting was killing him.

He was losing his mind.

He had put more time and thought into gifts for three little girls that had, in no uncertain terms, told him to back off their mother than he ever had on any female conquests. Somewhere, there was a laugh in that. If his former flames ever found out they had been outdone by three little cowgirls there was sure to be hurt feelings.

Since his return, he and his team had worked the Connors case, locking up most of the questions. It would be a pretty cut-and-dried case, what with no witnesses. He had gone on two very unfulfilling dates and tried his best to push Rainwash and Kali from his mind.

It was utterly insane. He couldn't stop thinking about the land, the territory, the way of life, the community living among the Jorgensons, and wondered if he'd missed his true calling. Sure, it was a throwback to the past, but it was where he wanted to be.

"Man, I don't know what the hell your problem is."

Sam spun around in his chair to see Mike standing in the doorway staring at him.

"You've had your head in a cloud since we've been back. What's the matter?"

"Just angling for all possible scenarios," Sam said, shrugging. Somewhere in the back of his mind, Kali lingered and it pained him to let her drift off. He wanted to pull the image of her back in.

"Well, quit angling," Mike said as he sauntered in and plopped into a chair. "Ashley Williams Nelson just signed off. She's no longer a threat. Guess she really doesn't want her small town knowing she did the dirty with Jeremy Connors." He chuckled and Sam scowled.

Sam hadn't known all the details of that affair and had been assured by Mike he didn't need to know. *"You're on a need-to-know basis, bro."* It was how they worked and it suited Sam fine.

"Unless Ms. Dillon takes out a full page ad in all the cities Jeremy has visited in the last decade, and she's not likely to do that, there are no more complainants at this juncture." An easy grin slid over his face. "I do believe the fat lady is about to sing."

Sam shook his head. "No, it won't be that easy, Mike." He stared at the file on his desk. "She's been too quiet for too long. You can bet she's digging somewhere."

"Well, she'll have to dig fast because she's only got two days. Sam, relax. This thing's locked up. We always contended there was another lover involved. Now we know. The jealous lover came back and killed her. Millions witnessed the fiasco at Rainwash Ranch. I'm a witness myself." He raised his arm still resting in a sling. "Jessica Stanten, God rest her soul, was raped and then brutally murdered by someone else, most likely a former lover. Jeremy Connors is, without a doubt, free and clear of any and all charges."

"Save it for the jury." Sam smiled and secretly let his mind return to Rainwash, hoping for just one more peek at Kali.

* * * *

Casey Dillon stepped out of the building and doubled over, letting her fingers first drag to the ground, then reach around to grab the back of her ankles, trying to get the full stretch in her hamstrings. She felt tighter than usual. Stress.

After the Connors case, she was running in the Bolder Boulder marathon. She had never been to Colorado but had seen pictures in her running magazines. She'd wanted to go for years, but there had never been enough time or money. This time, she'd decided she had earned it. Running had given her the stamina and personal drive to work harder in her career, which laid down a strong reputation among the judges and other lawyers, and the long work hours had fed her need to run to unwind and de-stress. Somewhere in the middle, her personal life had fallen through the cracks.

She stood and stretched to the right, then left. She gave friendly nods to people she recognized as she warmed up her arms and upper torso. As she adjusted her headphones, she resolved to get some semblance of a personal life. She didn't need to have a husband, but perhaps a more constant friend and part-time lover. That would be nice.

For the last few months, she had been seeing a man but knew very little about his personal life. She owed more to herself. She deserved the emotional ties. She deserved to know about someone with whom she shared intimate relations. Her perspective on her personal life had changed. It was something that Jessica Stanten had taught her. She felt a kind of allegiance or sisterhood toward Jessica.

She checked her watch and set out. Running eight-minute miles, Casey could knock out five miles and be back in time to meet with Luther.

Ashley Williams, the suspected high school rape victim, had been a bust. Not only was she not talking, but she was emphatically denying any wrongdoing on Jeremy's part. Casey had had another idea and was eager to talk to Luther about it. She wasn't ready to throw in the towel yet.

She set off at a strong pace, thinking about her approach.

It was a long shot but one worth taking. She could see the case slipping away from her, and while most people agreed Connors was guilty, they all spoke openly about how hard it was going to be for the prosecution to prove it. It was the "Run, O.J., Run" scenario all over again and a shame to the American judicial system. Connors had been dubbed a modern day Jack the Ripper, and despite the protests of various women's groups, new punch lines sprang up each day comparing his antics off the field to his treatment of players on the field.

One sportscaster had recently joked that at least his lady victims had a chance of enjoying what happened to them while the only thing opponents on the field got stuffed inside them was Astroturf. The masses had been expectedly aghast. The comments had been above the fold of newspapers and made the covers of magazines. The jackass had been forced to apologize, and the world had forgiven him, allowing him to keep his job. Men loved the fact that Jeremy Connors was a live wire, that he was ruthless, violent, and possibly criminal. For that reason alone, columnists and editorials candidly spoke about their desire to see him play another season—to see his temper unleashed.

No one seemed to doubt his guilt. Even his greatest supporters were willing to concede some portion of guilt on Connors' part, but no one wanted to see him stopped. So, with Jessica Stanten dead, Casey Dillon was public enemy number one.

She huffed.

She went after child abusers and molesters with a vengeance. She loved animals, children, nature, and life, and in that order, if she had to guess. She paid her taxes, honored her parents, never broke a law, overtipped people in the service industry, and usually drank coffee mixes she didn't ask for because she didn't want to get young baristas in trouble. Yet *she* was the bad guy.

Her steps quickened as her mind raced.

The entire situation set her teeth on edge, yet, as much as she hated it, she loved it. It gave her purpose and meaning. Winning this case wasn't about simply bringing one creep to justice. This was about serving notice to all creeps. Above all, it was the very least she could do for Jessica Stanten and her family.

Casey pounded the pavement, turning away from the courthouse and toward the construction. She eyed the site carefully. No workers. To her relief, it was after hours, and she didn't have to worry about how to handle the wolf whistles.

That was another tricky situation and another constant reminder to Casey how and why rape cases were always so confusing to so many people. Take the common wolf whistle. Half the women Casey knew admitted that when they were having a bad day, a run-of-the-mill wolf whistle secretly lifted their spirits. It was a sort of primal reminder that they still had the goods, but being professional women, they publically ignored the woofs and whistles. How was a woman to respond to such remarks and sounds anyway?

Most women ignored the calls. Some thought yelling back or flipping off the offending caller was the right thing to do, but that typically led to more come-ons.

Screw you!

My pleasure. C'mon, baby!

There was no winning.

Casey cut across the street and ran through the lot, hoping to shave a little time.

She would be glad when this case was over. She loathed and despised Jeremy Connors and all the rat snakes at Jackson, Keller & Whit—

The pain was blinding. The world was at a tilt, but it came at her at tremendous speed nonetheless. For a moment, she was confused—had she slipped? Fallen over something? But there was no time to process anything as the second blow was delivered.

It was her worst fear realized. Her mind flashed to Luther's lecture about a new running route. She had refused an escort because she never believed anyone would actually harm her

"At least change up your running habits, where you shop and walk," Luther had said again for the billionth time since all the anti-Casey websites had begun.

As always, she had rolled her eyes at him as she'd left the office. "They're pansies. What are they gonna do? Insult me to death?"

The third blow just missed as Casey rolled into a tight ball, opening slightly when she was on her back. She heard the loud *thunk* on the ground near her. Her eyes darted to the side.

A pipe.

It was raised again, and she rolled once more, trying to get to her feet. She might not be able to fight him, but she could damn well try to outrun him.

As she twisted to the side, her eye caught the glint of a second pipe, and she dove for it instead. The back of her hand scraped along the concrete, tearing the skin from her knuckles, but she felt nothing but the weight of the pipe in her hand. She tasted blood in her mouth, and she was pissed.

She was vaguely aware of a dull pain in the middle of her back but there was no time to think about it.

"Come on!" She pulled the pipe back ready to knock the bastard's head clean off his shoulders. She was going to kill him. She was ready to take on the world. She screamed again. "Fire! Fire!" It was the one word she had read a woman should yell in a dangerous situation. She wanted to make sure everyone within a two-mile radius heard her.

Someone appeared. Then another.

She laughed and licked the blood from her battered lip, widening her stance. She felt empowered and slightly insane. It was complete madness. She screamed again, laughing at the thug. "Come on, you little—"

Her assailant was small. The attacker wore a jacket with a turtleneck-like collar zipped all the way to the top and some kind of ball cap pulled low. Even at dusk, it was an absurd outfit to wear as Casey could see the face. Caucasian, very light skinned. Light eyes. Blue, maybe. Slight build. Maybe one hundred and thirty-five pounds. Maybe more. No more than five foot five.

There was a honk of a horn and more shouts. People were coming.

The little shit looked from the oncoming crowd back to Casey, and she saw panic on the half-covered face.

"Nowhere to go, sweetie," Casey said, seething as she shifted the pipe in her hand. Payback was going to be sweet. She flexed her fingers around the delicious weight of the pipe.

The little creep flung his own pipe at Casey.

She ducked and felt the shift. As her attacker tried to run, Casey felt no fear. Without hesitation, she ran after the guy, and in less than twenty steps, she brought her pipe-wielding friend down.

"Call 911! Call the police," she screamed. Casey was thrown off balance as they wrestled, but she swung a fist and heard a moan—a high-pitched moan that caught her off guard.

A woman? Another woman?

She shook her head and moved in again, determined not to be surprised this time. She delivered another hard blow, ignoring the searing pain in her hand. Sure she had broken something, she hit again and once more before a large man stepped in.

"Call the police! This little maggot attacked me!" Casey shrieked. "Call the police!"

"We did." The man's voice was calming. "My wife called the police," he said as he stepped in toward the assailant and ripped off the hat.

Both the man and Casey froze.

"He's a kid," the man said and staggered back. "Son of a bitch! A kid!"

Casey blinked.

A kid.

He couldn't be more than thirteen or fourteen years old. His face was bloodied, thanks to Casey, and he was glaring at everyone as though he were a helpless animal that had only defended himself.

An animal indeed.

Casey Dillon sank down to the ground, confused, hurt, and exhausted. She felt her hand again. It was definitely broken. Even as she sat there, catching her breath, she felt the swelling.

A freakin' kid.

Her back was on fire and her face began to throb. Only when another good Samaritan stepped in did she realize how much she was bleeding.

"Oh, Lord, honey," an older woman said to Casey as she inspected her face. "You need to see a doctor. Hey," she called over her shoulder. "Somebody needs to call an ambulance. Her face is all busted up!"

Gingerly, Casey reached up to touch her face.

The boy started to squirm, but mercifully, the man stopped him.

Casey was in no shape to stop anyone from anything now. The adrenaline was gone, and her body was racked with pain. As she pulled her fingers away from her face, she felt blood on them, sticky and thick.

She looked back at the boy. "Why?"

"You stupid bitch! I hate you." He practically spat the words, and Casey fell back on her bottom, speechless. "I should have killed you!"

The police came to cart him away, and the emergency crew tried to convince her to take a ride to the hospital. Casey never moved. She was in shock.

A boy.

She had been prepared for some beer-bellied monster with the IQ of yogurt to come at her, name calling and berating her, but a pipe-wielding kid? A kid who hated her guts and wished her dead? She just hadn't been prepared for that.

"Dammit, why do you have to be so hardheaded?" Luther asked between great gulps of air. He held her hand while the EMT applied butterfly stitches to her cheek. "I wasn't designed for sprinting." Luther half joked, trying to distract her from her pain.

She winced.

"Does this look like the body of a sprinter?"

Casey smiled slightly. "Stop it, Luther." She was glad to have him by her side, and patted his hand. The enormity of what had almost happened seeped its way into her brain. "He could have killed me," she said quietly.

"This isn't going to hold," the young man said about the stitches. "You need to let us take you in."

Casey just waved a hand at him in irritation. She didn't have time. Despite Luther's pleas, she wanted to get back to the office as soon as possible. That is, until the EMT said, "Let's take a look at your hand."

The pain was so intense it nearly shot Casey to her feet. She tried to recover but the exchange between the young man and Luther told her she was going nowhere but the hospital.

"You think it's broken?" She winced at the EMT, and he shrugged.

"You left handed or right handed?"

"Right," she said, and he smiled sympathetically.

"Too bad."

"What?" She blinked at her hand and turned toward Luther with big eyes. "What's he mean by that?"

Luther dropped his head with a shake. "Your hand is broken, Case. You won't be writing with it for a while, or anything else for that matter. You broke your hand."

"*I* didn't break my hand."

"No." Luther sighed. "But it is broken."

For a moment they only stared at each other. Casey let go, leaning into Luther, and he gave her a hug.

"I don't have time for this," she said.

"I know. I'm sorry."

"I don't have time for this," she said to the young EMT.

He nodded politely, shooting a look of concern to Luther.

"I mean, I've got all kinds of things I need to be doing to prepare for this case. I just don't have time for this."

"I know, Casey, but I can do all that."

"I just—" Her voice cracked. "Luther . . . a kid. A stupid kid." She almost laughed, but a tear began to work its way down her cheek. "A kid."

"I know, Casey. It's just not right. I'm sorry, babe."

Chapter Thirty

Sam's mind was still reeling when Mike and Ed walked into his office. The latest memorandum from the district attorney's office sat open on top of the pile of case folders on his desk. He had to chuckle. If nothing else, Casey Dillon had tenacity.

"I'm starting to like you, Ms. Dillon," he muttered and leaned back, lacing his fingers behind his head. It was an interesting tactic that left him wondering, but the expressions of his coworkers as they stood in his doorway brought new concerns.

"Oh, no," he groaned, prepared for the worst.

"Casey Dillon was attacked," Ed said.

"What?" Sam snapped forward. He looked back at the letter. It was just delivered so how . . . "When? Where?"

Mike dropped into a chair while Ed appeared the most shaken as he rubbed his temples and seemed to be using the wall to remain upright. Like Sam, Ed just wanted everything about the entire case to disappear.

"Some punk kid from Dallas ran away from home and attacked her. With a pipe, no less." Ed sounded exhausted as he supplied the first bit of information.

Sam's mouth fell open, and he wanted this to be a joke. He needed this to be some kind of stupid, pointless joke, but no one was smiling. "A kid?"

"Fourteen years old," Ed said and sighed. "He'd been on those websites calling for justice against Dillon. You've seen 'em. He got it into his head if he took her out of commission, the case would go away."

"A pipe?" Sam was still trying to digest the news.

"Yeah, you know," Mike said, as he yawned. "Dillon's activities are all posted, down to her dental habits. Apparently, the kid had mapped out her jogging route and attacked her when no one was around."

There was an awkward moment of silence, but Waters' yawn hadn't been missed by anyone. He had never been a fan of Dillon.

Ed seemed to have force his amazed stare away from Mike before he spoke. "Um, yeah . . . unsuccessfully."

"I just—" Sam shook his head in wonder. "I can't believe this. Where is she now?"

"She's got a broken hand, cuts, scrapes and bruises all over, and her face is swollen, from what I hear, but she's charging ahead," Ed said.

"That's our girl," Mike mocked.

Sam ignored Mike and pushed for more details. "So they caught the kid, then. Where is he? *Who* is he?"

"Name's Devon Buckley. Smart actually. He used his cell phone to place periodic phone calls so that his mom wouldn't figure out he was on a bus headed to Houston. A single parent, you know. Took her about two days to figure out he wasn't where he said he was. By then, he was lying in wait for Dillon, pipe in hand."

"Geez." Sam shook his head. "And he did this on his own?"

"Looks that way."

Mike sniffed, sighed, and kicked his legs out as if he was bored and ready to move on to a new topic.

"I hope this has no bearing on the case."

Mike and Ed both jumped out of their skins. Ed moved aside and Mike stood as Larson Whiteman stepped into Sam's office.

"Not at all." Sam moved around his desk with his hand extended. "Good to see you, sir."

Ed and Mike murmured in agreement.

Whiteman waved a hand.

The senior partner was the very core of Jackson, Keller & Whiteman. Grey haired, slightly stooped with osteoporosis, and well into his seventies, Whiteman continued to be an intimidating force in the courtroom, though he clearly hoped to turn most cases over to his new dream team.

"I'm reading things in the paper I shouldn't have to read," he said, looking down his nose at the men. "Witnesses dying, DA's being beaten up, rodeo round-ups, all while I'm getting phone calls from the league wondering how Jeremy will fare in all this. Talk to me, boys." He looked around the room. "Tell me you've got a strong case and I've got nothing to worry about."

Mike was the first to speak. "There's nothing to worry about, sir. Casey Dillon isn't a popular ticket among most sports fans, and unfortunately, there isn't much we can do about that but, I assure you, none of this can damage our case in any way. We are airtight, sir."

Whiteman pursed his lips together, squinted slightly, and stared at Mike before deliberately turning toward Sam. "I don't think I need to remind you how much this case means to all of us."

Sam nodded, groaning internally. It was only a matter of time before he had to deal with the partnership issue.

"We're on it." Mike stepped forward. "I assure you, sir. We know what needs to be done and how greatly this will affect the firm."

Whiteman nodded, virtually ignoring Mike. "Good then. I'm counting on you, man." Whiteman cocked and pointed his finger gun directly at Sam.

All three men were silent until Whiteman was well out of earshot.

Ed and Mike's attention returned to Sam as he hustled back behind his desk, hoping to dodge any unwanted questions.

"You got something you want—"

Sam held up the letter from Dillon's office and waved it at him. "I wouldn't say airtight just yet, Mike." He was hoping to distract both men.

"Oh?" Mike forgot about Whiteman as he held out his hand and moved toward the desk to get a better look at the letter. "What now?"

"In between annoying sports fans around the world and her recent trip to the emergency room, Dillon has found another witness to testify against Jeremy."

Mike's laughter cracked like a whip. "Who? Who in the—"

"Kali Jorgenson," Sam said and watched as Mike staggered back, stunned. Sam studied the paper again. "That's right, gentlemen. Kali Jorgenson, master horsewoman and cattle drive queen, is coming to Houston."

* * * *

Everything was spiraling out of control, and he felt as though he was coming unhinged. He had told that Devon kid in no uncertain terms to leave Casey Dillon alone, to let it drop, but no.

The kid worked on a rage all his own that had nothing to do with Casey Dillon or even Jeremy Connors. At least he wasn't blaming anyone else but was ready and willing to take the heat. Which, of course, he should since it was his own damn fault for being so stupid.

This new business with Kali Jorgenson, however, had officially tipped the scale, and he wasn't sure how much more he could endure. The bitch.

He laughed bitterly and pounded his desk.

All his hard work, all his time, all his effort, everything he had built . . . if not for her interference, he knew he could pull it off. After all, he had almost single-handedly destroyed what little evidence Dillon had and made a shambles of her case. He'd known by reputation that Dillon did not give up easily, but her persistence in this case might have been laughable if it weren't so damned annoying. Now this.

Damn, that bitch!

Killing her wasn't an option, not by his own hand anyway. He would have to find another way to get rid of Kali.

Discredit her?

Threaten her children?

He considered the latter. He had learned that the Jorgenson woman was deeply attached to her children, even more so than most mothers, if that was possible, as well as having a bizarre fear of crowded public places. Yes, that was something he could use.

* * * *

Kali sat atop Star and watched as the girls moved the herd in. He was restless but content to be working.

He'd been jealous lately having to watch from the corral as she worked Lightning more and more. The swelling in his knee has subsided, but she was worried about him. He wasn't the same horse he used to be. It was something she'd had to reluctantly admit after the fall. Star had taken it personally when he dumped her on the cattle drive. She knew there were people who argued that horses didn't have such thoughts and feelings, but she knew better. Just how much guilt and remorse a horse felt, she wasn't sure, but she had heard Star nicker and whinny, protesting loudly when she rode off on another horse. He hated it.

Star had been with her through the worst of times, and she wasn't about to bail on him either. She had to be careful not to let Star know just how much she enjoyed the youthful energy of Lightning.

Lightning was "dangerous friendly," as Tracy put it. He had no notion of how large he really was. He ran too eagerly and too quickly into everything and everyone, and just like a spoiled child, he deeply enjoyed taking a nip at someone and then turning to run as fast as he could. He was a handful and a wonderful distraction from the things that were going on in and around Rainwash. But today, Kali needed the comfort of Star for the day's work.

Matthew and Kali had rousted the girls from their beds early. A storm was coming, and they had to get the herd in. The reactions had been typical. Brooke had shot out of bed and scrambled for her boots, worried the animals were in immediate danger.

"We got time, sugar, settle down," Matthew told her.

She had been dressed in less than two minutes.

The twins, however, had been more difficult. Danni moved at sloth speeds and required constant supervision.

"C'mon, Dan . . . let's get the lead out." Matthew had stayed on her, handing her various items of clothing to put on.

She hadn't spoken but accepted each piece of clothing, dressing with her eyes still closed.

Jacks, however, had battled every step of the way. "Why are we doing this? What time is it? We're going out without breakfast? What time is it? It's still dark. Why can't Tracy do it?"

She had argued and whined while they had readied and mounted the horses but, as soon as she had settled into the saddle, she had come alive.

"Can I go ahead?" she asked for the fourth time in five minutes.

Kali was more than happy to be rid of the constant complaining. "Yes, fine! Go! Just be careful. It's still dark . . . keep an eye out for predators."

"Yip!" Jacks gave Mocha a slap to the behind with Danni and Fancy two steps behind.

Brooke lingered a moment longer, gathering more details about the storm.

Kali gave Star the lead. He knew where he needed to go and walked an easy line behind Danni and Jacks. He felt the storm coming, too, and his ears swiveled and scanned the territory for any unusual sounds.

"You remember last time we had the big storm in the middle of the night?" Matthew asked Brooke and she nodded. They had lost several cows, including a newborn. "It's probably gonna be like that, so we want the cows in close."

Brooke nodded again and rode off, leaving Kali and Matthew setting a comfortable gait with their horses.

"You should have brought Lightning," Matthew said.

"Naw, we'll be fine." Kali managed a smile. It felt like everyone was against Star. "This is pretty easy. The girls can bring in most of the herd." She watched the girls in the distance. Both Danni and Jacks had made good time and already reached the crest of the far pasture.

The sky had already begun to change from a dark purple to a beautiful canvas of brilliant oranges, yellows, reds, and purples. It was getting lighter as they moved along and becoming more and more breathtaking.

"This right here is why I guess I can never leave." Matt's voice filtered in, and Star's ears rolled back.

Kali had been lost in the light breeze and display of colors in the sky. She nodded, taking a deep, appreciative sigh.

"What's wrong, Kali?"

"What do you mean? Nothing's wrong. It's beautiful."

"That's not what I'm talking about," Matthew said as he led Redwing closer to Star.

Redwing glanced sideways at Star who couldn't have cared less, and Kali gave him an extra pat along his neck. He was working. Even at a snail's pace, he knew he was working.

"You're unhappy."

"Stop it." She wrinkled her nose as though he had said something absurd, but Matthew obviously wasn't buying the act.

"What is it, Kali girl?"

He would never know just how much that made her want to cry. Something about his tone, that deep affection in the way he called her 'Kali girl' that made her want to pour her heart out to him, but it was impossible. How was she supposed to explain something she didn't quite understand herself?

She shrugged and tried playing it tough. "Mattie, you worry too much. Just because I'm being quiet and want to appreciate this scenery doesn't mean something is wrong."

"No, you know what I mean. It's been going on for days now. I can feel it. We all can. What is it?"

She sighed. He wasn't going to back off.

Of all the brothers, she was the closest to Matthew, and she wondered if he had been put up to talking to her. She had to give him something because the fact was she couldn't remember being this sad since Nicky had died.

"Just restless, I guess. I can't . . . I can't really say what it is. I've just been a little down. That's all." It wasn't the whole truth, but the truth was too insane to share with anyone. Perhaps that was part of it. Deep down, she understood none of her reality was rational.

"I just wish . . ." Matthew shook his head and squirmed a bit in his saddle.

She turned to look at him and smiled. He looked so much like Nicky in many ways but particularly when he had something to say but couldn't say it.

His mouth was twisted to the side and his eyebrows furrowed. "I wish I had known . . . you know, that I had been there for you," he said, shaking his head at his own words.

"What are you talking about?" she asked and started to laugh. "You were there for me. All of you."

"No, no . . . I mean, with that asshole Connors," he said and her shoulders fell.

"Oh." She thought they had been talking about Nicky.

"I didn't mean to upset you. I just—look, I know from Tracy that something went down and—"

Kali raised her hand. "Don't," was all she said. She couldn't even think about it.

Together, they descended the sharp incline, and Kali watched as Star carefully picked his way down through the uneven rocks, plants, and cacti. His gait was uneven as he favored his left side.

Matthew fell respectfully quiet as they leveled out and picked up the pace to an easy trot.

Long out of sight, Kali was anxious to see where the herd was. Off in the distance, a deep rumbling could be heard, and although the sky looked beautiful, Kali knew better. That storm was coming.

She was distracted by Star's canter. It wasn't as smooth as she would have liked but she knew that he was happy, moving toward the herd. His ears were pricked forward, listening.

"Anyway, I just wanted you to know I was sorry," Matthew said.

Kali tried to smile for him. "You couldn't have done any more than Tracy did," she said, quietly stewing over that remark.

"Well, see, he feels real bad about that, too. He just didn't know what to do." Matt's voice jumped a little as they quickened the pace.

Kali said nothing but couldn't stop the sarcastic scoff from escaping her lips.

Matthew leaned forward in his saddle, studying her face. He never missed a thing.

"Whoa." Kali brought Star down a little to an easier pace and Matthew followed without question. "It was terrible," she said suddenly and quietly.

He whipped his head around toward her again, studying her face intently. "He thought he was gonna kill him. That's what he told Ms. Kat." Matthew shook his head. "I don't know exactly what he saw, but I gathered it was pretty bad. He didn't hurt you, though, right? I mean, that's the most important thing. Tracy said you weren't hurt, just scared."

"Yeah, I was scared." She blew out, trying to sound lighthearted, but it was impossible.

"He said he just didn't know what to do. He wanted to kill him. Shitfire, I know how he must have felt. I just can't imagine—" Matthew was talking more to himself than Kali, but he raised an interesting point that Kali suddenly wanted to hear.

"What would you have done?" she asked and tugged on Star's reins.

Star didn't want to stop. His ears were forward, anxious about something ahead of him. He tried to step forward a few times, urging Kali on toward the herd.

She ignored him and kept her eyes pinned on Matt.

"What?"

"What would *you* have done if you'd come up on us like that?"

"Shot him? Kicked the shit out of him? Cussed? Hell, I don't know. You're a hard one to figure, Kali."

"What? Me?"

He blinked, looking startled and suddenly unsure of himself.

"I'm hard to figure? What does that mean? Like it was my fault he attacked me?" Her voice rose with each word.

"What? No! That's not what I meant. I meant, you know, you never know how you might react to something like that. I mean . . . let's say he'd done, uh, whatever he did to you to *my* girl. I would have gone apeshit wild and whipped his ass right then and there. Excuse my French. But with you, you know, a guy just doesn't know how you'd react."

Kali opened her mouth then snapped it shut. She gave Star a kick, driving him forward again, and desperately restrained herself from making him gallop. She wanted to get away from Matt. No. She wanted to belt him across the mouth.

"What?" He caught up to her, Redwing's stride matching Star's. "What, Kali?"

"What the hell is that supposed to mean, Matt? Are you seriously saying that Tracy didn't defend me because he wasn't sure if I wanted to be defended or not? Because let me assure you, I was not having a good time!" She was almost yelling.

She knew Tracy had his reasons for reacting the way he had, but never, not once, had she entertained the notion that it was because he had been afraid of how she might react.

"Geez, Kali! I know that. That is—you're taking it all wrong. Tracy wanted to kill him and was afraid he might. But even later, when he wanted to go to him and talk to him man to man he didn't because he didn't know if he should be fighting your battles. That's how you are, Kali. You know that."

Kali's face turned to stone. She couldn't believe what she was hearing.

"You're not like other women," Matthew said.

"Oh? And how am I?"

"I don't know." Matthew fidgeted in his saddle and pushed his hat back to scratch his head. "Geez. You're just . . . you know, you're tough. You don't cry. You hold everything inside. You fight your own battles. You don't take anything off anyone."

Kali drew a deep breath. In retrospect, she was thankful for his remarks. It was the kick in the pants she needed. Nicky had always said she needed to get mad before she would speak up for herself.

"Let me tell you how I am. I actually like a guy fighting a battle for me now and then because, you know what, Matt? It's exhausting doing all the fighting by myself. I'd like someone to open a door for me, take me on a date, put an arm around me, and make me feel taken care of. Shocking, isn't it?" Her voice was hard. "As far as Jeremy Connors goes, I don't give two craps about him! That's not what *any* of this is about. To tell you the truth, I was more upset by the fact that Tracy never talked to me about it or even asked if I was okay. But as far as how he handled it? I'm fine with that. I just wish he could have, you know, checked on me.

"I've been thinking about leaving Rainwash because I'm dying out here. As much as I love it, I'm dying. And Sam Spann made me see that." Even as she spoke, she saw Matt twist in his saddle, hoping to make eye contact with her, but she didn't dare. She was still mad and hurt and ready to say it all. "But how do I tell Nicky's family that I've been thinking about moving on? How do I tell my own children? How do I take my kids away from the only life they've known? And how can I think about another man when I see Nicky every day? I see him in my children, in you, and Ms. Kat. I see him in Rainwash and . . ." She inhaled deeply and tried to steady herself. She did not want to cry. "I even see him in Star. I see him in everything and everywhere I look. I don't know what's right or wrong or up or down or . . . anything. I just know that I'm not right. If I'm hard to figure, Matthew, it's only because I can't seem to figure out anything on my own. But I promise you this, I'm just like any other woman. I like makeup and nice clothes. I like the idea of a candlelit dinner and romance and all that. I-I'd like to get flowers and . . . I don't know, have a picnic with some special person."

Matthew opened his mouth, not sure of how to respond when movement over the next crest caught both their focus.

Mouse was at full gallop and Brooke was screaming.

"Oh, God!" Kali moaned.

Chapter Thirty-One

"C'mon, Star. You can do this. Easy, boy. Steady. Steady." As she encouraged Star, she pressed him harder and harder, praying to God, the moon, the stars, and the sun that he could handle it. "Please don't buckle. Please don't fall!"

Her eyes were on Brooke as she and Matthew raced forward.

Redwing was just inches ahead of Star. Somehow, the young horse couldn't best him, but one stumble and both Star and Kali would be in dire straits.

Yet, it didn't matter.

Brooke was screaming. Brooke never screamed.

Kali felt sick.

He had been trying to tell her. He had known something was wrong. He had been listening and trying to move Kali along, but she had been distracted with talk of Jeremy and Tracy and Sam.

Star and Kali slowed slightly as they reached Mouse and Brooke, but Matthew and Redwing flew past.

He didn't stop to ask. He didn't need to know. He charged toward the twins and the herd.

"What? What is it?" Kali screamed as she neared Brooke.

Brooke's face was pale. "It's Ramrod." She panted, gasping for air and wrestling with Mouse as she tried to turn herself around again.

"What?"

"Ramrod. He crashed through the back fence. He got through . . . we didn't see him. He . . . he came . . . he got Fancy. He hurt Fancy, Momma." She began to sob hysterically.

"What do you mean hurt, Brooke?" Kali moved Star closer. "What do you mean, Brooke?"

"She's . . . I don't know." Brooke shook her head. "She's bleeding. She's down and bleeding, and Danni fell—"

"No, no, no!" Kali scanned the horizon but saw nothing.

From Brooke's description, they were on the other side of the hill, beyond the canyon. It was the only place where the Jorgenson property joined Buddy Mann's and his demonic bull Ramrod's grazing grounds.

"Brooke, go back to the house. Tell your uncles what's happened. Now! Go!"

Brooke could only nod as she rode off, sobbing.

Whatever happened, Kali knew it had to be bad. Fancy was a good, strong horse. She wouldn't go down and lose Danni unless something was very wrong.

Four strides into the hard gallop, Star stumbled and Kali screamed again. "No!" Why hadn't she switched horses? It was too late. "C'mon, big man! You can do this! C'mon, baby."

One ear rotated back toward Kali, taking in her words and the urgency of her voice, and the other was pricked with excitement. He steadied his hooves and bolted across the canyon.

In minutes, they were there, and then Kali faltered. It was Star who carried her forward.

The fence, or what used to be a fence, was flattened to the ground. It was crap wood that she had been after Buddy to fix for years, but he was too freaking cheap.

Brooke had been right. Fancy was injured. The herd was scattered throughout the canyon with Fancy near the top by a mesquite tree.

Kali scanned the territory for her babies.

Matthew was already in the mix, trying to lure Ramrod away from the horses and girls, but Ramrod was locked on to something.

Snorting and blowing snot everywhere, he pawed at the ground, moving slowly but surely toward Jacks, who was throwing rocks at him.

Kali's heart fell. Even if she had tried, Kali was sure no sound would come. Panic had frozen her lungs, and she nearly choked.

Jacks had secured Mocha in one spot, and it looked like Danni had tried to lead Fancy up the hill and out of danger.

It took a moment for the entire picture to register with Kali. Blood oozed from an open wound on Fancy's rear flank, and Danni was seated beside her, at the base of the tree, curled in a tight ball with her arms wrapped around her legs.

"Danni," Kali said almost in a whisper as she moved Star toward the edge of the slope.

He skittered a few feet, drawing the attention of the bull, and Matthew waved his hands at her.

"Kali, no! Don't even!" Matthew was trying to work his way behind the bull in hopes of starting a chase and, no doubt, leading the bull back to his own property, but it was futile. This time of the year, the bull had just one thing on his brain. He wasn't going to leave all the females without a fight.

"Jacks! Stop it!" Matthew hollered at her. "Get back on the horse and get out. Circle around to your momma. Git!"

Jacks wasn't listening. She was crying and throwing rocks as hard as she could at the bull. "You stupid bull! You damn, damned bull!" She cursed with great fervor. "You hurt Danni! You—"

At last, Kali found her voice and screamed at the top of her lungs. "Jaclyn Anne Jorgenson!" She surprised even herself. Her voice seemed to carry for miles. "You get your ass on that horse right now, and get over here! Now! Now! Now!" Kali bordered on hysteria.

Jacks seemed paralyzed with confusion.

Star slid a little farther, and more rocks clicked and skipped down the dry wall of dirt.

Ramrod snorted as the sounds echoed.

No one moved. No one breathed.

Kali winced internally as she watched Jacks.

Decked out in her bright red, white, and blue shirt she had gotten last year, she couldn't possibly have chosen a worse shirt to wear, but it was her sudden movement to get back on Mocha that alerted Ramrod. She had just one foot in a stirrup when Ramrod dropped his head and charged.

Kali screamed, "Go, Jacks! Go!"

Mocha took off with Jacks barely hanging on.

Matthew charged forward, hat in hand, whooping loudly at the bull, but there was no steering him off course.

Ramrod headed up the embankment hot on Mocha's tail.

Kali kept screaming for Jacks to move out.

There was no way a bull would continue to chase down a horse like Mocha. She was fast and strong. He would give up the chase as soon as she was no longer a threat to *his* cows. Jacks knew this, but would she act on her own instincts? Kali knew that all Jacks was thinking about was Danni.

Jacks and Mocha tore up and over the other side.

The hill had slowed the bull considerably, and he began to rethink his strategy.

"Easy, Matthew, he's coming back," Kali yelled, even though Matthew already saw it coming.

Redwing was agile enough to move out of the way as Ramrod doubled back. He moved a lot faster coming back down the wall of the canyon.

While Matthew worked around him, Kali urged Star west toward Fancy and Danni. Danni still hadn't moved, and Kali's heart began to pound harder and harder.

Neither Star nor Kali made an attempt to run, cautiously approaching instead as rocks still slid out from beneath Star's feet.

She wanted to rush in, to get her hands on her daughter and hold her close, but Kali knew she couldn't without endangering them all. She also knew she couldn't endure any more pain. Not Danni. Not her baby. She wouldn't be able to see her baby hurt. Or worse.

She whispered. "Danni? Danielle?"

Time slowed to a crawl as Kali looked for any sign Danni was still alive. "Momma?"

Kali's heart lurched. "Oh, baby!" She slid from Star's back and hit the ground hard. She wasn't thinking. She couldn't think. All she could see was her baby on the ground, curled up in the fetal position. She panicked as she slid like Star had, rolling over the tops of the rocks, and she fought to keep her position on the ground. She moved, practically crawling on her hands and feet, to get to Danni. "Oh, baby. What is it? What's wrong? Where are you—"

"Kali! Kali!" Matthew screamed, and Kali looked up to see Ramrod repositioning.

Her movement had drawn the bull's attention, and he was homing in on her. The only thing she could do now was run to Danni, scoop her up, and try to use the tree as a shield, but with her first step, she slipped farther down the slope, out of control and helpless.

"He-yah!" She heard Matthew whoop again, urging Redwing toward them.

Kali clawed frantically at the rocks trying to get her footing, and she realized she was screaming. She felt the earth shaking as the heavy bull charged forward.

Shit, shit, shit!

Everything was moving beneath her.

"Momma!"

The earth gave way beneath her, dragging her body along with it, and everything slowed. Kali watched as she slid right into the path of Ramrod. There was no stopping him. Kali did the only thing she could—she went with it. Using the forward momentum, she pushed her body up and attempted to run. Her escape was to get downhill, on level ground, and get some traction, but the bull was moving faster.

Noise. There was so much noise. Ramrod's snorts, and Jacks' screams, even Matthew's yelling was just noise.

It's all about timing.

In a moment of great clarity, she remembered telling Jacks that, in rodeo, timing was everything. One hundredth of a second meant the difference between first place and not placing at all.

And here it was.

It would come down to a millisecond. How quickly she could get ahead of him, miss his horns, throw Ramrod off balance enough to dodge him . . . it was going to be milliseconds.

Then, he was there.

She had heard him first, but in her moment of panic, it hadn't registered.

It was breathtaking.

It was exhilarating.

It was horrifying.

In the blink of an eye, the bull missed his target as Star thundered down the hill between them. Instinct took over as Kali reached up and she grabbed the saddle horn. Star didn't stumble or slow as she grabbed on.

Kali caught a knee and, with a second bounce to the ground, drove her foot against the rocks, catapulted up, and found her seat.

Ramrod tried to turn but lost his footing and slid out, allowing Star and Kali to slip past.

"Woo-hoo!" Matthew hollered, standing up in his stirrups. His voice echoed in the ravine. He led Redwing toward the bull, ready to turn and run as the shot rang out.

The sound was deafening, and everything seemed to stop. The silence afterward was even more deafening.

Kali whirled in her seat to catch a glimpse of it. Ramrod staggered and came to a stop. Nothing and no one moved. Then, with a final snort, Ramrod fell over with a heavy, loud thud.

Kali blinked.

On the crest of the hill stood Tracy on Toby with Evan and Buckshot behind him. Both had drawn a gun, but Tracy was frozen like a statue, his rifle still positioned on his other forearm.

Stephen appeared on the other side, rifle in hand with Brooke safely behind him.

Good girl.

Brooke had made good time getting back to the main house and alerting the others. Ms. Kat would be frantic until they returned.

Kali looked back at the bull.

"Son of a bitch," Matthew groaned, looking at the legendary bull. "He's dead." He ran his fingers through his hair and wiped sweat from his brow.

"Momma?"

Kali jumped from Star's back and clambered up the hill to Danni. "What is it, baby? Where are you hurt?" Danni looked so tiny and Kali wanted to cry. She fought the growing panic.

Danni moved a hand gingerly over her ribcage. "Here." She winced.

"Did Ramr—"

"No. I smashed into the tree." Danni gasped. "Fancy got hurt. Oh, Momma, how's Fancy?"

"She's right here, baby. She never left you."

Danni groaned again. "I know. I tried to make her run but she wouldn't."

Kali smiled, looking back toward Fancy. The wound was deep but not fatal.

"She wouldn't leave me." Danni sounded miserable, but Kali couldn't have been more pleased.

Fancy would live to a ripe old age and be rewarded daily for her loyalty to Danni. Kali would make sure of it.

"She's going to be fine, babe. A little gimpy, but she's okay." Kali scanned the area for Star. He'd saved her life, too. She digested that for a moment as she spotted the old horse. She looked back at Danni. "Let's get you out of here," she said.

Time and events swirled around her head as Kali mounted Star and led Fancy back to Rainwash. "Evan, go, call Dr. Thom. I'll be there soon enough." She brushed Danni's hair back. "You'll be okay, baby. Momma's coming."

Brooke and Jacks followed attentively behind their sister, talking all the while.

"Son of a bitch, what are you gonna say to Buddy?" Matthew wondered out loud.

"Like I give a damn!" Tracy's voice was unusually high-pitched. He was just as upset as the others. Ramrod was an expensive animal. It was a real loss for Buddy Mann and the rodeo circuit, not to mention no one on Rainwash liked the idea of killing an animal if it could be helped. "I wasn't going to sit by and watch him hurt one of the girls!"

"Hurt, nothin'," Stephen said. "He was going to *kill* Kali. You see that? Damn! And did you see Star in there? Like he was a two-year-old again!" He whooped with excitement.

"I'm just saying . . ." Matthew shook his head. "Hell, I just don't want to be the one to tell Buddy his bull is dead."

None of them was listening to the other.

"Damn bull's been tearin' down fence lines from here up to the highway. This has been a long time comin' . . ." Tracy blustered.

As their voices were drowned out by the increasing winds, Kali looked down to find Star's reins wrapped so tightly around her hands that her knuckles were white and throbbing and her fingertips turning a dark purple. She didn't know how she managed to do that. She flashed back to the only other time her hands had been in such a painful tangle.

Nicky.

She pulled her hands free of the leather and flexed the muscles. She collapsed on Star's neck, ignoring the ball of the horn poking into her stomach, and sobbed.

She cried for everything and everyone. Danni and fear at the thought of losing any one of her girls. Tracy and her conflicted feelings about him. Sam and how well he knew her. She felt like raw nerve and was utterly confused by the rush of emotions. She forced her breathing to slow and reminded herself that everyone was okay.

Thank you, Star.

Holding on to his massive neck, the world seemed to wash away. Fancy would be okay, she knew. Danni would be okay. Everyone was okay. And Star had proven himself again. She wished Nicky could have seen it. She wished—

"Ahem."

Stephen, Matthew, and Tracy had ridden up behind her.

Kali snapped straight up in the saddle and wiped her eyes.

"Well, I'll be damned. She cries. What do you know about that?" Leave it to Tracy. Shooting straight from the hip, he had to state the obvious.

"It's a bug. A giant bug flew in my eye."

A few chuckles behind her, and the small group continued on. Little else was said until they returned to Rainwash.

The damage had been surprisingly minimal. While Danni recovered from bruised ribs, Fancy was stitched up and temporarily stalled. Star had been stalled as well. Although a cortisone shot had relieved much of his pain and swelling, she wanted to keep him quiet and in his stall until he had healed.

Life, it would seem, could resume with everyone counting themselves very lucky.

Still, Kali was restless. Unhappy. Dissatisfied. As relieved as she was to have all her babies safe and sound, she felt empty and alone.

Tracy walked up on Kali as she sat outside Star's stall battling the urge to light a cigarette. "He's a good horse, Kali."

"Yeah, and you've been saying I needed to retire him," Kali said, huffing slightly and Tracy smiled. It was Kali's *I told you so.*

"He's still not the horse for you anymore," Tracy said. "He came through, though. I'll give him that."

Kali snorted.

Tracy found a place next to Kali and unabashedly studied her profile. "Just because he can't work doesn't mean you stop loving or caring for him." He gave her a weak smile that told her they weren't talking about Star anymore.

"He wouldn't understand it, Tracy. I don't care what you say. He doesn't understand being left behind."

As if on cue, Star nickered and rubbed his soft nose over her hands.

"No, what he won't understand is when his leg completely gives out or, God forbid, he falls on you and breaks your leg. That, my love, he wouldn't understand."

Deep down, she knew he was right. As much as she loved him, she wouldn't want her own daughters on his back. One hard stumble and they'd be thrown.

"Instead, you let him know you love him, but when you need to, you find another ride. Take Lightning. Young, strong. Full of life. He's . . ." He kicked at the dirt. "Oh, shit, Kali. I'm not any good at all this speaking metaphorically stuff. I ain't just talking about Star. I think you know that. You need to go, Kali. Find what makes you happy. Whatever it is, whoever it is, it's not here. We all know that. And we don't thi—"

"Do you guys sit up at night discussing my personal life?" she asked, turning on him. She was annoyed with this topic, but she hadn't expected his candor.

"Yes'm. Yes, we do. We talk about you all the time. We talk about how we can bring our old Kali back. We talk about what's good for the girls, and darlin', your happiness is part of that. You think they don't see how unhappy their momma is? You need to stop being afraid, Kali. I can't say it any more plainly than that. You act so tough all the time that you actually had us fooled for a long time. I—" He shook his head. "I regret how I misread you, but enough is enough. You need to step out into the world, find someone to hold on to, find that kind of wild happiness you used to have."

Kali stared at him, openmouthed.

"And we'll be here when you get back." He reached over and patted Star. "Just like the old man, here."

Chapter Thirty-Two

The timing of the call couldn't have been better.

She'd had no business working with Axel with her focus splintered in so many directions. Her attention had been on Danni and Tracy and Sam and Star. It had been on things said and things left unsaid. It had been considering threats from Buddy Mann and a potential lawsuit over the death of a bull that had earned his bullet. Her attention had been everywhere but focused on the unusually high-spirited horse throwing his head around and charging her. He had been sizing her up, but she hadn't taken him seriously.

Stallions do not like to be ignored. He reminded her of that quickly. She'd turned away for a moment—just a moment—allowing him to spin around and kick out. She narrowly escaped a hoof in the mouth but caught it in the shoulder and back. She would be wearing a bruise for days for that mistake.

It hadn't been the mustang's fault. It had been hers, but it didn't stop her from grumbling and stomping into the main house, chucking her hat against the tree rack, and practically growling into the receiver when the phone rang.

She'd almost hung up, thinking it was another reporter, but the woman on the other end had begged her to listen. Kali wasn't entirely sure why, but something she said had caught her attention long enough to hear what she needed to hear.

The woman identified herself as a Casey Dillon, the prosecutor on the Jeremy Connors case. She admitted that she was desperate and didn't know where else to turn to for information—any information—on Connors. Anything Kali could provide would be helpful. She asked if Kali had overheard Connors talking about the case. Specifically, Dillon was looking for names connected to the rape victim's murder.

Though she never asked directly, Kali got the impression that Dillon had hoped she might impart information gleaned from Connors' legal team, but

Kali had nothing.

"I'm sorry," Kali said. "There's just nothing I can think of. In fact, when the helicopter appeared out of nowhere, they were all surprised. I really don't think Jeremy knew what was going on. It was a shock to everyone."

"Oh, you were there?"

Kali nodded as the memories of that day flooded back. "Oh, yeah. It was a bucket of fun," Kali said flatly.

"And Connors never said anything? He never spoke about the case or any of the women in his, uh, life?"

"No, nothing. But . . ." Kali hesitated.

"Yes?"

"Nothing. I was just going to say, if it helps, I know he did it."

"How's that?"

"He's guilty. I know he's guilty."

"Why do you say that?"

Kali heard Casey Dillon's intense interest, and she sighed, revving herself up.

By confiding her certainty of Connors' guilt, she knew she had to explain. She needed to. It was the right thing to do, yes, but she also needed to do it for herself.

"It was the change in his voice," Kali said. "The look in his eye. The way he changed so suddenly from one personality to another."

"You sound as though you've been through something."

Kali heard the sudden inflection in Casey Dillon's voice and knew she was testing the waters. "You could say that."

She had spent countless hours since that horrible night reenacting the events, and she couldn't imagine how she'd have handled it had she been actually raped. To have a person turn on her, ripping at her, and ignoring her pleas had been humiliating and terrifying and infuriating all at once.

There had been no love or affection involved. She hadn't been a person, but an object. It had had nothing to do with lust or sexual attraction. It had been about an animal gratifying his own warped desires.

For that reason alone, Kali had to talk about what had happened. Who knew how many others there had been, or how many more there might be? And as much as she hated to admit it, she needed to know that it was not her fault. So even knowing Ms. Kat and Gina were within earshot, Kali relayed the events of that night.

Casey Dillon never spoke. Even when Kali couldn't find the courage or proper words to describe her feelings, Ms. Dillon remained silent, taking in every word.

"It didn't matter how much I fought him." Kali gnawed the side of her nail before admitting, "I've always thought I was a strong woman, but it had no impact on him. He was in his own world. I tried to punch him, kick him, but . . . I couldn't fight him off.

"He told me I was a man-tease, and that I needed to know what it was like to have a real man." She sighed and fought the shaky feeling that threatened to topple her.

Gina emerged from the kitchen, towel still in hand, and moments later, Ms. Kat stood behind her. Their expressions almost broke Kali, and in some ways, Kali realized that telling a total stranger over the phone was her way of being able to tell the women in her life.

She took another deep breath, locked her eyes on Ms. Kat and Gina, and continued her story. "I tried to remind him why he was here at Rainwash, remind him about the woman who had accused him of rape, but he laughed."

Ms. Kat shook her head, and Kali thought she heard Gina groan.

"He said those men wouldn't blame him for doing what he was doing to me. And . . ." She put her hand on her throat, whether to move the lump past it or steady her voice she wasn't quite sure. "He pushed me down. He had his hands on my . . . b-b-breast." She cleared her throat. "And he pulled my legs apart . . ."

"Oh, dear Lord," Gina said, moving toward Kali.

Kali reflexively shrank back.

Gina froze.

Kali knew that if Gina touched her, tried to hug her, she would crumple. She stared at the floor and kicked the ground with the toe of her boot.

"Gina, honey, come here." Ms. Kat's voice was a whisper, but it echoed loudly in Kali's brain.

"I couldn't do anything. He was on top of me and was jerking at my pants when Tracy stopped him." Kali peeked at Ms. Kat and Gina.

They stood like two statues locked arm in arm, eyes unblinking as they watched every move she made.

"Would this Tracy—"

"Tracy Sommers," Kali said.

"Would Tracy Sommers be willing to testify to what he saw?" Casey Dillon asked.

"If I asked him to, yes."

There was a pause, and Kali braced herself. She had opened this can of worms and had to be ready to deal with the fallout.

"Ms. Jorgenson, are you prepared to come to Houston and testify to what you just told me?"

Kali looked up at Ms. Kat and Gina.

"Ms. Jorgenson?"

She couldn't speak. It was as if every emotion had crashed into her at once.

"Kali?"

Her heart began to pound, and she squeezed her eyes shut.

"Okay, Kali. Would you be willing to come to Houston to testify? I'd need you to retell everything you just said."

Leave Rainwash? Fly? On an airplane?

Kali had traveled to nearby cities for the girls' rodeos, but she wasn't sure she was ready for this. She had been quite content staying on the ground ever since . . .

"Kali? Are you still there?"

She felt the tempo of her breathing change. "Yes." Kali swallowed the hard chunk of fear stuck in her throat. "I'm here." She slid against the wall and rubbed her head. She had to think.

Gina rushed forward. "What is it? What? Are you okay?"

"She wants me to come to Houston," Kali said.

"Who's she?" Gina asked and Kali wiggled the phone in front of her.

"A lawyer—Casey Dillon . . . the lawyer prosecuting Jeremy Connors. She wants me to come and testify against him."

"Give me the phone." Gina snatched it from Kali before she could react.

Kali's heart still pounded. She felt the walls closing in. She had never noticed how dark the interior of the main house was. All dark wood. The leather upholstery was dark. So dark. And stifling. It was hard to catch a breath.

"Yes, she'll be there," Gina said.

"Gina!" Kali dove for the phone, but Gina evaded her, putting her back against Kali.

As Kali groaned audibly and covered her ears in disbelief, Gina identified herself to Casey Dillon, verified more information about the lawyers' stay at Rainwash, and the general demeanor of Jeremy Connors and his posse.

Kali staggered to the big table and fell into a chair. "I can't believe this." Kali groaned, letting her head fall to the table.

As Gina wrote down information, Ms. Kat rubbed her back. "Oh, precious baby. I had no idea. Tracy told me something went on, but I don't think even he realized how bad it was. Oh, honey. I am so sorry."

"This is horrible. I can't go to Houston." Kali moaned and rolled her head back and forth on the cool tabletop. "I just can't."

"Yes, you can and you will," Gina said from behind them.

Kali snapped upright.

Gina glided toward the table, reaching for Kali's hands as soon as she was close, and looked deeply into her eyes. "I know this is going to be hard, sweetie, but you have to do this. You have to go and tell what happened. I'll go with you if I have to and hold your hand the whole way, but you have to do this. You have to do this for yourself, but you have to do this for the poor woman who was killed. She can't talk, Kali. You have to talk for her."

"I can't . . ." Kali gasped for breath. "I can't fly."

"Yes, you can." Gina's voice was stern, but, a second later, she turned to Ms. Kat and faltered. "I had no idea. Oh, Evan would just die. I had no idea."

Kali shook her head. "I can't do it. You know what will happen to this place? All the reporters and phone calls and . . . and . . . hate mail? I just can't."

Gina was shaking her head. "Kali. It's out of your hands and you know it. You have to do this . . . for you, for your daughters, for that Ms. Stanten. You have to do this for victims without a voice." She took a deep breath, looked at Ms. Kat, and then let Kali have it. "Nicky would want you to do this."

"I can't fly." Kali almost laughed.

"Yes, you can," Gina said. "And I know you, Kali girl. You will."

Kali looked to Ms. Kat for some kind of support.

"You know Gina's right."

And that was that.

Tracy was not so easily persuaded. He used every excuse he could think of not to go but, in the end, Ms. Kat wouldn't hear another word. Tracy was going with her.

Ms. Kat had pulled Tracy to the side before they climbed into the truck. "And when you take off, you hold her hand. Don't ask and don't take no for an answer. She's terrified and needs someone to reassure her."

"Hell, what about *me?*" Tracy asked, eyebrows raised. "I've never been on a plane in my whole life."

Ms. Kat chuckled. "Fine, then. You can hold each other's hands. It'll be perfect."

They did just that . . . when they took off and again when they landed.

* * * *

That son of a bitch couldn't keep his pecker in his pants for one minute! Once he had learned about Jeremy Connors and Kali Jorgenson, he'd understood exactly what Casey Dillon was after. Kali Jorgenson's testimony would illustrate how little Connors cared about women or the legal system. What better witness than a still-grieving widow? She was a doting at-home mother, animal lover, girl-next-door, still living with her in-laws. Not only had the woman not had sex since the death of her husband, she hadn't even dated. To make matters worse, the woman's husband had died serving his country, leaving her with three small children. There wasn't enough dirt in the world to discredit this witness. The jury would hang on her every word.

Casey Dillon had locked up a beauty this time.

For all the work he had put into Connors, it was going to end with a mindless pass at a grieving widow. And Kali Jorgenson wouldn't be bought off as easily as Ashley Williams Nelson. Sex and money didn't mean anything to this woman. She was acting on a moral high ground.

He sighed.

It would be up to him to fix the situation and reason with the Jorgenson woman. If reason didn't work . . .

He was running out of time. And patience.

* * * *

Just as Tracy picked up the last suitcase, Kali tapped him on the shoulder and pointed toward a large well-built, black man in his early forties holding a sign with the name Withers on it.

It had been the first thing that came to Kali's mind when she'd been asked about a code name.

Although the man had no way of knowing who they were, Kali had noticed that as the man scanned the baggage claim area, he kept coming back to her. Kali had given a very brief description of Tracy Sommers and herself. Clearly, the man had been told what to look for and he smiled broadly as Tracy and Kali made their way toward him.

"Mr. Sommers? Ms. Jorgenson?" He stuck a hand out, giving both a firm handshake and quickly took a bag from Tracy. "Name's Luther Monroe, assistant DA and sometime chauffeur. How was the flight?"

"Well, we're here," Tracy said, scratching his head.

Luther Monroe didn't miss a beat. "And that's all we can ask for, isn't it? Let's go. I'm parked out this way." He assured Tracy and Kali that they would get to meet Casey Dillon as soon as they were checked in and settled under their assumed names. For their own protection and for the good of the case, no one knew they were in Houston.

"Well, Connors' team knows you're here, but they are under a gag order. That means no talking to the press or anyone else." What Luther didn't tell them was what a difficult time they had had keeping intimate details of the case, including names, from the press, gag order or no gag order.

Tracy and Kali stole private glances toward each other.

They already knew. Before they had left Rainwash, they had scoured the Internet and learned more than they had ever dreamed possible about the nastiness of the case, including details about Casey Dillon. While much of the information was unflattering about the hard-hitting attorney, Kali had decided she liked the woman. She didn't take any guff from anyone and wasn't about to back away from the Connors case. As Ms. Kat had said, she just might be the one woman capable of stopping Jeremy Connors, and for that, Kali was ready to support her in all ways.

She had spoken to the girls before she left, fearing they would ask difficult questions, but they seemed to understand that Uncle Tracy and Momma had to go talk to a judge about what they knew of Jeremy Connors.

"You can't worry any more about it," Ms. Kat had told her. "After it's all said and done, if you want, you can tell the girls a little more. But, for now, they know as much as they need to know. You've got more important things to worry about."

While she had tried to focus on what she would say at the trial and how she would try to present herself, she'd kept going back to one person—Sam Spann.

As Mr. Monroe discussed check-in and meeting Casey Dillon, she grew more anxious. It was all becoming real. She realized she was more nervous about seeing Sam than she was about testifying. It was ridiculous that one man she hardly knew should be on her mind so much. Yet, there he was. In her dreams, in her thoughts, and about to be in the same courtroom—only he was the enemy. Her heart ached thinking about it.

Vaguely, Kali heard Mr. Monroe talk about dinner and meeting times as she looked out the back window of the car. Houston was a sea of construction, skyscrapers, and cars. It was a far cry from Rainwash, and Kali was homesick for her babies. Justice or no justice, Sam or no Sam, she wished she had never come.

While she withdrew, Tracy was unusually animated with Luther Monroe, asking questions, taking in the sights, and making personal comments, all of which entertained Mr. Monroe so mightily that he never even saw the tail.

Chapter Thirty-Three

Kali looked out the window of the hotel just off Highway 12 in Clear Lake. The suburb outside Houston—and the city of Houston, for that matter— was nothing as she had imagined. Kali had believed it was skyscrapers, bookstores, and Starbucks on every corner, but twenty minutes outside downtown Houston, and Kali was staring at an older highway with strip malls lining both sides. Cleaners, karate schools, salons, and shoe stores were everywhere. Simply put, it wasn't Rainwash.

She turned to look at the room again and tried to remember the last time she had been in a hotel room. She had a king-sized bed with a patterned bedspread she was sure no one would ever actively choose for their bedroom. Still, it matched the maroon carpet and heavy satin-looking drapes. The wooden bed frame, table, and dresser were a deep cherry wood, rich in texture and design. The state was paying top dollar for their stay. It was a beautiful room, but the bedspread had to be questioned.

Tracy had the adjoining room, and while Kali had not seen it, she assumed by his excitement it was similar to hers. A miniature bar, fully stocked, was the highlight of his furnishings.

With Nicky—that had been the last time she had been in a hotel room. She hadn't traveled since his death except for the girls' riding competitions, and they slept in the trailer. No, the last time she had been in a hotel was when she and Nicky had traveled to New York to check out possible neighborhoods and houses. It had been particularly wonderful because they had gone without the girls.

Her eyes drifted toward the bed again. It hadn't been wild, crazy lovemaking. It wasn't rough or scandalous. It was just . . . nice. It had been gentle, sweet, and caring. It had been very Nicky.

Oh, how she missed being touched, caressed, and loved by a man. She missed being held, the feeling of snuggling and smelling that musky, male scent on her sheets. She still loved and missed Nicky, and always would, but the ache she felt now was less about Nicky than the actual physical need.

Her mind had begun to wander when a knock at the door startled her. "Yes?"

"It's Luther Monroe, Ms. Jorgenson. Ms. Dillon is with me."

"Oh, yes. Just a minute." Kali knocked on the door separating her room from Tracy's. "Trace! They're here."

She opened the hallway door to find Mr. Monroe and a petite, meticulously dressed woman who could only be Casey Dillon. Kali stuck out her hand. "Ms. Dillon," Kali said, pumping her hand a few times. It was a nice, strong handshake that Kali both appreciated and expected.

"Casey, please."

"And I'm Kali."

Tracy entered the room behind them, hugging an ice bucket under his arm, and loaded down with a candy bar and two cokes.

Kali grinned. "And this is Tracy Sommers. He's having a little too much fun with the miniature refrigerator and vending machines," Kali said with a laugh.

Since they had checked into the hotel room, Tracy had managed to lock himself out of his room twice, forgetting his key while raiding the floor's vending machines.

"Hey, as long as it helps him talk." Mr. Monroe chuckled and politely pushed past Kali.

Kali stepped back, letting Ms. Dillon in, and together, the four went over the events that had occurred between Jeremy Connors and Kali on the night of the helicopter fright. They discussed possible questions Sam Spann and his partners might ask, cross-examination tactics Kali might expect, and how Tracy's interpretation of what had happened could be reinterpreted. Within an hour, Kali and Tracy were emotionally exhausted and completely irritated.

After three, Tracy no longer held his tongue. "Look here. I saw what I saw. I know what I saw, and no one can try to make me say different. We came here to do what's right but, I gotta tell ya, I got better things to do with my time than repeat myself over and over again and listen to insultin' questions. I ain't stupid."

For the fourth time, Mr. Monroe pacified Tracy. "We know, Tracy. But you've got to remember, Connors' lawyers have millions at stake as well as their reputation. They are going to grind you down on the tiniest detail and if you say just one thing, move in one direction, or get angry in any way that can be used against you—against *us* . . . it's over."

They discussed and rehearsed how to approach the stand, how to hold their bodies, and how to direct the court.

Casey looked over Kali's wardrobe, helping her select the proper outfit, and Kali found herself apologizing for everything she had brought. She suddenly felt very insecure and out of place.

"This is fine. Perfect, in fact," Casey said, in reassurance. She looked at her watch. "What do you say, Luth? We've been at this long enough. Let's all go get something to eat."

"No, thanks." Kali rubbed her hands over her face and scrubbed her tired eyes. "I'll just order in." In truth, she wasn't even hungry.

"You sure?" Tracy asked.

Kali knew she should go just to keep Tracy company, but he'd had a wild look in his eyes. He was far too excited to be held back. She was pretty sure that without her in tow, Tracy might venture out to a few nightclubs, having a far better time alone.

She nodded and smiled. "You go, Tracy. Soak in Houston. Just try to control yourself."

While Mr. Monroe cautioned Kali against opening the door to strangers, they had not appeared overly concerned. No one knew Tracy and Kali were in town much less which hotel they were in.

"Stay in, watch some television and relax." He smiled an easy smile. "You'll be fine."

Kali nodded, eager to be alone to relax.

"I'll leave a message at the front desk to give you a wake-up call around eight in the morning. Is that okay with you?" Casey asked as the men walked out.

"That's great," Kali said, knowing she would be up long before then.

"And, hey."

Kali looked back at Casey standing the doorway.

"You're going to do great, Kali. I can't thank you enough for coming. This means a lot to a lot of people. You're doing a really good thing." She gave Kali a little thumbs-up sign and Kali smiled.

When the door shut with a heavy clunk, Kali fell back against the pillows on her bed.

She couldn't remember the last time she had felt so incredibly uncertain. She wasn't uncertain about testifying against Jeremy Connors. It was the one thing she felt right about. He was a monster and had to be stopped. She had seen it in his eyes and heard it in his voice. If ever the word *predator* could be applied to one man, it was Jeremy Connors.

She was uncertain how well she would present herself, and how she would feel once she saw Sam. She began to question herself again. Was this a case of a lonely woman building one man into something he really wasn't? Was she so desperate that she imagined a budding relationship that didn't even exist?

She kicked at the pillows on her bed in disgust. For all she knew, he had a girlfriend. Or more. It had been more than a month since she last laid eyes on him.

The girls had loved their gifts from Sam, and for days he was all they had talked about. She hadn't known how to take the gifts. Were they genuinely gifts from the heart to three special little girls? Or were they attempts to get closer to Kali?

The girls had wanted to call him, but she had resisted—a thank-you note would suffice. Beyond that . . . well, she just hadn't been sure. Dating and the rules of dating had become foreign to her. Truly, Kali did not know what to make of the entire situation. All she knew was she couldn't seem to stop thinking about him.

She remembered the lawyers' comments and the lady-in-wait theory of his, and snorted. What kind of man represented a man like Jeremy Connors? She had spent so many years alone she had actually lost perspective on what a good man really was.

She spent the next few minutes trying to create a list of everything that was wrong with Sam Spann when a knock sounded at the door.

She rolled her eyes and scooted off the bed.

"Trac—" She opened the door, but it wasn't Tracy.

* * * *

He pushed her so hard and quick that she stumbled backward and caught her heel on the carpet, falling to the floor.

There she was. Kali Jorgenson in the flesh.

He glared down at her. Her eyes were huge.

She crab walked backward, looking confused and frightened.

A small corner of his mouth flickered.

Good, at least she's got the good sense to be scared. She should be. Bitch.

His heart pounded.

Okay. Now what?

No one had seen him come in the hotel and no one had any reason to suspect him. Not here. Not with her. He could make it look like a random attack in a hotel room. It was believable, but her being who she was, her sudden death would be obvious.

He continued to stare at her while her mouth began to move.

"What are you doing here?" she asked.

She started to get up but he moved in, and she dropped back against her hands again, still sitting in a crab position. He wanted to keep her that way for a moment longer while he decided what to do with her.

He ground his teeth.

Oh, the options.

Kick her in the face and knock her unconscious.

Bitch!

Rip her clothes off and have his way with her.

She was a strong woman, but one good punch to the face and she'd crumple like a ragdoll. His eyes roamed her body, considering. He risked too much by leaving possible hair or skin DNA and the little wench wasn't worth it.

"What are *you* doing here?" he asked her.

"I'm . . . I'm here to—"

He watched as she fumbled with her words and they both knew what was going on. She didn't want to say. She didn't have the balls to say it, but they both knew why she was in Houston. She shook her head and began to stand. Again, he felt his pulse race.

Do something!

As she crouched and moved her hands in front of her, he knocked her back with a knee, slamming it against her shoulder. She fell too easily, and he decided she wasn't even trying to fight him. She was genuinely shocked by his sudden appearance and didn't know what to do about it. But as he went over his options, he saw Kali gathering her nerve.

She rolled to the side, avoiding his knee and hopped to her feet.

"Get out!" Her eyes flashed. The fear was gone.

He smiled.

He had rehearsed what he was going to say many times but standing over her, he'd temporarily lost his edge. It wasn't until she stood again, challenging him, that he regained his focus.

"Not before we talk business," he said. His voice was calm and cool.

"What business?" she said.

Although she did her damnedest to appear confident, he saw that she was shaking and worked it to his advantage. "A little unfinished business before you go to court tomorrow and ruin an innocent man's life."

She laughed. "Innocent? I don't think so. But I also don't think I should be having this conversation with you," she said and moved toward the phone. "You need to get out before—"

Dammit!

He hit her from behind, knocking her to the bed, and rolled on top of her, pinning her down. Once again, he had the advantage.

"What are you doing?"

She was so shocked she had allowed him to get completely on top of her, pressing her shoulders to the back of the bed.

She began to scream and he hit her again.

He waited, wanting to hit her more, but she stopped and stared back at him.

He smiled down at her. "That's better," he said, his voice dripping with sarcasm.

She struggled, but he could tell it was halfhearted. She had decided to see what he was going to do next, waiting to conserve her energy.

He admired that in her.

He had spent too much time listening to her talk about reading an animal's body language. What was it she had said? *Feel the body. Is it bunching up? When you feel your horse's middle bunch up, he's ready to explode. Be ready to handle the reins . . .*

And here he was, sitting on top of her, waiting to feel her body bunch. It was exciting.

"What do you want?" she asked through gritted teeth. "Tracy is going to be back any minute."

"You can't testify tomorrow," he told her.

She didn't move.

"I don't suppose you care, but should you testify, you ruin many lives. And we don't want that, do we?" He stared down at her. He felt the tension rising in her body.

The mare was about to bunch.

"You can go straight to hell," she snapped.

* * * *

With a sudden explosion from her hips, she pitched him forward, and he raised his hands to brace himself against the wall or be smashed into it. He was only using one arm, and it was all she needed. She rolled to the side, scrambled out from beneath him, and wiggled off the bed. She was off the bed and half running, half crawling toward the door when he pounced on her again, smashing her to the floor.

She grunted loudly.

The pain was horrible. It felt as though her rib cage was crushed and all the air was pushed out of her. She felt the wheeze and struggled to catch her breath, but it was too late.

He was on top of her again, forcing her to roll over so he could sit on her.

She'd spent far too much time fighting with livestock to go down easily. Although she had almost no breath, she managed to bring up a leg and kick him away from her. The kick was hard and powerful.

Take that, asshole!

He flew backward and slammed into the table.

She heard him grunt and tried to run, but she didn't have enough time. She was very aware of him coming back, and panic swelled inside her. She tried to scream for help but had nothing. More than his oncoming assault, that scared her the most—she had nothing. She gasped and coughed and tried to catch her breath. She vaguely recalled a competition when Danni had landed on the horn of her saddle, knocking the wind out of her lungs. The rodeo physician had told her to try to take big, even breaths.

Kali tried, but he was back, pushing her down, sitting on her, and shoving his face in hers. Only this time, he was extremely angry. He was hurt and he knew he was running out of time.

Was this what happened to Jessica Stanten? Was this how it happened? She was confused. It couldn't have been him. No, the timing was off. He wasn't there when she was attacked, but nothing else made sense.

"How do you think I found you, bitch?" he asked, and Kali closed her eyes.

He was going to kill her . . . she knew it. It wasn't fair. She needed more time to catch her breath then, she swore, she would beat the shit out of him.

She knew she could. She had no doubt she would. She just needed to . . .

"I knew what time you arrived. I knew what hotel you were in. I know everything about your personal life—your family and your horses. I know what bank you use, what credit cards you have. Hell, I even know what books you've ordered online. I know what time you go to sleep, wake up, what kind of shampoo you use.

"I have a lot of money, Kali, and I swear to you, I intend to use every bit of it to destroy you should you testify tomorrow."

She watched as his face contorted right before her.

"And I have already employed two men to do a very nasty little job."

She swallowed.

"Believe me, it wasn't easy. It's not that hard to find men willing to do such things, but there are those who make it their specialties."

Gradually, her breath returned. She needed to catch him off guard and get to the door. She needed to take advantage of his injury. If she could just make it to the door . . .

"Little girls, Kali." He leaned in and she froze.

Again, her breath was gone.

He laughed a low, menacing chuckle. "That right, Kali. There are men who specialize in little girls. Specifically, yours."

Oh, God.

Chapter Thirty-Four

Sam leaned back in his chair. He was sure he would regret the amount of coffee he'd sucked back, but it had been a long day that had stretched into a long evening with Jeremy.

While Mike had concentrated on attacking the defense, Sam and Ed had drilled Jeremy on his demeanor, his body language, and his choice of words. Jeremy reeked of privilege and conceit—the poster boy for elite, overpaid athletes. Part of their defense had to be Connors' admission of guilt. They planned to present Jeremy as a man who would and had said almost anything to get a woman into bed, but never had he resorted to rape. They had a long list of women willing to testify to Jeremy Connors' appeal and eligibility, and confirm that they would and had said just about anything to get in bed with Jeremy. He was guilty all right. He was guilty of not having the wherewithal to walk away from fast women and an even faster lifestyle. Jeremy may be a victim of his own circumstance, but he was guilty of perpetuating that sinful living.

The problem was getting Jeremy to show any sense of remorse for that living.

"Just a little," Sam had pleaded. "It's all we're asking for here. Just a little."

Instead, Jeremy had shown uncooperative restlessness as he fidgeted and continuously checked his watch.

"Are we keeping you from something?" Ed asked.

Jeremy had been sitting back in his chair, legs spread apart, slumped down with the attitude of a teenager being grounded. "Yeah." He came to life for the first time with a smile that was slow and hopeful. "I'm supposed to meet some of the boys for a little, you know, get-together at Chelsea's."

Ed and Sam exchanged glances while Mike looked up from his paperwork. Disbelief washed over the boardroom as all three men went wide-eyed and slack-jawed.

"Chelsea's?" Sam knew there had to be a punch line coming. Jeremy couldn't be serious.

"The strip club?" Ed asked. He almost choked on an incredulous chuckle. "You're going to go to a strip club the evening before your court date." He let his reading glasses drop to the table and rubbed his eyes. After a long pause, he began to laugh.

Jeremy looked around the room, puzzled by their reactions. "What?"

" 'What?' That's your line of defense? Brilliant!" Ed slumped back in his chair and stared up at the ceiling. "I don't know. Maybe tomorrow we should enter this in as evidence." He continued to talk to the ceiling. "If nothing else, it shows the jury how completely idiotic and clueless Jeremy Connors is. Maybe our new line of defense should be that he's too stupid to be a predator."

"Hey!"

"Jeremy," Mike said patiently as though talking a petulant toddler out of his tantrum. "It's not going to happen. You have to call your buddies and say you aren't coming. You will not go to a titty bar tonight."

Jeremy jumped to his feet. "I'd like to see you—"

Sam held his hands up. He'd hit his breaking point. He wanted nothing more than to punch Jeremy square in the mouth for being the arrogant, insolent little bastard that he was. When Jeremy had first come to Jackson, Keller & Whiteman, much of the staff had been elated to have such a big name come through their doors, and they had bent over backward for the little prick. Sam hadn't been impressed then and he wasn't now. Jeremy had represented a corner office and a partnership in the firm. It had been everything he thought he wanted in life. Now, two pots of coffee and zero sleep later, he was changing his mind.

Always, his thoughts wandered back to Rainwash. He found himself wondering how Lightning was doing and how he was responding to the next rider. How were the girls and, most importantly, how was Kali?

He thought about Kali a lot. She loathed Jeremy, and Sam couldn't blame her, but he wondered and worried what she thought about him. He had outed her over her cigarettes. He had played the scenario over and over in his mind. The way she had looked. The way her clothes had lain against her body. The way she had muttered, "You got me." The way she had walked off. He couldn't imagine what she thought of him.

He rubbed his jaw, refocusing on Jeremy.

Jeremy had kept his phone on during their conference, taking one call after another, doing that little finger flick to the staff. That *hold that thought, I've got to take this* gesture that made Sam irate. As if this wasn't the single most important event of Jeremy's life.

"Jeremy. Stop right there. We're on your side, man, but Mike is right. You can't go to a, uh, an establishment of ill repute when we are trying to show you're the victim here. Women are throwing themselves at you." Sam pointed a finger at him.

Jeremy nodded.

"That can't be happening if you're stuffing singles down a G-string, got it?"

Jeremy snorted. "Shit, man, I just wanted to be out with the guys the night before. You know? Think of it as a pre-celebration." He chuckled. "Ill repute. Ha, you gotta love that." He gestured toward Sam with his thumb and looked to the others for support. "An establishment of ill repute. I'll have to remember that one."

"It's no joke." Sam sighed.

"We don't celebrate until there is actually a *reason* to celebrate," Ed said.

"See, you're going about it all wrong. Damn, man. We've been here all day. I got it, man. I got it all down. I know what to say, what to wear, how to walk and talk." He pressed a hand to his chest. "This is what I do, remember? I know how to put on the show. Come show time, I'll perform just like I'm supposed to, but you got to give me some downtime."

"Right, as opposed to the downtime you might be getting in prison," Ed said and Mike shot him a hard look.

"Right now!" Sam pounded a fist on the table, catching Jeremy's attention. "I guarantee Casey Dillon is pounding in every detail to Kali Jorgenson's head." He felt a slight tug in his chest. It was going to be difficult to see her, but he had to deal with it. Somehow. He had to deal with it. "Every point Dillon wants made, every little nuance she wants the jury to get, she's pounding into Kali's head. And I promise you, Kali's not going to a strip club. She's going to come off as—"

"Yeah, well, or good ol' Tracy Sommers is," Jeremy said with a sneer.

"I bet not," Ed said.

"Yeah, you're right. He's out taking in the sights." Jeremy chuckled as he looked around the room. "You tell me where an old cowboy, alone at night in Houston, is going to go but to a titty bar?"

"How do you know what Tracy is doing?" Sam asked. Hell, no one even knew where they were being kept.

Once again, all eyes were on Jeremy as the smirk faded almost instantly and Sam sat forward.

"You're serious?" Ed asked, incredulous. "You know about Tracy?"

"How do you know where Tracy is and what he's doing?" Sam repeated the question.

Mike's chair squeaked as he leaned forward as well.

Jeremy shifted his gaze and tried to smile, but it was all wrong. Since they had met him, all he had done was smirk and sneer at everything. While it was obnoxious, it was a natural expression for Jeremy. This was strained, forced, awkward.

No one said a word.

"I dunno." Jeremy shrugged and laughed. It was a nervous laugh. He had stepped into it now. "Maybe Perry told me."

"Perry?" Mike said.

"What does Reginald Perry know about it?" Ed asked.

"More importantly, why are you even talking to Perry? I thought you were done with him. Wasn't that part of the agreement?" Sam asked.

Someone's fingers drumming the table echoed in the silence, and Jeremy shifted his weight to his left leg, looking around.

"Hey, what's the big deal?" He spread his hands out and shrugged again. "No big deal, man. So I talked to the guy."

"You talked to Perry about this case?" Mike stood and walked around the table.

"You talked to Perry about Kali and Tracy? What about?" Ed asked, growing more urgent with each word.

"Wait! Stop!" Sam shook his head. "Back up. How does Perry know where Kali and Tracy are staying?"

"No, Sam!" Mike exploded. "*Why* does he know where they are? That's the question here. Why? Why?"

"Shit, I dunno," Jeremy said sounding a great deal like that petulant toddler once more. "I guess he wanted to talk to them."

"What?" Ed slammed his palms down on the table, scattering papers.

"Talk to them? To possible witnesses? About what?" Mike's voice was alarmingly high. "What the hell does he think he's doing?"

As a certain panic began to rise in the room, Sam stayed very calm, watching Jeremy's facial expressions. Jeremy looked like a little kid, looking from one angry adult to the next.

"Why are you talking to Perry? He's a piece of crap, Jeremy. I thought you—" Ed shook his head in disbelief. "You call him or did he call you?"

"Will someone please tell me why Reginald Perry, a little snot-nosed piece of shit, is putting the screws to us again?" Mike stopped pacing only long enough to pose his question. No one had an answer or seemed to hear him and he was back to walking a hole in the carpet.

Sam leveled a hard look at Jeremy. "Why?"

Jeremy focused on Sam. His eyes widened as his mouth dropped open, closed, and dropped once more.

Sam asked again. Calmly. "Why, Jeremy? Why is he talking to them?"

"I don't *know*. Shit! Maybe . . . maybe . . ." Jeremy paced alongside Mike. He cleared his throat and held up a finger as though his mental lightbulb had gone off. "Maybe he thinks if he could get Kali Jorgenson to not talk . . . maybe, you know, Perry could represent me again."

Mike stopped.

Ed stopped.

Sam collapsed into his chair.

"Unbelievable."

"Let me get this straight," Ed said and laughed sardonically. "You told Perry if he stopped—"

"Hey! I didn't tell him shit." Jeremy's face flushed with anger as he stepped forward. "You can all go to hell. I didn't tell him shit. He's been callin', sending messages and crap. Hell, since I've been back. He's callin' all the time and begging for another chance. Says he's got some big fat contract lined up with a show and some liquor company in Europe. Millions. He says he's got it all locked up. Keeps calling me and shit, begging for me to take him back. I never called him. He always called me!" His voice had gotten louder and louder with every sentence, and by the end, Jeremy was yelling.

"And you didn't feel the need to set him straight, remind him how royally he had screwed up." Ed cocked an eyebrow.

"Look, man, I don't know how bad he screwed things. He's trying to help. He's got my interest—"

"No, Jeremy! He sees a fat paycheck slipping away and wants you back because his screwup made worldwide news. No one wants him as an agent. He has to get you back to prove his worth. He doesn't give a shit about you. He's in this for himself, but he needs your name to redeem himself." Mike jabbed a finger in Jeremy's direction.

Jeremy shrugged. "Whatever."

If Perry could deliver on his promises, however, Jeremy could triple his money. Jeremy didn't care about anyone but himself either. It was a perfect marriage.

"If you don't believe me," Jeremy said, a smirk returning to his face, "here, check my caller ID." He fumbled for his phone. "That last call. That was him. See?" He found the number and waved the phone around for all to see. "He's there, at the hotel, to talk to Kali Jorgenson. I got nothing to do with that. You know that 'cause I've been here all day."

Sam's heart jumped.

Reginald was with Kali? Where was Tracy?

"Oh, shit," Ed murmured, and Sam realized he wasn't alone in his concerns.

Perry, the same man who had arranged to have a helicopter crew record the cattle drive and nearly killed everyone. The same man so desperate to restore his reputation to the sports world, he would do almost anything to get Jeremy back.

"What hotel?" Sam demanded. He could see Kali's face as he imagined Perry pressing her up against the wall, forcing her to sign something, or threatening her in some way. His chest tightened.

"Hell, it's not like he could hurt her." Jeremy tried to laugh. "She's strong and he's a little pencil-necked—"

"Aw, geez." Ed groaned.

"His arm is still in a cast for cryin' out loud." Jeremy went on, but no one was listening.

Mike's pacing had practically turned into a jog, and Ed could only groan as he held his head in his hands and rocked back and forth.

Jeremy stammered as a rage welled inside Sam. He had been dealing with this punk for too long.

"The hotel! The name of the hotel!" Sam's voice roared, echoing across the near-empty office building.

Even Mike froze.

Sam's priorities shifted so rapidly he almost felt the room tilt.

Even as Jeremy mumbled the name of the hotel, Sam was already running, yelling for someone to call hotel security. Forgoing the elevator, he headed for the stairs, praying he would get there in time.

Chapter Thirty-Five

She stared at him, her eyes wide with fear, and he felt a primal satisfaction. The bitch was getting a dose of her own medicine. He was not to be trifled with and was not about to be undone by some Suzy Homemaker with a penchant for horses.

He told her as much. He reminded her that she was nothing in the big world of business and sports. There were men who would love to get their hands on her, who could have her disappear forever.

How would her girls like that?

"I'm not asking you to even do anything," Perry whispered in her ear. "I'm asking you to do nothing. It's pretty easy, Kali." He felt her cringe against his breath.

He liked that. He liked everything about the position he was in. He felt her caving. He watched the panic in her eyes and felt the heat rising from her body.

He was sure she was a regular wild cat, but she didn't fight. She had been paralyzed by his words.

Again, great satisfaction.

He was a spin doctor. It's what he did. Words were his weapon. His words and creative ideas were what million-dollar corporations wanted. It was what was going to win Jeremy back.

He licked his lips.

It would be sweet justice when all those who had written him off received notice that Jeremy Connors was back. The world would know the truth—Reginald Perry was too good to go without.

* * * *

She winced.

The little piece of crap had blindsided her with a crack to the back of the head and body using his cast as a weapon.

She seethed.

There was no way he would have been able to take her down without a weapon. The ache at the base of her skull was debilitating. She could only blink and listen. The pounding and burning was so strong she thought she might be bleeding. Rather than fight, rather than treat him like insolent livestock and stomp the snot out of him, she listened and felt the throbbing pulse in the back of her head.

She closed her eyes and swallowed hard.

"Even if you have me arrested, knock me out and throw me off the balcony . . ."

She shivered against his dank breath and shrank into the carpet as much as her body would allow.

"The contract with my friends is on. They will get your little girls, Kali. They've already been paid. They will snatch them up in the middle of the night, even with all your brothers-in-law around, and disappear forever. Only I can stop them." He lowered his head and kissed the side of her face.

She whimpered. Not out of fear but out of disgust and fury.

"Only you can stop me." He traced a finger along the side of her face and neck following the bead of sweat that rolled down as she fought her gut instinct.

She squeezed her eyes shut. "Maybe I will be the one to stop you," she said, finally finding her voice, which sounded tight and uncharacteristically high. She moved and Perry shifted, pinning her shoulders tightly against the floor.

He pressed his cast against her throat in an attempt to remind her who was in charge.

"Maybe I will kick the shit out of you and disappear *your* miserable ass forever." She struggled against the cast and took a deep breath. "Maybe I'll make it home and hide my children away so no one will ever find us. I have lots of friends, too. I could go places no one would ever find on a map."

He chuckled. "Don't think I didn't think that through. Or that I failed to mention that very thing to the gentlemen I've employed. These guys have traveled through the deserts of the Middle East. They've survived on nothing but water and sand bugs, evading terrorists and high-tech surveillance equipment. They can't be caught, and they can't be stopped. Maybe you'll evade them for a month or two, but they will catch up to you eventually. Do you really want to live in fear for months or years to come?"

She didn't speak.

"What do you care about Jeremy Connors anyway? Is his freedom really worth the life of your girls?"

"Is having Jeremy Connors as a client really worth going to prison? Or being killed? Why do you care about him anyway?" she shot back.

"Fair question. Jeremy is everything to me. Once I have him back, I go solo. I build my own business. With a name like Jeremy Connors, I can go as far and as high as I want. You understand that, Kali. I know you do. The quality of a horse has a lot to do with how well you ride, right? Do the right thing, Kali. Make life easier for everyone."

Kali's head was spinning. She wanted to cry. She wanted to rage. Even if she agreed to remain silent, there was no guarantee he wouldn't send the hit men anyway. Who was to say she would ever be safe? She was now a witness against Perry, too. This was . . . her mind raced to think of the word. *Witness tampering.*

Certainly, Perry had already thought of that. She'd seen firsthand how he worked with the helicopter disaster at Rainwash. He obviously didn't care about anything outside Jeremy Connors and himself. Perry was a man of unscrupulous desires. He would do anything he wanted or needed to have his way. There was no way she would be safe from him. Ever.

He had been whispering in her ear when he suddenly lowered his head and kissed her again, dragging his lower lip against her cheek.

She felt the moist heat on her face and wanted to scream. She wanted to throw him off her but was terrified to move. She felt him pressing against her in ways that he shouldn't, in ways that revolted her.

She swallowed.

What did Jeremy mean to her? If she really thought about it, sure, she disliked him, but she didn't care enough to actually hate him. He was nothing to her. When she returned to Rainwash, her life would in no way change whether he went to prison or not.

She choked on the absurdity that she was only doing this as a favor to two women she didn't even know—Casey Dillon and Jessica Stanten—and her life, as well as the lives of her daughters, was in jeopardy.

He made disgusting sounds and rubbed against her body.

She cringed and began talking to herself, willing herself to get through the next moments with Reginald Perry. The first matter of business was to get free.

"Okay," she said and winced. "I won't . . . I won't testify. I'll be sick tomorrow. I won't show."

He studied her face, not ready to believe.

She turned toward him for the first time and locked eyes. "I mean it. This . . . you . . . aren't worth it. I just want to go home."

"That's my girl."

She cringed again. Nicky used to call her that. Hearing it come from Perry made her want to vomit.

"Please, get off of me," Kali said finally finding the strength to push against him.

"Now, now . . . just a few more little details," he said as he brushed her hair from her face.

She jerked her head, not wanting to be touched, and considered the idea of head-butting him as the door burst open.

A large man wielding a pistol charged into the tiny hallway of the room.

His gun was leveled at Perry's head.

A second man rushed in, half tackling, half pulling Perry's weight off her, and they landed with a heavy thud a few feet from Kali's body.

She blinked.

It was all so surreal. Somehow, her mind had been playing tricks on her just like it used to when she would smell Nicky in her bed or hear his voice across the room even though he had been dead over a year. Her mind had only let her digest half of what was happening to keep her from screaming hysterically. The sight of Perry slammed onto his stomach and his hands cuffed behind his back panicked her.

The large security officer struggled against the cast, not knowing quite how to secure it.

Perry raged on, threatening lawsuits and abuse. "They won't stop. I've already paid them. Even if you throw me out the window or put me in jail, they'll still come for the girls!"

Kali rose to a seated position. She felt a hand on her shoulder and cried out, scrambling away from the hand.

The second guard asked if was she okay, but she could only stare at him, blinking and gasping wildly for breath.

They'll come for the girls.

She leaned back on her hands and inched away from the man.

He took a step toward her, hands up, and she gasped.

This wasn't happening. She had to get to a phone. She had to call Ms. Kat and—no, she had to tell Mattie to—no, he needed to wait until she—he had to watch them day and night. She needed to—where the hell was Tracy?

She felt a stab of anger. He wasn't here when she needed him . . . again.

She crawled farther away from the hand and Perry's voice.

He was saying something to Kali, but she only heard every other word.

The guard was yelling.

She had to keep her promise not to talk. She couldn't testify.

"Shut up! Shut up and stop resisting!"

Perry wasn't giving up, and Kali heard him call her name again and again.

She couldn't take her eyes off Perry, but she continued to crawl out of the room, into the hallway. Her head throbbed even more when she sat up, making her feel slightly disoriented.

"Hey."

Another voice.

Another hand.

A sound came out of her that panicked her even more. It wasn't like any noise she had heard before.

"Hey! Are you—"

Kali slapped wildly at the hand and bit the inside of her cheek to keep the sound from escaping again.

"Kali!" Large hands grabbed either shoulder and gave her a firm shake.

She looked up to see Sam Spann and thought she'd finally slipped over the deep end. She had wanted to see him for so long she was sure this must be another trick of her mind.

"Sam?" She reached up and as soon as her fingertips actually made contact, she grabbed him, hugging him so tightly he staggered.

"Remember our deal," Perry said over and over.

Kali leaned heavily into Sam and tried to block out his voice.

"Shut up! The only deal you'll be making is between a good lawyer and the police," the guard said.

"On what charges?" Perry sneered and called out to Kali again, but Sam swept her into the room, out of Perry's sight, and slammed the door.

Kali was only aware of Sam. She was incredibly grateful for him. If nothing else, he was a safe body to hug and hold on to.

They sat on the edge of the bed, Kali between his legs and her head balanced on his chest and right shoulder. She closed her eyes, unconsciously petting his forearm, and recounted what had happened.

"Damn!"

Kali's eyes flew open, and she jumped. Standing at the mouth of the room were Jeremy, Ed, and Mike.

* * * *

Sam felt her reaction and looked toward Ed. "Get him out of here," Sam yelled. "Get out! You shouldn't be here." He held her close and squeezed her tighter then said, "None of us should be. Kali, sweetheart, this is highly improper."

But she wouldn't let go.

"Ed, get him out." He looked around the room for a moment. Although it wasn't horrible, there were definite signs of a struggle. His heart ached. Something had happened between Perry and Kali, and he prayed she hadn't been hurt. "Did you call Casey Dillon?"

Ed nodded as he took in the entire scene.

"Did he hurt you?" Sam asked.

Kali petted his arm.

"I think she's in shock," Ed said, staring at her.

Ed had admitted fearing Kali Jorgenson of Rainwash on more than one occasion. She had held his life in her hands, and he had trusted her experience and wisdom on the trail. This was not the same woman.

"I'm not in shock." Kali's voice made everyone stop.

"Are you okay? Did he hurt you? What did he want?" Sam wanted to know. It took everything he had not to hug her and refuse to let go. He stayed as still as possible. It was insane how deeply he felt for this woman. There was no rational explanation. He barely knew her and, from a legal standpoint, she was the enemy, but she was exactly where he wanted her to be.

He felt her body go rigid in his arms and he attempted to let her go, but she made it clear he shouldn't.

"He told me not to testify," she said flatly. "He told me . . . he would have the girls killed!"

"What?" Ed knelt down and looked at Kali directly. "Exactly what did he say?"

"No, Ed." Mike stepped forward, pushing Ed back. "We don't need to be hearing this. No. That's between her and her lawyers, not us. We don't need to be hearing any of this."

But the floodgates had opened for Kali. "All he cares about is getting Jeremy back as a client," she cried, leaning against Sam. She didn't seem to care that Jeremy was there to hear it.

But Jeremy tried to protest. "Hey, I don't know anything about any of this, man!"

"Ed, get him out. He can't be here." Sam brushed Kali's hair in an attempt to calm her. "Kali, I need—"

Jeremy hung on, fighting against his own lawyers.

Sam knew what he was doing. He was trying to make Kali understand why she should just leave everything alone. But he needed to shut up. Jeremy needed, for once in his life, to shut up.

"I didn't do this to get even," Kali said looking at Sam with wide blue eyes. "I didn't even want to come. She called me. I didn't call anyone. I didn't want to be here, I didn't ask for this," Kali said, the adrenaline and realization of what happened finally setting in as she began to tremble uncontrollably.

"I know that." Sam squeezed her arm and kept rubbing her hair to reassure her. He was in a compromising position, and he knew it.

"Then let it go, Kali," Jeremy said.

"Shut up! Get out of here." Sam kicked at him, still holding Kali close.

"I'm sorry if you—" Ed pulled at Jeremy's arm but the large man deflected him and stood his ground.

Kali's eyes were downcast. She was completely unaware of any of them. "And he was kissing me, licking me." Tears began to form as the words came. Kali winced. "It was horrible."

"I never did that!" Jeremy started.

Kali snapped her head up. "Not you!"

"Get him out of here." Sam was almost growling as he held Kali a little tighter. He felt a sense of possessiveness taking over as rage welled inside him.

"I-I-I couldn't believe it was happening. That icky little weasel. He's so . . . but I couldn't fight him. I was afraid. He was talking about sending someone after my girls. Sam, what am I going to do? I've got to get to a phone!"

"Kali, by the time the police are done with him, we'll have every name of every person he even thought about doing business with. Don't worry." He tried to shush her.

"It was horrible. Just like when Jeremy had his hands all over me, only it was different." It was as if Kali didn't hear anything Sam had said. "He was all over me and I just . . . I couldn't make it stop."

Sam was seething, yet all he could do was comfort her.

"That's bullshit!" Jeremy shouted.

"He didn't attack you," Mike said. His voice cut like a razor and both Kali and Sam looked up, stunned.

"Shut up, Mike," Sam said.

"What? We can't just sit here and let her say this without . . . it has to be said, Sam. For shit's sake we're still Jeremy's counsel." He raised his eyebrows at Sam and stared at him in disbelief.

"He did attack me." Kali tightened her grip on Sam's arm, and Mike waved dismissively and scoffed.

Jeremy shook his head. "I didn't. You misunderstood."

"I'm sorry, Ms. Jorgenson. You know I like you and this isn't personal, but he did not attack you. I was there, remember? Sam, we need to get out of here. This is a definite conflict."

Kali held on fast to Sam's arm, and he felt the tension rising in her body.

"What I remember, Mr. Waters, is that you were unconscious," Kali said quietly.

Mike waggled his finger. "Dazed, not unconscious."

"You were completely unconscious!" Kali said incredulously.

"Hey! I beg your pardon?" Casey Dillon's voice rang out as she and Luther Monroe entered the room. "What the hell is going on here?"

"I know what I saw, Ms. Jorgenson," Mike said flatly.

"Good Lor—what are you doing here?" Casey looked first to Jeremy then to Sam. "Sam, have you lost your mind?"

Sam opened his mouth to explain, but Kali wasn't done yet.

"You don't know what happened because you never saw a thing, but I guess you're being paid enough to lie."

"Enough!" Casey snapped, but no one seemed to hear her.

For the first time, Kali released Sam's arm, almost shoving him away as she started toward Mike. "Do you know that he took special joy in trying to rip my clothing off while you were right there, Mr. Waters?"

"Didn't happen."

"Shut up, Mike."

"He told me I was asking for it, that I wanted it, and that he was going to be the man to give it to me. Even while I held your head and gave you water, and you slipped in and out of consciousness."

There was only the slightest flicker of emotion on Mike's face.

Kali laughed, but there was no joy. Tears flowed from her eyes as her voice shook, but she stood her ground.

"We're not having this conversation, people." Casey tried to push Mike out of the room.

"How could you pretend to know?" she asked Mike. "How? How could you do that? I was taking care of you."

Her voice sounded so small, and it shattered Sam. Somewhere in the back of his mind, a voice began to talk to him, but there was no time to listen.

"I was so scared for you, Mr. Waters. You were in so much pain, and I was so scared for you. I held you, tried to keep you warm, and made sure you were hydrated. I kept thinking about the family you might have and . . ." Her voice cracked, and she struggled for composure.

The room was still as everyone stood in stunned silence. The powerful, confident, almost robotic Kali Jorgenson was falling apart.

"All I could think about was your family and making sure you made it back to them. You were hurt. I stayed with you, making sure you were safe, but you weren't. You were in so much pain. You passed out." Her voice changed. "And when you were completely out of it, this . . . this scumbag didn't care about you one bit. He didn't give one shit about you or your family or your pain. All he could think about was coming after me. In front of you! And you . . . you pretend to know about that?! How could you do that?"

Mike opened his mouth.

They heard the pounding first.

Heavy.

Footsteps.

Coming fast.

Tracy Sommers appeared in the doorway, panting. He opened his mouth as if to ask what was happening. No doubt, he had seen the action in the lobby and heard there had been some kind of scuffle.

If Sam had had any question about what had really happened out there on the range, every answer he needed was right there in Tracy's expression.

Tracy scanned the room, his gaze landing on Kali, and Sam watched his eyes widen with fear. He loved Kali like a daughter. She was like blood. Tracy saw the tear beginning to form in her eye and his face blackened.

Then he saw Jeremy.

"Why, you son of a bitch!"

There was no time for reaction.

Even the high and mighty professional ball player stood like a deer caught in headlights as Tracy steamrolled into the room, laying a full-body tackle on him. "I'll kill you, ya dirty, rotten son of a bitch!"

"Tracy!" Kali screamed, but Sam wrapped both arms around her and held her close, pulling her toward the bed and away from the fighting.

The hit knocked Jeremy across the table and both men skittered across the top and off the other side, slamming against the heating and air unit. Jeremy staggered to his feet, but Tracy was right on top of him, pounding fists into his gut and face. Jeremy simply covered up.

"I told you if I ever saw you put your hands on her again I would kill you and so help me, I will. I should have shot you that night!"

In three steps, Luther Monroe was in the middle, trying to separate the two men while dodging Tracy's blows.

Jeremy wasn't trying to fight but simply hold his ground. "I wasn't doing anything!" he bellowed, dodging behind Luther Monroe.

"Call the police. Someone call the police!" A woman screamed. She and another woman stood in the hallway, watching the spectacle.

"Tracy, stop!" Kali cried.

But Tracy had become a wild man, frenzied with rage. There was no stopping him.

Even Jeremy knew it. "I was just standing here," Jeremy yelled.

Mike jumped in, pulling Jeremy backward toward the bed and, eventually, out the door while Luther used his size to block Tracy.

As Jeremy eased by, Sam looked at him, and all doubt disappeared.

He had done it. Jeremy had attacked Kali.

Chapter Thirty-Six

They heard Jeremy struggling against Ed and Mike, along with a security guard in the hallway.

"Hell, just shut up, Jeremy," Mike said.

"This was not what we needed," Ed said.

There was a ding, their voices trailed away, leaving the hotel suddenly very quiet.

Inside the room, Luther still blocked Tracy who no longer posed any threat of attack.

Covered in sweat and breathing heavily, Tracy plopped back on the bed and braced his elbows on his knees. Large, calloused hands covered his head.

Casey Dillon was the first to break the silence with a heavy sigh. "Okay, this is good. We can use this—" She was thinking out loud but stopped short when she locked eyes with Sam Spann.

Still holding Kali, Sam shook his head. "No. Casey, don't say anything else. I can't—I'm not supposed to be here. I can't hear any of this," he said and he released Kali.

"Which poses a great question." Casey leveled a hard stare at Sam. "Why *are* you here?"

"I got a tip that Reginald Perry, who, by the way, has nothing to do with —"

"Kali," Tracy's voice broke in. "I'm sorry, baby girl. I'm so sorry."

No one moved.

"I didn't realize until tonight how angry I was. I just kind of shut it all out, but I shouldn't have. When I come up on ya like I did, I should have kicked his head in." He wiped a hand across his face, stroking his stubble absent-mindedly. He turned halfway on the bed to face her.

Although Sam had released her, he hadn't stepped away, and Tracy locked eyes with Sam instead.

"You're representing a monster. You know that, don't you?" he asked.

Sam said nothing.

Tracy stood and waved a hand. "It's all right. I know you can't say nothin' to that, but I just wanted you to know it. From me to you. You're a good man, Sam. I know that much, and I suspect you didn't know one way or the other if Jeremy had done all those things. That isn't your job. You just defend him. But as sure as I'm standing here, on my word, I can tell ya, Sam. He done it. He done it all, and then some."

"You're right about that, Tracy." Luther's deep voice interrupted whatever Sam might have said back. "He can't talk about this. For that matter, we shouldn't be either. We need to just, what?" He looked around the damaged room. "We need to get Kali a new room. I'll call Johnson." He looked at Casey, who nodded. "If at all possible, get some sleep."

"Johnson?" Tracy asked.

"A bodyguard we use from time to time. He's the best. I don't think it's really necessary." He started to give Kali reassurances, but she cut him off, shaking her head.

"I don't need that. I've got Tracy."

Tracy puffed up. It clearly meant the world to him that, after everything that had happened, she believed in him, and he nodded. "No one's gonna touch her."

Casey held up a hand this time. "That's fine, but we're changing rooms, and calling Johnson all the same." Kali opened her mouth to protest, but Casey shook her head. "This is my show now, Kali. I know you can appreciate that. You have to let me do this my way."

The two women stared at each other until Kali relented, and with that, Operation Protect Kali was in motion. Within a few minutes, Casey Dillon had found a new hotel and had Luther carrying bags to the elevator.

"I don't need a new room," Kali protested. "What I need is—"

"Already done." Casey held up a finger and shook her head. "All is safe at Rainwash, and local and state police have been alerted. No one is touching your family."

Kali deflated a little, the tension visibly leaving her body. She turned to Sam. She thanked him and actually said she was sorry.

Sam thanked her as well. He thanked her for Rainwash, Lightning, and the girls. With a slight squeeze to her shoulder, he said goodbye and stepped out of the room.

* * * *

Don't leave.

That was what she had said to him.

I don't want you to leave.

It was a whisper. A sweet, delicious whisper in his ear that set him on fire with wonder and want, but his hands had been tied. He had to leave.

His heart pounded as he watched and waited. His career hung in the balance.

He momentarily considered the wild notion that all this had been an elaborate plot to upset the defense. An imaginary headline flashed through his mind and he winced. Imagine being caught in Kali Jorgenson's room with her crying foul.

He stopped.

Kali wasn't that way. She never would have been part of something so devious. No, she had reached out to him because she wanted him. In the most unexpected manner, she had been bold and had expressed herself to him.

This doesn't have anything to do with Jeremy or the case or anything except you. I wish you could be with me.

For all the time lost thinking about her and wondering how she felt about him, he knew now.

She wanted him as well.

It wasn't time lost.

He smiled. Just that thought alone empowered him. It wasn't time lost at all. Kali Jorgenson felt the same way.

* * * *

During the car ride she had tried to reason it all out, to understand why she felt the way she did. She wanted to go home. She wanted to feel secure and safe. She wanted Sam. The need to have Sam with her was powerful and overwhelming. Almost desperate. He had stood behind her as she lashed out at Mike, giving her strength. She wasn't ready for him to leave her, only to do battle against her in court the following day. The thought was too horrible to imagine. It had been easier to ask him to stay.

A giant of a man named Brent Johnson met them in the parking lot and wasted no time on small talk as he informed Tracy and Kali how they would enter the hotel, where the elevators were, and how they were to walk.

Kali's brain hummed. She only half listened as Johnson gave both Tracy and Kali their assigned rooms, explaining the layout, and where he would be. She glanced toward the lobby and her heart skipped a beat when she spotted Sam Spann.

He had come.

"I need for you to distract Luther and the bodyguard guy." She feared Tracy questioning her. She didn't want to have to tell him that she was interested in another man besides Nicky.

Instead, a slow grin spread across Tracy's face. "You bet, baby girl." He gave her a pat on the knee.

Tracy insisted on ice, special drinks from the house bar, and became such a nuisance for Johnson that Sam Spann, lead council for the defense, slipped unnoticed into Kali's room.

"Hi," he whispered.

Although Kali couldn't see his face, she knew he was smiling. "Hi." Her heart slammed against her chest. Even her ears were ringing. Only the hum of the air conditioning unit offered noise.

In the distance, Sam and Kali heard Tracy call down the hallway. "You got Bacardi?"

"Get back inside," Johnson hissed.

"What? It's just room service." Tracy sounded innocent and Kali smiled.

"He's a good man," Sam whispered.

She tilted her face up toward him to answer and found him alarmingly close. His breath, his smell, his presence were incredibly powerful and she inhaled deeply and tried to calm herself.

"Yes," she said.

The air unit hummed on and Sam took a small step forward. "Why, Kali? Why did you want me here?" He bent his head toward her, taking in the smell of lilacs and shampoo. He didn't know the fragrance but he liked it.

"I—"

Sam's right hand pressed against the door, leaning over her while his left brushed her cheek.

Kali jumped and Sam immediately withdrew.

"Sorry," he whispered.

"No." She managed a small laugh. "I asked you here. I wanted you here."

The humming stopped as the unit registered a desired room temperature and stopped producing cool air.

Kali felt as though she was on fire. Sam's body heat was intense, only to be matched by her own. Her heartbeat had steadied, but her body was tingling all over.

His hand was back, tracing along her cheek and jawline and up to her hairline. Gently, his fingers laced through her hair and behind her neck, pulling her toward him.

Then she felt it, the electric shock of his lips against her. Unconsciously, she drew in a sharp breath, but when he started to pull away, she held him tight. Kali brought her hands up to his shoulders and up around his neck.

He was tense, bunched up like a wild animal ready to spring.

As she felt him press into her, his arms wrapped around her, she wanted to let out a grateful sigh but didn't dare. Instead, she let her hands roam freely over his magnificent body. His shoulders were broad and powerfully shaped. His neck was thick and strong. His touch tender and loving.

He kissed her, his lips covered her own before moving to her neck, jaw, and eyelids. He was taking in every bit of her. He gently parted her lips and pushed his tongue against hers.

She returned his kiss and felt her body melt into his when he sighed a soft moan that sent waves of passion through her body.

Kali's hands slid behind Sam's neck as his own hands drew up against her body, fighting gently against her T-shirt and moving up under the fabric. His hands, while large and strong, were soft as they glided over her body.

He pulled her in closer and their contact became more passionate as they became lost in the taste and touch of each other, both jumping at the hard knock that sounded against the adjoining door between Kali and Tracy's rooms.

"Yes?" Kali gasped.

"You okay in there?" Johnson's gruff voice carried through the door.

"Yes," she squeaked. "I was just going to bed. I . . . I'm hoping to sleep through the rest of the night."

"I'll check back," Johnson called out.

"I should go," Sam whispered as he tried to pull away from Kali.

"No," she whispered back, taking his hand and leading him to the bed.

If Kali had expected some small voice to question her, yell at her, ask what she thought she was doing, it never came. She knew what she wanted, and Sam never fought her.

With certain ease, Kali laid back and tugged him toward her. She felt the width of his chest and the restraint he used as he lowered himself down. First his chest pressed gently, warmly against her then his lips burned against her neck. She tilted her head back and repressed a heavy sigh. His hot kisses felt so good against her flesh. Then he shifted and she finally felt all of him.

She wanted to shout. Or cry. Or simply breathe.

He felt like home.

Kali's fingers went to work, unbuttoning his shirt and peeling the sleeves off him. She had admired his body for some time, watching him ride Lightning, wondering how he would feel, and always stopping herself from going any further, but he was here and on top of her, pressing against her as her fingertips explored his upper torso.

Sam wasted no time in doing the same, pulling her shirt over her shoulders and head. He did it so gently she barely moved. Their lips only parted for the brief moment her shirt went over her head. He kissed her so passionately, exploring her mouth, she felt as if she was melting into the mattress.

The air conditioning unit kicked on, and Kali sighed along with it, unable to hold herself quiet any longer.

* * * *

Only later would he consider how happy he was with Kali's traveling wardrobe. Unlike the snug jeans he was used to seeing her in, she wore loose-fitting trousers that slid easily down her soft, round hips.

As they did, it was Sam's turn to sigh.

How long had he imagined holding her in his arms, feeling her warmth, and running his hands over her incredible backside? Here she was, in his arms, beneath him, sighing for him.

Kali's skin was smooth and unbelievably warm as he ran his fingers beneath the fabric of her panties.

Another unexpected sigh brought Sam back to Kali's lips. In the dark, he felt the soft curl of her lips as she smiled.

He pushed her trousers down to her knees, leaving only the sheer fabric of the panties in the way.

"This is your show," he whispered to Kali. What he wanted to do and what he was going to do were two entirely different things. This was all Kali's call.

Her hands slid over his hips, pulling against his clothing. Her hands, though small, were strong and sure.

He dug his heels into the mattress and lifted his hips so Kali could remove his pants. Otherwise, it was all Kali.

As the air conditioning unit hummed along, so did Kali, pressing herself against him, working her hands over his body until he could no longer control himself. It was Kali's show, but she was driving him insane.

She rolled with him when he shifted, and her hands found him in the dark. She stroked him and moved in ways he hadn't imagined possible. She made small noises that drove him mad.

When the air conditioning unit clicked off again, they never broke stride, but their moans and groans, their rapid breathing and gasps of passion were silent.

Where she wanted to scream, she whimpered.

Where he wanted to moan, he buried his face against her and hummed.

Just as he could hold on no longer and exploded inside her, she released.

She pulled against him, holding him another few seconds. Then, with a quiet laugh, she fell back against the pillows.

Sam rested against her, listening to the pounding of both their heartbeats.

"Kali, that was incredible." He had had a wild impulse to say he loved her. He hadn't wanted to frighten her, but as he felt her wrapped around his body he knew couldn't resist. It was how he felt. It was what had made him
—

He felt a drop of wetness roll onto his hand.

"Hey," he whispered against her ear. "Are you okay?"

She had said she was but he could feel the change in her. No longer giving, she pulled away. It had been Kali's show, and now she regretted it.

Chapter Thirty-Seven

They were careful not to smile. After the verdict was read, they took the obligatory walk down the courthouse steps, talked to the press, and recapped their personal beliefs about the judicial system. Yes, it still works, they had said. They accepted congratulations, shook hands, and nodded to show their satisfaction. They ignored the boos and moved through the crowd as quickly as possible.

It was not until the door shut behind them that Luther Monroe broke into a huge grin.

"Well?" He held his hands out and Casey dove, throwing herself into his arms. They laughed and hugged for several minutes, each reveling in their hard work, persistence, and a victory that they hadn't been at all sure they would ever see. Luther's hugs were a bit too hard for her still very sensitive ribs but she didn't care.

"Oh, life is good!" Casey laughed, throwing her head back.

"Amen!"

Still holding hands, they began talking to each other at rapid speed, neither really hearing the other.

"Did you see the look on his face? The gasps—"

"Oh, man! I couldn't believe it when they read—"

"Did you see Mike Waters' face? I thought he—"

"What was the deal with Sam Spann?"

"I think there's something going on with him and—"

"You think? Did you see Connors' face?"

"Pfft! Did you see the look on his teammates' faces?"

The phone rang and Casey pounced, said a few words of thanks, and smiling, she passed the phone to Luther. "It's Vanessa," she said.

Word had spread quickly. Vanessa's emotional investment in the case was equal to Luther's. Luther had worked long, hard hours on the case, barely seeing his own wife. Secretly, Casey knew Vanessa was just glad it was over—win or lose.

As Luther spoke in low, sensitive tones to his wife, Casey rounded her desk and fell into her seat. Jeremy Connors was going to prison for three to six years. It wasn't great but, based on what they'd had, it was a victory. She owed it all to Kali Jorgenson and Tracy Sommers.

She leaned back, kicked off her heels, and propped her feet up on the desk.

As if they hadn't had enough against them from the start, a huge scandal had broken out over Houston's police crime lab. An audit of the lab had revealed that its analysts lacked proper training, had insufficiently documented cases, and may have allowed evidence to be exposed to contaminants.

Jackson, Keller & Whiteman had done an extraordinary job of proving at least one other man was involved with Jessica Stanten. That compounded by the jury's complete lack of confidence in the DNA testing from the crime lab, had Casey and Luther sunk. Witness after witness had stepped forward to show the jury how the most long-legged beauties to grace the earth were willing and wanting of Jeremy Connors' company and that he had never resorted to violence with women, nor had he ever needed to.

The strong testimony of a grieving widow and her sidekick, Tracy Sommers, along with the sudden leave of Samuel Spann, had tipped the scales of justice.

When Sam had recused himself, the often hotheaded Mike Waters had been left in charge. Mike was great at closing, but as he lost control with the unbelievably calm and cool Kali, his statements had become more erratic and temperamental.

Casey said a silent prayer to Kali, wherever she was. And, although she'd never thought she would, even threw in one for Sam.

A light rap on her door broke Casey from her thoughts. "Come in," she called, without moving her feet.

Sam Spann poked his head in.

Casey dropped her feet to the floor and began to stand.

"I gotta go, baby. I'll call you back," Luther said to the phone, not waiting for a response, and hung up.

"Sam," Casey said solemnly.

Luther offered a polite head nod.

"I thought you'd be out running a marathon by now." Sam flashed a white smile to Casey.

Although she was startled, she played it cool, easing back into her chair. She gestured dismissively. "Well, you know, my wings have been clipped for a while . . . doctor's orders." She glanced at Luther. "Luther, too. The body's still a bit banged up."

"Yeah. Sorry about that." He ducked his head, a silent request to come inside.

"Yeah, man. Come in. Here." Luther pushed a chair toward Sam. "Have a seat."

"Thanks, but I'm not staying." He scratched his head, a weak smile on his face. "You, uh, you guys did great. It was a great job."

"Thanks, Sam." Casey said and exchanged another look with Luther. "What can we do for you?"

Sam wasn't much for social visits and they all knew it. There was a reason he had pulled out of the case. While Casey and Luther had secretly discussed theories, they hadn't been about to complain. But now it seemed Sam had come to collect on a favor.

Casey settled herself back into her chair while Luther folded his arms across his chest. They waited.

"I'm looking for assurances that your office will follow through with the Wilson Burrell case," he said, looking first to Luther, then Casey.

"We're handling it," Casey said, frowning.

Wilson Burrell and Reginald Perry were one in the same. Under the name Burrell, Perry had set up and falsified information on several websites linked to the "Save Jeremy Connors" fund, trafficked pictures and information about Jessica Stanten and Casey Dillon over the Internet, and in his desperate quest to hang on as Jeremy's agent, Perry had also engaged several chat room users into discussing, among other things, violence against the women who fought Jeremy in court.

Despite his threats against Kali Jorgenson, there was no real evidence that Perry had paid for, much less solicited, the services of militia hit men. He was crazy but he hadn't been that stupid. Still the threat, along with his lascivious activities on the websites, had gained him the attention of the Feds as well as ATF. In short, Perry had no chance.

"I'd like to offer my services," Sam said. "That is, if you need any help."

"Oh." Luther smiled broadly. "We'll be keeping Mr. Perry, AKA Burrell busy for some time." He grinned at Casey.

"Yes, between his association with Devon Buckley—"

"Buckley? Oh, right, the kid who attacked you," Sam said and Luther and Casey nodded.

"Between that and the murder of Jessica, we hope to be quite successful against Perry." Luther gave two thumbs up to indicate just how positive he and Casey were about everything.

"You got someone on the murder?" Sam's eyebrows shot up.

"Been working with a detective in Shreveport who thinks he's got someone." Casey shrugged.

"Some nut job, sports lunatic, but they found the connection to one of Perry's websites," Luther said.

A coworker knocked and stuck their head in the office. "Great job."

Luther and Casey nodded in appreciation then refocused on Sam.

"It's pretty clear that Perry was leading the guy on, presenting him with motive and opportunity to kill Jessica." Luther snapped his fingers at Casey. "What was his name? The guy has been in and out of psychiatric wards for years. He was prime pickings for Perry."

"Of course, Perry is claiming he can't be held responsible for the actions of others," Casey said.

"But we'll make short order of that, too," Luther said.

"Anything I can do to help," Sam said.

"We can always use help." Luther shrugged. "But we've got this one pretty much locked up," he said with great confidence.

"Does this interest have anything to do with Kali Jorgenson?" Casey asked, eyebrows raised.

Sam chuckled. "It's unfinished business, is all." He shrugged and she looked at him skeptically as her phone rang.

Casey waved a finger in the air as she answered it. She made short order of the call, giving her thanks to the well-wisher, and hung up.

"Tell us, Sam." Casey leaned forward, her elbows planted firmly on her desk. "What happened? I mean, one minute you were the leading crusader for Connors' defense and then . . ."

"I just thought Mike could better serve the client. That's all."

They all knew what it meant. Sam Spann, in good conscience, could no longer represent his client.

Casey cocked her head to the side, eyeing him hard, and Sam's smile broadened.

"That's all, Casey. No big mystery."

"Drinks at Charlie's?" A man stuck his head in the door, pointing to everyone in the room. If he recognized Sam Spann, he didn't give any indication.

Luther gave him a thumbs-up. "You bet. We'll be there in about twenty minutes," he said and the man disappeared.

They could hear the man call down the corridor, promising the team of Dillon and Monroe would be on hand.

Luther turned back to Sam. "And what about Kali Jorgenson?"

"What about her?" Sam asked.

"I . . . we . . ." Casey said, her eyes shifting between Luther and Sam. Her eyebrows shot up. "We presumed there was something more to your relationship. Yes? No?"

"I guess we'll never know," Sam said sullenly.

"Man, that doesn't sound like the Sam Spann I know," Luther said, a slow smile spreading across his face. "You've been a pain in our ass since this trial began. And, I might add, not just this one. You've earned yourself a reputation for being a relentless, persistent, pain-in-the-ass pit bull, but you're gonna let a woman like Kali Jorgenson go without so much as a single word?" He winked at Casey. "I don't mind telling ya, I'm disappointed."

"Stop it, Luther." Casey waved a hand at him. Although she did not smile, there was definite amusement in her eyes. "We're going to have a celebratory drink," she told Sam. "On us. You want?" Casey stood and grabbed her purse.

"You kidding?" Sam tried to grin, though it never reached his eyes. "You're the enemy."

"Okay, your loss. Sorry." She smiled sheepishly. "Look, I don't pretend to know exactly what went on between you and Kali, or why you dropped out. I know we are indebted to you—" She looked at Luther. "Although I'll deny ever saying this, but whatever your reasons, and I'm betting they were good ones . . . it helped us immensely.

"I've known you professionally for many years, Sam. I'd hate to see you just sit idly by and watch something or . . ." She slung her purse over her shoulder and stopped just before Sam, leveling her courtroom gaze at him. ". . . *someone* slip away." With that, she turned to Luther and they stepped into the hallway.

Instantly, the hall was filled with congratulations as Casey Dillon and Luther Monroe walked along. Their excited voices faded as they exited the building.

"You know, your closing was excellent."

"No, you fed them what I needed. I think it was—"

"Kali was key. Did you see how calm and collected she was? We couldn't have asked for a better witness."

"Tracy Sommers wasn't bad either. You know when he . . ."

Chapter Thirty-Eight

"Rider two fifty-seven, Ms. Jaclyn Jorgenson of Horse Canyon, Utah, straight out of the Rainwash Ranch, and I'm told she's called Jacks. Let's give it up for Jacks from Utah, people!"

Kali shifted in her seat as the crowd lit up. When the announcer stopped, the buzzer sounded, and Kali's heart thudded against her chest. It never mattered how many times Jacks or Danni performed, Kali's heart always slammed against her chest when she saw them come out but, this time, she was more nervous than usual.

When the new rodeo season had begun, it had seemed like a good idea to jump on the circuit, hitting small towns from Oklahoma to North Dakota. While the boys stayed back at Rainwash to help Tracy, Wade had joined Kali for the three-month jaunt. Although the district attorney's office had assured Kali and the Jorgenson clan that the girls were not in any jeopardy and that Perry's claims had been lies, it felt safer to stay on the move. At least, for a short while.

The girls were in heaven. While Jacks and Danni had competed in every event offered to them, the fiercely independent Brooke had aligned herself with the traveling vets, becoming an unofficial vet tech. Right before her eyes, Kali had watched Brooke mapping out her own future. Brooke had never been particularly interested in the competitive aspect of riding. She enjoyed handling the horses, caring for, and nurturing the animals themselves. It was who she was—mother to all.

For Kali, the time away from Rainwash had allowed her to think and not have to face questions.

The men had let it go, simply believing the entire experience had been overly traumatic for Kali and even brought up ghosts from Nicky and Afghanistan, but, truly, those wounds had healed. It was the new emotions she had been feeling that had her perplexed, exhausted, confused, even cranky. While Kali had tried to sort out her thoughts, Ms. Kat and her sisters-in-law appeared to have figured it all out. The sly grins and passing comments about Sam Spann had been more than Kali wanted to hear. Secretly, she'd wondered how much information Tracy had divulged. Seeking refuge along the rodeo circuit had seemed a fine idea indeed, and much to her delight, Wade wasn't much of a talker.

A month had passed since her testimony in Houston but, on some days, it felt like yesterday. The wound of leaving so abruptly was still raw. She had wanted to see Jeremy's face when he was convicted, but she hadn't. She had wanted to see Mike's disappointment when he realized his lies and insinuations had not fooled anyone, but she couldn't. She had wanted to say goodbye to Sam and reckon with her feelings toward him but had not. She'd needed to get home to lay her hands on her babies and hug them and assure herself that they were okay. She had needed to know that everyone she loved and cherished was safe and sound in the confines of Rainwash. Including Star.

She had realized that whatever delusions she'd had about leaving Rainwash were just that. She could never leave. It was where her people were, her horses were, and where her heart lay. She had once believed it was because it had been Nicky's home, but that was no longer the case. It was her home. Her place. Her sense of comfort and well-being.

That, she decided, left Sam Spann nowhere. At least, nowhere where she was concerned.

Jacks was out of the shoot and hunched over the saddle in perfect form.

Kali jumped to her feet.

Mocha looked strong. Her strides were long and powerful as she headed toward the first barrel and rounded it masterfully, bunching up at the last second and exploding out of the pocket. She ripped across the arena to the next barrel.

Kali whooped.

Jacks was settled back nicely into her saddle, pumping her legs furiously against Mocha's sides—all cues to keep the horse moving. Like many of the riders, Jacks also used the end of her reins, appearing to slap either side of Mocha to keep up the pace. But Jacks was sure to slap the saddle not her beloved Mocha. Just the sound alone urged Mocha on at a strong pace. Mocha was all muscle and speed.

Again, they rounded out nicely, and Jacks steered them toward the middle barrel at the opposite end of the pen.

Mocha's lines were great.

It would be a good time. A really good time.

Jacks was pressing Mocha harder than usual. She had an ax to grind. At the last competition, as Jacks and Mocha had neared the finish line, Jacks' hat had flown off—automatic disqualification, but the time on the board had placed her in first. She had been forced to watch a two thousand dollar purse go to Kitty Harrelson out of Butte, Montana. It had consumed Jacks to no end. She had made all their lives a personal hell, and in a small RV, there had been no way to get around her. Kali had finally had to get tough and threaten not to let Jacks ride at all if she couldn't get over it.

"Watch the hat, watch the hat," Kali said under her breath.

Once the final turn was made, Jacks howled. Legs flapping against Mocha's body, reins slapping, Jacks hunkered down for the final sprint.

Kali noted the reins were hitting hide—Jacks was on pure adrenaline.

Mocha was stretched out. She was a gorgeous symmetry of power, grace, aggression, and beauty. She was breathtaking.

Kali smiled.

Jacks had dropped the reins and leaned in, hands clasped in Mocha's mane. Back home it was how Jacks roared across the territory and it had made Kali furious.

You have no control like that! Stop it, it's too dangerous!

Hold the reins, Jaclyn Jorgenson! Hold those reins or no more Mocha!

But they were there, together, lost in their own world, racing across the territory, and loving it.

As the crowd cheered, Mocha crossed the finish line, and disappeared in the exit tunnel. She was moving too fast and too hard to suddenly stop.

Kali looked up at the clock and gasped.

The crowd saw it, too, and broke into thunderous applause. National standing—Jacks had beaten the record by one one hundredth of a second.

With a final whoop, Kali hurried down the stands toward Jacks.

She couldn't wait to tell Danni and Brooke. Danni had stayed back at the trailer, preparing Fancy for their competition in the next hour with Wade, while Brooke remained at the mobile clinic with Dr. Rook. She hadn't even thought about the purse, just the time.

A new record.

Kali's heart swelled. This would set Jacks in a new standing.

Although she could see Jacks, getting to her was another story altogether. Jacks was surrounded by well-wishers and promoters. She saw a photographer talking to Jacks and . . .

Kali froze.

Sam Spann!

All the breath was yanked out of her.

Jacks was smiling down, holding Sam's hand, and nodding while he spoke to her.

She was beaming.

At Sam.

Jacks was talking to Sam.

Sam was here.

Kali couldn't seem to stop her mind from running over the same thought —he's here!

She felt her heart skip. He was here. But . . . why?

Panic quickly replaced any feelings of joy she had and she began pushing through the crowd. There were periodic sounds of protest as she bullied her way through, no apologies. She had to get to Jacks.

Sam was here which meant something was horribly wrong.

The FBI had found evidence of a hit man after all. The girls were in jeopardy!

By the time she'd almost reached Mocha, Jacks, and Sam, Kali was frantic. With a final push, she was through, almost stumbling against Mocha.

"What?" Kali gasped. "Why are you here?" She looked around frantically.

Sam's smile slipped away and he frowned. "I, uh . . . I just thought . . . I was just congratulating Jacks on her win," he said, looking both confused and hurt.

"Yes, but why are you here?" Kali demanded.

"I just, uh," he stammered. "I just wanted to see you."

Kali blinked. "What?"

"Man, you're not making this easy!" He raked his fingers through his hair. "I just wanted to see you, you know, so I thought I would, um, come up here and, uh . . ." He tried laughing, adding a deep shrug. ". . . see you."

"Oh." Kali relaxed ever so slightly. She looked around.

More pictures and the promoter of the rodeo began to lead Jacks to the center of the pen.

More applause.

"There's no threat?"

"Threat?"

"From Perry? No threat against the girls?" She leaned in as she asked so he could hear her above the crowd.

The announcer read off Jacks' stats as everyone applauded.

"What? No! I just . . . geez, Kali. I just missed you."

"Oh." She felt heat wash over her cheeks, and she looked toward Jacks. She was having the time of her life, and so was Mocha.

Kali eased her gaze back to Sam. "Hi." Her smile spread even further.

Sam laughed, smiling back with a matching grin.

Seconds ticked away.

"No doubt you know about the case," he said and she nodded.

"I'm sorry I had to leave so suddenly."

He shrugged, allowing her a way out.

"I was so worried. I just needed to know the girls were okay."

"Oh, hey. I understand."

"But you . . . I'm sorry for you. Not for Jeremy or Perry or Mike, for that matter." She kicked up some dirt with the toe of her boot. "But I am for you."

"Don't be. It was long time coming."

"But . . . why?" she asked, but he waved her off.

"Turns out it's not what I wanted."

They stared at each other.

"What is it you want?" Kali asked softly, her heartbeat spiking a bit.

"Well, I'll be damned!"

They turned to see Wade, Brooke, and Danni approaching.

"Mr. Spann!" Brooke cried and ran forward. "Thank you so much for the . . ."

Brooke rattled off the list of gifts Sam had sent the girls, but Kali heard very little. The blood pounding in her brain blocked everything out.

* * * *

Wade shook Sam's hand, and Danni leapt around as Jacks headed back toward them.

"I just figured since I've never seen a rodeo before—"

Brooke gasped. "You've never seen a rodeo!"

"But you live in Texas," Danni said, though it was more of an accusation. "How could you never have seen a rodeo?"

"An oversight, I assure you," Sam said and grinned at the girls. He looked up to find Jacks almost on top of them.

"Jacks," Sam declared. "That was about the coolest thing I've ever seen!"

Mocha nosed everyone, receiving many kisses on her soft muzzle.

Sam's eyes grazed over Kali for a moment. He tried to be quick about it, but he needed to look. He needed to take in what he had missed in the dark, making love to her. She looked incredible. It was her standard look—T-shirt, jeans, boots—and one that he cared for very much. He made himself look away, but the memory lingered on.

Luther Monroe's words had burned in his brain for days following the trial. Sam Spann was not one to sit idly by and let someone as amazing as Kali Jorgenson simply float out of his life

He had been sitting at his desk, cleaning everything out, when Mike had sauntered in and demanded to know what had happened.

The loss had been blamed on Sam Spann, which had been fine with him, but whatever contacts he'd thought he might leave intact had been gone after the fight with Mike. Whatever hesitations he had about traveling across country to see Kali just once more had been gone after the fight with Mike, too.

In typical fashion, Mike had opened up on Kali, blaming her for their loss. It hadn't been Jeremy Connors' fault. It was Jessica Stanten, Kali Jorgenson, and "all those other lady-in-wait, money-grubbin' bitches."

Sam had taken him down with one solid punch.

While he'd had no idea what lay ahead of him, he had never looked back.

Danni grabbed his hand, insisting that he watch her competition, too. It hadn't mattered how many times he promised to sit in the front row, she kept after him until he laughed, claiming to have traveled this far to see her, and *only* her, compete.

* * * *

Kali's throat began to close up. It had been so long since she had felt this good. She patted Mocha, gathered the reins, hugged the girls, and squeezed Wade, touching everyone but Sam. Oh, how she wanted to hug him. Instead, she cut her eyes toward him and smiled.

He had come. Sam had come to find them at the rodeo.

Chapter Thirty-Nine

Danni had taken third place but was immensely happy with her successes. She had competed against and lost to a national champion horse and a local champion who was in her teens. Danielle Jorgenson had done an outstanding job, as had Fancy, and she promptly fell asleep wearing her ribbon.

With all three girls tucked in and tuckered out, Wade emerged from the RV and shoved his hands in his pockets.

Kali and Sam had been standing near the trailer and portable pen where Fancy, Mocha, and Mouse swatted flies and dozed. They recapped the day, all agreeing it had been great until Fancy stamped a hoof, impatient with the flies and mosquitoes.

"I'll spray her down again if you like." Wade offered, but Kali waved him off.

"No, you've done enough, Wade," she said and he nodded.

"Well," he said and took a deep breath, uncertain as to how he should make his exit. "Some of the boys are going to town, to some bar . . . I guess I'll shove off."

Kali nodded and smiled.

"Uh, I should tell ya, Brooke would have you believe she's sleeping, but she's not. She's peeking out the window at you."

"Be careful. No rowdy stuff," Kali teased.

" 'Night, Wade. See ya tomorrow," Sam said.

Still walking, Wade turned backward to face them. "I hope so, man. We like having you around." And he disappeared into the night.

Sam and Kali turned back to watch the horses, neither speaking for a moment.

"One more vote for me," Sam said lightly.

"You're taking votes?"

"As many as I can get." He smiled down at her.

"Okay," Kali said with chuckle. "I'll give you a vote."

"Yeah?" His eyebrows shot up, and Kali laughed out loud.

"Wait! What am I voting for?" she asked with a huge smile. They were just a few inches apart, leaning against the pen, and Kali felt like a teenager.

"For me to stick around for a while." He frowned, looking suddenly embarrassed, and Kali couldn't help but grin. He looked so shy. "I mean, you know, if it's okay."

"Here?" she asked and pointed at the ground. "I mean, while we do the rodeo circuit?"

"Well, yeah. I could be of some help, I think. I rode Lightning, didn't I? I can fall off a horse and run screaming from danger with the best of them," he said and wagged a finger at her. "Plus, I am incredibly cheap and will resort to bribery with your children."

"Ah, yes. That's already been established."

They both chuckled and stared at the horses. They had managed to talk about everything but their night in bed in Houston.

When Kali straightened and brushed her hair back, Sam watched her.

"Geez, Kali. You are so pretty," he said and Kali froze.

It had been a long time since anyone said anything like that to her and she felt her cheeks flush.

"You could drive a man crazy."

Kali's eyes strayed toward the RV where she saw a small figure in the window leaning against the glass. "Brooke's watching us."

But Sam wouldn't be thrown off course, and he stepped in a little closer. "She's just watching out for her momma. I don't blame her. But . . . I'd like to have that job."

Kali blinked. "Wha?" Her heart pounded against her chest.

"You know, in exchange for free horse riding lessons."

"Don't you have a job?" Her smile was teasing but her eyes were serious.

"No. It seems I am suddenly out of work." He grinned and shrugged.

"What? Because of me? Oh, not because of me, I hope." Kali faced him with a look of concern.

"No, because of me. I promise."

"Is this because of the Connors case?" she asked.

"Kali, I am forever indebted to you. That's all I have to say about that. I've been dealing with guys like—"

"Oh, no," Kali groaned, but Sam took her shoulders and gave her a reassuring squeeze.

"No, Kali. Listen to me. It's the best thing I ever did. I promise." He stared at her for a moment longer. "Damn, you are so pretty."

She flushed again. Her mind was racing, desperately trying to think of something, anything to say. Nothing came. She simply stared up at him. His eyes were so clear, so kind. She wondered why she hadn't noticed that from the beginning.

"If I don't say this now, I guess I never will. Kali, since the first time I laid eyes on you, I haven't been able to get you out of my head. And, believe me, that's not how I usually am. I'm not really the romantic type. I'm . . . I don't know. I don't know if I've ever really been in love before but . . . dammit." He dropped his hands away from her and stepped back, pressing his hands against the sides of his head. "I want to be with you all the time. I'm willing to move to Rainwash and clean out stalls if you'll have me. I don't . . . hell. I'm not sure what . . ." He tried to laugh. "I don't know what you think of that or if you even want me. I just had to tell you. I just couldn't go on doing anything else until I knew how you felt.

"Since that night in Houston—"

She shushed him and looked toward the trailer again.

Sam withdrew. "It's all up to you, Kali. Whatever you say . . ." He took a deep breath but his eyes never broke from hers. His gaze was intense.

A flood of relief and joy went through her. Everything she had been wanting and feeling and thinking, Sam had magically summed up in his wonderful speech. She wanted to scream, yell . . . shout. Instead, she cried.

"Hey." He stepped forward, stroking the tear that slid down her cheek. "Don't cry. I don't want to upset you . . . I'll leave—" He turned, but she grabbed him.

"No!" She regrouped quickly. "I mean, no. As it happens . . . " She sniffed and grinned. ". . . we're in need of a good lawyer. Rainwash is being sued for killing a bull named Ramrod."

Sam stepped closer, pressing against her, and Kali felt the pen give a little against her back.

"What are you saying, Kali?" he asked. He sounded urgent.

"I'm saying," she said and gulped. "I'm saying I'd like you to stay on at Rainwash." There was so much more she wanted to say but couldn't.

He bent down and kissed her.

It was a soft, sweet kiss that almost caused her knees to buckle. Butterflies soared through her body as his hands slid around her waist and pulled her against him. He was hard and warm and wonderful. She had ached for this feeling of closeness for so long and, more specifically, for the feel of Sam. His smell filled her nostrils. He tasted delicious.

She slid her hands up around the back of his neck and felt his hair through her fingers. He felt so good, so strong, so loving, and she couldn't stop the tears of joy.

"What?" His eyes searched her face.

She shook her head, smiling back at him. "Tears of joy." She tried to brush the tears away but he wouldn't let her. With her face cupped in his hands, she could only stare back at him.

"And that night when we made love?" he asked, leaning heavily against her. "I didn't know if I hurt you or . . . if you were regretting what we . . ."

"Tears of joy," she said with a smile. "Well, first tears of ecstasy then joy."

He pumped his fist into the air. "Yes!"

* * * *

Brooke pressed her face against the window, watching her mother carefully.

Momma sat against her smoking tree, legs tucked up against her chest, and she was smiling.

Sam Spann was kneeling on the ground with his arms encircled around her.

Brooke thought Momma fit perfectly in his arms and looked happy.

She liked Sam. He felt like family. It was hard to believe that he had only lived with them for four months. It seemed like she had known him forever. He helped Brooke and her sisters with homework, worked hard alongside her uncles, and made Momma smile. A lot.

Even his work had been good for Momma. Every now and then, Sam had to travel across the state, taking cases about environmental issues. At first, it had been Momma's idea, but when business had picked up, she had been afraid. She was afraid he would get hurt like Daddy had and didn't want to let him go.

She was learning to relax, though, and not be so scared.

They had finally gotten Danni to try barrel racing, but she had been so scared at first. She was afraid of wiping out at the barrel, that Fancy would lose her footing and take them both down, but eventually she had learned to trust and had been giving Jacks a run for her money lately.

Brooke smiled.

Sam was good for everyone.

She gasped and both Danni and Jacks sat up in their beds.

"What?" Jacks asked. "Is Momma smoking?"

"No, you dope. Momma doesn't smoke anymore," Danni said.

Jacks rolled her eyes and crawled out of bed.

"No, dummy, she never smoked," Brooke shot back over her shoulder. "She just did that to fool you guys."

"What's she doing now?" Danni asked and clambered out of bed.

Just as Danni reached the window, Brooke drew in a deep breath. "He's gonna ask her to marry him," she said.

Jacks dove at the window.

The three girls rested their chins on the windowsill, their noses steaming up the bottom window panel.

Sam had said something funny, and Momma rocked to one side, allowing Sam to tighten his grip around her hips and pull her in closer. Whatever he was saying to her, Momma's eyes gleamed as she looked down at him. Then, releasing her with one arm, he reached into his shirt pocket and pulled out a small box.

"He gave her a ring. He gave her a ring," Danni said, her breath fogging up the glass.

Momma's jaw dropped. She looked first at the box, then at Sam. Her fingers shook as she carefully took the box from him.

No one said a word as they watched.

Momma tucked her hair behind an ear as she examined the ring. She was saying something to him when Sam moved his other arm, coming up so that he was perched on both knees, and leaned against her.

From where the girls stood, it was hard to see their mother's face. Her head was bent down and she was nodding.

Sam bent down a little, leveling his face with hers, and he cupped the side of her face with his hands then he pulled back, and bent down to kiss Momma's belly.

Brooke smiled again. Secretly, she hoped for a little brother.

"If she marries him, he'll be our dad," Brooke said.

"I like Sam okay," Jacks said a little grudgingly, but Brooke just rolled her eyes. Jacks loved Sam and everyone knew it.

"I like Sam a lot." Danni grinned.

And they all watched as Sam tilted his head to the side, giving Momma a kiss.

"Eww!" Jacks and Danni scrunched their faces and moved away from the window. As they crawled back into bed, they scrutinized this Sam Spann, a citified man who played a mean game of Crazy Eights.

Brooke moved closer against the window. She watched as Momma closed her eyes and kissed Sam back. She looked so happy. So pretty. She smiled and placed Sam's hands against her tummy. Together, they laughed about whatever she said.

And for the first time in so very long, Brooke moved away from the window and readied herself for bed without a worry in her mind. She understood why the smoking tree had once been so important and was so much more grateful to the man who couldn't ride horses very well but could make their mother cry.

The End

About the Author

Alexandra Powe Allred graduated from Texas A&M University with a BA in History, saying, "As everyone knows, once you get a degree in history, all you can really do is teach or write. I'm just doing what I can!"

As the daughter of a now-retired US Diplomat, Allred traveled all over the United States and around the world. Her writing career began before graduation with several pieces on bilingual education with national education publications. But the real stories began while living as a youth in Moscow, Russia. Under a communist regime, imagination and the ability to create stories are the very best way to beat boredom not to mention the freezing cold!

As her career was taking off, Allred embraced her second passion—sports. She trained for and made the US women's bobsled team in 1994, becoming the first US National Champion. She was named Athlete of the Year by the United States Olympic Committee and garnered worldwide attention as she was also four and a half months pregnant at the time! Her training regimen was (and still is) used by the United States and International Olympic Committees for pregnant athletes. Following her retirement from the sport in 1998, Allred returned to the literary world with *The Quiet Storm*. While living in the Olympic Training Center in Lake Placid, New York, she was able to talk to Olympic and National athletes from all disciplines and share with sports enthusiasts. From there, her career was launched. She did adventure freelance writing for *Sports Illustrated*, *Muscle & Fitness for Her*, and *Volvo* magazines. She held a sports column, worked as an editor for *NOW* magazines outside Dallas, Texas, and began working as a clean air advocate, often testifying before the EPA.

Today, she writes (mostly) fiction and teaches kinesiology classes for Navarro Community College while enjoying her family and animals in Texas.

Acknowledgments

She Cries was inspired by my family and friends. Thank you for always allowing me to be bold and creative without fear. Few people realize, however, the magic of editors. To Andrea, Shaina, and Lea, thank you for your patience and attention to detail. I know, I know . . . I do tend to wander at times.

To Sugarsmack Supreme–thank you for the hilarious editorial comments, your endless patience, and your devotion to each and every project. You make the process not only painless but fun. Luv ya, smoochie.

CPSIA information can be obtained at www.ICGtesting.com
Printed in the USA
LVOW07s0421230714

395614LV00010B/89/P